Here Come[

MW00460498

Author
Santa Dan

An adult novel by Dan Slipetsky

To DAVE —
Hope
You enjoy
my
LUNACY !
Santa Dan
4-20-'12

This book is a work of fiction. The characters, incidents and dialogue are based on the author's wacked-out imagination and are not to be construed as real. Any resemblance to actual events or persons, living or dead, is entirely coincidental.

Photo of Santa Dan Slipetsky courtesy of:

Craig Lampa, Jack'N Jill Studio

Easton, PA

ISBN-13: 978-0615592251

ISBN-10: 0615592252

This book is dedicated to my family: Shirley, Apryl, Hope and Danny. You all mean so very much to me. Thank you with all my heart. I love you all (You too, John. I hope you make the cut).

They are your next-door neighbors; the kind we all pray to have – especially when one of them moves away. *Oh, please God, don't let some asshole move in next door!* They are not too loud, keep to themselves, wave when they see you in the driveway, and never, ever come over to borrow a cup of sugar, the lawn mower or just to chat. No kids yelling and screaming, no yappy dogs, no wild parties, and NO cops – just a real nice family. Get it? They are Donald and Susan Kaminski and may God bless them and their two children, Donald Jr. and Anne – Junior and Annie as they like to be called.

In a way, they remind you of the Cleaver family in that old TV sitcom. "Leave it To Beaver." There are no surprises when it comes to the Kaminski family – that is until the fall of this year. That's when it all started.

Part 1

IT BEGINS

Santa Claus, or Santa, is a figure in North American culture with legendary, mythological and folkloric aspects, which reflect an amalgamation of the Dutch Sinterklaas, the English Father Christmas, and Christmas gift-bringers in other traditions. Santa Claus is said to bring gifts to the homes of good children during the late evening and overnight hours of Christmas Eve, December 24. Santa Claus in this contemporary understanding echoes aspects of hagiographical tales concerning the historical figure of gift-giver Saint Nicholas, the man from whom the name of *Santa Claus* derives and in whose honor Santa Claus may be referred to as Saint Nicholas or Saint Nick.

From Wikipedia, the free encyclopedia

"It's easy being humble when you're a success.
The tough part is being arrogant when you're a flop!"

George McGorman

With Thanksgiving and Christmas rapidly approaching, Donald Kaminski finds himself on a mission at the local mall. Let's follow him and see what he's up to as he makes a beeline to "The Three Wise Men" (that's what he calls it). We know it as Bailey, Banks and Biddle...a jewelry store! Oh, oh, this is going to be expensive.

Don passes by Victoria's Secret and of course turns his head to look at the window displays. What man doesn't? In the entrance to the store he spots a store employee on a ladder attaching a huge string of plastic holly with big colored shiny balls on it just above two scantily clad mannequins bedecked in candy apple red nighties and Santa hats. This catches Don's attention and without realizing it he begins singing out loud.

"I'll be home for Christmas. You can count on me. Please have snow and..." Don stops suddenly, looks around for any witnesses and blurts out, "Oh my God, what am I doing? It isn't even Thanksgiving yet!" The worker on the ladder overhears Don and laughs. They spot each other, exchange smiles, and Don, red-faced and embarrassed, shirks his shoulders as if to say, "My bad." He continues on down the mall while the employee on the ladder goes back to "decking the halls" with the big colored balls.

Don enters the home of the "Three Wise Men."

"Good morning sir" the salesman who won the honor and a huge commission for *selling the most diamonds last year and can spot a sale a mile away,* pipes up. "Have you ever seen anything like this?" He holds up a gorgeous bejeweled necklace that looks like the one from the movie "Titanic." "What a great holiday surprise this would make for the wife."

Without missing a beat Don replies, "I'm sure the surprise comes in January when I get the bill for that beauty." That's Don's humor – sharp and witty. Words just pop out of his mouth before he can think about it and sometimes he ends up with both feet in his mouth as a result. "Sorry pal, but that's a bit much for me right now.

Heck, I'm only a school teacher and by the way, I expect my educational discount and anything else you can do for me."

"No problem sir. I'll take good care of you," Mr. *Sold the most diamonds last year,* replies.

That's what I'm afraid of, Don chuckles to himself.

"And what can I show you today?" as the "Titanic" is placed back into the showcase and is securely locked up.

"Got a minute for a quick story?" Don says.

"Go ahead, I've got all day," the salesman says while sizing up Don for the kill.

"My wife and I joined a mixed league bowling team not long ago. We call ourselves the 'Alley Cats,' and believe me that's where we should bowl – the alley. We really are terrible but we have a lot of fun. Anyway, we bowl once a week on Friday nights with a nice bunch of people. You know: pizza, beer, a few laughs. Well, just to keep things interesting we sometimes bet each other on difficult shots. Believe me pal, Sue, my wife, is so lousy at bowling that I never once had to pay off."

"Let me guess," Mr. *I've got a big sale now, baby,* cheerfully responds. "She made the shot and you owe."

"Do I!" Don fires back. "I owe big time! Do you know that TV commercial where the Mrs. gets that three-stoned diamond ring for being a good wife? You know, the one that represents the past, the present, and the future? Well, Susan gets hers for making the 7-10 split!"

With that, Mr. *I've got just the ring you want,* has it out of the case already and in Don's face.

"And here it is – even more beautiful in person than on TV."

Before you know it, Don has the ring boxed up, wrapped, bagged with fancy colored papers, bowed with gift card filled out, charged, and even the extra maintenance guarantee – warrantee contract filled out to include a free cleaning and check-up once a year for only $4,250.95 plus tax. Not a bad way to start the day for Mr. *And I'm going to sell the most diamonds this year as well!*

Upon departing "The Three Wise Men," Don Kaminski stops to take a look at the mall Santa all dressed up in his crisp, bright red Santa suit with whiter-than-white Angora fur and matching hat with holly trim.

Sure he looks great, Don thinks. *It's early in the season yet. Give it another two weeks and let's see what Santa AND the suit look like. I'll bet they both won't smell so great either! And look at that, would you. Santa has on real boots and not those fake tops the kids can spot a mile away. This guy's a top-shelf Santa!*

Don watches the process and then spots the elf working with Santa. *Is he a midget, or is he a dwarf?* Don can't remember the difference, but he is fascinated how efficient the little guy is in prepping the kids for Santa. The elf is bouncing and skipping all over the place and laughing in that elfish voice of his. The kids seem to love him. They watch his every move.

Santa's elf bounces over and greets the little red-headed, gap-toothed lad at the head of the Santa line. "Hi munchkin! I'm Buddy the Elf. What's your name?" the elf asks while placing his hand out for a "low five."

"Tommy," says the boy, as he "low fives" the elf. Don observes little Tommy quickly turn from being a little hesitant to willingly follow Buddy the Elf to the ends of the Earth! Buddy grabs the lad by the hand and says, "Come on Tommy. Let's go see Santa!" They both skip over to the "big man."

"Here's Tommy, Santa." Before you know it, Buddy the Elf, as small as he is, hoists Tommy onto Santa's lap with little to no effort, then returns to the next child in line and begins the routine all over again.

Don ponders, *Buddy the Elf, huh. I wonder where the little guy gets all this energy? He's great!*

"Ho, Ho, Ho!" bellows Santa. "Why hello there, Tommy – my-oh-my, look how much you've grown since you were here last year!" Santa pats Tommy on the head as if to prove he's much bigger this year. Little Tommy grins with pride. "And how did you get to be so big?" Santa asks.

"I had a birthday!" Tommy replies grinning and showing his missing front tooth.

"Why yes you did!" Santa chuckles. "And your mom must be making you all kinds of good food to eat, that's for sure!" Tommy nods his head in agreement.

"I've heard you've been a good boy this year, Tommy. Is that true?"

"Yes."

"All of the time, or most of the time?" asks Santa.

Tommy looks over at his parents for an answer then back to Santa.

"Most of the time," he answers while he looks back to his approving parents.

"Well that sounds good to me, Tommy. What would you like for Christmas this year?" That's all Tommy had to hear. The *okay* has been given. The coast is clear. It is now time for the good stuff – presents! And Tommy's had his list memorized for three weeks now.

"I want a LEGO Star Wars – General Grevous Starfighter, a Transformers Dark of the Moon Ultimate Optimus Prime, a Marvel Regener8'rs 1:64 Scale Spider-Man Cruiser, a Nerf Vortex Nitron Blaster…" Santa gives Tommy a sour look.

What in the hell is this kid talking about? What ever happened to dump trucks and G.I. Joe?

"…a Power Rangers Samurai Mega Blade, some DC Universal Action Figures, you know – the one with five in a pack?"

"I see. Is that it?" Santa cuts in. "You must have been awful good to want all *these* presents, Tommy. I'll do the very best I can." As if on cue, Santa turns his head and is smiling for the camera, but Tommy is too busy trying to remember the rest of his toy list to be posing for some dumb picture with Santa. Meanwhile, the photographer is frantically waving a Buzz Lightyear whirligig complete with sound and flashing lights while whistling and making bird calls to get the kid's attention. Don cracks a smile at the dilemma and continues to watch.

"Oh, yeah," Tommy remembers. "I want a Big Buck Hunter…Did I say a SpongeBob SquarePants Motion TV Game?" While still looking straight ahead and holding the smile, Santa shrugs his shoulders. "I want the Ideal Electronics Super Slam Game, an iPod, a Wii and Wii games like: New Super Mario Bros., Wii sports, WipeOut, and the Ultimate I Spy Game…"

"Tommy! Tommy!" dad yells from behind the photographer. "Smile, Tommy! Smile for the man!"

"Come on, Tommy," mom cries out. "It's time for you to smile for the picture!" Tommy tries to comply. "No! Not *that* smile – smile normal!" Tommy remembers there's more on his list.

"…a Razor Electric Dirt Rocket Bike, and oh, I almost forgot, a talking globe." Tommy smiles – not for the photographer – but because his list is complete. He looks at Santa to see if he got all of this or does he need anything repeated? Santa seems to be ignoring Tommy and continues to smile and face the photographer.

Come on for Christ's sake! Take the goddamn picture! That's when dad gets one of his brainy ideas.

"Hey Tommy!" yells pop. "Why don't you pull Santa's beard and see if it's real!" And this is exactly what the kid does. Tommy grabs two handfuls of hair and pulls down hard.

"Yeeeeeeooooooooowwwwwwwwww!" Santa lets out a yelp like a dog that has just had his long tail stepped on and grabs for his beard. And wouldn't you know it. That's exactly when the photographer took the shot. Buddy the Elf holds back the next child who's trying to get to Santa before he forgets *his* list of toys and thinking, *this kid blew it and now it's MY turn.* All the moms and dads in line are laughing. The children are all speechless. Most of them think, *This kid ain't gettin' shit this year!* Even Tommy's mom is biting her lip to keep from laughing out loud and starts yelling at Tommy. Dad doubles over in laughter and stomps his foot, "That's my boy. That's my Tommy." The photographer just shakes his head in disgust.

"Just wait until you come down off Santa's knee!" threatens mom. She has a half-smile on her face as she turns to slap dad playfully on his shoulder. "And shame on you! Santa's going to bring you coal – again!"

Santa recovers as best he can. There are still a few tears in his eyes as he says something to little Tommy and points to the camera.

Probably told him to smile or else he wasn't getting SHIT for Christmas! Don thinks.

Both are smiling now and the photographer snaps the picture knowing it's a "keeper." Tommy slides off Santa's lap, Santa grabs for a tissue, Buddy the Elf is skipping up with the next child in line, mom claps her hands in delight, grabs Tommy by the hand and heads on over to the high-priced silver frames, and dad – well, dad's smile turns into a frown as he digs out his wallet.

Paul Waxman, the mall owner, and some say silent partner of the Chicago Bears, is briskly walking down the mall concourse to the Santa set with mall manager, Wayne Jarusinski. Waxman is pointing out stores whose rent will be raised soon after the holidays are over in order to force them out of the mall. He's pissed because several store managers did not go along with his plan to switch to a more expensive trash hauler which, by the way, is owned and operated by Anna Marie Mancuso, who just happens to be Mrs. Paul Waxman and the daughter of one very highly connected mob type who set up Anna Marie in the trash business in the first place.

Paul Waxman and Wayne Jarusinski stop just short of the set to observe Santa.

"Wayne," Paul questions, "How's the new Santa making out?"

"Fine, Mr. Waxman, sir, just fine. We are lucky to get him. The kids love him and the moms and dads are buying up the pictures, sir – and lots of expensive frames!"

"That's great, Wayne. He sure does look the part doesn't he? They both observe Santa for a while when Waxman says, "Where did you find this guy? And who is Santa's helper? Is he a midget or a dwarf or something? What is the difference, Jarusinski? I can never tell one from the other. It *is* a *he* isn't it?...the dwarf...the midget, I mean – whatever it is?"

"First off, Mr. Waxman, sir, we found this Santa through the Amalgamated Society of Santas, right here in Chicago. This organization..."

Waxman cuts him off, "The Amalgamated Society of Santas? You have got to be kidding me, Jarusinski! You got a Santa from *ASS!*"

"Ass?" repeats Jarusinski turning to the boss with a confused look on his face. Then he gets it. "Oh, no sir! No, No, No! They don't call it that, Mr. Waxman, sir. No acronym is used because...well...you can see why. They call it what it is, the Amalgamated Society of Santas. Anyway, sir, as I was going to say..."

"I can't believe in this day and age that Santas work for *ASS!*" Waxman snorts then lets out a laugh. "Think about it, Wayne. Now that's funny!"

"Yes, sir, Mr. Waxman, sir, I guess that does sound a little peculiar, doesn't it? I mean Santas working for *ASS* and all." And now Wayne has a grin on his face. "But this is a first-class organization, sir, which hires out over two hundred Santas in many states."

"That must be some operation," says Paul Waxman. "I'd hate to see their dry cleaning bill! That's a lot of *ASS* cleaning, if you know what I mean!" He can't control himself with the play on words and is laughing again. "I'll bet if each Santa gets a kiss on the cheek that would be a lot of *ASS* kissing! Wouldn't it, Wayne?" He doubles over in laughter but mall manager, Wayne Jarusinski is not sure how to take all this humor from a guy who never, ever jokes around about anything – especially when money is involved.

Waxman settles down a bit and continues, "Okay, what about the little guy?"

"That's Buddy Holly, sir."

"Buddy Holly is dead, Jarusinski!"

"Not *that* Buddy Holly, sir. This is Buddy Holly the Elf. And yes, he is a male, and he *is* a dwarf, not a midget – he told me that himself, but I'm not sure of the difference, Mr. Waxman, sir. I checked and his legal name is 'Buddy Holly.' I met him through ASS – now you got me saying it – through the Amalgamated Society of Santas."

"You met 'Buddy Holly' through *ASS?*" Waxman slaps his side and is almost on the floor with that one. "That's the funniest thing I've heard all day, Jarusinski!" Waxman pats him on the back.

"His name really is 'Buddy Holly,' sir." Wayne checks to see if Waxman is still laughing. "He told me so when I interviewed him. He said 'Holly' is his last name and his mother liked the movie, 'The Buddy Holly Story,' and so she named him, Buddy Holly."

"Good damn thing she didn't like 'Frankenstein!'" Waxman almost wets his pants with that one, and rapidly settles down when he realizes that he is becoming *way* too chummy with Jarusinski.

"You know Wayne, in the old days we used to hustle up a town wino from the alley behind the old YMCA and put him in a Santa suit for three dollars and fifty cents a day. Can you imagine that, Jarusinski? They were cheap but they smelled so darn bad from the booze and the body odor, and they never smiled at the right time – but you couldn't beat the price."

"I know what you mean, sir. I had my picture taken with one and I cut my toy list short just to get away from the smell," said Wayne.

"What's that supposed to mean, Jarusinski?" challenged Waxman. "It was a good deal and business is business!"

"Yes sir, Mr. Waxman, sir," Wayne answers while checking the paperwork he's carrying. "And guess what else, sir? This here Santa legally changed his name to Santa E. Claus. You see according to him, now he really *is* Santa Claus and not "lying to the kids," as he puts it. And, by the way, the 'E' is for his real name Eddie. I know. I saw his Indiana driver's license."

"Santa *E.* Claus?" bellows Waxman. "Are you sure this guy's okay? Did you do a background check? Does this clown come certified or are we going to have problems like last year?" Waxman starts dancing a nervous jig. "Christ, we're still in litigation over that one and God only knows how much longer it will remain in the courts. Not to mention the bad press we got – 'Santa Drops Tot on Head – Beats Up Bystander!'"

"No, no, no, Mr. Waxman, sir. Santa E. Claus comes highly recommended and is certified by ASS, I mean the Amalgamated Society of Santas; complete with a recent background check and a drug test from just last month, sir. Heck, he even attended the Santa College in Fresno, California and he has his beard insured and registered through the National Beard Registry." Jarusinski rechecks his information. "He's number 1737. I looked it up on the internet, sir – number 1737."

Waxman starts to say something smart about ASS again, but changes his mind and waves on his mall manager to continue.

"Not to worry, sir. I've done my homework this time," Wayne pleads. "And besides, sir, the Santa from last year wouldn't have bolted out of the Santa set like that if he hadn't spotted someone coming out of Victoria's Secret who owed him money."

"Damn it all, Jarusinski!" Waxman turns off the humorous mood he's been in – big time. "Just make damn sure this one doesn't go bouncing kiddies on their heads or get locked up or something! Got it? We don't want any more bad press!"

"Yes sir, Mr. Waxman, sir. I'm right on top of it, sir." Wayne looks up to the heavens for some sort of sign. "I'm right on top of it, Mr. Waxman, sir."

"Well you'd better be!" threatens Waxman. "I'll give you one thing," his tone changes again. "That's one hell of a good looking Santa set, and it cost a small fortune. I ought to know – I got the bill!" Waxman turns to Jarusinski. "What did you do with the old set?"

"Mr. Waxman, sir, believe me when I tell you we tried to save it to perhaps sell it to the Windy City Farmer's Market or to St. Ignatz the Martyr Church down on Pulaski St., but to tell you the truth, sir, it was just too darn old. We did invite the Patriarch, Zoltan Shimko, from over St. Ignatz the Martyr to take a look at it. The Patriarch did come over one day last week all dressed in his black robes with gold cords and a funny pointed black hat with black veils streaming down his back." Waxman is struggling to get the right picture in his mind. *This clown sounds like he's dressed for Halloween?*

"The Patriarch takes one look at the set, gets pissed off and starts yelling at me in Ukrainian," Wayne continues. "I didn't understand most of what he was saying, sir, but I do know a few Ukrainian words because my wife Stella is a 'Ukie' and speaks the lingo to her mom and dad all the time. Anyway, I'm almost sure the Patriarch told me to…" Jarusinski looks around to make sure no one is listening and whispers, "…go fuck myself."

"Tell me we're not getting sued by St. Ignatz the Martyr, are we, Jarusinski?" Waxman pleads.

"I don't think so, sir, because right after the Patriarch tells me to 'go fuck myself,' he then switches to English and says, 'You should pay *me* for taking all this shit off your hands!' Then the Patriarch blesses me three times, makes me kiss the icon of St. Ignatz the Martyr he wears around his neck, and then *he* kisses *me* on both cheeks and then on the lips!" Waxman looks at Jarusinski as if he has totally lost his mind. "The next thing I know the Patriarch turns away from me and leaves the storage area followed by two altar boys. One is chanting and brushing tinsel off the Patriarch with a large brush, and the other is burning incense in a silver-chained-thing he was waving all over the place. It still smells like high mass back there!"

"Pay *him*? Pay *him*!" Waxman spits out almost chocking on the words. "Fuck those Polacks *and* St. Ignatz the Martyr!"

Wayne Jarusinski is not surprised one bit by this verbal attack by his boss. He's seen it before – many times. After all, no one knows better than Wayne that, *No one had better mess with Paul Waxman when it comes to the almighty dollar!*

"So what did happen to the old Santa set, Jarusinski?" The boss cools down a bit.

"Well sir, the Santa chair is falling apart so badly it can't be fixed any more, and the entire set needs a paint job. Sir, it's simply falling apart. The red holly has turned purple with age and looks like rotten grapes. The silver tinsel has faded so badly it turned pink, and if you just breathe on it, it flakes apart like snow – only *pink* snow. You couldn't walk by the set without turning pink, sir," Wayne says. "We finally had to toss the whole thing out just last week in a special dumpster we had to order from the Hanson brothers. Those are the boys who haul away our trash, sir."

"Not for long they won't if I have my way!" scorns Waxman. Nothing is said for the next few minutes as they continue to observe the action at the Santa set. Owner Paul Waxman settles back down again. "You know Wayne, I'll bet we've had that old set for over twenty-five years," he chuckles. "I remember one old Santa we hired from behind the YMCA, leaned his chair too far back and fell right through the set with three kids on his lap. The guy was so damn drunk he says the Santa chair turned into a cobra and bit him in the ass! And guess what? Nothing happened – not a thing! We helped them all up from the heap they ended up in and, believe it or not, the kids were all fine. One kid's hand was folded back the wrong way with his little fingers damn near touching the inside of his elbow – and the little bastard wouldn't shut the hell up for nothing – just kept crying and complaining about his dangling hand. We ended up giving mom the picture for free – Christ, I hated doing that! Anyway, she was as happy as she could be to save the two dollars."

"That set was much older than that, sir," Wayne cuts in. "It's the same one I had my picture taken with the smelly wino, sir, when I was a kid."

Waxman looks at Jarusinski as if he'd just spotted an employee loafing on the job and changes his temperament once again.

"Get back to work, Jarusinski!" he barks – another mood swing back to reality as Waxman does a military about face and marches back to his office.

"Yes sir, Mr. Waxman sir," Wayne quickly responds. *And screw you Waxman, you old Jew bastard!* Wayne says this to himself and begins walking to Orange Julius for a free drink and to look at the new girl – Patsy with the big tits.

Jimmy D. Mays was the pride of the black neighborhood once. Located in a bad-ass section of Chicago; just behind the Burr Oak Cemetery, Jimmy D. (that's what everyone called him since Jimmy was a baby): went to school, paid attention to his teachers, respected authority, and went to church faithfully every Sunday with his grandmother, Miss Shirley. Miss Shirley raised Jimmy D. since he was a baby. He never knew his mother, an alcoholic prostitute who turned up dead on the shore of Lake Michigan early one morning – right across from the Conrad Hilton Hotel. No one knows what happened to her and only God knows who the father might be. There are no other family members to speak of. All Jimmy D. had in life was Mom-Mom Shirley and she was the world to him. Miss Shirley taught little Jimmy a lot about life and especially to, "be good, Jimmy, and always do the right thing!"

Jimmy D. graduated from high school with decent grades and got a good job on the Ford assembly line where he drove brand spanking new Mustangs out of the plant and into the yard. He loved his job and loved driving those Mustangs even more. He was making big plans to buy one any day now but couldn't make up his mind which color he liked best. He leaned towards "grabber yellow," especially when he drove one off the assembly line, but then he would change his mind with the next color he drove, like "grabber green," – decisions, decisions.

And then a little thing like Vietnam came down the road and so did a draft notice. That ended the color war in Jimmy D.'s head and replaced it with a real one.

The local newspapers reported that Army Cpl. James Douglas Mays received a Purple Heart and was further decorated with a silver star by General Milton M. Hershey himself for bravery in action while being pinned down under enemy fire for over six hours. Even with two slugs in his left shoulder, Jimmy D. kept on firing and held back the Viet Cong and all while nursing three wounded buddies. When help finally arrived, Jimmy D. let out the piss he'd been holding for so long and passed out. They all made it home though, thanks to Cpl. Jimmy D. Mays.

After a long stay at the Ira Hayes Veteran's Administration Hospital, Jimmy D. is declared fit for an honorable discharge and is turned out onto the streets with the clothes he had on his back, and a brand new toilet kit – a parting gift from the Polish-American War Vets. Miss Shirley has long since gone to the "great beyond" and never even knew about a place called Vietnam.

No one seemed to care about another "baby-killer" Vietnam vet and subsequently Jimmy D. was all by his lonesome except for the clothes on his back and that new toilet kit. But Jimmy had changed some since he walked the streets of Chicago as a young man. He did have some extra baggage, so it seems, and not the kind with roller-wheels either. Now poor Jimmy is hooked on cigarettes, caffeine, pills, pot, booze and whatever else he could get to ease the pain with – both mental and physical. And Jimmy D. has very little money, and no place to go but the streets. Sure there were programs to sign up for and meetings to attend but Jimmy was too busy looking for his next fix or cool sip of wine.

So how did he end up, you ask? Well, right now Jimmy D. is half fried on some pills he swiped last night from some other passed-out war vet and a half pint of some cheap-ass booze he bought with the money he had pan-handled earlier today. Jimmy swilled the booze down in about five gulps.

Presently "Jimmy the wino," as he's known on the streets, is rummaging through a big dumpster out back of the shopping mall looking for anything that resembles food, clothing and shelter.

"Holy shit!" yells Jimmy. His voice is raspy, scratchy and low after all those cigarettes he's smoked. Man-oh-man, did he love those French cigarettes he got back in 'Nam – "Gauloises" or something like that. He wishes he had one of those now instead of that butt he picked up off the floor of the liquor store that had long since gone out.

"Dis here dumpsta bigger 'an a house! Jimmy D. can lives in here," he says as he begins to rummage around through the trash. "My oh my, look at all dis Christmas shit!" Jimmy is so excited he almost swallows the butt hanging out his mouth. "Da man mussa throwed Sanda out da North Pole or somepin' 'cause all his shit is right here!" The old Jimmy who graduated high school and held down a good job did not speak this way. Unfortunately, the new Jimmy, the one who graduated from 'Nam, – "Jimmy the wino," does.

Jimmy shivers a bit from the evening chill. "Man, it sure is col' out tonight," he says. Jimmy spots something red in a box and bends over to check it out. "An' look what I foun' – Sanda's own suit!" Respectfully, Jimmy D. holds up the Santa jacket and gives it the once over. Convinced he will be a lot warmer in the Santa's duds, he quickly slips on the jacket and pants right on top of his own soiled clothes and instantly feels warm all over. "I wonner what they done to ol' Sanda?" He finds the hat and puts it on his head. "Mus' be they chase Sanda out o' town 'cause he left all his shit right here!"

Jimmy D. has a field day checking out box after box in the large dumpster. "An' was all dis here shit?" Puzzled, Jimmy holds up some faded-out holly garland that looks like purple grapes on pink snow. "Too bad dis shit ain' real. Squeeze dis grape shit out an' make me some home brew. Ha, ha," he laughs. Jimmy tosses the garland behind him and digs a little further. Next, Jimmy finds a life-size cardboard Rudolph folded up under another box and proceeds to set up the "most famous reindeer" in the dumpster. "Now, Jimmy D. gots hisself a reindeers who gonna keep Sanda comp-ny!" He stands back to admire Rudolph as he lights up another cigarette stub. Getting back to the business at hand, Jimmy opens another box and finds even more surprises.

"An' here's dinner!" Jimmy D. says as he unwraps two almost-fresh hotdogs complete with buns, mustard and relish – all wrapped up in tin foil like it was prepared for him to take home. He simply cannot believe his good fortune. "Thank you Jesus," he prays and takes a big bite out of one of the hotdogs. "You bin lookin' out for ol' Jimmy D. for a long time now an' I 'preciate it Lord, I really do. Sure wish I had some nice wine or some shit to go along wid all dis but I ain' complainin', Lord, I really ain't."

All of a sudden, a flying missile of something in a glass bottle comes flying past Jimmy D.'s head, hits the cardboard Rudolph in the nose and rolls back towards his feet.

"Incoming!" Jimmy yells and dives for cover. Jimmy lies on the floor of the dumpster waiting for something to happen – nothing does. He is startled about the relapse into his military mode. It brings back bad memories and Jimmy is sweating now. He mentally works hard to regain his composure and knowing that he is safe from harm, he slowly gets up off the floor to locate and inspect the "grenade."

"Grenay, my ass!" Jimmy bends over to look at the missile. "Some gook done throwed Jimmy D. a bottle o' wine!" He picks up the bottle to inspect it. Lucky for Jimmy D. the bottle didn't shatter all over the place. Jimmy is stunned when he realizes it's almost a full bottle of Mad Dog 20/20 – Jimmy D.'s favorite bottom-shelf wine. "Thanks be to Chrise," he prays out loud and picks up the bottle. "Sure hopes there ain' no shit or VD in here."

Tires screech from a black-primered, Monte Carlo low-rider with green neon lights under it as Tito cuts the wheel to the left to avoid hitting the large dumpster and the green neon lights barely scrape the blacktop. He's angry and his right shoulder hurts like hell from hurling the Mad Dog 20/20 from out of the sun roof and into the dumpster. He turns to yell at his younger brother, Carlos. "And what the fuck kind of Puerto Rican are you, dude? Go and buy that nasty-ass wino shit! I told you to get some tequila – dumb ass!" Carlos shrugs his shoulders as they peel wheels and zoom out of the parking lot leaving a trail of fire from the duel exhausts.

Jimmy D. unscrews the cap and enjoys the Mad Dog as he polishes off the second dog. He belches liked he ate a five-course dinner at the Ritz and then lets out a fart that further helps to warm his body. Life is good.

"Yeah man, maybe dis gonna be Jimmy D. home for a while anyhow." Jimmy spots what looks like a Santa chair under a pile of cardboard and two-by-fours which was once part of Santa's North Pole Workshop, and goes over to investigate, careful not to lose his balance.

"Damn grapes is all over da flo. Shit!" Jimmy stumbles and catches himself as he almost falls into a large box of almost-white cotton, sprinkled with pink glitter, and what looks like the top of a chimney. "Whoa, Jimmy D.," he cautions. "Doan go fallen down da chimney. You ain' da real Sanda an' it ain' Christmas yet," he snorts and chuckles.

After a minute or two of struggling, grunting and cussing, Jimmy frees up the Santa chair and moves it to the center of his new home. He clears out more room in the middle of the dumpster and cleverly fashions four inner walls and a roof from the old Santa set. With plenty of room to move about, Jimmy decorates the place with strands of pink holly and purple grapes. He picks Rudolph up off the floor, carefully flattens the reindeer nose back into shape, and sets him up next to a small artificial tree that has purple balls on it. Finished, and proud of his work, Jimmy finally sits in Santa's chair.

"Ow! Man, what da fuck?" Jimmy D. bolts up out of the chair and feels a wire spring finally let go of the seat of his newly found Santa pants. He grabs for his sore behind and rubs it a little as he surveys the spring. "Shit! Feel like a snake or some shit done bit Jimmy D. in da ass! Shit!" He's really rubbing the soreness out of his behind now. "Some-bitch hurt like a mutha!"

Once his posterior returns to normal, Jimmy D. bends the end of the spring back into the Santa chair, looks around at his new home, and begins to daydream about when he was a kid and all the wonderful Christmases he had spent with Mom-Mom Shirley. They didn't have much, that was true, but Mom-Mom Shirley made everything right, especially around the holidays.

"Ain' dis some shit? If Moms could only see me now." A tear rolls slowly down his cheek. "Now I bein' Sanda," says Jimmy. "Who ever hear of a black Sanda? Well Jimmy D. gonna be da firs. Ho, Ho, Ho, all you little muthafuckas!" Jimmy laughs so hard he pees a little in his pants. Not to worry though. It really won't change the smell any.

With a short candle he had in his pocket and some wood matches he managed somehow to keep dry, Jimmy D. lights up Santa's workshop and in doing so kicks an open box of tinsel with his right foot. The pink flakes explode into the atmosphere and come falling down all over.

"Holy shit!" Jimmy yells. "Look like it be snowin' pink in here!" Jimmy starts to violently sneeze as it continues to snow inside the dumpster. At one point he sneezed so hard he peed his pants for real this time. "Oh well," he says. "At lease dis snow ain' col' like da real shit is." Jimmy laughs at his joke and begins to sing out loud in that raspy voice of his as he re-lights the candle that went out either during the snowstorm, the sneezing fit, or from the piss.

"Chesnuss roasin' by a open fire. Jack Fross stealin' all your shit. Yuletie stockin's being hung by da fire, and folks dress up like a bunch o' 'Skimos'"

"Skimos," Jimmy recalls, is a derogatory name for Eskimos, Jimmy found out from one of his buddies in 'Nam – his squad leader and one of the men Jimmy kept alive – Army Sergeant Jaykoasie Atagootak. "Jay," who prefers to be referred to as a "Inuit Native American" and not "Eskimo," is back home in Anchorage, one-hundred percent recovered, with a wife and two children, and serves as a state legislator. He often wonders whatever happened to the man who saved his life that day.

Realizing the Mad Dog is all gone, Jimmy flings the bottle over his shoulder and begins to admire how he looks in the Santa suit and tries to impersonate Santa. "Ho, Ho, Ho, Jimmy D. gonna be da Sanda now an' he be bringin' your ass some good shit for Christmas. But *please* don' leaves me no milk an' cookies on a plate. If youse gonna leaves me somepin', how 'bout some roas' beef or turkey wif stuffin'. Das what Jimmy D. want. None o' dat cookie shit, oh no."

Jimmy reaches up with both hands and struggles to close the heavy metal dumpster lid and before long, Jimmy D. is fast asleep in his new mansion. With the Santa set for walls and a roof, and all the holiday cartons stacked up for insulation, it is rather warm and cozy in there.

Goodnight Jimmy. Sure hope you have visions of sugar plums in your dreams tonight and not the Viet Cong.

6

Donald Kaminski is back in school today bright and early. Don's an eighth grade English teacher at the John F. Kennedy Middle School located in a nice suburb where he lives, just north-west of Chicago. The school district Don works for is a progressive one and is independent from the large Chicago school system.

It is the Monday of Thanksgiving week and the students are off due to a special teacher's inservice day called for by the district. It's just as well. The kids are anxious about the holidays and wish that Thanksgiving had come and gone already so they could get to the good stuff – Christmas.

Don makes his way into the auditorium and spots his buddy, Chick Falzone, the phys. Ed. teacher. Chick seems excited and is motioning for Don to grab a seat by him.

"Hey, Chick – same old shit, right?" Don checks the seat first for gum, ink, spills, thumbtacks, wood splinters, and any other hazards before he sits down.

"Hell no, Donny-boy – something's up!" A nervous Falzone leans over into Don's face. "This is really serious, man. I mean, look – they called for a special inservice for the *whole district* and the entire school board is here!"

"The school board's always here when there's a free lunch," Don replies.

"No, man, no!" Chick fires back. "Listen Don, I'm telling you right now that something's up! I can feel it in my bones. Something is definitely wrong here! Trust me on this, will you?" And why shouldn't Don Kaminski trust Chick Falzone? After all, they've been friends for a long time now. In fact Chick was in Don's wedding and always reminds Don's wife, Sue, that she married the wrong guy. Sue just laughs whenever he teases her. She knows she's got the right one. Chick is the one with the problem. He's on his third marriage if you count the one that lasted less than a month.

"Relax, Chick. Believe me, this is nothing more than another 'dog and pony' show, you'll see." Don and Chick agreed a long time ago that there hasn't been an inservice day since John Dewey himself walked this Earth that was worth a flying shit!

"I hope you're right, Don – but I've got a real bad feeling about this one, buddy." Both Don and Chick acknowledge many of the district teachers seated near them. Most of them know Chick from his antics at the holiday parties and consider him to be a "typical phys. ed. teacher."

Donald Kaminski, on the other hand, has gained the respect of his peers as being a great teacher. Don's classes always go well and because he whips those kids into shape early on with his "learning should be fun" and, "by the way, I'm not putting up with any of your crap" routines, he hardly ever has any discipline problems. There was one kid a few years ago, Mike Moffett, Jr., who just about drove him crazy with his antics. The best was when Mike, who has a slight resemblance to a garden gnome, especially with those googly eyes, lit an M-80 firecracker under Patty Mooney's chair. The class got a laugh, poor Patty rushed to the Nurse's office to call home for some fresh underwear, Don was furious and felt this was the last straw, and Mike got suspended from school – again. And then one lucky day in March, Mike's dad, Mike Moffett, Sr., a respected pesticide field representative specializing in premature potato rot, got transferred to Boise, Idaho. Sure hope Boise survives the potato rot and Mike Moffett, Jr.

Principal, Ralph Emerson stands hoping to attract the attention of the assembled staff and open the session.

Ask any teacher and they will probably tell you that whenever you have a room full of teachers, they are worse behaved than the students ever were! They talk while the presentation is going on. They like the stories and the jokes, but really – what teacher, with any classroom experience at all, is seriously going to listen to some school administrator tell them how they can perform better? – or better yet, some asshole from the local university, who probably never taught public school one day in his life (and yet is noted in his introduction as being an "educational leader"), explain why "Billy can't read." Hogwash! Thus, for the most part, teachers simply do not pay any attention to what is being said and what's more, they really don't give a damn – especially the older ones like Millie Cramer, the librarian who would often voice out loud at many a faculty meeting, "We tried that ten years ago and it didn't work then!"

Principal Emerson is standing up at his portable lectern, made by the boys in wood shop last year, trying to get everyone's attention by waving his arms like he was landing a 747 jumbo jet at LaGuardia and calling out, "Okay guys…all right. Can I have your attention, please?"

Emerson is nervous because all the big wigs are here. He hides this with a big fake smile on his face. He grabs for a pencil lying on top of the lectern in the pencil groove. Principal Emerson just thought of something important he wanted to say. He continues to hide his nervousness. *If they only knew what it is they're going to hear today,* he says to himself. The smile disappears as he thinks about today's subject. A frown is next as the pencil point breaks off *because those dumb ass shop kids thought it would be 'real cool' if they carved my initials on the WRITING TOP of this friggin' lectern! What A BUNCH OF dunces!*

It seems every time Principal Emerson tries to write something on a piece of paper on the top of that darn lectern, the pen or pencil point tears through the paper because of the fourteen inch long, hand-carved initials! Emerson carefully re-writes the note, avoiding the grooves, and nervously looks up at the faculty and staff. He is beginning to sweat.

School superintendent, Raymond Wilkins, a tall, strikingly-handsome man, stands up alongside Emerson and things quiet down. Wilkins stands six foot-three, with not an ounce of fat and dressed in a dark-blue pin-striped suit with matching accessories. He doesn't say a word – simply surveys the auditorium with a smile. Sort of looks like mom did when you got home later than you said you would and you think, *Am I going to hear something pleasant or am I going to get kicked in the ass?*

Pleased with the crowd reaction, Principal Emerson begins. "A heart-felt thanks to all of you for keeping things running so smoothly since the beginning of the school year." He pauses waiting for his thought process to catch up with his mouth, then spits out, "…especially with the holidays coming up…er…well actually they're right here aren't they?" The nervous laugh and exaggerated smile give him away as he looks around at blank faces. He takes a deep breath.

Okay, here we go. Emerson steadies himself and holds onto the lectern for reassurance.

"Okay people, let's get started, shall we? We have a lot to go over today." Principal Ralph Emerson stands erect, as he should, before the group he is in charge of, and draws another deep breath. "As you have no doubt noticed, we have the school board with us this morning and we greatly appreciate their taking the time to be here." Emerson looks to the right and to the left of the lectern while smiling and nodding in acknowledging the board members present. By the looks of them, one might think they were "bored" members. There are no smiles in return. Most of the staff clap their hands out of respect – some do not.

"I have been asked to turn over this morning's session to our superintendent, Dr. Raymond Wilkins." Most all the teachers applaud out of respect for Ray Wilkins. As superintendents go, they probably have one of the better ones in the state. They like Dr. Ray and appreciate his leadership. And after all, they were the U.S. Department of Education's nationally recognized Blue Ribbon School of Excellence recipient for the past three years and are always being recognized for excellence in something or other.

All the auditorium seats squeak and squeal as everyone in attendance settles their butts in as comfortable a position as possible on those hard wooden seats.

"Get ready for the 'dog and pony' show," Don whispers to Chick.

"Dr. Wilkins," Principal Emerson gestures with his hands for the superintendent to use the lectern as he steps back a pace. Ray Wilkins already made up his mind to stand right where he is, behind the table and facing the audience, begins in a loud voice.

"Good morning," he greets the staff and surveys the audience with a no expression on his face what-so-ever. "I want you to hear this from me first." Wilkins now has the look and expression of a surgeon addressing the bereaved family with, "I'm sorry. We did everything we could."

"Believe me when I tell you that you will be reading about this in tomorrow's newspaper." This statement draws dead silence and everyone is listening, even Millie Cramer.

"I told you something was up!" Chick warns Don.

"This district is in financial trouble," Wilkins continues.

"Heck, we all know that already," Don whispers to Chick. "What district isn't?"

"As a result of the State of Illinois cutbacks in educational funding over the past few years, we have had to make many changes because of the lack of funding, but you already know that, I'm sure." Wilkins cocks his head to the side and appears to look like FDR during a fire-side chat.

"It looks bad folks. It looks really bad. In short, the state has squandered our money. I should say the Illinois Department of Education has squandered our money…the money our school system should have gotten this year…the taxpayers' money…and has funded way too many pet projects across Illinois that have had very little impact on the education of the children."

Wilkins pours a glass of iced water from a silver pitcher on the table. He takes a long drink of water like a parched alcoholic who has just entered the bar and hears, "Last call!"

"And the state let them get away with it," he adds as an after-thought.

"It will be reported today that the governor of our state will sign an emergency bill this afternoon to, among other things, cut administrators, teachers, and staff pay by ten percent, effective immediately!"

Groans, moans, and threats erupt from the mob, because that is what this group instantly turned into – a mob – and quicker than Spencer Tracey turned from Mr. Hyde to Dr. Jekyll in the classic movie. Eight or nine in attendance stood up at the same time and began to yell at the superintendent and the school board all at once.

"Give me one good reason why we are to take the blame for the stupidity of the state?"

"Why should *we* be the ones to take a cut in pay? What about the *other* state employees?"

"What about the Chicago school system?"

"Where was the state auditor while all this was going on?"

"You mean no one saw this coming until now?"

"If the governor signs that bill today, we'll be on strike tomorrow!" Cheers are heard from the staff.

"The Department of Education and the state legislators caused this mess. Why shouldn't they take a cut in pay?"

By this time, the mob was up on its feet like the founding fathers were when the latest tea tax hit the colonies. Principal Emerson is frantically trying to get the crowd under control and is waving his arms as if to say, *Please take a seat. We will listen to all you have to say. We will answer all of your questions. After all, we are all in this together, right?* The mob disagrees verbally.

"THEY HAVE!" Wilkins yells out so loudly he surprises himself with the volume. All turn and look in his direction.

"They *have* agreed," Wilkins booms across the auditorium. "They have agreed to take the same pay cut; ten percent across the board, including the governor," replies Wilkins.

"Oh, they are not happy about it one bit," he pauses, "but the governor and the state legislators realize that something has to happen and it has to happen right now, and it has to happen from the top down if we are going to save this state from financial ruin. That's how bad things have gotten." Wilkins takes another long drink and polishes off the water wishing it were something else a lot stronger.

More yelling erupts from where the custodians and cafeteria workers are sitting. "I can tell you right now, AFSME will not tolerate this move and for all I know we might be on strike right now!" boasts the chief of custodians, Cleon "Tiny" MacDaniels.

"Thas right!" the remaining custodians and cafeteria workers chime in like an inner-city church choir responding to the minister's call. Cleon turns, smiles, and waves to all "his people," white, black, Mexican, and Puerto Ricans alike, for their show of support.

A cacophony of custodial and cafeteria voices erupts as if on cue and with more harmony and flow than Verde's "Sextet from Lucia." These operatic voices of all ranges, sopranos to basses, all flow together as each voice range sings their lines in unison: "Thas right! Thas right! We ain' takin' no pay cut from nobody! We will strike firs'. If strike is what they wants, strike is what they gets! Strike! Strike! Strike! Thas what we sayin' – STRIKE!"

Cheers and applause thunder from the multitude. Everyone is up on their feet. Some are even standing on the chairs, and if the band was there, the lot of them would have marched out in unison and paraded down the streets singing "We shall overcome!"

Talk to some folks who attended that meeting and they will swear they saw strike signs of all shapes and sizes miraculously appear from out of nowhere bobbing up and down. "Strike! Strike! Strike!"

"Quiet please! Quiet!" Principal Emerson yells for order. No one listens – of course not. You just hit them hard where it hurts – the pocketbook; and right now, they're madder than hell! In fact, this group appears to be solidified already. They truly are ready to strike.

Chick pokes Don in the chest while grinning and climbs atop his seat for a better view. He nearly falls off as his weight shifts and the old, wooden auditorium seat starts to fold up entrapping his right foot in the fold. He throws up his hands to quickly balance himself better than Karl Wollenda, of the "Flying Wollendas" high wire circus act, ever did. Actually, come to think of it, Chick did a better job of it and remained balanced on the chair. Old man Wollenda, who was seventy-three at the time, and should have retired years ago, fell to his death in Puerto Rico back in 1978, when he tried to balance himself on a scary high-wire walk between two ten storied towers during a wind storm! Both Chick Falzone and Karl Wollenda must have felt the same rush of energy and excitement. Karl felt his a little more, perhaps, especially when he hit the sidewalk!

"Strike! Strike! Strike!" the mob chants in unison.

"Damn right!" Chick yells out, "Strike!"

"Let me have your attention, please!" booms Superintendent Wilkins. "PLEASE! Let me have your attention!" The thunder dies down some as Wilkins attempts to continue.

"There is an answer! There *is* an answer!" Wilkins announces. The mob quiets somewhat to listen out of respect for the superintendent.

"We are fortunate that we live in this suburb of Chicago and have our own school system separate from Chicago's, and, as a result, we are much better off. Most of you live in this suburb and your children attend our schools." The unruly mob begins to turn into orderly citizens once more. After all, now you are talking about *our* kids.

"We all care about our children and we all care about our schools. And these are *our* schools. And this is *our* community! We live here. We teach here. And we care about what goes on here, especially in our schools. We care because these are *our* children." Wilkins has the crowd now and they are listening to every word he says hoping for an answer.

"The Chicago Independent School District will announce to the press tomorrow morning that our community, our schools, teachers, parents, and everyone else who lives in our school district will unite to pass a school referendum this coming January for the funding that we need – that our children need – to continue to run *all* of our educational programs for the rest of the school year." Shock leads to dead silence. *The referendum will never pass!* They all think.

"Furthermore," Wilkins smiles, "As of this point forward, *this* district will continue to fund *every* teacher, *every* administrator, and *every* staff member, at full pay, for the rest of the school year, and with *all* benefits, REGARDLESS of what the State of Illinois does! Our people will get full pay and benefits because YOU deserve it!"

Pandemonium lets loose! Wilkins could have gotten elected Pope this day if he had wanted it (If not Pope, at least Patriarch down at St. Ignatz the Martyr). Everyone in the room stood, faced front, and applauded one super-superintendent, Dr. Raymond Ellis Wilkins, as if they each had a share of a winning multi-million dollar lottery ticket and *with* the power ball number! Hallelujah!

Then all of a sudden, an old withered voice, dusty from all the library books shelved over these great many years, echoed from the back of the auditorium, "We tried that ten years ago and it didn't work then!"

"Shut up, Cramer!" came the response from about fifteen teachers at once. "Just shut the hell up!" And she did.

Wilkins knew it was only Millie Cramer speaking her mind. He had known her for years now and he knew she was harmless. In fact, he worked with Millie many years ago when he was the new, young principal of this very school and Millie was transferred here when the old high school burned down on Mischief Night many years ago. Millie was old then, come to think of it.

It really is a wonder that he didn't laugh out loud when he heard her voice because every time he sees Millie Cramer, hears her voice or her name, he thinks about the "Dick Hurts" incident and smiles.

Years ago, Millie Cramer was the only librarian at the old high school and we are talking about the days when kids really did use the library to look things up and check out books and not just each other; you know – before computers. Well, during one school year, veteran librarian Millie Cramer was assigned a study hall group which met every day in the library during period seven – the last period of the day. She complained bitterly about it from day one. "How am I supposed to monitor the students normally in the library at this time, stamp and check out books, return books to the shelves, look for back issues of magazines in 'stacks,' and watch these kids in the study group at the same time?" she would cry out with anguish.

She could have added but did not, "And take a drink from the back room!" which she was suspected of doing quite often but never got caught. You don't become the longest serving librarian for the State of Illinois by getting caught mixing cocktails in the "reserved books" room.

Well one day, Wendell Marsh, the class clown for that year, signed the attendance roster with the name "Dick Hurts." You see it coming, don't you? Tired out from a hectic day and wishing it would end so she could revisit the "reserved books" room for a well-needed taste of gin, "Old lady Cramer," as she was fondly known, stood on the second story walkway bridge that went directly over the middle of the main library, looked down at the seated study hall group and called out the names on the sign-in list.

After eight or nine totally bored "here" and "present" responses, she finally gets to, and blurts out the name, "Dick Hurts." Nothing, not even a giggle is heard. The students are in shock and can't believe she fell for it. Again she tries only a little louder this time. "Dick Hurts!" she calls out clearly like the bailiff does down at the court house. Still there is nothing – no response at all. The entire group at the study hall table is looking at Wendell Marsh. They knew what he had done, and suddenly a low level of laughter begins.

"Okay, listen up, people!" Cramer threatens even louder. **"Who's DICK HURTS?"** That did it. The entire library breaks up and laughs so hard many of them had tears in their eyes, especially their new principal, Ray Wilkins, who had just walked in to hand Millie a phone message from the police that her car she had reported stolen last week from Wallowich's Frog Pond (what ever the hell that is), was found stripped in an alley located one block behind the Thaddeus Kosciusko War Memorial, not far from the Polish Am. Vets. on Pulaski Street.

Wilkins back-stepped out of the library that day and never let on he was there to witness the "Dick Hurts" incident. And just about everyone in the library that afternoon, including superintendent Wilkins, tells that story at least once or twice a year without fail.

Wilkins regains his composure but still smiling says, "I know exactly what you're thinking. Maybe Millie Cramer is right? Maybe this won't work?" Wilkins sighs. "But I have been assured by our finance department that it can work. It *can* work and it *will* work. And we will see to it that it *does* work! All of us will! All of us in this room right now will spearhead this referendum effort into the community and into the hearts of our citizens. We will do this for our schools. We will do this because we must. We will do this for the children...*our* children!"

More clapping and cheers echo throughout the auditorium for all the good intentions expressed by the superintendent, but you know what they say about good intentions, don't you?

7

That morning session seemed to have lasted forever with feelings and emotions rapidly changing from high to low to high again. And all the questions – most of them were downright stupid! And all the answers – most of them were stupid as well, and all because no one had a crystal ball. Needless to say, they were all wound up by lunchtime and gorged themselves with sub sandwiches, macaroni salad, huge oatmeal and raisin cookies made by the cafeteria ladies, and a multitude of sodas and flavored iced teas. Most of them were too full, on a sugar high, and their brains too jumbled to do much of anything else that afternoon. The superintendent dismissed the lot of them after lunch and told them to get a good night's rest and not to worry – but they all did. He needed the rest of the afternoon to meet with his steering committee and come up with a strategy on how to get the referendum passed this coming January.

They all left the school in fairly good spirits, but they were still a little antsy. Sort of like knowing you have killed all the vampires but wondering if there could be one or two who escaped into the night? And there were, for later that afternoon the Education Association and the local Federation of Teachers voted to strike immediately when they incorrectly learned that until the local referendum was passed to make up the difference in pay, and they were doubtful it would pass, they would still have to take the pay cut. Later that evening the great State of Illinois did announce that the ten percent reduction in pay would take effect immediately.

Don got calls from all his neighbors, friends and relatives who heard the bad news and wanted to know what they could do to help. This made him feel good to know he is this well thought of in the community and the facts are – he is!

Don Kaminski knows all of his neighbors, their children and all of their names. He is very active in the community he lives in. He served as president of the civic association for over three years and worked hard to construct a playground for the kids in a neighborhood park, an annual summer picnic for all to enjoy complete with concert band and home-made ice cream, and still set aside money for snow removal.

Some might tell you that no one else wanted the job, but this is not the truth.

Don also organized the community yard sale and the UNICEF drive until one of the other community activists, old man Barney Rakestraw, who secretly wanted to be the UNICEF chairman just to get the respect, and who was always jealous of Don Kaminski, complained about Don at one of the public school meetings making the accusation that, "Maybe some of the UNICEF coins didn't end up in the jar?"

Sure Don's feelings were hurt. Wouldn't yours be? Don turned over all the records he had in his possession and gave up both positions that night, but not until matching the UNICEF pot with his own personal check. Just about all of the people at that meeting, and in the community for that matter, knew that Don Kaminski would not do something like steal UNICEF money and urged him to continue to be the UNICEF chair. Besides, no one really liked old man Rakestraw, who always attended the community and school meetings and was the biggest pain in the ass there ever was! Don resigned anyway and that was the end of that.

The community hated old man Rakestraw even more after that. Most believed he deserved everything he got because a more bitter old man never existed than Barney Rakestraw. He never had a good thing to say about any thing or any person – just complained about everything. When it rained, he wanted sunshine. When the sun was out, he complained about it being too hot, and besides, "We need the rain, don't we? There's a water shortage goin' on, ain't there?"

Very few people wished him a good day or a happy holiday. If they did, all they got back was a grunt or a negative comment and sometimes both, so why bother? Rakestraw did not know the meaning of a "good" or a "happy" anything.

No one ever visited him over the holidays either. The neighborhood kids know they are not going to get any treats at the Rakestraw house on Halloween. On Halloween night, old man Rakestraw, who lived by himself these many years since his wife Stella died in the '70's from an acute case of Asperger's syndrome, would shut his house up tighter than a drum, then turned off all the lights and pretended that no one was at home. All the neighborhood children knew he was home because old man Rakestraw never went anywhere except to the doctor's once in a while, and naturally to every community and school meeting.

On Halloween night the kids would chant things from the sidewalk like, "Old man Rakestraw hides in his house – afraid of his shadow and afraid of a mouse." On Mischief Night they would bang the daylights out of his front door and soap up his old Plymouth in the driveway.

Some of the boys might even take a pee in his flower beds and that really made him mad since he took great pride in his exotic plants and flowers – especially the one he called his prize "Aficanus Aunt Jemimus."

A few years ago, one young rascal scooped up some dog poop in a paper bag and set it afire in the middle of Barney's porch. A nearby trellis caught fire and things looked like they were going to get out of hand until the Parker brothers bravely jumped up on the porch and whipped out their *schlongs* in front of everyone, boys and girls alike, and proceeded to pee on the flames, and put out the fire.

The girls, who watched, squealed and giggled, thinking this is truly a heroic act. Not once did they turn away. Instead, all the kids seemed to be amazed, not that the fire went out, but that the Parker brothers each had the longest penis they had ever seen! Heck, most of the girls had never seen a penis up close before. Certainly not ones as long as these were! Both Parker boys needed to wrap both hands around it like a fire hose gone wild in order to take aim at the burning trellis.

Needless to say, since that day, the Parker brothers gained a deep respect from their peers and the "well never went dry" on dates for the junior and senior proms, the church carnival held each summer at St. Ignatz the Martyr, and the ice cream socials held each spring down at the Polish-American Veterans on Pulaski Street. And, get this – both Parker brothers want to be firefighters for the City of Chicago just like their old man, Luke Parker, Pop-Pop Harry, Uncle Dan, Uncle Pat, and practically every male in the entire Parker family.

By the way, old man Rakestraw passed away unnoticed a few years back, and so did the UNICEF collection.

Later that evening, Don got a call to be on the picket line tomorrow morning at seven a.m. and "be prepared for a long one."

A long one? A long one! How long? What about the holidays? Thanksgiving?...Christmas?...and Christmas presents! That diamond ring that cost a fortune and had been charged? Damn that seven-ten split all to hell! Now what? What in the hell do I do now? Don wonders. He was so upset that night he could hardly eat. He tried his best to explain the situation to his wife, Susan, but Sue already knew. She got all the latest gossip from her neighbor Caroline Fletcher, who accurately reported everything that went on at the school and at the union meetings. Caroline was better than "Action News" in finding out what was happening in the community. Somehow she even knew about Sue's new ring and Don had not told a soul!

Long into the night Don and his wife Susan discuss the unforeseen problems associated with this mess and try to second-guess the future. They play out different scenarios in making plans. It did not look good and it sounded even worse. Good thing the kids were not home that night to hear any of this. They will find out soon enough.

Sue could readily see Don was encased in doom and gloom and does her best to cheer him up. "Come on Honey, this will all work out. We've been through these kinds of things before. We'll get through this just like we always do," Sue said. "Hey, I've got an idea," Sue's voice is about an octave higher then it usually is and she has this big smile on her face. "Why don't you let your beard grow a little longer and get a job as Santa Claus at one of the malls!" she jokes. "You can use a pillow to stuff the suit with."

Don is caught by surprise with this one and immediately begins to laugh. "You know Hon, you're right. I'm not going to worry about it. We'll get through this somehow even if I do have to fatten up a bit to fit the red suit."

Sue gives Don a well-deserved hug and they go to bed early that evening, both of them exhausted. Sue is asleep in five minutes. Don brushes his teeth and stops mid-stream and looks at himself in the bathroom mirror.

"Holy Christ," he says. "I really do look like Santa! And how in the hell did my hair get so gray?" Shocked at the revelation, Don, still not moving, has another thought. "Hey, maybe that's not such a bad idea after all?" He thinks about the Santa he saw at the mall the day he purchased Sue's ring. "Damn seven-ten split!"

"I wonder how much money a Santa can make in a season? Hell, I'm good with kids and I sort of look the part now. Beard's a little short – but maybe not." Don turns sideways and sucks in his belly. "And I might not have to use a pillow!"

Donald Kaminski is presently in his mid forties and is not a bad-looking man by any sense of the word. Sure, he has a touch of middle-age spread like some of us do, but he does have all of his hair, even if it is gray. Actually, Don's hair is really silver, not the mousey-gray like some folks have. He sports a matching Hemmingway beard and mustache which he likes and grooms very meticulously. He calls it his "writer's look." Claims he's going to write a classic novel one of these days just as soon as he finishes his screen play, which, by the way, he hasn't started yet – but he will.

With his six foot-one frame, Don stands erect, has excellent posture, and carries his weight well. People ask him all the time if he ever played professional football – which he did – high school and college – mostly tackle. What is most notable about Don Kaminski are his piercing blue eyes and devilish smile. He used to be quite a ladies man in his day.

Don always dresses for the occasion and you never see him in public where his hair isn't combed and his clothes aren't clean, fresh and appropriately styled for his age. He loves to wear different after-shaves and colognes depending on his mood – but when it's date night with the wife, he wears Polo, his favorite.

The family has not come to an agreement about the beard. His children like it and Susan agrees it does make him distinguished looking, but she thinks it makes him look a bit older than his forty-six years. His students at school think it is "way cool."

Lights out, Don is in bed, finds his position, and is also asleep in record time. Several times that night, Don dreams about candy canes, long lines of kids, having his beard pulled once or twice and having to pee really bad while in the Santa chair.

8

Jimmy D. is up bright and early this Thanksgiving morning. It is only ten thirty so there is plenty of time to hustle up some breakfast money and maybe even a little extra. "Man o' man – Jimmy D. hungry dis mornin'. Hungrier 'an shit!" Jimmy rolls over, sits up and brushes off some pink snow from his Santa jacket, and sneezes several times. He stands, admires his new home again, grins like the Santa at Macy's Department Store, always ready for the picture, and walks through the opening he figures ought to be his front door and into the rest of the dumpster.

"Betcha no Jehovah Witness gonna fine Jimmy D. house, for sure," Jimmy laughs. "No donation dis year, an' no Girl Scout cookies either! Das too bad 'cause Jimmy D. sure do like dem Girl Scout cookies! Wish I had some o' dat shit right now, too. Shit on a stick – is always somepin ain' it?"

Jimmy lifts up the heavy dumpster lid and surveys the surroundings. "Oh well, my guess is da sooner I starts pannin', the quicker I gonna eats." Jimmy's over the side of the dumpster in two shakes and starts down the alleyway behind the mall when he realizes he still has on the Santa suit and turns to head on back to the dumpster.

"Wade a minute. Wade a minute!" he says while thinking out loud. "Maybe dis Sanda shit gonna do good for Jimmy D.? Maybe peoples say 'Hey look, dere goes Sanda,' an' give Jimmy D. some money and shit."

Jimmy does an about face and heads on out to the main parking lot dressed up like Santa and wishing he had some reindeer and a sled to pull his sorry ass down town.

Today is Jimmy D's lucky day though. He no sooner gets to the very edge of the parking lot, when two elderly white ladies walking to their car, spot him, begin an excited conversation and while nodding their heads in agreement, change direction and are heading his way.

"Now what da shit gonna happen? Jimmy D. ain' done shit an' two ol' white bitches gonna yell rape or somepin an' Jimmy D. goin' back to jail again on Thanksgivin' Day an' dress like Sanda. Why oh why da mall gotta be open on Thanksgivin' Day?" The ladies hurry over to Jimmy and he covers his head with his hands in preparation for the inevitable pocketbook assault and those bags look like they are carrying bricks or worse yet, forty-fives.

"Good morning young man," says Miss Emma in the sweetest voice. "You sure do look like Santa," she continues. "Miss Martha and I just had to come over and give you this." Jimmy, hands and arms still over top of his head, peeks through his fingers and recognizes a twenty. That's when the hands went down and Jimmy gently grabs the bill and smiles at the two old white ladies.

"That's for the children you're collecting for," Miss Emma continues.

"We wish we could afford more," Miss Martha chimes in, "but we haven't received our Social Security checks yet." Miss Emma shakes her head to confirm that fact.

Jimmy D. is beside himself with his good fortune and cracks a smile from ear to ear. "Ladies," he begins to turn on the charm in that low raspy voice of his. The snake at the Garden of Eden could take a lesson or two from Jimmy D. – the charmer. "I can assures you dat da chil'ren will all be taken care of due to your gen'rosity. Thanks to you bof." Jimmy takes a deep bow careful not to loose his balance or drop the twenty.

"Our pleasure for sure," says Miss Emma.

"Good bye, Santa," says Miss Martha.

"Yes, yes, goodbye Santa," repeats Miss Emma. "We'll be sure to leave you some cookies and milk!" They happily walk away convinced they did a wonderful thing today and will be blessed by the Lord himself come judgment day, which both secretly agree isn't too far off.

"And besides," Miss Martha says, "I'd rather give money to a black Santa knowing it's going to the kiddies instead of that Patriarch fellow down at St. Ignatz the Martyr. His after shave smells a little too expensive for my taste. Don't you agree, Miss. Emma?"

"Why certainly I do, Miss Martha. I don't like the looks of anyone who goes around wearing black all the time. He looks like he's a friend of Zorro's, if you ask me," says Miss Emma."

"Well now, Miss Emma, don't be so quick to judge. Johnny Cash wears black *all* the time and I'd give money to him if he needed it," answers Miss Martha.

"Why Miss Martha, you would have given Johnny Cash more than money if you could, I'll bet."

Both old gals continue walking at a slow pace and laughing all the way to the car.

"Why did you park so far away, Martha?"

"Just to piss you off, Miss Emma!" – more laughter.

9

From the make-shift security closet (because the mall owner is too cheap to provide a real room), Security Chief, Paul Simpkins spots Jimmy D. on one of the many black and white security monitors stacked from wall to wall and almost reaching to the ceiling. Simpkins is sweating like a stuffed pig in these tight quarters due to the heat in this tiny space (his three hundred plus pounds probably adds to the problem a bit), and the heat from all the equipment is not helping much either. In fact, it feels like a blast furnace in there.

Simpkins is darn near speechless and tries to rise up out of the chair to move closer to one of the monitors for a better look, but his "spare tires" hold on to the arm rests and so the entire chair laboriously rises up off the floor because it is stuck to his ass. Gravity finally wins out and the chair, plunges back down to the floor with a crash that shatters two of the four plastic rollers.

The Chief immediately leans forward for a closer look. Unsure of what he is seeing, Simpkins crashes back down into the chair with a confused look on his face and even more plastic breaks off. He tries with all his might to roll the chair back away from the monitors and think a bit about what he's seeing on the security monitor. Next, he struggles like a bulldozer to move the chair forward again for another look. In doing this, the broken rollers manage to gouge out long strands of floor tile that curl up like colored party ribbons all over the floor. He stares in total disbelief at what he sees on one monitor. His mouth is wide open now and the stub of that cheap cigar he had been chewing on for the last two hours falls to the floor.

"No way!" he says, "No fucking way!" Simpkins pokes Officer Billy Watkins in the ribs. "Hey! Wake the fuck up!" he yells at Watkins who is asleep and tightly wedged between the wall and Chief Simpkins in the security closet.

Newly hired Security Officer, William P. Watkins is no more than a hundred and twenty pounds, soaking wet. That's really why the Chief hired him – God knows it was not for his brains. Watkins just lost a good-paying job as a guard down at the Serta Beds factory for repeatedly sleeping on the job. There is no doubt about it, in the Chief's mind that is, that Watkins was hired from the thirty some applicants because they both could fit in the security closet at the same time.

"Look at this shit, would you!" the Chief grunts. "Seems like we got us a nigger dressed up like Santa Claus and talking to two old white ladies in the parking lot!"

"What?" says Watkins as he bolts upright out of the chair from a dead sleep when **POW!** Watkins bangs his head on one of the lower security monitors. This sends him reeling back down into his chair with an instant Excedrin headache. He reaches for his forehead on the way down and feels the blood welling up in his right eye.

The Chief looks over at Officer Watkins as if someone had just opened the security closet door and thrown in a hand grenade. Realizing that this did not happen, that they were safe in the closet, and that Watkins, although bleeding a lot, didn't look all that hurt to him, the Chief returns to the monitor and the little black Santa. Simpkins points, then shakes his finger at the monitor and says, "Please tell me what in the Sam Hill is going on here?"

Officer Watkins comes to a bit and leans way over in his chair to take a closer look with his one focused eye. "I can't tell for sure Chief. It's a little fuzzy, but it looks like one of them old ladies just gave the nigger Santa some money!"

"What the fuck?" Simpkins quickly checks the other monitors and sees nothing unusual going on; then back to the monitor with Jimmy D. and the two old ladies. "Is this some kind of freaking scam or something?" he yells at Watkins. "That's all the hell we need is for some lunatic, Santa-wannabe, sicko, mother-fucking, skinny-assed nigger to go raping and killing two little old ladies for their welfare checks and K-Mart coupons in our parking lot! Mother of Christ!"

"Hold on, Chief. Hold on a bit," cautions Officer Watkins. "Look! Look at this, Chief! They're parting and going in separate directions. See, nothing's happened. They're all smiling like they're long, lost relatives or something." The Chief and Officer Watkins watch as the ladies turn from Jimmy D. and head towards the main parking lot.

"Christ on a cross if you ain't right, Billy! I don't get this at all – not one fucking bit." Just then, the Chief realizes he forgot to turn on the recorder to catch all this on tape because the mall, in his words, "is too fucking cheap to put in a first-class security system!"

BAM! The angry Chief of Security, Paul Simpkins pounds a meaty fist down on the long desk in front of him and Officer Watkins with such force that several of the monitors way up on the top shelf come crashing down. This starts an avalanche of security monitors and equipment onto booth of them. That's when the power went off in the security closet and it got darker than hell in there. It got quiet as well – not a sound, and that's because both Security Chief Simpkins and newly hired Security Officer Billy Watkins lay knocked out on the floor jumbled up in each other's arms and with Chief Simpkins fat ass still stuck in the chair. And that's when the urine eased on out from under the door.

"So long, ladies," Jimmy says as he bows. "An' thanks again for the twundy." He realizes what he just said out loud would perk up the ears of any derelict within five miles. Carefully, Jimmy D. turns slowly and checks for any rapid movements in the parking lot the entire three hundred and sixty degrees. Rambo himself couldn't have done a better job in surveilling the perimeters. Convinced that he is safe, Jimmy inspects both sides of the bill and is convinced it is genuine.

"Steaks an' eggs, here I comes! To hell wid dat cookies an' milk shit." Jimmy D. just about skips through the parking lot as he heads for town and perhaps more good fortune. He spends most of this time daydreaming about some wine he might buy, perhaps from the second shelf from the bottom, like maybe: Vampire, or Mother's Time Out – they are both pretty good; or perhaps Old Bastard – the red, not the white. "Maybe some o' dat shit be on sale today?"

Jimmy D. Mays skips off whistling and singing, "Here come Sanda Claus. Here come Sanda Claus. Right down Sanda Claus Lane. He gots a twundy and he byin' breakfas' and maybe some wine again…"

Somehow Thanksgiving got here and even after several days on the picket line, Don forgot all about his troubles and got lost in the savory smell of turkey, stuffing, and home-made pumpkin pie. Dinner was on the holiday table and Currier and Ives couldn't have painted a prettier picture. Sue loves to go all out for the holidays and it shows this year. The best of everything is laid out on the dining room table complete with a Thanksgiving centerpiece which Don remembered to pick up this morning at the local flower shop.

And the food! Homemade pumpkin soup to begin with that tasted so good it hurt a little behind your ears. That started the slurping contest straight off. *Gentlemen, start your engines!* Max Kaminski, Don's father, won the slurping contest hands down this year. That's only because Bobby Lee Chambers, Sue's dad, managed to remember to bring his teeth. No teeth – and Bobby Lee would have slurped loud enough to clog up the ears on a Coon dog. Lucky for him they were laying next to the car keys on the kitchen table back home or poor Bobby Chambers would have left them at home again.

You plan and cook a Thanksgiving dinner with all the trimmings for the family and invite Don's almost-kosher parents, Marsha and Max Kaminski from New York. They're really not that Kosher at all. Max just likes to wear his *yarmulke.* He boasts and complains at the same time about his Jewish heritage, and what a great/tough life he's lived. Mix the Kaminskis in with Sue's parents, Eunice and Bobby Lee Chambers, and you'll end up with some pretty interesting conversations. Bobby Lee, Sue's dad, is straight out of West Virginia, while her mother, Eunice, was born and raised in Boston, Massachusetts. Now that's a strange mix to begin with: Max is quiet and very opinionated while his wife, Marsha, is more open and friendly. Eunice might be "Miss Manners," but can hold her own in any conversation or situation – and Bobby Lee? Bobby Lee can talk your ears off.

Last year, Bobby Lee Chambers spent over an hour explaining how they were related to the McCoys, and later corrected himself when he thought about it and realized it was the Hatfields. It seems the more whiskey he drank the longer and more interesting the stories got. Bobby had everyone's attention when he presented a historical rendition of the infamous feud over a pig and something about a fiddle contest and a busted still. He described to a "T" what the leader of the Hatfields looked like – old Devil Anse Hatfield himself – how ruthless he was, and how Bobby's great, great, great grandmother was a captured Black Foot Indian woman, (or was she a Shawnee?) Bobby wasn't all that sure.

He went on to tell about the strict Baptist services they all attended in West Virginia and how you could not dance or drink (but a lot of them did anyhow, especially Bobby). Bobby Lee Chambers could hold your attention for hours talking about the traveling preachers, tent revivals, and the snake handlers who practiced out in the sticks – "out in the sticks?"

Bobby's whole family (Granny, four other brothers and three sisters plus all the kids), lived on the side of a big hill (looks like a mountain to some), miles from anywhere, located "just above the hollar," where you "threwed the trash you didn't want, over the side of the hill." Trash could be anything from leftovers from dinner, rags that "wasn't no good no more," hog bones and hide, mash from the still, an old ice box, or perhaps that '42 Buick that "ain't run so good for some time now." The Chambers are the "Waltons" in real life, and yes, at the very top of the mountain is the family cemetery where all the Chambers are laid to rest including the old Indian woman – who is way off to the side "'cause we weren't all that sure she believed in Jesus?" Bobby explained.

While Bobby Lee Chambers delivered his oral dissertation on "mountain people" (good God, don't ever call him a "hillbilly!"), Marsha Kaminski, Don's mother, sat frozen with a fork full of turkey in her hand, mid-way to her mouth, which was frozen wide open. She had an expression on her face that said, "Please kill me and end this suffering!"

Max Kaminski, on the other hand, never said a word, but looked down at his dinner and ate while shutting out all the noise in the dining room. He wanted quiet. *It should be quiet when you eat, and with no noise!* Max isn't going to eat cold turkey again like last year. He did manage to stop once or twice, however, to adjust his *yarmulke* and take a sip of Mogan David wine, which he liked served at room temperature. Cold Mogan David made his teeth hurt – at least the ones that were his.

Max would roll his eyes to the ceiling as he heard the same old stories he had heard the year before, much longer and with more detail. More than once he would fish out a Rolaids from his inner jacket pocket, where he always kept a fresh pack, to help ease the indigestion he was sure he was going to have. *Oi, gevald!*

Eunice Chambers, Bobby Lee's wife, could be the odd duck at times. She was always dressed smartly in fashion classics that somehow seemed a bit out of style on her. She had the manners of a Rockefeller even though she grew up just like Bobby did – poor as dirt – only she didn't know it. Some people think she's "uppity," but she isn't. She's behaving the way she was taught by her mom – *Always know your place and be respectful!*

Eunice has puffy, dyed, yellow hair which she spends a great deal of time with every morning getting it just so. No hair is out of place. Bobby Lee swears she has them all numbered. Her hair is usually as hard as a rock from all the hairspray she uses. And her nails! Eunice should do TV commercials with her hands and nails – always expertly manicured and painted. "Did them myself," she would boast. In her defense, she could be quite sociable and liked Don for the man he is and how he has always taken good care of his family, and never once made them move to West Virginia and live with those "heathens from the hills" like Bobby Lee did her.

Eunice likes Don's parents, Marsha and Max Kaminski, and goes out of her way to find out how they are doing, and what is new with them. In fact, Eunice likes darn-near everyone. The one person she does not seem to care for all that much is Bobby Lee – her husband. People who meet them for the first time, as well as people who know them well, cannot figure out what these two have in common, including Bobby Lee and Eunice.

Don and Sue are used to all this by now. They continue to smile through it all and occasionally throw in a word or two. Most of the time, they shrug their shoulders, laugh a little and say, "Family – God bless 'em." Only once did they come to an agreement that their fathers actually had something in common. They both slurped their soup.

On one holiday soup course, the slurping became quite rhythmic and got so loud that Junior started tapping the table with his fingers and sang the Harry Bellefonte song, "Day-O." Everyone laughed hysterically except Bobby and Max. Neither one got it. Bobby looked around the table with a puzzled look on his face and Max just shook his head wondering what the hell all the noise was about. After all, he thought, *It should be quiet when you eat, and with no noise!* And once again that evening Max adjusted his *yarmulke* atop his head. It almost slid into his soup this time – must have been the vibration from all that slurping and table tapping. It wasn't long before both dads went right back to "Slurp Fest 2000."

One can readily see how this combination of heritage, habit, and old age can make for an interesting holiday dinner! Like, two years ago, when Bobby Lee had forgotten his teeth. Seems he left them on the front seat of that old '57 Chevy he had up on blocks in the front yard. He had been working on that piece of junk for the past seven years, on and off, and it still didn't run.

Bobby had purchased that car "almost new" back in 'seventy-three for only three hundred dollars. He had only owned it a week when he darn near knocked down the town's lighted holiday tree and Christmas display when he got blind drunk at the union meeting down St. Ignatz the Martyr Social Club and drove home like a bat out of hell. He was all "lit up" and probably reenacting the good old days back home when he used to run moonshine down to the city. A trunk full of shine and a potent "big gulp" up front for the driver.

Bobby Lee raced through the center of town and forgot about the new traffic circle. He hopped the curb and just kept right on going. That's when he ran into the forty foot Christmas tree with all the lights and trimmings. Lucky for Bobby he wasn't hurt none because the holiday nativity display slowed him down a bunch before he slammed into the decorated tree. For some strange reason, he could never figure out to this day, no one was around to witness the crash even though he spent over an hour wrestling with the hood of the car, which had flown off on impact, and was now firmly lodged in the back of the makeshift stable for the Nativity scene. In the process of removing the hood he knocked over one of the wise men and dumped baby Jesus from the manger. Bobby finally maneuvered the hood out of the back of the holiday stable and tied it on top of the car with some rope he had in the trunk. The hood is still tied to the roof of the car to this day.

Bobby Lee tried his best to right the wise man but "Balthazar" was just too heavy and Bobby was just too drunk. He got a little scared when he saw St. Joseph standing there beside the manger with his head knocked clean off and lying by the feet of the camel. It seems the hood of the car shot through the air, sliced off St. Joe's head without knocking him over, went through the sound box that played Christmas carols twenty-four hours a day, and wedged itself into the back of the stable. A staggering Bobby Lee Chambers picked up St. Joseph's severed head from the frozen ground and tossed it into the trunk of the Chevy hoping that no one would notice it was missing, seeing as how it was Jesus' birthday and St. Joseph played a very small part in the pageant anyways. Bet you that head is still in the trunk of that old Chevy, too!

The crash didn't seem to hurt Bobby's car much other than the hood flying off. Even the tree, which was planted in honor of the Chicagoan native sons who died in Korea, appeared to be okay minus a few dozen badly damaged Christmas ornaments, tenderly created and hand-painted by the veterans down at the Ira Hayes Veteran's Administration Hospital. However, since the day of that accident, the tree lights never did seem to work right. And the holiday sound system – well you can for get all about that.

So now it got real quiet since the music wasn't playing any more. Bobby Lee went to work trying to put things back together and remove any evidence that he had been there that night. Some of the residents who live near the circle are kind of glad this happened though, because now they could finally get some sleep for a change – but they'll never voice this opinion out loud.

"They ought to shoot the bastard who fucked up Jesus' manger and torn up the town's decorations!" That's what they'll tell you, all the while happy that the bags under their eyes are slowly going away because now, finally, they can get some sleep. And what the town council can't figure out to this day is how St. Joseph totally lost his head that night and why was there blue paint on his neck?

Anyway, Bobby Lee forgot his teeth one year, remember? Poor Susan did her best to cut and mash things up for daddy to gum on. She did not mind a bit. It wasn't the first time and it won't be the last he had left his teeth somewhere. Last summer he came over for the annual crab fest by the pool. He brought his teeth sure enough, but then threw them out with the crab shells. Poor man bought three pair of false teeth these last two years! Eunice was forever yelling at him, "Bobby Lee, did you bring your teeth this time?" She always managed to bring hers. And Bobby would usually smile to show off his brand new "pearly whites" or he would drop his head in shame and say, "No, I forgot my damn teeth."

"Dumb ass!" Eunice would lash back.

On with the dinner – out came the turkey, the stuffing, mashed potatoes and gravy, candied yams, both cranberry sauces, with and without the berries, and on and on it went. Mix all of these special dishes with a chilled Prosecco (Italian champagne, but they can't call it that), and some room temperature Mogan David and you had a feast.

"Better save room for the fresh baked pumpkin pie, complete with home-made whipped cream," Sue cautions with a smile. She just made that whipped cream only five minutes ago and took great pride in going that extra mile with her holiday dinners.

"And don't forget the two different kinds of New York cheesecake we brought from Myer's Deli." piped Max as he adjusts the *yarmulke* atop his head. "Made fresh," he almost sings. "That's what Myer said when we picked them up in the wee hours before we drove all the way here, 'Made fresh this morning.' And Myer wouldn't lie about something like that. His reputation is on the line," Max said in a serious vain.

No one valued one's reputation more than Max did. A man's reputation and family traditions that went back centuries were sacred to him. That and to live by the "golden rule," – "Do unto others before they do it to unto you!" This was the true meaning of life to Max Kaminski.

"It's really all a man has left in this world – his reputation. The government owns everything else," Max would exclaim.

Throughout dinner, (and it's a marvel how Bobby Lee Chambers ate anything at all with all his rambling about living in the mountains of West Virginia, but somehow he managed to help himself to just about two servings of everything), Bobby Lee informed the family that he just talked to his sister Pearl this morning on the telephone, and got a whole bunch of news about the family.

Eunice would cringe at the thought of West Virginia and the whole Chambers clan wishing the lot of them had been wiped out by the McCoy's.

"Pearl says she's 'ailin'' some these days with her lumbago. Uncle Hunter bought himself a new Cadillac that had only a hundred and fifty-some thousand miles on it." *Hunter sure did love his Cadillacs*, Bobby thinks. "Cousin Tammy might have gotten herself 'knocked up' during the last barn dance. Don't know yet 'cause the pregnant stick she used got wet when they tapped the keg the wrong way and everything and everyone got soaked down real good with 'Old Milwaukee.' So the poor kid either got pregnant, got drunk, or both!"

Bobby's wife, Eunice humphed at this and warned, "It was bound to happen sooner or later. That Tammy Chambers girl was not raised the right way, that's for sure!"

"And Doke Candy growed up to be over three hundred pounds and still don't have a job," Bobby said. "Pearl says that Doke don't do nothin' but fight them cocks all night long." Bobby is shaking his head, laughing and sort of proud of the man Doke Candy has become and a little envious that Doke got to stay on the farm and Bobby had to go off and find work.

Marsha just about chokked on a mouth full of cranberry sauce on that one – the one with the berries in it. She took a big swallow of Prosecco to hold the berries down and belched out loud. Everyone looked her way.

"Please excuse me," Marsha said embarrassed by the social blunder.

"Don't worry about it, Mom," Bobby Lee chuckled. Bobby always called Marsha "Mom," even though he had ten years or better on her. And did Marsha hate it when he did that!

"Think nothing of it, Marsha dear." Eunice said sweetly. "Bobby Lee does that all the time at home and sometimes worse." Eunice gives Bobby a nasty look and he returns the favor.

"You know, in some countries when you belch out loud like that," Bobby Lee, the world-wide traveler explains, waving his fork in the air; "it means you like the food or the owner's horse or something like that. Maybe it was his sister you liked? I forget which." He turns away, shaking his head in confusion and reaches for the mashed potatoes.

Don thinks to himself, *this is from a man who never left the hills of West Virginia until recently, that is.* Oh sure, there was that three-year stint in Korea, but that doesn't count for much because all Bobby Lee did was haul water down from the mountains for the troops. Bobby loved it there because he loved the mountains, even in Korea, except it was "too darn cold!" He drove those trucks like a bat out of hell in Korea too, come to think of it.

Don listened to all the news from back home but he had some other things on his mind that had an awful lot to do with the word "finance." *Oh well,* Don says to himself. *Things could be worse. I could be broke and have to feed Doke Candy for the rest of my life!* Don snickers and gets back to eating and enjoying Bobby's latest down-home dissertation.

Sue never did think much of Doke Candy and wasn't the least surprised that he just "layed around and ate." When they were all younger, they grew up together on Chambers' hill, mountain, whatever the hell it was, and Sue had to wear Doke's old hand-me-down overalls, long johns and such, which never seemed to fit her right and had about twenty safety pins in them to keep them on. That was back when Bobby Lee lost his job making dental floss at the Gortex plant in Delaware and they had to pack up and move everything back to West Virginia and stay at granny's for the next few years.

That was a tough period for them to get through. Bobby went back to work at the mines, and Sue's mom, Eunice, raised as a prim and proper woman from Boston, and yes, definitely related to the Adams family (John and John Quincy, not Gomez), had to pitch in with the cooking and the farm work. You should have been there to have seen that one. Why Eunice was as much out of place as a pork chop at a kosher dinner.

Even little "SuzyAnn" (that's what they still call Sue back home), had to gather eggs and feed the ducks which she hated because they would always peck at her legs, make her drop the feed and run back to the house crying – only to get "bopped" in the head with a broom by granny for dropping all the feed in one spot.

And Doke Candy didn't do anything at all to help out. Nothing! He was granny's boy for sure and all day long she would coddle to him and give him fresh buttermilk to drink out of a baby bottle. No wonder he, "growed up to be over three hundred pounds!"

"Did you have nice holiday dinners back in West Virginia?" Marsha asked Bobby, trying to add to the conversation but a little afraid of the answer. After all, she might end up hearing about some Hatfield massacre or rape of another Indian girl.

"Why sure!" he answered. "Dinner was always at granny's house, even the special ones. In fact, just about every meal was at granny's house, except lunch. We ate lunch down in the mines and half the time you couldn't see what you were eatin' 'cause it was awful dark down there." Marsha is frozen in thought of the miners eating lunch in the dark.

"Granny always had a big pot of beans cooking on the back burner of that old wood stove," Bobby explains. He's grinning because he can taste those beans right now.

Those damn beans were horrid! Eunice thought and she made a face and turned her head.

"And we always ate the same way," Bobby Lee said. No doubt this was the beginning of a long one so Max Kaminski took a slurp of his room-temperature Mogan David and said something in Yiddish to himself.

"Come on, Pop," whispered Don while tipping his head in Bobby's direction as if to say, *be respectful and listen to the man.*

"*Feh! Kish mir en tooches!*" Max whispers back. "Dinner should be quiet, and with no noise!"

Bobby Lee overhears Max talking to Don and looks to see if he wants to add to the conversation. Max keeps his head down staring at his plate and goes back to eating his hot dinner. Bobby looks around at the others a bit confused but no one says a word so he continues.

"The menfolk always ate first. That's the way it was. Then the women ate. And then the children ate last – whatever was left over."

"I remember that," Sue said. "When we children sat down at the dinner table, Doke Candy would always tease me and eat the food right off my plate!…especially my corn on the cob. That corn we grew was the best corn I ever ate!"

Eunice chimes in again, "You know, Susan, the corn was grown mainly for the "shine" – not to eat, as I recall." Everyone heard Eunice but not exactly sure how to react, they just ignored the comment and kept on eating and listening to Sue. Fact was, just about everyone who knew her, ignored Eunice Chambers, especially when she did get a little uppity and made it sound as though she was better than everyone else.

"Granny knew Doke Candy would always eat the corn on the cob right off my plate," Sue said. "Then she got smart and would save two ears just for me and hide them so Doke wouldn't get to them." Bobby laughed and shook his head as he remembered all the fighting between SuzyAnn and Doke.

"And with all the brothers and sons who were old enough to work the mines," Bobby Lee continued, "well, we just about had enough time to wash the black from the mines off our hands when granny would call us to come eat. And we'd better hop to it if we knew what was good for us 'cause granny ruled the roost!"

"But what about the holiday dinners?" Marsha interrupted.

Holiday dinners! Eunice rolled her eyes on that one.

"Well," Bobby looks at Marsha and pauses to think. "We didn't have to wash up much then 'cause we weren't all that dirty, unless it was shit spreadin' day or castratin' day. We washed up real good then." And with that thought in mind, Bobby raises both hands mid air and checks to make sure they are clean today. Satisfied, he lowers them to the table and looks at Marsha.

Marsha felt a gag coming on and reaches for the Prosecco bottle. The kids, Junior and Annie, just laugh quietly through the whole ordeal and make faces at each other. They hardly got a word in once gramps got started. They didn't care. It was much more interesting to listen to gramps and watch Grandma Marsha get all worked up.

"We would march to that long oak table made years ago by Grandpa Riley," Bobby Lee began again on a mission to educate the masses. At that, Eunice stood up, marched over to the server, and helped herself to a small portion of three-bean salad, and returned to the table without saying a word. Bobby watched her do it, then twirling his finger along side his head, motioned to all that she was a little nuts.

Bobby looked back at his audience and said, "I'll bet that there table sat at least fourteen. By golly, that was a sight to see, 'cause our hands were clean but when we worked the mines our faces were not."

"Yuck!" Eunice said disgustedly recalling that whole scene straight out of "Coal Miner's Daughter."

"Each and every one of us had a black face except around our eyes where the goggles went." Bobby traced around both eyes with his right index finger and looked around the table for all to get the picture.

"That's the truth," said Sue. "They looked like the end men at the St. Ignatz's Annual Springtime Minstrel show they used to have years ago. At any minute you'd think they might start playing banjos and break out in a song like, 'You are my sunshine,' or start cracking jokes about the local politicians."

Sue looked around the table. "For years I thought my father was black!" she said. "That's the honest-to-God's truth. I thought my mother married a black man." Laughter around the table except for poor Marsha who is now coughing up a wad of candied yam she carefully spits into her cloth napkin hoping no one has noticed.

Eunice tries hard to remember if there were any black men who worked the mines in those days, and decided, *I never saw a black man in West Virginia back then until I went to Yeager that time when Tammy Chambers won second prize showing off her heifer at the 4-H competition. And when I did see one, I thought he was just coming home from the mines like every one else!*

Marsha's eyes have watered some and she thinks she might have lost a contact lens in her plate as the vision in her left eye is somewhat blurred. She grabs Max's napkin off his lap and gently wipes her watering eyes. Thank God, her vision returns to normal, and then she polishes off an almost full glass of Prosecco and looks for the bottle.

Max grabs back his napkin, shakes his head in disgust and grumbles to himself, "Dinner should be quiet, and with no noise!"

Bobby Lee is lost in his epic and never heard a word. "We'd all be talking and joking about work and things. We had to shift over on them long benches and a bunch of mismatched chairs so every body could fit – and hungrier than a man has a right to be. And onced we were all seated and dinner commenced, nobody said a word. This is the way it was. No body spoke at dinner…ever."

"And that's the way it should be," chimed Max. "Dinner should be quiet, and with no noise! No noise! No noise what-so-ever!"

"I agree with you Max," Eunice added. "There should be no talking at the dinner table! And your elbows shouldn't be on the table as well!"

Don and Max both shift their elbows off the table hoping this went unnoticed. Junior and Annie just laughed and pointed in Don's direction. Don noticed but pretended he didn't.

12

Having hitched several rides from the locals wondering who the skinny black Santa is and how utterly wrong it would be to leave Santa stranded in the road, Jimmy D. is now making a beeline for Guilday's Family Restaurant, which he knows is open and always has a special holiday meal for Thanksgiving. He knows this because when Mom-Mom Shirley got too old to cook, she would take him to Guilday's where he would eat himself full.

Guilday's even made sweet potato pie – not as good as Mom-Mom Shirley's, mind you – but good enough. The owners, Mitsy and Mike Guilday (brother and sister) ran the place for years now after the old man died, and they had a pretty good business going. Mom-Mom Shirley even worked there for a while but she liked Miss Mitsy as a friend better than she liked her as a boss. And no one ever talked much to Mr. Mike, the main cook, who was two busy in the back breaking the eggs. If you wanted two eggs over easy for breakfast, you had better order four of them because Mr. Mike would invariably break at least one or two and then try to hide them under the home-fried potatoes.

Miss Mitsy and Mr. Mike always did like Jimmy D. and thought he'd gotten a bad deal from the V.A., so when they saw him coming through the door dressed like Santa, they both came over to say hello.

"Hey, it's Jimmy D." said Mitsy.

"What's up, Santa," said Mike. "Bring us any presents?"

"Hell yeah," smiled Jimmy. "I bringin' you all my love for sure," Jimmy says as he gives Miss Mitsy a big hug. "An' you, Mr. Mike…Jimmy D. bringin' youse a whole basket of unbroken eggs." Jimmy laughs along with most of the folks sitting at the counter who have eaten their fare share of Mike's broken eggs.

"Hey Jimmy," questions Mitsy. "Whatcha doing in the Santa suit? Got a job at the mall or something?"

"Nah, it's a long story, but I came here for some sweet potato pie, if youse have any?" Jimmy asks.

"We got plenty, Jimmy," says Mitsy. "But first, come with me. I got something for you." Mitsy leads Jimmy to the back of the restaurant and into the employee lounge. "Look, Jimmy," she hands him a bag of goodies: toothbrush, toothpaste, soap-on-a-rope, shampoo, washcloth, towel, after shave, and a few other odds and ends, including some underwear and socks. "How about you go on into the dressing area where you can take a nice hot shower and clean up a bit, okay? You can lock the door from the inside."

"Thanks youse, Miss Mitsy. Sure thing, thas really nice o' youse. You and Mr. Mike always bein' good to me and Moms a long time."

"Don't mention it, Jimmy. Take your time and when you finish up, how about you go through the restaurant and wish all the customers a happy holiday!"

"Sure thing – Miss Mitsy. I be wishin' these folks eatin' here all the bess for the holiday." Jimmy D. heads on into the dressing area to inspect all the presents he got and indulge in a real shower, "An' clean unnerwears!"

Later, refreshed and smelling great from soap and Old Spice, Jimmy made the rounds at Guilday's Restaurant bringing season's greetings to one and all. Everyone there smiled and wished the little black Santa "many happy returns." They loved that he was all decked out as Santa and they started giving him money. You couldn't help but like Jimmy D., especially when he turned on the charm. Jimmy circled the rest of the tables and booths and by the time he got back to the counter, he had the two pockets on the Santa jacket filled with dollar bills and change.

Jimmy throws himself up on the swivel seat at the counter and dumps out all his new-found loot to see what he had gathered.

"Holy shit! Sweet Jesus hisself," Jimmy says in a hushed voice. "Jimmy D. got over thurdy-five dollar jus' here an' it ain' even dark out yet, an' Jimmy D. smells good too!"

Miss Mitsy steps over to Jimmy with a big smile on her face and says to Jimmy, "Put your money away, Jimmy D. and get ready for a big Thanksgiving dinner with sweet potato pie – on the house. And thanks Jimmy, for saying hello to all the customers." She leans over the counter and gives Jimmy a kiss on the cheek.

"Gee, that sure is nice o' you, Miss Mitsy" says Jimmy. "You always treat Jimmy D. like he special or somepin"

"Well you are special, Jimmy. You just made every one in this restaurant very happy and that was a good thing to do, Jimmy," says Mitsy.

Miss Mitsy turns away from Jimmy who is still a little shocked by how much his luck has changed all of a sudden.

"Muss be dis here Sanda suit?" Jimmy says to himself, puzzled. Oh well, he'll figure this all out later as soon as he polishes off the first good meal he's had in a very long time.

13

Bobby Lee Chambers went on and on that Thanksgiving night but somehow they had gotten through dinner and into dessert. Eventually, the old man started coughing and took a few more gulps of Dickle or Jack Daniels and quieted down a bit but his brain was still lost in "them thar hills."

Sue Kaminski began to daydream as well about the time she couldn't take Doke Candy's teasing anymore. It was well after dinner one fine hot summer day, she remembers, and Doke had taken the only corn on the cob left right off of Sue's plate before she even got one bite. And she fixed that ear perfectly, too. Buttered and salted just the way she liked…not too much…not to little…just right.

Sue remembers how she had cried her eyes out because that was all there was. Granny had forgotten to save her any corn that day and fat Doke Candy stood next to her and just laughed and laughed; smelling like corn and with buttered kernels splattered all over the front of his dirty overalls.

That was it! Little SuzyAnn couldn't take it any more. She closed her right hand into a tight fist and with one good roundhouse swing, she nailed Doke Candy right square in the jaw which shut him up immediately. Poor Doke didn't know what hit him as he went spinning out of control through the parlor, tripped and actually dove, head first, clean through the screen on the front door.

As hot as it was that day, there was a real nice breeze blowing that evening which made things peaceful like and so the grown-ups were all seated comfortably on the front porch that evening, sipping fresh lemonade granny made and listening to the Philco radio playing softly from the parlor.

Bobby Lee had won that radio in a card game and brought it all the way back from Korea. He had to fix it up some, now and again, but it played real nice. Sue can still hear the Philco playing an old blue grass tune Bobby liked and tried to recall the name. Something like, "Why did I leave the plow in the field and look for a job in the town?"

When **KA-BOOOOOM!** Someone had dropped a bomb or something right in the middle of the front porch! No! Something was thrown through the screen door that hit the porch like a refrigerator and was moving! No, that wasn't it either. What ever it was, it flew through the screen door alright, but it looked like Doke Candy wrapped up in a fishing net and flopping on the boards like a freshly caught tuna!

Folks jumped out of their seats in complete horror and shock as they stared in disbelief at the creature on the floor. Granny stood up so fast she pitched her lemonade and ice, clean out of the Mason jar it was served in, clear across the porch and onto Eunice's head. More than one Chambers lost control of their lemonade that day as ice cubes and small Mason jars began bouncing all over the place like Mexican jumping beans with liquids flying every which way and even a few jars rolling across the porch headed for the cement steps.

Eunice, who always dresses proper no matter what, and had her hair fixed just right that evening (because that's they way she was raised in Boston), immediately jumps up and violently brushes the ice cubes from her wet chest as if she had been bitten by a rattler. That's when she felt the cold lemonade rushing through her hair and down her back. This gives Eunice a chill as the yellow ooze makes its way clear down to her shoes. Eunice couldn't take it any more and let out one murderous scream that Alfred Hitchcock would have been proud to direct. Now she realizes her hair is a mess and isn't as proper as it started out that evening and now she is madder than a wet hen and has the face to prove it.

Granny jumps up and flies over to her poor Doke who is twisting all over the place being bound up tighter than a spare snow fence in a Vermont DOT storage shed, and muttering something about "corn on the cob." Granny couldn't free Doke from that devil's grip of wire screening he was twisted up in. The harder she tried, the more frustrated she became. He was wound and bound up so tightly, and crying like a banshee trying to get loose.

It took four grown men about ten minutes to finally free Doke Candy, but before they did, granny jumps through what was left of the front door and into the parlor. With the support wood shattered all to hell and a big gaping hole in the screen that was big enough to drive a cement mixer through, granny easily gets into the parlor without opening the screen door.

You could hear her yell clear across the hollar wanting to know, "Who tied up Doke Candy and pushed him through the screen door!" Man, was she burned up.

All the cousins point to SuzyAnn as she stood there in sheer fright, tears welling up in her little eyes, and feeling like a bulls-eye at the county fair shooting match on finals night – unable to move and waiting for the broom to magically appear and start "bopping" her in the head from now 'til kingdom come.

Granny gave little Susan a look that would have vaporized Superman and went off looking for the broom just as Eunice made it through the door, dripping wet. Being a proper woman, Eunice opened what was left of the door to enter the parlor. The little bit of screening and door that was left fell out of the doorway and landed on top of Doke Candy and his rescuers. Doke let out a cough and said something like, "Please, no more corn!" then blacked out.

Realizing that her daughter, little Susan, has something to do with all this, but what, she didn't know, Eunice quickly grabs Susan by the hand and hustles her up the stairs two at a time and out of harms way. Little Susan is probably more surprised to see mom all wet and not looking the way she usually does, than she is that she had just put fat Doke Candy in his place forever. From that day on, the corn snatching that went on in the past would never happen again. And to this day, all the cousins still laugh and tease Doke Candy about the day little SuzyAnn Chambers knocked him clean through the screen door.

"You okay, Hon?" Don asks as he gently places his arm on Sue's shoulder.

"Sure, sure I am," Sue answers as she comes back to the present and checks to see if anyone else caught her daydreaming. Instead, the family, Max included, was enjoying one another in good conversation, and the amount of drinking that went on didn't hurt none either. It seems Bobby Lee had finally run out of stories for the time being and was actually listening for a change. Even Marsha is smiling and saying something to Bobby and Eunice. She begins to laugh and pats Bobby Lee on his arm. Bobby laughs back and gives Marsha a pat on her back that makes some of the Prosecco jump wildly from the glass she's holding. Eunice, who doesn't drink often, had been sipping Bobby's whiskey every now and again. After all, no well brought up, respectable girl from Boston is going to upset her stomach by mixing good liquor with sodas.

Eunice Chambers has mellowed out quite a bit and actually has a smile on her face, Don notices. *She's quite an attractive woman for her age*, he thinks. She is laughing now at something her husband, Bobby Lee, said to her. *That's the first time I've ever seen these two get along so good!* Next, Eunice pats Max on his back, but a lot more gentle than Bobby did Marsha. Max didn't seem to mind. He always did like Eunice because she reminded him a lot of his Aunt Dorothy – his mother's sister, from the old country, who never got captured by the Nazis because she ran a respectable whorehouse in Minsk and frequently gave away samples. The difference being, Aunt Dorothy always smelled good – like sausage and onions. Eunice smells good too, mind you, but more like lavender and lilac. And besides, Eunice never gave away anything for free.

Marsha steps forward a bit to keep her balance while laughing even louder, grabs Eunice by the hand and heads for the drinks table. Bobby Lee, who needs a refill of Dickle, motions to Max to follow him, Eunice and Marsha. Max Kaminski, who never turns down a nice glass of Mogan David, as long as it is room temperature, motions *after you* and both join the parade to the liquid refreshments. Junior and Annie have disappeared somewhere in the house, no doubt to call up their friends and make plans for the weekend.

"All is as it should be," Don whispers in Sue's ear and kisses her on the cheek. "This is a family. Thanksgiving is when families get together to celebrate all that is good in life. And this Thanksgiving was perfect, thanks to you." They both watch as the odd couples continue to kid each other as they refill their glasses.

14

Thanksgiving Day is rapidly coming to an end, and all over the United States dishes are stacked up on the sink, football is on TV, the top buttons on several million pairs of pants have been unbuttoned, and the Pepto Bismol, Brioschi, and a hundred different kinds of stomach pills are being swallowed with some flat soda and maybe even a little Mogan David…room temperature.

Jimmy D. Mays, on the other hand, is feeling fine with all his buttons intact. He left Guilday's Family Restaurant a while back with a full belly topped off with sweet potato pie and still has all his loot. It was great to see Miss Mitsy and Mr. Mike again and it was even better to scarf up on a free meal.

What a great day this has been for Jimmy. Hitching rides in the Santa suit made life much easier. Even Habib Constantine, the owner of Bee Bee's Cash and Carry, laughed when Jimmy D. strolled in and wished him a "Happy holiday, Bee Bee!"

Habib smiled back and said, "Where you been, Jimmy D. Ain't seen you around much lately?"

"I been 'round," Jimmy answers. "I been 'round and 'round and 'round an' here Jimmy D. at Bee Bee's an' happy you open on Thanksgivin'." Jimmy D. makes his way to the wine section of the Cash and Carry, and looks over the shelf – the second one up from the floor. "An' dere it is," Jimmy smiles, "Fat Bastid – da red, not dat white shit – an' on sale too!…Only four dollar, niney-nine cent a bottle!" Jimmy can't believe his continued good luck. It just seems to never end. "Gotta be dis here Sanda suit bring Jimmy D. all dis here luck."

Back to the counter where Jimmy slings up four bottles of Fat Bastard – the red, not the white.

"Hey, Jimmy D.," Habib teases, "Hey, you buying *four* bottles today? What did you do, win the lottery or something?"

Jimmy pulls out a wad of cash and throws a ten and several fives on the counter. "Yeah, Bee Bee – Jimmy D. done won da lottery alright." He puts the wad of cash away and slaps his side pocket.

"Now Jimmy D. have two rich ol' lady frien's and he in line for some 'heritance."

"Oh yeah?" questions Habib. "What kind of 'heritance' are we talking about? How much you get?"

"Hey Bee Bee, don' youse worry your brains out on dat. Youse worry 'bout if youse needin' to order more Fat Bastid – the red, not the white, in case the shelf be empty for Jimmy D. Got it? Jimmy D. got enough to pay for it. Thas for sure. You jus' be knowin' dat it's da squeaky wheel gets da worm. Dat's all youse gotta know. Okay, Bee Bee?"

"Jimmy D. buying *four* bottles of wine this time," says Habib grinning away. "Hey Jimmy. How come you buyin' Fat Bastard and not Mad Dog 20/20 like always? Mad Dog is on sale too!"

"Listen, Bee Bee – anybody who be drinkin' wines like I do, knows Fat Bastid tases more better 'an Mad Dog every day o' da week, das why. Da red, not dat white shit!"

"I don't know, Jimmy? That priest-fella from over St. Ignatz the Martyr? He comes in here once a week and buys a case of Mad Dog 20/20 for all them Jews over at St. Ignatz. It must be good if St. Ignatz drinks it?"

"Listen, Bee Bee…them Jews over St….what?...St. Bignuts?"

"Ignatz, Saint Ignatz the Martyr down on Pulaski Street," Habib corrects.

"Yeah, soun' like 'big nuts' to me, Bee Bee. Anyways, dem Jew boys don' know nuttin' 'bout no wines like Jimmy D. Das all dere is to it, Bee Bee."

"If you say so, Jimmy."

"I say so, 'cause I knows so! Hey, Bee Bee, you sell unner-wears in here?"

"No, Jimmy D." Habib answers. "We sell just about everything else, but we don't sell no underwear. You need some toothpaste or some Pepto Bismol?" he asks.

"Pepto Bismo? What da fuck is Pepto Bismo? Jimmy D. don' drink no Pepto Bismo – jus' dis Fat Bastid shit be plenty for now, Bee Bee. Oh yeah, and gimme two pack o' Camels."

"Okay, Jimmy D." Habib reaches behind him for the Camels, hands them to Jimmy along with the change and then suddenly draws back his hand with the money in it and says, "Unless this is my tip?"

"Tip, my ass, Bee Bee. Jimmy D. ain' livin' no life o' luxury. At lease not yet, anyhow." He gathers up his Fat Bastard, Camels and change, and heads for the door.

"Hey, Jimmy!" yells Habib.

"Hey what!" yells Jimmy.

"Hey – That priest-fella from over St. Ignatz the Martyr – he be giving out clothes and underwear to the people in the neighborhood. Why don't you go see him and get some for free?" says Habib.

"Hey, thanks, Bee Bee. Jimmy D. be sure to see dat priess-fella over at St. Bignuts."

"Hey, Jimmy D. – don't take no wooden nickels!" Habib laughs at his joke and throws Jimmy some matches which hit the floor.

"Oh yeah, thanks Bee Bee – I be needen dese." He bends over to pick up the matches and puts them in the bag. "An' don' worry, Bee Bee. Jimmy D. ain' taken nuttin' made o' wood," ... *unless it be a new Sanda chair. The one I gots is tearin' up my behind wid dat cockeyed snake-spring be bitin' Jimmy D. in da ass all da time!*

Jimmy exits the Cash and Carry and hears the bell tinkle as the door shuts. This reminds him, all of a sudden, of the old black and white movie that he and Mom-Mom Shirley would watch each holiday season (Actually, everything they watched on TV was in black and white because Mom-Mon Shirley never owned a color TV in her life!).

"Yeah," says Jimmy as though he has just deciphered the Da-Vinci Code. "Da one wid Jimmy Stewar' and Donna Reeds in it. What da shit was dat called?" he ponders. "Oh yeah, 'Is a Wonnerful Life.' Dats it! – 'Is a Wonnerful Life' – when da bells keep on ringin' and dis here angel be doin' shit to Jimmy Stewar'. I wonner if dat bell ringin' at the Cash and Carry gonna be doin' some shit to Jimmy D.?" Jimmy ponders this question while heading out to the highway to thumb a ride back to the dumpster.

"Hey, wade a minute," Jimmy stops dead in his tracks. "At da end o' dat movie, everybody in da worl' come to Jimmy Stewar' house with 'cordians and shit an' give him all da money pile high on da table! Even da ol' black lady give Jimmy Stewar' all her money!" He raises his eyebrows and looks up to the heavens. "Bess be getting' my ass home, case maybe lotsa peoples be bringin' monies and shit over to Jimmy D. house an' da Jehovah Witness peoples an' Girl Scouts be sayin' Jimmy D. ain' home!"

Jimmy D. opens up a pack of Camels and lights one up, careful not to drop the Fat Bastard – the red, not the white. He takes one drag and inhales so deeply that half of the cigarette becomes ash. Jimmy skips the rest of the way down the block and out to the highway where a black-primered Chevy low-rider, with green neon lights shining under it, jams on its breaks stopping to pick him up before he has his thumb out. And Jimmy hops in hoping he gets home before all the money gets there.

15

Bobby Lee Chambers is back in form and telling tall ones better than Samuel Clemmons ever could. Who would have guessed that all it took was a couple of drinks (actually it was way more than a couple), to get Don's parents, Max and Marsha Kaminski, so dog-gone friendly with Sue's parents, Bobby and Eunice Chambers? But there they all are; laughing it up and having a merry old time. Bobby and Marsha stroll over to Don arm-in-arm.

"What's this?" Don questions. "Mom, are you two-timing Dad with Bobby Lee?"

"Not to worry, Son," Max pipes in as he follows up with Eunice on his arm. We have decided to switch partners for the evening."

"Max!" yells Eunice blushing as she lightly gives him a smack on his arm. "I didn't think you cared?" she says laughingly.

"Marsha, my love, I have something to announce," Max says while pushing the *yarmulke* back on top of his head and glancing over at his wife. "I'm out of Mogan David." Marsha and Eunice laugh as if on cue and Marsha says, "And Don, Eunice and I are out of that lovely bubbly stuff you bought. What did you say that was?...Popsico, or Pepsico or something?" She looks to Eunice for an answer, but right now Eunice is in no shape to start answering questions.

"Hold on, ladies and let me go to the kitchen and get you some more of that 'Pepsico,'" Don laughs.

"Say, Don, if it ain't too much trouble, I'll take some of that Wild Turkey you got hidden under the sink," Bobby Lee chimes in showing his empty glass to all.

"You don't miss much, do you, Pop?" Don says heading out the doorway and into the kitchen.

"And don't forget the Mogan David – room temperature, please! It must be room temperature to be any good." Max Kaminski reminds his son.

"Sure thing, Dad – Mogan David at room temperature coming up."

"He's a good boy," says Marsha, "but I'm worried about him with this strike and all going on." She turns toward Max.

"He'll be alright," Max proclaims with his index finger in the air. "He's a Kaminski! And we Kaminskis have made it through the Tsars, Hitler, Stalin, the Pogroms, and even Siberia. Donald can make it through a strike."

"My father, Hiram Kaminski, may God rest his departed soul, was one of seven children. He and my Uncle Saul were in their prime during the war and worked for the Polish underground. If caught – instant death – no questions asked. Oh, they knew for a long time that they were marked to be sent to one of Hitler's concentration camps where they would be either be murdered in the ovens or worked to death, but it took a long time for the Krauts to catch up with them. They knew all the little Polish towns and its people, and they were very street smart. It looked like they might make it to freedom, but, eventually things went bad. The Nazis hunted them down for almost two years when they caught up with them in a little village called Lipsk, famous for their home-made *czarnina* – duck's blood soup." Max's eyes begin to water as he remembers the stories told to him often by his father when he was a young boy and by the tangy taste of the of the duck's blood soup which he always enjoyed as a boy if there was any left.

"My Uncle Saul, who left my father briefly at one of their hideouts, was captured by the Gestapo on a street corner eating a sausage he had stolen from a vendor down the block. Saul ended up in a Nazi concentration camp called Camp Slivovitz in Lithuania." Max is now visibly shaken and has to hold on to the back of a chair for support. "I'll bet you never heard of that camp, did you? Camp Slivovitz was run by those rotten Lithuanian bastards who worked for the Germans. This was not one of those camps with the ovens, although many people died there. This camp was a factory – a special factory. Want to know what they made there?" Everyone shakes their head yes.

"Chrome hubcaps for the Mercedes Benz people! That's right! This was a big Nazi secret during the war. No one was ever supposed to find out that there was a big hubcap plant right in the middle of Lithuania. And there was no Otto Schindler there to save the Jews either!" Max is visibly shaken but continues with a little Kaminski history.

"Somehow word got back to the Allies about the hubcap plant and so it was never touched during the heavy bombings that took place in that area because Mercedes had big connections in the U.S. Everything else was bombed to hell – military or not: villages, towns, factories, whole milking herds, egg farms, breweries – that was a damn shame because no one made better beer than the Lithuanians! – ski resorts, monasteries, and the huge Schultheiss Lederhosen plant the Allies thought made 'heavy water' for nuclear experimentation. None of this was true, however. The underground got big money to spread that rumor by Horst Radamacher, who owned the only other lederhosen plant in the area – *Der Drei Schweinen*.

Max adjusts his *yarmulke* back on top of his head and continues, "The underground convinced Eisenhower that the Schultheiss Lederhosen plant was secretly manufacturing 'heavy water' for the Krauts, and so the Schultheiss plant and every pair of lederhosen in it went up in flames. Later, after the war, Simon Wiesenthal, the Israeli 'Nazi Hunter,' caught up with Radamacher in the Cayman Islands, running a dry cleaning business and living like a Saudi Prince. The Mossad – You know what the Mossad is don't you? – Israeli Secret Service. The Mossad, was led by that one-eyed guy – What was his name? Diane something…Diane Carrol? No, that wasn't it. Oh yeah, now I remember – it was *Moshe*…Moshe Dayan – that was it – Moshe Dayan."

Max is visible shaken and caught up in the story but rages on, "Now mind you; what I am about to tell you because this IS highly classified information. Very few people know this. Moshe and his men, disguised as pizza delivery boys, got into the Radamacher mansion, captured Horst dressed in drag for a *Cinco de Mayo* party he was getting ready to attend, and drug him out kicking. He couldn't scream so good because they had duct-taped his mouth shut. And that was the end of Horst Radamacher – no trial, no jail, no nothing – and no Horst. No one ever heard from him again. Some say his remains were ground up with the chicken feed. Others are convinced he was buried alive in the cement foundation of the David Ben-Gurion Motocross and Sports Palace (Israel's equivalent to NASCAR). Some even say he's still alive somewhere in a Jerusalem jail, but I doubt it. No one dressed in drag ever lasts long in a Jerusalem jail. And for about four years after he disappeared, all the dry cleaning trucks that drove through the Cayman Islands had a bumper sticker on the back which read, 'Where's Horst?'"

"Miraculously, thanks being to the one living God, Camp Slivovitz was saved and the hubcap production didn't slow up one bit. They had so damn many hubcaps stockpiled they tried to sell some through the black market to General Motors, but GM wouldn't fall for it. They knew the Mercedes emblem would not go well on Cadillacs and Buicks, especially during the war years. And besides, they were all metric! Oh, yes, GM tried them out because 'a deal is a deal.' Sadly, however, every time they put the Kraut hubcaps on a GM car and made a sharp turn on the test track, the Mercedes hubcaps would go flying off! Sorry, Mr. Mercedes – no dice!"

"In a way," Max continues, "the secret hubcap plant was the best thing that could have happened for my Uncle Saul. In fact, it saved his life, because Uncle Saul knew all there was to know about chrome and hubcaps. He was…" Max points upwards with his right index finger, "a hubcap expert! From a block away, Saul could spot a dented hubcap lying by the curb and tell you not only the kind of car it came from but also the year, make and model, and sometimes, if he was really 'on,' he could tell you the color of the car it came off of!" Max tries to take another drink from the empty glass, then looks toward the kitchen for Don to return.

"It wasn't long after he was captured that the Krauts found out about Saul's talent and made my Uncle Saul in charge of production. They started to give him extra food and clothes – and once or twice they gave him a woman – usually a Gypsy, never any thing worth bragging about. Eventually, as the Germans figured out they were going to lose the war, Uncle Saul was given his freedom. And what did Uncle Saul do? He stayed right there and continued to supervise the hubcap making. Right there in the new Lithuanian town of Slivovitz. He kept the job as Head of Production for Mercedes Benz, only this time he got paid – not that much, but it was a living. He married the Gypsy woman, has three children now, and lives there in Slivovitz today – still!" Again, Max looks toward the kitchen for the new bottle of Mogen David – room temperature.

"My father was lucky too that day. He saw the Gestapo coming just in the nick of time and shimmied under a dead horse lying by the side of the road where he pretended to be the dead rider. The Gestapo rushed Uncle Saul and arrested him. They saw my father but he didn't move a muscle – which would have been hard to do anyway with a dead horse on top of you – and, as I said, my father was playing dead and since he already smelled the part, he got away with it. Later he caught up with the underground and escaped." Marsha looks at Max in amazement and wonders if Bobby should be telling this story.

"My father…" Max pauses to swallow down a sigh and with pride continues the saga. "He made it!" A single tear begins to roll down Max's cheek as he adjusts his *yarmulke*. "Thanks be to the one and only true God from above, he made it! He made it all the way to Latvia where he worked the tourist trade by selling picture postcards of the shrine of 'Our Lady of the Weak and Downtrodden' to the wealthy Krauts who would come to Riga to vacation. You know, to take in the salt baths, swim in the Baltic, and visit the shrine of Our Lady of the Weak and Downtrodden – Riga is the capital city of Latvia, you know."

"Later on, my father, who was always the entrepreneur, sold crucifixes made from olive wood with mother of pearl inlay. He claims these were made by the Little Sisters of the Poor who, some say, began their order in Riga and were originally called just the 'Little Sisters' because they were all pretty well off at that time." Max again tries to take a long sip of Mogan David but the glass is still empty. Again, he looks toward the kitchen.

"Ancient history tells us the poor Little Sisters lost everything," Max shakes his head in pity. "Churches, convents, highway toll booths, collection boxes, the chocolate factory – everything! …on that fateful night of Friday, October 13, in 1307 when King Philip the Fair of France rounded up and arrested the Crusaders, specifically the Knights Templar. They were all caught partying with the Little Sisters who happened to be in Paris on vacation that year. Now they really are poor!" Marsha is convinced this was the Mogan David speaking and not Max, but the story got so interesting, she didn't dare interrupt.

"Somehow…Somehow!…My father, bless his sacred heart, made it to America with nothing. Nothing!…not even a crucifix to sell!" The tears return and begin to well up in Max's eyes as he begins to reach for his hanky and quickly changes mid stream to catch the *yarmulke* sliding off his head and without realizing it, he blows his nose in it with a loud 'honk,' and slides the *yarmulke* into his back pocket.

Don is returning from the kitchen with several bottles when he thinks he hears a horn blast from a semi-tractor trailer driving by the house and wonders why these guys aren't home on Thanksgiving?

"That's when my father, bless his heart, decided to start the funeral business in Queens," Max finally ends the saga. "After all, who knew more about death than my father?" Max feels for the *yarmulke* that should be on top of his head, but it isn't there. He looks around questioningly then checks the floor around him and not seeing it, he shrugs his shoulders and holds out his glass to Don for a refill.

"Son, I hope…"

"Don't worry none, Pop…"

"Room temperature," they all sing out and break into a laugh.

16

"Hey, Homes," Tito says while looking through the rear view mirror at Jimmy D. Mays sitting in the back seat and trying not to laugh. "What you doin' dressed up like Santa?" Carlos turns around to get a better look at Jimmy and cracks a smile.

"Yeah, man, whatchu doin' – workin' at the mall or something like cousin Domingo?" Carlos adds. The two brothers look at each other smiling and do a high five.

"Hey, Carlos," Tito says quietly. "Hey man, don' be raggin' on Domingo, man. You know he ain't right in the head, man. Dumb shit is doin' the best he can, man, especially for a retard."

"I know. I know," say Carlos. "But it's funny, man – And I ain't sayin' it to his face."

"You do that, *pendeho*, and you're one dead Puerto Rican."

"Thas right…thas right…go on an' laughs 'cause Jimmy D. gots hisself a job and you two lazy 'Ricans riden' roun', no job, no place to go, an' wonder where you gonna eats nex'! Look to Jimmy D. like the joke on you two jokers. Ha, Ha, Ha," laughs Jimmy. He knows both of these characters – Tito and his younger brother, Carlos. And Jimmy D. knows they're harmless or he wouldn't have gotten into the car.

"You that wino Jimmy D., right?" asks Tito.

Jimmy nods his head as if to say, *well I ain't da real Sanda! Dumb-ass Poor-Ricans!*

"Yo, Jimmy, Yo…look at this," Tito asks. Shouldn't you be sayin' 'Ho, Ho, Ho,' 'stead of 'Ha, Ha, Ha?'".

Another high five between the brothers who are almost doubled over with laughter now.

"Das funny comin' from a Poor Rican, can' even talk English right," Jimmy responds. "Look…Was your name? Topol, Timo, Teaso or some shit?"

"Tito, man, T-I-T-O, *TITO*, man – it's Tito!" Tito yells through the rear view mirror.

"What ever – Looks Tonto, my man, how 'bout jus' takes Jimmy D. to da mall – das all – to da mall – okay? Is late, man, an' Jimmy D. tire."

"So you do works at the mall!" quips Carlos – and another high five is in progress.

"Yeah, somepin like dat," Jimmy snorts and reaches for a Camel. "Hey, Tonto, okay if Jimmy D. smoke?"

Tito, man – it's *Tito*! You can light 'em up, homie-dawg, as long as you got one for me an' Carlos." Another high five is shared between the brothers.

Jimmy hands out the smokes as they drive on down the highway, red flames roaring out of the dual exhausts and the road lit up with green neon.

17

Looks like the party's over at the Kaminski's and everyone's grabbing their coats and neat little packages and bags of leftovers from Thanksgiving, carefully packaged in Tupperware. Don is helping Max on with his coat. "Dad, are you sure you don't want to stay over and get an early start tomorrow morning?"

"No, son," Max says. "I'm a little tired, but I can drive some before we retire for the night."

"Sure wish you'd change your mind, Dad."

"You know your father," Marsha says. "When it's over – it's over and he has to get home as soon as possible so he doesn't miss any of his shows. You know your father is 'The Price Is Right' junkie and he likes Drew Carey."

"Look, Marsha. If I've told you once, I've told you a hundred times – 'The Price Is Right' is a terrific show because not only is Drew Carey funny, but he's also Jewish. You can count on it. Drew Carey is Jewish."

"Oh, he is not," Marsha fires back.

"He is too Jewish, Marsha," says Max. "Drew Carey is as Jewish as they come, I tell you. Nobody can be that funny and not be Jewish!" Max would argue with Marsha at least once a week on whether or not Drew Carey is Jewish or not.

"Come on, Dad," Don pleads. "You can watch 'The Price Is Right' here. The spare bedroom has a TV in it with remote control."

"Is it a flat screen?" asks Max.

"I don't know what it is, Dad. It's Annie's old TV but it works great."

"No, son – we're going to go. Motel 6 has flat screen." Max is heading for the door motioning to Marsha to come along.

"We're going to head on out too," Bobby Lee says. Eunice and I will drive some, then stop over Uncle Gavin's place in Ohio." Eunice cringes at the thought because Bobby's brother Gavin is a Civil War buff and always talks about how the South should have won if it weren't for, "them damn Jew bankers in New York who backed the Yankees!"

"Gee, Dad," Sue has an arm around her father. "Don't you think that's a bit far?"

"Nah," Bobby answers. "Don't you worry none. If I get tired, we'll stop somewhere and rest up."

"We are not sleeping in the car like last time, Bobby Lee!" Eunice bellows out.

"Yes, Eunice. I mean, No Eunice. We won't sleep in the car. This here Ford Escort is too damn small, anyways."

All the goodbyes are said and hugs are given making sure no one is missed as they pile up outside heading for the cars.

"Hey, Dad," Don says, pulling him aside. "Do you think it would be wrong for a Jew to play Santa Claus at the mall?"

"Santa Claus at the mall?...A Jew play Santa Claus at the mall? Are you kidding? Who? You? You're playing Santa Claus at the mall?"

"No, Dad, no." Don looks around hoping no one heard. "I was just thinking about it – that's all. You know – just to make a little money until the strike is over. I could sure use it."

Max turns and looks Don in the eyes. "Son, do you need some money?" He starts reaching for his wallet.

"No, no, no." Don whispers as he grabs Max's hand. "No! We're fine. Believe me. We will get through this alright. It's probably a bad idea anyway." Don reaches in his pants pocket and pulls out a newspaper ad. "Actually, Dad, I saw this in the paper the other day and I got to thinking," Don gives the ad to Max. Max fishes out his reading glasses he always keeps next to the Rolaids and reads to himself – although he mouths the words:

SANTAS WANTED
Natural-bearded Santas wanted in the Chicago area.
No experience necessary!
Earn between 50-75.00 an hour, full or part-time!
Clean Santa suits provided for each job.
Free training and padding provided if necessary.
Call 362-5001 between the hours of 10:00 am to 9:00 pm.
Ask for Jackie.
Gigante & Associates, LLC
An equal opportunity employer

Max hands back the ad to Don and says, "Actually, son, it's not such a bad idea at all. Your grandfather Hiram, bless his mortal soul, would have done it. And so would your Uncle Saul, if he wasn't such a big shot for the Nazis!" Max shakes his head thinking about Uncle Saul – still alive, living with that old Gypsy woman, and still working at the Mercedes plant making hubcaps.

"Tell you what," Max says. "Let me ask the Rabbi – Rabbi Peckerman – He'll know what to do. I'll give him a call and let you know what he says."

"Thanks, Pop."

They all make it to the cars – buckled up and Tupperware containers carefully positioned on the back seats. The new Buick and the used Ford Escort slowly drive away with horns tooting (the Buick horn is a cord of notes which sound regal, whereas the monotone Escort horn sounds flat and tired even to the untrained ear), windows are down, and hands are waving good byes and "I love you" echoes down the street. Don and Sue, arms around each other (both out of love and to keep warm), are waving back and wishing everyone a safe trip home and a thanks for coming. The cars turn down the block and out of sight. Windows are rolled up, heaters turned on full blast and Marsha is already asleep.

"Don't knock over that pumpkin pie, Eunice – You've had way too much to drink," Bobby Lee warns her.

"Me? You just shut up and drive, Bobby Lee!" Eunice answers. "Just shut the hell up and drive!"

That ain't so damn prim and proper, now is it? Bobby thinks.
Damn Boston bitch!
Dumb Hill Billy!

18

With a loud roar that can be heard a mile away, the black Monte Carlo low-rider pulls up to the front of the mall. The parking lot is empty.

"Hey, Homes," laughs Tito. "Looks like you missed your gig."

"Yeah, Jimmy," Carlos grins. "This place is locked up tighter than a drum and ain't nobody home." High fives all around.

"Look fellas," Jimmy lights a Camel from a Camel and throws a couple of new ones up front. "Jus' drop Jimmy D. off at da cornah an' go 'bout your own damn biness." Jimmy grabs his wine, which he manages to keep hidden from the occupants in the front seat, careful not to let the bottles clang.

Tito rolls on down to the corner of the mall and asks, "Here?"

Yeah, Tito – righ' here be good," says Jimmy. "Thanks."

"Whatcha got in the bag, Jimmy D.?…Somthin' good?" asks Carlos.

"No man. Jimmy D. ain' got nuttin but some form'la for da baby and a box o' rags for some ol' ladies been good to Jimmy D. – das all."

Jimmy eases on out of the low-rider and just closes the door when Tito floors it. The tires squeal erasing a whole lot of rubber and send up a shower of cinders and dust onto Jimmy D. as red flames mixed with green neon light can be seen racing through the parking lot.

"Hey! You crazy Poor Ricans almos' made Jimmy D. drop his form'la and shit!"

Jimmy coughs a little, sneezes, and checks inside the bag and sees all four bottles of Fat Bastard – the red, not the white, are intact and an unopened pack of Camels. Next he feels the Santa pockets from the outside and feels a wad of cash on both sides. Jimmy smiles, shakes his head, and heads for the dumpster. Wheels peel again and he spots the red flames and the green neon exiting the parking lot.

"Crazy-ass Poor Ricans!" Jimmy yells.

Jimmy D. strolls down the short side of the mall enjoying the crisp night air and doesn't seem to mind the cold as much tonight. It must be that full belly and the "green" insulation that makes all the difference in the world. "It don' gets no better." says Jimmy looking up to the heavens in thanks and he breaks out in song. "Here come Sanda Claus. Here come Sanda Claus. Righ' down to da Sanda Claus dumster. Jimmy D. bein' da Sanda this year and he ain' taken' no shit. Especial' from all youse little tiny rug rats hangin' out at da mall. 'Less you leaves Sanda sompin good to eat, Jimmy D. ain' bringin' you no shit at all!"

      Jimmy stops dead in his tracks. "My-oh-my, what has we gots here?" Jimmy bends over to pick up a black, man's wallet (notice the comma). He knew ten steps before he got there what it was lying on the sidewalk with a big invisible sign that said, 'Yo, Jimmy D. – Look down here!' He looks around to check the perimeters like an accomplished Ninja warrior on a mission from the emperor. Silence – bag with wine and cigarettes touches down without a sound – the wallet comes up – another look around – nothing – wallet is opened – *cash!* – about forty-five dollars worth – and no, repeat, *no* identification what so ever (not that this makes any difference). "Course not," says Jimmy D. "Is mine now! Finder – keeper. Loser – cryin' his ass off!" Jimmy picks up his possessions and heads for the dumpster.

None of this is on any of the mall black and white security monitors or on a security tape because half of the monitors do not work any more after the blackout. At least four of them were so badly damaged they had to be thrown out in the trash. And anyway, the mall has been closed for about four hours now and no one was manning the security closet. Too bad though, because security Chief, Paul Simpkins swears, as soon as he gets out of intensive care he's going to, "find that nigger Santa and bust him in two!"

      Newly hired Security Officer, William P. Watkins, was discharged from St. Joseph's Hospital several hours ago. He stopped by to see the Chief in the ICU, not to check up on how the Chief was doing, but to leave off the hospital bag containing his mall security uniform which was full of glass, blood, and piss, and to leave him a little note that said, "Fuck you! I quit!" That's too bad. It will be tough to find another skinny security guard to fit in the security closet with the Chief and that fat ass of his.

19

The day after Thanksgiving – Black Friday – and Don doesn't have to serve on the picket line. Sue and the kids left early this morning to scarf up on all the sale items and Don has the day to himself. Showered and shaved, he jumps into his old Volvo with the morning paper under his arm sans ads Susan took and adjusts the seat belt.

Might as well treat myself to a little coffee and sweet roll at Dunkin' Donuts, he thinks. The Volvo starts – always does – and off Don goes, excited about having a day to himself with no list of chores, no kids, and no plans except to bite into a fresh coffee roll.

The sun is out and Don has his satellite radio on and is listening to Frank Sinatra sing, "My Way." He sings along pleased that over the years his voice got better and not weaker – and right on tune. Poor Sue cannot carry a tune in a bucket if she had to, and neither can Annie for that matter. Now Junior!…Ha!…Junior could sing the song and jazz it up on the trumpet with no fuss at all.

"My Way," really is Don's song. He is living the life he wants to live and has always "called the shots" when it came to his career. Years ago, several of the Chicago school system supervisors approached Don to see if he might try administration to see how he liked it. Perhaps school administrators, in general, think that the reward for being a good teacher is to become the principal of the building? Well, they are dead wrong!

Don was offered a principal position several years ago but a little voice in the back of his head told him that this wasn't going to work out well at all. Don gave it a try though. After all, he was always going out of his way to help new teachers and often reminded them, "You must remember that, for the most part, students in grades seven and eight are neither fish nor fowl, and with all those hormones flying every which way, well, the job of teaching the little rascals isn't going to be easy!" Becoming the principal, and especially the assistant principal, in a school in Chicago would be a challenge for Gandhi, General Pershing, and even John, "the Father of American Education," Dewey himself for that matter…(although Stalin might have been able to do it, but there would have been a number of missing people:

students, teachers, cafeteria workers, custodians, crossing guards and a few bus drivers).

Well, Don couldn't! He struggled as the assistant principal at the Richard J. Daley Middle School for about three months or so and the little voice was right – this isn't working out at all! As any school administrator will tell you, the assistant principal is the "hatchet man" for the school and gets to do all of the dirty work; and there was plenty of it to do at the Richard J. Daley Middle School.

Poor Don tried so darn hard too, but he just could not solve everyone's problems and got frustrated when he couldn't. He was too soft with the kids, the teachers, and the staff. And day after day staff and students sat in his office for a plethora of reasons: Clarice yelled obscenities to Janice, Randy took markers from Booker, Rudy made an inappropriate comment to Suzanne. And these were the teachers! Truth be told, Don did not want to be responsible for getting little Johnny back on track if he didn't have the child in a classroom. This made no sense to Don at all. Don soon came to realize, especially after meeting some of the parents who thought they knew it all and in reality could not do anything right for their kids, school administration was not for him.

Don got real tired of hearing about the leaks in the roof and how the school system could not make the repairs any time soon due to funding problems (and yet the entire administrative office was outfitted earlier that year with new ergonomic office chairs costing well over eight hundred dollars a piece).

He hated it whenever he got complaints from the teachers – like the time Doris "clicking heels" Jenkins (for over thirty years now, Doris always wore high heels to school and you could hear her coming down the halls a mile away), complained that the new box of red pens she had requested over two weeks ago, "finally got here and they are all fine point!" A few weeks before that, the heat wasn't working and the entire staff, just about, called his office at the same time! Don raced down to the basement and found the chief custodian, Cleon "Tiny" MacDaniels ("Tiny" weighed over three hundred and fifty pounds and was said to be the smallest of the four MacDaniels brothers), wedged in behind the boiler and the basement wall, ASLEEP, snoring away, with, of all things, a fried chicken leg in his right hand! Meanwhile, the boiler was all torn apart with parts mixed in with chicken bones lying all over the basement floor next to an open box of KFC.

And then there was the time Don caught the metal shop boys spinning the substitute teacher, Otis Strekfuss, in the teacher's swivel chair perched atop the desk. Just how in the hell this happened, he hadn't a clue. The Chicago school system still believes that all eighth grade boys should rotate through the metal and wood shops. Noble idea when you have someone in complete control around all that potentially dangerous equipment like Matt Ohmler, the regular metal shop teacher who was recovering from a bad vasectomy. Otis Strekfuss on the other hand, was goofy enough to begin with without the joy-ride provided by the shop kids.

Look, the facts were plain and simple – being the assistant principal all but destroyed Donald Kaminski. Yes, granted, he tried really hard to do the best job he could; all the teachers there loved him for it and the district office heard nothing but praise for Don Kaminski. When Don got home, and we're talking late at night (way past a normal dinner hour), Donald Kaminski turned into Vlad the Impaler – Dracula himself!

He was moody, short-tempered and no fun to be around at all. Why once he even kicked the family dog, Peaches, in the butt for taking too long to go outside to pee. And Don loved that dog. He lasted about two months as Assistant Principal then begged out of the position to get his old job back, which, thanks being to God, he did. Don was never happier to get back into the classroom. Ask him. He will tell you all about it. But that's another story. Let's get back to the present-day Donald Kaminski, shall we?

Don's thoughts go all over the place this morning as he drives to Dunkin' Donuts. He's still upset over the assistant principal thing. The next minute he's thinking about his wonderful family and the great Thanksgiving they had, Camp Slivovitz and the Mercedes hubcap plant, the damn strike and picket lines, and Millie Cramer and the "Dick Hurts" incident. There – that got Don back to smiling.

In two shakes, Don's out of the Volvo and into the shop. He places his order, and sits at a table ready to enjoy. The coffee is mixed just right and the coffee roll is sweet and tasty. The world is perfect, according to Don Kaminski, and it's nice and quiet, *with no noise! I wonder how Dad's doing?*

Don begins to check out the front page of the Chicago Daily News and one headline catches his attention: "FBI Sting in New Jersey Ensnares Mayors, Rabbis – Wide-ranging probe brings 44 arrests so far." The accompanying picture, just below the sub-headline, shows five men, all in handcuffs, being lead to a police bus. The last two suspects have on long overcoats, are wearing what appears to be black Fedoras, and have long beards and those side curls of orthodox Jews. *These men look like rabbis to me, alright. There's no denying that.* Don thinks. Curious, he reads the article.

It appears a long-term investigation has uncovered the sale of black-market human kidneys and fake Gucci handbags leading to wide-spread political corruption, "ensnaring more then 40 people, including three mayors, two state lawmakers and several rabbis." Don reads on baffled about the mix of people involved – *human kidneys and fake Gucci handbags?…several rabbis?* Don continues to read.

According to a top-flight foreign investigative-reporter, Alf Blomqvist from the Svenska Dagblader, the investigation centers on a money-laundering network operated between Brooklyn, New York; Hoboken, New Jersey; Stockholm, Sweden; Tel Aviv, Israel; and Marcus Hook, Pennsylvania and is alleged to have laundered tens of millions of dollars through a number of Jewish charities mostly controlled by rabbis in New York, New Jersey and Stockholm.

Don can hardly believe what he is reading. *Controlled by Rabbis…not the mob? Stockholm, Sweden? How the hell many Jewish charities can there be in Stockholm, Sweden? What's this world coming to?* Don thinks.

Don reads further into the article and sees the name "Rabbi Joseph Peckerman of the Beth Shalom Synagogue located in the Lower East Side of New York City."

"Holy Moses," Don says out loud. "This is Dad's Rabbi – Rabbi Peckerman!" Don looks around and realizes everyone in Dunkin' Donuts is looking at him like he's a crazy man or worse. Several retired Chicago cops who meet here just about every morning, are checking Don out to see if he moves any hand toward his coat pockets. Ex-Detective, Carlo DiSabatino, reaches for his "piece," which he turned in a long time ago when he retired from the force, and found air instead. And the donut shop owner, Shuly Patel (Shuly isn't his real first name – but it works), comes around from behind the counter thinking the neighborhood gang of kids ran into his shop again to yell nasty things about people from India.

Patel sees Don, and says in very good English, having worked many years for Comcast Cable before he came to this country, "Is everything okay, sir?"

"They locked up Rabbi Peckerman!" Don yells without thinking.

"Perhaps you would like a free Old Fashioned donut, sir?" Patel counters.

"Rabbi Peckerman! Rabbi Joseph Leon Peckerman! It says it right here – Rabbi Joseph Leon Peckerman among those arrested!" Don shouts while smacking the paper with his right hand. "Dad's rabbi! The one he was going to ask if it was okay for me to be Santa!"

No donut-eating customer in the store that morning, including all those ex-cops, has any idea what the hell Don is talking about, and if ex-Detective Carlo DiSabatino did have his "piece," Don would have had two slugs up his ass by now.

Shuly Patel keeps his cool, however, having dealt with many irate Comcast customers all those years and re-negotiates. "Perhaps, sir, I can call you a cab?" Shuly smiles graciously showing just about all his teeth. The one front tooth, enameled in solid Indian-grade gold, sparkles and shines like Dudley Do-Right's does in the cartoons.

Don looks at Patel and his sparkling tooth, grabs his coffee and newspaper, and bolts out the front door. All the ex-cops start breathing again and Patel already has the table cleaned off and ready for the next customer. He turns and heads for the storeroom happy that this is over and he can get on with business as usual.

Ex-Detective Carlo DiSabatino grabs for his throat when he realizes that he can't breathe and sags to the floor knocking over the table and all its contents. The ex-cops at the table rush to Carlo's aide in a panic, and Shuly Patel comes running out from the storeroom swinging a wet mop over his head like a Bantu warrior and screaming like a lunatic, "Goddamn kids!"

20

Sue parks the old Pontiac behind the mall near the dumpsters. It is so crowded today, the only spots left are as far away from the mall entrances as you could get. This is to be expected on "Black Friday." It did not make any difference to the girls, however. They were on a mission and knew exactly what they were after, which stores had the items they wanted to buy at the best prices, and whether or not they needed a coupon.

Junior, on the other hand, is not quite sure why he is here. According to him, *it's way too early to buy Christmas presents* and besides he is dead broke. He sees the jammed parking lot and the crowds heading for the doors.

"Mom," he cautions. "Are you sure we want to do this?" He walks behind the girls at a much slower pace.

Both Sue and Annie turn to face Junior while still rapidly heading for the entrance to the mall and yell in unison, "YES!" Junior shrugs his shoulders and keeps moving along.

"Wait up," says Junior. "Do you hear that?"

"Hear what?" in unison again.

"Stop and listen," Junior says and stops to do just that. The girls also stop.

They faintly hear something, that's for sure, but what is it? Above the car engines, the doors slamming, and the parents yelling at the kids to behave or they're "going to tell Santa." One grandpa, parked next to them in a red Jeep, yanks out a little girl sassing about something. Grandma gets out the other side and yells, "Keep it up, Hope, and you're getting a bag of coal for Christmas!" Still, there's something else. They can hear something or someone, but can't quite tell what it is. And there it is again – only clearer this time – this deep, gravely-throated voice singing as loud as it can, echoing from somewhere nearby, "Joy to the worl' 'cause Jimmy D. rich. Let all the peoples come. Be bringin' all da money. To Jimmy D. house. Jus' like Jimmy Stewar'. Jus' like Jimmy Stewar'. Jus' like – jus' liiiiiike Jimmy Stewar' and Donna Reeds!"…and then silence – no more singing.

"What was that?" asked Annie to Sue and Junior. They look at each other puzzled.

"I'm not sure," answers Sue. "I think it came from over where that large dumpster is." They all look at one another in wonderment, turn and continue on to the mall entrance along with the multitude – all flocking to the doors. It looks like a scene from the original "Night of the Living Dead," except these zombies are in overdrive to reach the doors. And they're not after flesh – they're after sales!

They finally make it to the mall entrance, enter through the one unlocked door in single file like everyone else and wait for each other to assemble right outside the JC Penney store. The mall is beautifully decorated for the holidays. Christmas isn't around the corner. It's right here, right now, and at the mall. Junior is studying the Victoria's Secret windows when all of a sudden a fight breaks out just inside the entrance to Penney's.

Two rather plump moms, who look like they would be more comfortable in a K-Mart, are tugging at something red and fuzzy that looks like an Elmo doll. They are screaming and yelling obscenities at one another. The entire mall, it seems, stops to watch.

"Let go of it, you fat shit!" K-Mart mom number one yells and gives a tug that almost rips Elmo's head off. She is dressed in a faded pink sweatshirt and gray sweat pants that did not fit her two years ago. The sweatshirt has an ad on it from Bob's Restaurant in the Outer Banks which reads, "Eat and get the hell out!"

"I had it first, you trailer trash pig!" K-Mart mom number two spits out between her missing teeth and yanks even harder throwing K-mart mom number one off balance. Somehow, mom number one holds onto Elmo. Mom number two also has on a sweatshirt, a grayish-white one (it was white when she bought it at the K-Mart), with the message, "Any Complaints Dial 1-800-EAT SHIT."

"The hell you say, you nappy-haired bitch!" from number one – Elmo is jerked to the left.

"Who you callin' 'bitch,' bitch?" From number two – Elmo is now jerked to the right.

No movement now – a standoff? – No – Elmo drops to the floor. The switch on his back is turned on due to the fall and Elmo starts to laugh hysterically, pounds on the floor with both furry red hands, and then begins to turn over and tumble all by himself while the two K-Mart moms go at it swinging, pulling and kicking at each other and anything else that gets in the way. There is a lot of hair pulling, swearing and screaming going on and bitch number one gets off at least two good punches that definitely hurt bitch number two. But when bitch number two kicked bitch number one in the crotch with those roach killer shoes she has on, it was all over. Down bitch one goes for the count. You can almost hear the crowd counting her out – *ten, nine, eight*…Junior thinks he saw two onlookers exchange money, but he's not exactly sure it was over the fight.

The winner is K-Mart bitch number two. She bends over to claim her prize but Elmo is gone! Seems another sneaky K-mart bitch snuck into JC Penney's, saw what was happening, scarfed up the last Elmo doll off the floor, and is now rushing through the store like O.J. did in the airport commercials. But Elmo is still laughing, giving away her location and both K-Mart bitch combatants begin to run in that direction and screaming at the Elmo thief.

"Hey bitch, wait up! You don stole my fuckin' Elmo!"

"He ain't your Elmo! I had him first – bitch!" All of this said while running, then, POW! – both K-Mart mamas begin to duke it out all over again in the middle of the shoe department. Screaming, yelling, and cussing, shoes flying in every direction, mothers hustling kids out of harms way, security running in from all sides, and two enormously fat bodies rolling around on the floor like a dust storm in Kansas, sucking up slippers, high heels, bags, socks and plowing into shoe boxes and knocking over holiday decorated trees.

And while all of this is going on, the sound system in Penney's is playing and Perry Como is singing, "Peace on Earth. Good will to men."

"I'll kill you, you fat bitch!"

Back in the dumpster, Jimmy D. Mays slumps over in the Santa chair, passes out, and then oozes out onto the cardboard floor like a liquid. Next to him are the two empty bottles of Mad Dog 20/20. His foot kicks into the side of a box and PUFF – it's snowing pink again in Jimmy D.'s house.

21

"Hello?" a husky female voice says. "Can I help you?" the voice continues taking time to exhale a smokestack full of cigarette smoke.

"Yes you can," Don says into the receiver while reaching for some paper. "Good morning. My name is…"

"Good morning to you, too," the voice interrupts followed by a huge inhalation of Marlboro heaven.

"Yes, thank you. My name is…"

"You're very welcome, I'm sure." Again, another interruption erupts by the voice on the other end followed by a quick breath of air for the lungs.

Look lady – just put Jackie on the phone, would you?

"My name is Don Kaminski and I…"

"So nice to talk to you, Mr. Kaminski, I'm sure. How can I help you?"

Are you for real, lady?

"Could you put Jackie on the phone, please?"

"This is Jackie."

Don pauses in frustration and just looks at the phone receiver debating whether or not to hang up.

What is it with today? Maybe I should go back to bed and try again tomorrow? The Rabbi Peckerman blowout at the Dunkin' Donuts this morning and now this confusion – What the hell is going on?

"I'm calling about the Santa jobs," Don says hoping not to prolong the greeting formalities any further.

"What would you like to know, Mr. Kaminski?"

I'd like to know if you have a brain in that tiny head of yours?

"I'd like to know if I can work as a Santa?"

"To be truthful with you, Mr. Kaminski, I don't really know if you can be a Santa or not. You have to come down here in person for an interview.

"That's fine," Don says. "Who schedules the interviews?"

Exhales – "I do. Would you like to schedule one, Mr. Kaminski?"

Not really. I just called up to see how you are getting along these days with the economy being so bad and all...oh, yes, and to remind you it's time to call that "Don't Call" phone number so you don't get all those annoying sales calls, and finally to get your head out of your ass and throw away those damn cigarettes!

"That would really be nice. When is your next available time slot?" Don asks.

"Right now is fine." – inhales – exhales – "I'm not doing anything important right now."

"And I take it you do the interviews?"

"Why of course I do," says the voice. "I have been interviewing Santas for seven years now. Mr. Gigante himself says he trusts nobody but me to do the interviews. Mr. Gigante says I'm good at interviewing Santas and I should do just that and nothing else. 'Let Jackie interview the Santas,' Mr. G. always says. 'She's good at it.'"

Why am I not surprised.

"Where are you located, Jackie?"

"You mean right now?" – inhales – exhales – "or where I do the Santa interviews?" the voice answers.

Assholes of the world unite!

"I'm coming to you right now for an interview, Jackie. Where do you want me to meet you?"...*Michigan Avenue, the old Playboy Mansion perhaps, The White House, Afghanistan?*

"Oh, you can meet me right here, Mr. Kaminski."

"And where might 'right here' be, Jackie?"

"Do you know where North Belmont Drive is, Mr. Kaminski?"

"Yes."

"Do you know where the Belmont Harbor is, Mr. Kaminski?"

"Yes, again."

"Do you know where the Belmont Yacht Club is on North Belmont Drive, Mr. Kaminski?"

"Ah, yes once more."

"Well," Jackie inhales both lungs full of Marlboro smoke. "Come to the main building where all the big yachts are, you know – those big ships. Park in the back behind the yacht club, and then come inside and ask at the bar for the Harbor Master's office. I'll be waiting for you, Mr. Kaminski." Jackie exhales.

She is probably the harbor master too!

"I'll be there in an hour," Don says.

"Don't rush, Mr. Kaminski." Jackie inhales again. "My nails aren't dried yet. See you then." – exhales.

22

Junior separated from the girls hours ago after making several trips to the Pontiac loaded down with bargains that are going to help make this Christmas a perfect one. He had arranged for them to call him on his cell phone for the next run. He figures he'll stroll down to the "We Be Coffee" shop for a double dark chocolate and peanut butter mocha-almond latte with caramel sauce, whipped cream and a cherry on top. On the way, he might stop at the gadget store for a quick self-massage with the chrome Magi-cure Hand Massager that's always at the end of aisle one near the store entrance. Junior swears if he ever has three hundred dollars in his life he doesn't need for something important, he is going to buy one of those chrome beauties. It feels so good!

Don Kaminski, Jr. might be broke just now but lately he's been feeling pretty darn good about himself. He's a high school senior this year and captain of the baseball team (a hell of a pitcher – southpaw). Junior is a good musician for his age. He plays trumpet for the school marching and concert bands with a flare for jazz. He's an excellent student with the grade point average to prove it. Junior is excited about his future and is torn between becoming a lawyer, architect, football star or jazz musician. Both mom and dad like the lawyer-architect route but still encourage him to do something he likes (please Lord – don't let him become a jazz musician!).

So far, Junior's been offered academic, sports, and music scholarships locally and from several prestigious colleges all over the country. No doubt, once he zeroes in on an occupational goal, he will be successful.

Junior is just itching for baseball season to start. He knows the scouts will be there and so will his groupies which now include just about every good-looking girl in the school and even a few who aren't so good-looking.

His biggest worry now-a-days is whom to ask to the senior prom (It seems the Parker brothers have claimed the two "hotties" on top of the list). However, several other fine lassies, including "number three," feel Junior has more than hinted that they are the "chosen one." One dizzy chick (with a body from heaven itself), even made plans with her mom to start shopping for a prom dress. Junior recently found out about this tidbit of information last week when he was approached and openly challenged by Ramona Hallman who just happens to be pretty high up on Junior's prom list. Ramona raced up to Junior while he stood in the cafeteria line and demanded to know, "Was it true or not that you already asked that Irish tramp, Katie Moran to the prom?" Ramona had just heard this from her big-mouthed friend, Janet Sweeny. It took a minute or two for Ramona to get the words out because she was out of breath and her chest hurt so darn bad from bouncing up and down the entire length of the cafeteria. Naturally everyone heard what she said because she already had everyone's attention – especially the boys!

Junior's face turned beet red and while still in shock, and deeply embarrassed by the whole ordeal, somehow managed to get out of the entanglement and calm Ramona down to Earth with as few words as possible. Junior spoke so darn low you could hardly hear him. Ramona must have accepted his answer because she walked away smiling like she was still in the race and with all her pride and status in tact. Poor Junior just stood there in cafeteria line with his head down, wishing he could just disappear, and patiently waited for his over-done pizza pocket. Only time will tell how this will all end.

Junior gets half way down to "We Be Coffee" when his cell phone rings. He knows it's Annie on the other end because he set the ringer to play the "American Idol" theme song whenever she calls. Mom's ring is set for Kermit the frog's "It's Not Easy Being Green," and Dad's is the theme song from the old police show, "Dragnet," because Dad rarely calls and when he does, it is usually a more serious conversation. Once, while chatting up one of the more popular cheerleaders after a pep rally, "Dragnet" went off and Junior nearly soiled his pants right there, it surprised him so.

Junior about falls into the window of the candle store on hearing the "American Idol" theme since it was only about five minutes ago he ran a load to the car. *What the hell did they buy already?* He wonders. They took Mom's old Pontiac because it has a large trunk. You could fit a five-foot step ladder in there sideways. That's how big it is. *And right now, the damn thing's almost full!*

"What?" he challenges into the cell phone.

"Junior?"

"Yeah, Annie," he says. "Who do you think you called, 'Dial A Date?'"

"Very funny, kiddo. Just tell me your underpants size will you?"

"Oh, is that all…thirty-four."

"Thanks, skinny."

"Don't mention it. Anything else I can do for you? Any more fights? Have you run into Elmo, perhaps?" Junior laughs. He can tell Annie put her hand over the mouthpiece and says something to Mom because now he can hear them both laughing in the background.

"No, Junior," Annie chuckles. "We haven't seen Elmo. Call you later."

Junior holsters the cell phone and heads on down to "We Be Coffee." He's smiling now thinking about Annie and the talking Elmo. As far as brothers and sisters getting along with each other goes – well, Junior and Annie are right up there at the top.

Annie's the oldest by three years and is growing up to be a real sweet, delightful young lady. A sophomore majoring in education, she wants to become a school teacher just like her Dad. She takes after her father for her common sense and work ethics and has her mother's good looks and charm. You can already tell Anne Kaminski is going to make a fine teacher – just like her dad.

Anne Kaminski lives at home and has a part-time job at Guilday's Family Restaurant where she waits on tables several days a week. This semester, Annie is knee-deep in a teaching methods class at the local junior college. She has always been a good student and works hard to get good grades. Her one problem this semester is that she has just figured out that her instructor, newly hired Regina Huffy from down south somewhere, doesn't know a teaching method from a good fried chicken recipe. Someone please call Paula Dean to help this lady!

Annie constantly complains about the instructor to the other students in the class and they all tell her to just keep her mouth shut and put up with it because, supposedly, Ms. Huffy is an "easy A." Oh well, you know the old saying, "Those who can't *do* – teach; and those who can't teach – teach phys. ed." Perhaps Ms. Huffy would have made a better gym teacher?

Junior finally makes it to "We Be Coffee" and walks inside. Lo and behold, who is working hard behind the counter mixing, stirring, frothing and serving?...Ramona Hallman, that's who! And Ramona is looking super fine in her "We Be Coffee" get-up.

"Hi, Ramona," he says. Junior smiles and looks down at his penny loafers. He knows damn right well if he tries to look at her face now, especially the way she's dressed in that super-tight "We Be Coffee" pink t-shirt and with no bra either, he won't be able to keep his eyes off her chest, and lucky Junior has met these two bad boys in person – once!

"Hi-ya, Junior," Ramona says in that honey-coated voice of hers. "Want some...coffee?" She giggles at the hesitation she used just before the word "coffee."

"Sure thing, Ramona." Junior's head isn't thinking right – at least the one on his shoulders isn't and so he's forgotten all about his fancy drink and is now getting a regular coffee.

"What size will it be, Junior?"

He's afraid to look down, but he feels confident it's got to be a *grande* by now.

"Make it a large, please."

"Anything in it?"

Oh, it's loaded alright!

"Just cream and sugar is fine, Ramona."

"Extra cream? Extra sugar?"

The 'Extra cream' is coming right up as we speak. Better hurry with the coffee!

"Extra cream with four sugars, please."

That's really not what the hell I came here for, but what the hell. Oh my God! Look at those tits! I think the left one just winked at me!

Ramona puts the coffee on the counter and presses her tits tightly on the glass case which Junior can plainly see from his side. He hands her some money. Might be a hundred for all he knows. He can't keep his eyes from those two heavenly orbs Ramona keeps rubbing up against the glass. She sees his eyes and knows damn right well what he's looking at and it isn't the Gelato.

"Keep the change, Ramona," he turns to leave.

"Why thank you, sweetie-pie," she says. "Don't forget your coffee, hon." Junior, red with embarrassment, turns to collect his coffee from the counter and takes one more look at heaven.

"Good seeing you," says Junior, finally looking her in the eyes, "but I have to go, Ramona. Mom and Annie just called me to carry some heavy bags back to the car. See you later."

"You be sure and call me real soon, Junior…promise?"

"Yeah, sure, Ramona, I'll call you tonight. I've been thinking about you."

"I'll bet you have, you sweet thing you." Ramona smiles and winks at Junior. "I have a couple of heavy things I'd like you to help me carry with those great big, soft hands of yours," she whispers across the counter.

Junior grabs for his coffee and just about dumps it down the front of his school jacket. *That would have looked cool – lettering in hard-ons!*

23

Don is driving along the North Belmont Drive and sees a sign up ahead for the Belmont Yacht Club. He sees the spars on many a tall sailboat and pulls into a well-manicured parking lot that is quite large and seems pretty full.

My God, what a beautiful day it is today, he thinks. The late afternoon sun is dazzling bright and everything seems to be alive with color – even the bare trees seem to have sprouted buds; and even though it is still winter out there, the car heater is turned off and it feels rather pleasant. In fact, it is warm out today. Don remembers hearing the weatherman on TV last night report that everyone in Chicago should get outside today and enjoy the sunshine and fresh air. *He's right-on this time. It's magnificent out here. And this little patch of Mother Nature has the look of elegance in shades of green.*

As Don casually drives around the parking lot, he can't help but notice all the fancy cars parked row after row in parking spaces with names of big companies and prominent families painted on the cement barriers. When he was a teen, Don could tell you the name and model of just about every car and truck he saw coming down the highway – even the foreign ones. Wonder where he gets that trait? Today, however, not only does he not know the names of these "high-end" cars, but he also cannot pronounce some of them. He knows one thing for sure. They all shine like down on the showroom floors. Don drives on looking for a sign that perhaps says, "Regular slobs like you, Don – park here,"

While driving and looking for the visitor's lot, Don spots a Bentley with all the bells and whistles that makes him drool. At first the car looks like a deep burgundy, but as he drives buy and continues to admire this luxurious, driving creation, the Bentley appears to change colors to an acrylic black. *What a paint job! I'll bet that one is Jackie's – the harbor master!*

Ah, here we go. Don drives around to the side of the building and far in the back he can see about half-a-dozen cars that look like they should have been turned in for the "Cash for Clunkers" deal. Some of these things (Don has a hard time calling them cars), really look out of place parked in this lot, that's for sure. Look at that old rusted-out VW Westfalia camper with a handicap tag hanging from the rear-view mirror. It looks like the same one he had in college at Western Michigan University, in Kalamazoo. *And the same faded-out blue and white paint job.* Don bends his head almost clean off his shoulders as he passes by the camper. *I wonder?* A smile comes to Don's face as he thinks about: Rosemary Kowalski, Janet Wilson, Annette DiCostanza, Faye Rubinski, and all the others whose names he had forgotten. *No wonder the thing rusted out!*

Next to the camper is a black Harley Fat Boy with a side car. The Harley has seen better days, however. It has no shine left to it at all. The chrome is a yellowish-brown, and it looks like the thing is covered in dead stink bugs and K.D. Lang stickers. *Now that's peculiar!*

Next to the Harley is a shiny, clean Dodge Sebring convertible – with the top down. The car is painted in that Mary Kay – Pepto-Bismol shade of pink that's enough to make you sick just looking at it. *I thought Mary Kay gave out pink Cadillacs! – Must be the economy. I wouldn't let that car out in the main lot either.* Don is wondering if this is some sort of exhibit or car show. *For what? – The world's oddest car collection!*

It gets worse! After the "pink puke" is what looks like a "clown car" from the circus. Don is sure this is a Yugo that has different colored fenders, hood, and trunk. *What the hell is going on here?* he wonders.

Don pulls into an empty spot next to the Yugo and a black-primered Chevy that is so low to the ground he wonders how anyone can get in and out of the thing. The Chevy's engine is running, and inside the car, two Puerto Ricans are smoking and laughing. They spot Don and rev up the engine as he gets out of the Volvo and walks behind the rear of the Chevy. The Chevy revs up louder this time as if to warn Don, *You are too close!* Not only did the noise hurt his ears, but he jumped a foot in the air when he saw the smoke and red flames blast out of the duel exhausts with a roar! Don checks to make sure his pant legs aren't on fire and then sees the two Puerto Ricans laughing like hell and giving each other high fives. *Assholes!* Don says to himself.

Next to the assholes in the Chevy is a boxy-looking Honda Civic from the seventies painted in lime green with a humongous red Chinese dragon realistically painted on the trunk, roof and hood of the car. Long talons scrape down the sides of the doors giving the perception that the dragon has just caught the Honda unaware and will, at any second, take fight while clutching its prey and flying off to the dragon's lair for a Honda snack. *Bazaar! That's all I can say – Bazaar!*

As Don walks a few steps, he's sees a sign that identifies this section of the parking lot is indeed for visitors. He shakes his head in amazement and continues to the front of the building and back to a beautiful day, Mother Nature, and a better class of people. Don checks and sees that the entire lot is paved in mauve colored pavers in a herringbone pattern which really blends in nicely with the professionally placed and tendered shrubs and trees.

    Look at all these yachts! One bigger than the next – and still in the water! There's one that is twice a big as my house! I'll bet some of these rich folks celebrate Thanksgiving on their boats! Don sees a green sign with gold lettering "Harbor Master" and an arrow pointing to a swanky building, probably designed by Frank Lloyd Wright himself.

    Up a few steps to the portico that reminds Don of the Thomas Jefferson mansion at Monticello and he enters the building through a huge stained-glass door. The foyer looks inviting with dark oak wood paneling (the good stuff – not the veneer), and with real art hanging on the walls. The paintings are all seascapes with grand sailing ships from all over the world. Each painting has its own light above it and a brass plaque identifying the name of the ship, the painter and the year it was painted. There is a grand fire flaring and popping against the back wall giving off a wonderful heat with a scent of cherry wood. A bar and lounge are off to one side serving grownup refreshments and interesting tidbits to nosh on. Surprisingly, there are quite a few people here sitting in comfortable, over-sized brown leather chairs, sucking down different colored martini-type cocktails and chit-chatting away. *Probably talking about how much they made today on the stock market,* Don thinks, *and I'm looking for a Santa job because I'm broke!* There's a pianist, sax, and bass player on a tiny stage off to the side in the middle of a jazzy rendition of "When Sonny Gets Blue." Don stops to listen a bit. "These guys are good," he says.

    "Can I help you, sir? Are you a member?" pleasantly asks a rather distinguished-looking older gentleman, who in fact reminds Don of the old guy on the Monopoly game.

"Why yes," Don answers. "Can you direct me to the harbor master's office?"

"You mean *suite*, sir." "Mr. Moneybags" gives Don a head to foot look-over as if to say, *I don't believe you are here to park your yacht.* "Right this way, sir," "Moneybags" gestures with his hand the direction to the harbor master's suite.

Don remembers the nautical term he's searching for and casually delivers, "I'm not here to rent a slip."

"I didn't think so, sir," "Moneybags" responds.

"To tell you the truth," Don tries for a come-back line. "I don't think you have one big enough for the "Lisa Marie!" *'Lisa Marie?' What in the hell am I thinking of?*

"Quite frankly, sir, with that wonderful-looking beard of yours, sir – I would say you are looking for Miss Jacqueline DiSanto to apply for one of the Santa jobs, *n'est pas?*" "Moneybags" says in French.

"Okay, you got me there, Inspector Clouseau. Where do I find Miss Jacqueline DiSanto?"

"Right this way, sir." "Moneybags" leads the way.

24

Don walks through an ornately carved solid oak door that must have come from King Arthur's castle and there she sits, in the center of a beautifully decorated parlor behind a quaint little desk done up in white enamel with gold leaf trim, Miss Jacqueline DiSanto in all her glory, buffing her orange colored fingernails.

Jackie looks up from her buffing and smiles at Don. "And you must be my Mr. Kaminski," she says standing up and offering her hand after she crushes out her Marlboro into a silver ashtray. As beautiful as this room is, Don can hardly see her for all the smoke that immediately makes his eyes tear up.

"Yes, Jackie – I can call you Jackie, can't I?" Don coughs a bit as Jackie lights up another Marlboro. "It's me, Don Kaminski." Don shakes her hand and realizes, when his eyes clear up a bit, that Jackie is rather a good-looking broad for her age – he guesses her to be about fifty-five-sixtyish – but in great shape and very smartly dressed. *If she could only ditch the smokes, she'd be much more interesting. Too late now, I suppose. Probably been smoking since she was twelve.*

"Sure – you can call me Jackie," inhales – "if I can call you Don," – exhales – she says.

"It's a deal."

"Don, why didn't you tell me you had a natural beard? And such a beautiful one! I would have had you come sooner!" Jackie gives Don and his beard the once-over and smiles in approval.

Don, a little confused, says, "Right, Jackie. I should have come over sooner. So listen, where do we begin?" he asks.

"Well, I can already see you fit the bill and believe me, we want you to be a Santa for Gigante and Associates, LLC. First, I'll need to have you fill out some paperwork and then I have to ask you a few questions. Is that okay?"

"Sure thing, Jackie – Can I do that now? – complete the paperwork?"

"Oh, sure, sure – you can do this right here at my desk if you like." Jackie moves the silver ashtray off her desk to a small side table – inhales – exhales. Next, she removes a rather large vase of beautifully fresh-cut flowers onto the floor besides a silver trash can.

"Say Jackie," Don says. "I've got to ask you – Are you the harbor master?"

"The what?"

"The harbor master – This is the harbor master's suite, isn't it?

"Oh, *that* harbor master – Oh, no – I'm not the harbor master. Mr. Mimo Gigante, Jr. is the harbor master. His friends call him 'Momo, Jr' or 'Little Mo' because they call his father 'Momo, Sr.' or 'Big Mo,' get it? Know what I mean? – Mimo, Sr. and Mimo, Jr. – 'Momo, Sr.' and 'Momo, Jr.' – 'Big Mo,' and 'Little Mo,' – see? Well his suite – 'Momo, Jr.' that is, is just behind those doors." Jackie points to the right. "'Little Mo's' the harbor master but Joey and Paulie help to park the really big boats, collect all the money and bring it back here. I do all the banking, by the way. I make several deposits every day at Mr. Gigante's bank. 'Big Mo'…but I don't call him that; I call him, Mr. Gigante. In fact I call them both 'Mr. Gigante,' but that's beside the point. But anyway, 'Big Mo' isn't here right now. He's attending a banking convention in Las Vegas."

"He has his own bank? – Mimo? – Momo? – Mr. Gigante, Sr.?" Don asks.

"Oh sure he does. Mr. Gigante, Sr. owns the Gigante Savings and Loan Association, LLC."

"Never heard of it," Says Don. "How many branches are there?"

"Branches? – There are no branches – It's a bank not a tree, that's all – just a bank."

"Well, where is the bank located?"

"Right over there, behind those other doors." Jackie points to the left. "Sal and Vic are in there right now waiting for me to make a deposit so they can count the money."

"Listen, Jackie, I never asked you anything, okay. Why don't I just fill out the paperwork for you right now?" Don hustles over and sits down at the front side of Jackie's desk and begins to complete the forms. *What in God's name am I getting myself into? – Mimo – Momo – 'Big Mo' – 'Little Mo' – Sounds like the mob to me. Just shut up Don and take the money! Your family and Christmas are counting on you! Doke Candy and Rabbi Peckerman can take care of themselves!*

Okay, let's take a look at these. Let's see what we have here: a standard application, a W-4, emergency contact form, and a disclai-

mer. A 'disclaimer?' – for what? Don flips to the disclaimer form and reads:

DISCLAIMER

The Gigante and Associates, LLC is not responsible for anyone or anything that happens on the way to the Santa job, at the Santa job, or returning from the Santa job **PERIOD!**

_____   _____
    Jackie signs here   Santa signs here

_____
  Today's date goes here   Notary gold sticker goes here
                                                            (do not forget to use the seal!)

What the hell is this all about, 'not responsible'... ***NOT RESPONSIBLE!****...Nice set-up!*

"Let me guess, Jackie. You are the local Notary Public, right?"

"How did you know that?" She whips out the metal notary crimper and a circular gold seal. "I'm ready when you are, Don."

It doesn't take Don long to complete the forms and he hands them over to Jackie.

"Say, Jackie. What about a back-ground check and a drug test?" Don asks.

"Look, Mr. Kaminski," inhales – exhales – "if you want all that you're going to have to pay for it yourself. Neither Mr. Gigante, Sr. nor Mr. Gigante, Jr. is going to pay for a back-ground check or a drug test. And besides," she adds, "You look pretty smart to me. I'll bet you could pass both of those tests on your own."

Don is taken aback by this and isn't sure how to respond. His brain is so mixed up and full of smoke, he's not sure what to ask and he knows he has a hundred questions in his head somewhere. *Come on, brain – work!...PAY! That's it – Pay.*

"I hate to ask this, Jackie – but what about pay?"

"Oh, don't worry about that, Don." She brushes him off with her hand. "You're going to get paid in cash."

"That's nice to know, Jackie. But can you tell me how much and how will I get the money?"

"Oh, sure, sure – I'm sorry, Don." – inhales – exhales. "First of all, you get paid after every job right here at the Gigante and Associates Savings and Loan, LLC. And did I tell you that you get paid in cash?" She points, "Right through those doors to the left. Just remember to come back here after each job to turn in your Santa gear and get paid"

"I got it," Don says, "Joey and Paulie, right?"

"No, Don. Joey and Paulie park the big boats for Mr. Gigante, Jr – you know – 'Momo, Jr.' Sal and Vic work in the bank. They have nicknames too, but I don't know them."

Probably Sal 'the enforcer' and Paulie 'the executioner!' Don thinks. "Again, forget I asked that! Okay, Jackie?" Don hands her the completed forms.

"Sure thing, Don. Let's see now." Jackie licks the gold seal and carefully attaches it to the form. Next she crimps it with the seal. She holds the form up with her hands and admires her attention to detail.

"Almost there, Don," she says. Jackie pulls out a silver-plated clipboard from her desk that has a checklist on it and grabs for a long pink feather-pen from the desk-top holder.

I'll bet Mozart used that very pen to write the opera 'Don Giovanni' Don thinks.

"You have your own beard," Jackie says and checks a box on the checklist.

"You have your own teeth," she checks another box.

Don smiles to show that he does.

"And you have a very nice smile," checks box – inhales – exhales.

"You have both arms and legs," checks box.

Don looks to be sure.

"You aren't cross-eyed, no hair-lip or obvious disfigurement," checks box.

Don crosses his eyes to make sure they go back in place. They do, however, they also begin to water again from all the smoke.

"You don't have acne or bad skin…and you smell good," check, check, and check.

"Looks like all you need is a Santa suit," Jackie says.

"Yep! All I need is a Santa suit." *Might as well go along with the lunacy,* Don thinks, wiping his eyes.

"Let's see…hmmmmmmm." Jackie is checking more boxes and muttering to herself.

"No, none of that." She looks down at the form. "Probably not." She looks at Don and shakes her head from side to side while marking more boxes on the form.

"Doesn't look like it to me," she says to herself and then checks off several more boxes.

"Ah, Don?" Jackie asks. "Have you ever sued anyone since you were born?"

"Never, Jackie, so help me God!" Don raises his right hand.

Although there was that one time, in the ninth grade, when Roscoe Stokarski asked Connie Blevins to the school dance and got to 'second base,' and that fool knew damn right well I was going to ask her – I told him so! I wanted to sue his ass off but I didn't know a good lawyer then and besides I didn't have any money.

Jackie is now rechecking the form and counting up the checkmarks. Beads of sweat begin to form on her upper lip like Richard Nixon during the presidential debates.

"Got it!" she says. "Congratulations, Don. You qualify for sixty-five dollars an hour."

"Sixty-five dollars an hour!" Don coughs, "What about taxes?"

"Look, Mr. Kaminski, if you want to pay taxes, *you* pay them. If we pay your taxes, I'll probably have to charge you for it." She looks him in the eyes and winks.

"Got-cha, forget I asked the question."

"Already forgotten."

"Sixty-five dollars an hour! When do I start?" Don finds himself in total shock over this whole experience.

"Now hold on a minute, Don. Remember, I said I have to ask you some questions?" warns Jackie.

"Ask...ask! I'll answer anything for sixty-five dollars an hour!" Don is downright giddy with his good fortune and is having a hard time controlling himself.

"Okay, Don. Here goes." Jackie flips over

to the next page on her clipboard. "Actually, there's only one question I need to ask," Jackie realizes.

"When can you start?"

"When can I start? When can I start! – NOW! I can start right now!" Don jumps up out of his seat and gives Jackie a big hug and kisses her on the cheek.

"You're going to make a good Santa, Don." She smiles having been kissed by Don.

"I am, aren't I, Jackie? Say, wait a minute. Where do I go? What about the photographer? – the Santa suit? – the times? – potty breaks and stuff?"

"Not to worry, Don." Jackie points again. "Just go into the harbor master's suite and see Mr. Gigante, Jr. He's waiting for you right now to attend a Santa class. He'll answer all your questions."

Don laughs at himself and says, "I should have known that." He skips over to the doors on the right while waving to Jackie. "See you, Jackie. Be good! Remember, Santa's watching!"

"Bye-Bye, Don. Talk to you later," – inhales – exhales. *Gee, Mr. Kaminski is going to make a good Santa. I wonder if he speaks any Italian?*

25

Don points to the door with the big carved wooden sign and sailing ships that says, "Harbor Master."

"In here?" he asks.

"Yes, in there," Jackie points to the same door.

Don opens the door and enters into another beautifully decorated suite and sees six other men sitting in folding chairs, listening and taking notes. *Thank Christ – No smoke!*

"Please, excuse me," Don says. "I'm looking for Mr. Gigante, Jr." He looks around and spots the guy he thinks is Gigante, the shortest of them all, "Italian-stallion" type, and is facing the group probably teaching the Santa class.

"Hi. You must be Don Kaminski? I'm Mimo Gigante, Jr. but you can call me "Momo." Mimo extends his right hand. He seems friendly enough.

Don was right. It is the "Italian-stallion." He walks over to shake his hand.

"Pleased to meet you, Mimo…er…Momo."

"Nice to meet youse too, Don. That's a great beard!" Mimo laughs and points to Don's beard. Don hears laughter coming from a dark corner. Don figures it's Joey and Paulie. No, that's not right. Joey and Paulie are out parking the boats. It's Sal and Vic – must be. They are still waiting to count the money Jackie is supposed to bring them.

"Please. Don, grab a seat and come join the other Santas, will ya?" Mimo gestures invitingly.

Don gives them the once over and realizes he is the only one in the room with a natural beard. *That's why I'm getting the big bucks!* Not only that – These guys do not look like Santa at all! Not in the least bit! Don is introduced to them one by one: Santa Bruce, Santa Rick, Santa Anita (Don couldn't tell at first that this Santa is a woman), Santa Rajneesh (*Santa Rajneesh?*), Santa Lee, and Santa Domingo. All the Santas say "Hi" to Don except Santa Domingo, who just looks at the floor and snarls out, "Gringo!" Don takes his place in one of the chairs at the back and listens to Mimo resume his teaching on how to be a good Santa and not fondle the kids or the parents. He can't help but size up the others in the room and figures that:

1). Santa Bruce is a flaming fag with all the trimmings: looks, walk, speech, high-pitched voice, makeup and clothing. The squealing and nervous giggle gave him away at the onset – not to mention the hand gestures that made everyone in the room just the slightest bit uncomfortable. Like the time Sue and Annie invited Don to go see that cowboy movie, "Brokeback Mountain." Don's still not sure he'll ever forgive them for that one. He did stay for the whole picture because the woman who sat next to him was so darn fat that when she wedged herself into the theatre seat – well, there was no way in hell Don was able to get around her to get out! And he thought about leaving more than once, especially during the tent scene. Sue and Annie still talk about Don's reaction to the movie and how he had to close his eyes and groan several times. Sure, they thought that was real funny. And when those beautiful panoramic shots of the outdoors came on, Don missed the whole thing because the fat lady pestered him about how her husband loved the "wide open spaces," and worked as a security guard in some mall somewhere.

Back to Santa Bruce – And later, when Santa Bruce got up from the chair during break, his walk was rather strange, perhaps leading one to believe he had a huge love-making session recently and Santa Bruce was the "catcher!" *Let me guess,* Don ponders. *Santa Bruce owns the "Mary Kay" car.*

2). Santa Rick is sitting in a wheelchair. *A Santa in a wheelchair?* Santa Rick's lap is covered in a Tartan plaid. No problem there. However, there are no shoes, or feet for that matter, showing below the Tartan on the foot supports! Santa Rick has no feet! He does have a lap, Don can see that. *It's probably one of Jackie's checkboxes – 'Lap – check!'* There are definitely no feet, however. *I guess that saves a little on Santa boots! They probably use the fake tops anyway.* Don's giddiness returns and he begins to laugh. *I got it! Santa Rick drives the VW Westfalia with the fold-down tailgate on the side. Probably has all he needs to drive the thing on the steering wheel.* Don cracks a smile and laughs out loud.

"Do you find something funny here, Kaminski?" Mimo asks. "Do I amuse you?" Laughter breaks out from the dark corner. "Please inform the other Santas what's so damn funny about a law suit?" Mimo challenges.

"Nothing, sir, Mr. Mimo-Momo, sir. I was just excited about finally getting to play Santa, sir. That's all," Don responds.

"Can you believe this guy?" Mimo smiles again to the dark corner of the room. "He's excited about being Santa!" More laughter erupts from the dark corner.

"Okay, Don. Pay attention, will ya?" Mimo continues on about law suits, the disclaimer, and the need for each Santa to have a good attorney "in his" (or her, as the case may be), "pocket." Mimo hands out business cards to each of the Santas in the room.

"Here's our attorney," Mimo says. "Abramowitz, Abramowitz and Laganelli."

Don inspects the card and thinks he's read about this firm in the paper recently, but it had nothing to do with the Santa business. Don seems to recall something about trash being the issue.

"Laganelli is there just so we can understand Abramowitz and Abramowitz, and to keep Abramowitz and Abramowitz on the 'up and up,' if you know what I mean!" Mimo explains.

From the dark corner, either Sal or Vic says, "You don't want to fuck with Abramowitz and Abramowitz, that's for sure."

"Who you shittin'?" the other says. "Laganelli's the one you have to look out for! They don't call him 'ice pick' for nuttin'! Remember old man Jimmy DiPietro who came up short time after time on his gambling debts? And I kept telling that *stunad,* 'Don't fuck with Laganelli!'"

"Oh yeah, I forgot about that."

3). Santa Anita is the biker chick who looks like she could take out any one in the room, except for Sal and Vic, perhaps. Don is pretty sure they are "carrying." Santa Anita is dressed all in shiny black leather with silver chain piercings from her ears, eyebrows, nose, and lips which interconnect all of these parts. It is difficult to look at her without following one of the chains to see where it might go. It also appears to be quite painful for her to talk and she groans a little when she walks! *Can't wait to see that picture on the mantle Christmas Eve!* Don thinks. *This chick probably owns the old Harley. No wonder she limps a little!*

Mimo is still talking about law suits and what happened to the Santa who mysteriously disappeared two years ago, Santa Willard.

4). Santa Rajneesh is from India, Sri Lanka or some place near there. He has a make-shift turban on his head that looks like a dirty bar towel. He speaks English rather poorly and has a very heavy accent. At one point he asks Mimo, "Please telling me, Mr. Mimo-Momo, sir. What is proper way to ask child if he has to go make a duty in case some bad odor surrounds him that you do not recognize, sir? How to doing that, Mr. Mimo-Momo, sir?"

Mimo looks to the corner and says, "What the fuck is this rag-head talking about?"

"He wants to know what to do in case a kid has to go *caca?* You know, Boss – take a shit!" This is from the dark corner.

"Whatever you do – what's your name – Ragmop?"

"Rajneesh, sir"

"Yeah – Raghead – for sure. Is your paperwork all filled out?"

"Yes, sir, Mr. Mimo-Momo, sir. Mr. Jack has all my papers, my shot records, and recommendations from Seven-Eleven and Dunkin' Donuts, Mr. Mimo-Momo, sir."

"Mr. Jack? You mean Miss Jackie, don't you? No wonder you people are so fucked up." More laughter erupts from the dark corner.

"Good damn thing your papers are in order, Dothead, or I'd send you back to Hawaii or where ever the fuck you come from!"

"He don't look like no 'pineapple' to me, Boss!" – more laughter from the dark corner.

Don can't believe this "Comedy of Errors" unveiling right before his eyes. *This clown has to own the multi-colored Yugo!*

"So listen up all of you – and especially you, Raghead."

"It's Rajneesh, Mr. Mimo-Momo, sir."

"Yeah, whatever, Ragmop, Ragweed, Raghead – If the kid has to take a shit – dump the little bastard off your lap as soon as you can! Whatever you do, don't go coming back here with shit on your Santa suit and expect to get paid, because I promise you, you won't!"

"You get to clean off the shit this year, Vic," – from the darkness.

"Fuck you, Sal! It's your turn! I did it last year!"

5). Santa Lee looks like a left-over Ninja dressed all in black with black driving gloves. He smiles and glares at Don at the same time like Don is some sort of target or something. He is probably a black belt expert, twice over, in some martial art form or something: Karate,

Jujitsu, Kungfu, Kendo, Feng Shui, Cyrillic – something. *And yes my friends, Master Lee drives the lime-colored Honda with the red dragon! He probably is a professional jewel thief like in the "Pink Panther" movies.*

6). Santa Domingo is one scary Puerto Rican type who, if you met him in some alley, looks like he would slice you up quicker than Ron Popiel, the guy who sells those onion-slicers on TV, and steals your wallet just for the fun of it. He never spoke the entire time – just sat there with his head down muttering. Once in a while you would hear him mutter, "Gringo!" That was about it. Even during the break, Santa Domingo never said a word. No one seemed to care much about it, either. *Santa "Scary-ass" Domingo probably rides with the two Puerto Ricans in the Chevy low-rider that almost burnt the pants off of my legs! What state would grant this ghoul a driver's license? – Delaware maybe!*

Just when things looked to be about over, in walks this tall, bulky guy with the grandest Santa beard and hair Don ever saw. *Now this truly IS the Coca-Cola Santa!* He is wearing a long, double-breasted, black, camel's-hair overcoat with a silver fur collar that looks just elegant on him. *He looks like the Tsar of Russia!* Don thinks. The "Tsar" stops, looks at Mimo and in a heavy Eastern-European accent says, "I am wery sorry, Meester Momo, sir, for being late, but I had some werry important busyness to attend to, your excellency, sir." And with that the "Tsar" bows to Mimo.

          "I'll be damn! – He IS the Tsar!" Don says in a whisper.
          "I remember you," says Mimo. "You did this last year, right?"
          "And the year before that, your excellency, sir."
          "That's why I like you so much. You know how to show re-spect – Mr. Patriarch, right?"
          "No, No, No, Meester Momo, Sir. Today, I am just Zoltan Shimko, your excellency, sir.
          Patriarch? – as in orthodox church Patriarch? Don gives the "Tsar" the once over. *Are you telling me that an ordained priest and Patriarch of an orthodox church is running around playing Santa?*
          "Welcome back, Zoller!"
          "ZolTAN, you excellency, sir. It is pronounced, ZolTAN!" The "Tsar" says this with a flare waving his arms.

"Yeah, ZolTAN," Mimo apes with his arms moving every which way.

More laughter from the dark corner, "ZolTAN my ass! Who the hell ever heard of a Jew Santa? Tell me, Sal, who?"

Don looks to the dark corner and says to himself, *Yo, fellas! Yo! Right here, in the light – it's me – Don Kaminski – and I am a Jew!* Don's brain begins to stray a little. *And now it's time to play 'Who's the Jew?' How about you, Brucey-boy? Are you a Jew, perhaps? Santa Anita? Besides being named after a highway, are you a Jew or a Jewess? Probably not – hey, Rajneesh? No, you are definitely not a Jew. One thing's for sure. The 'Tsar' here AIN'T NO JEW! Never heard of no Jew becoming the Tsar! He might be an orthodox priest. He might even be a Santa, but he AIN'T NO JEW!*

"He ain't no Jew, Vic! He's some kind of Armenian or Slovak – some kind o' shit like that," from the dark corner. "Jackie was tellin' me about him last year. The guy drives a fancy, black car came over from Russia called a Zhil or Zil – something like that. Miss Jackie says he bought it from his boss in the old country – a guy by the name of Metropolitan. Honest – he ain't no Jew!"

"Metropolitan! Listen, Sal," from the dark corner again. "If this schmuck bought a Metropolitan, then he bought a Nash! Nash made Metropolitans – you dumb ass! Don't you even know your cars yet? And besides, Sal, what the fuck do you know about Armenians or Slovaks? Don't give me that shit about 'Miss Jackie says'! There're all fucking Jews…He does make a good Santa, though. I will give you that one, Sal."

Don is listening to all the aside comments and is about to wet himself at the sheer lunacy of this whole ordeal.

"If youse guys are all done the chattering over there, I'd like to finish up here with dese fucking Santas if it's alright with youse two clowns," challenges Mimo to the dark corner.

Zoltan Shimko immediately stands up, blesses Mimo three times, and then sits back down muttering, *"Oy, Boshe moi! Boshe moi!"* (Oh, my God! My God!).

"Sorry, Boss," in two-part harmony from the dark corner.

"Okay, ZolTAN," Mimo begins. "Have you been sued this year by anyone or have YOU sued anyone this year?"

"No, sir, your excellency, sir. We worked it all out after the fire." Zoltan smiles and bows again to Mimo with a flurry of hand gestures.

"Everybody!" – Mimo says. "This is our best-looking Santa, ever! – Meet ZolTAN!"

All the Santas applaud except Santa Domingo who looks up at Zoltan, then puts his head back down and snarls, "Polack-Gringo!"

Well I'll be a monkey's uncle! – A Patriarch-Santa from the old country who bought his car from the Metropolitan of the church. This keeps getting curiouser and curiouser, don't it?

"Any youse Santas got any more questions?" Mimo asks.

"I do. I do," Santa Bruce says like the existence of mankind depends upon the answer to his question. "Which side of your head does the ball hang on, Mr. Mimo?"

Laughter erupts again from the dark corner. The Santas all look at one another unsure if this made a difference.

Who knows? Don thinks. *Maybe Santa Bruce is onto something here? What if the ball hanging on the right side of Santa's head means Santa's a child molester or something?*

"That's it – All o' youse Santas – get the fuck outa here and come back tomorrow morning at eight sharp for your assignments and Santa suits." Mimo exits into the dark corner and laughs it up with Sal and Vic.

"Fuckin' flamer!" he says – laughter from the darkness.

26

Don is the first Santa to exit the Harbor Master's Suite and into Jackie's parlor which is jammed full of smoke. His eyes begin to tear again. Don can hear the others asking all sorts of questions to one another, but he's had way too much fun for one day and is anxious to head home for some normal conversation with the family. He can hardly wait to tell them about all of this. He looks around and doesn't see Jackie. *Probably went on a cigarette break.* Without warning, and there should have been one, two hellatious smoke-eaters anchored to the roof comes on with a roar and in less than four seconds, the entire room is cleared of all smoke. Not only did the smoke disappear in a hurry, but so did several papers off Jackie's desk, three or four long-stemmed flowers from the vase, and Jackie's feather pen; all gone high up into the rafters and into the smoke-eaters. *Damn! Hope that isn't my sixty-five dollars an hour voucher! And who made those smoke-eaters? – Pratt and Whitney?*

Don makes it through the country club area. It's still crowded and smells great, but the band must be taking a break. *Just as well,* Don thinks. *I have got to get out of here.* He turns around and looks back as he's walking for some reason and spots the Patriarch, Zoltan Shimko, hot on his heels. *Probably has a baptism to perform!*

Finally outside for some fresh air and a drive home in the setting son, Don continues walking to the Volvo and passes by the Bentley and sees the driver, a silver-haired old gal who looks like 'Lovey' the millionaire's wife on 'Gilligan's Island.' She's got the door open and is standing outside carrying on a heated conversation with a security guard who is driving an enclosed silver golf cart with a blue light flashing on top and has his window zippered down. As Don gets closer he hears the argument.

"Members should not have to park in the same lot with the likes of these cars," Lovey says. "Just look at these things? What are they? They don't even look like cars! I never thought the day would come when commoners would be welcome at a distinguished place like this. It just goes to show you how much this world has changed thanks to those damn Democrats! And shut that annoying light off, young man. It makes me squint and it hurts my eyes! What are you trying to do – make me go blind?"

The blue light goes off in a flash.

"Yes ma'am, Mrs. Powell. I'll see to it right away, ma'am. They probably belong to workers, Mrs. Powell."

"Are you telling me, officer, that the workers are allowed to park their cars in the same lot as we? I find that very hard to believe that you do not have an employee lot somewhere off the premises, young man?"

"We do have an employee parking lot, Mrs. Powell," the guard answers. "Perhaps they are new employees and don't know where it is, ma'am. It's way behind the tree line next to the dumpsters, Mrs. Powell, ma'am."

"I don't care where it is, young man. Just see to it that those horrendous vehicles are moved at once! Most of them belong IN the dumpster, if you ask me." The door to the Bentley closes and Lovey presses one button which automatically starts the car, adjusts her seat and steering wheel, locks the doors, turns on the classical music (Vivaldi's "Four Seasons" for the drive home is rather nice), and warms up her tush.

Don agrees with Lovey on this one. *All these cars belong IN the dumpster.* And then he sees a car the likes of which he has never seen before in his life. This yacht is low, long, shiny jet black and with lots and lots of chrome. It looks like something out of the nineteen-forties, like a Cadillac LaSalle or something like that. And what the hell is this? Two teens dressed up like altar boys are busy working by the car. One is wiping down the high-gloss black finish with some sort of fancy towel like you see on those TV commercials, and the other…*The other altar boy is waving a gold incense burner, hung on a long gold chain! Oh my God! He's spreading incense smoke all around the car like they do during high mass!* Don can see the smoke from where he is in the lot and he can smell the incense. *It IS incense!*

Patriarch Shimko passes Don without a word and heads straight for the Russian car. Don watches as the Patriarch puts on a pointed black hat (not a witches hat, but the kind that orthodox priests wear), with black veils streaming down his back almost touching the ground. *Am I really seeing this?* The altar boy with the special cloth stops, comes to attention, and then opens up the driver's side door. He bows as the Patriarch reaches him. The second altar boy runs around to the Patriarch and begins to incense him from head to toe. The Patriarch sneezes once, then blesses the boys three times and says something in a foreign language. Once Shimko is in the driver's seat, the door is closed for him and both altar boys hop in the back seat. A split second after the back doors are closed, Zoltan floors the black yacht out of the parking lot and onto Belmont Drive. The windows of the car are all down and Don stares stupefied at the sight. The Patriarch is still wearing his pointed hat and the black veils are streaming outside the car window about five feet and blowing in the wind like the torn sails of a haunted pirate ship. Don can hear chanting and loud church bells gonging, all coming from the car stereo which is turned up to the max.

"I've seen it all and now I'm going home!" Don confesses.

27

After the Black Friday "shop 'til you drop" marathon, you would think Sue Kaminski would stay in bed for a little extra sleep for those tired feet of hers this morning? Not the case. She is working harder than ever at the V.A. hospital for tonight's big BINGO party.

Susan Kaminski nee Chambers is Don's wife of twenty-three years. She works as a volunteer at the Ira Hayes Veteran's Administration Hospital three days a week. Quite an attractive woman for her age (same age as Don by the way, except she looks younger), – well, let's just say Sue Kaminski is a "real keeper." She has short strawberry-blond hair that is cut stylishly to accent her facial features which aren't hard to look at. She is fit and trim, watches what she eats, and exercises at the YMCA on a regular basis. Sue especially loves to participate in the deep water exercise program at least twice a week. Her mother used to say, "Susan could melt butter with those big, dark brown, puppy-dog eyes of hers." They were the first thing Don noticed about her when they first met in college. In addition to her volunteer work, Sue Kaminski is a darn-fine cook, keeps an immaculate house, and takes good care of Don and the family.

Sue has a right to be nervous about planning for tonight's BINGO party. Events like this one can be a problem since many of the veterans try to sneak booze into the common room. Almost had a major riot last month when retired Marine, Gunny John L. Sargeant, that's right – Sgt. Sargeant, tried to punch retired Army Major James Michael "Bug-eyes" McDermott in the mouth when he accused Gunny of cheating – which he was. How do you cheat at BINGO and expect to get away with it?

Sue and several other orderlies had a tough time separating the two from all the ex-service men, especially the Marines, who joined in the fracas yelling, "Semper Fi" while swinging and jumping on one another. The whole thing looked like a D-day reenactment, with the G.I.s struggling to take the beachhead in hand-to-hand combat.

When it finally ended and the armies were separated for triage and aspirin, almost every soldier involved was covered from head to toe with blue and red dots from the BINGO markers. Once the punch bowl was emptied and refilled with only punch this time, things got back to normal, whatever that was.

So tonight is the big night. This is a fundraising event and not just a bunch of veterans with mental and physical disabilities playing BINGO for chump change or complementary shaving kits donated by the Polish Am-Vets down on Pulaski Street. The public is invited to this one and they expect a large crowd. The big jackpot of the night is worth well over two thousand dollars, depending on attendance. All the locals will be here, especially the band of fifteen to twenty professional BINGO players who do nothing but go from BINGO game to BINGO game, and some of these old BINGOphiles play up to fifteen cards or more at a time.

Sue has been working since eight o'clock this morning and all she's had to eat or drink was a large Dunkin' Donuts coffee – black, and a free Old Fashioned donut the little Indian man at Dunkin' Donuts gave her. She didn't even want the donut but the nice man at the shop (Sue thinks he's the manager or owner), always insists she have an Old Fashioned donut for free. Not having anything yet for lunch, Sue is starting to feel a little light-headed and figures she will take a break soon – but the success of tonight's event is so dog-gone important and everything has to be just right for it to go off well. Sue has to see to every detail and that everything is ready for tonight's action. She has a ton of pizza being delivered throughout the night from Mario's Chicago Pizza Palace, and many of the workers at the hospital brought in cakes, pies, brownies, and cookies to be sold. They all had to be wrapped, sorted, bagged, and tagged this morning. *Gee, I wonder how Don's doing? Today is his first Santa gig.* Sue cracks a smile thinking about Don in a Santa suit dealing with all the kids. *Sure hope no munchkin pulls his beard or pees in his lap!* Sue's brain resorts back to BINGO and the planning mode.

There will also be all sorts of soft drinks, teas (hot and cold), and coffee for sale. No alcohol can be served on the premises – legally that is – and that's just as well with all the problems trying to keep the vets and alcohol from mixing. This fundraiser needs to be successful in order to fund the entertainment for the next six months or so.

Sue eyes the punch bowl – free punch for the residents of the hospital. It's all set up; spic and span and ready for action. The paper BINGO cards are secure in the trunk of her car and won't come out until the last minute to keep this an honest game (who knows what anyone has up their sleeves these days, resident of the hospital or not). New colored BINGO markers have been purchased down at the dollar store and are ready for sale – and these are the washable ink kind.

All the orderlies got their pep talk this morning about keeping an eye on the punch bowl and for cheaters – especially ex-Sergeant John L. Sargeant.

Looks like everything is just about ready in preparation for to-night's big event, Sue thinks. *Doors open at six. Please God, don't let there be a big brawl like last time when we had to call the cops.* Sue remembers all too well the big fight that took place during the last BINGO game earlier this month. Retired Gunny John L. Sargeant and some humongous black lady tore up each other, the recreation hall and just about everything in it. It took days to clean up the mess. Shards of glass from the punch bowl and punch all over the tables and floor, not to mention the zillion plastic bits and computer chips from the brand new neon lighted BINGO ball machine AND squashed BINGO balls lying all over the place which shot out of the BINGO ball machine like a cannon when it exploded. And TEETH! – There were at least six or seven teeth lying on the floor! *Please God, don't ever let that happen again! We just got that new machine almost paid for!* Sue thinks about the ordeal in finding and ordering a new BINGO ball machine. *If it hadn't been for Patriarch Shimko down at St. Ignatz the Martyr and his connections, we would never have been able to do it. God bless the Patriarch and St. Ignatz the Martyr.*

Sue looks around and decides things are pretty much in order.

Sure hope that black lady with the big bosoms doesn't show up. Maybe I'll step out now for a quick bite to eat.

28

It's one-o'clock on a gorgeous Saturday afternoon and time for Jimmy D. Mays to rise and shine. He's not sleeping in the Santa suit any more. He has the suit hanging up on a wood hanger right next to the cardboard Rudolph. Jimmy figures the Santa suit is some kind of magic and should be respected and definitely not pissed in. He found some Santa's helpers and elf costumes in a box and sleeps in those (the elf pants are a little tight, though). Later he figures on going over to St. Ignatz the Martyr and round up some extra clothes for free.

"Yeah – Jimmy D. gonna build up a collection of fine outfits an' shit. See what da good priess Bee Bee tole me 'bout ova St. Bignuts gonna give to poor ol' Jimmy D. for free. Who knows, might be getting' some o' dat wine too. Wonner why dat priess be drinkin' Mad Dog when he prolly can afford some good shit from da top shelf? Don't make no kinda sense? He gots money enough to be drinkin' Fat Bastid like Jimmy D. drink. Maybe he don't like dem kinda words in his church? Yeah, das it – you can't be saying 'Here's to you, Jesus' and be drinkin' Fat Bastid."

Lickety-split Jimmy is up, in the Santa suit, and out of the dumpster. He's headed for the back of the Penney's store where he knows the outdoor water spigot still works and hasn't frozen solid yet.

"Bess be washin' up for today's aventure! Jimmy D. might hit da jackpot or some shit today an' he gonna smell the bess he can."

As Jimmy strolls to the water spigot he looks to the left and right hoping to see Miss Martha or Miss Emma. No such luck. Jimmy rolls up the white fur on his sleeves and washes his face and hands as best he can. Next he cups his hands for a cool drink and is reminded how great an ordinary drink of cold water can be, so he takes several more handfuls. Now his fingers begin to sting a bit and he notices the cold.

"Damn! Jimmy D. better be watchin' out or some frossbite be bittin' on his ass instead that old Santa chair!" Jimmy rubs his behind in remembrance.

Ready for the day to begin, Jimmy lights up a Camel and heads out to the main parking lot. When out of the clear an older, gold-colored Lincoln appears along side Jimmy and the driver's window goes down.

"Is dat you, Jimmy D. Mays, all dressed up like Santa hisself? Lord oh Lord – tell me it's you, Jimmy D."

Jimmy cracks a smile when he recognizes an old friend.

"Hey, Wanda, how you doin', girl? Man, Jimmy D. ain't seen youse in a long time?" Jimmy peeks inside the Lincoln and sees Wanda's enormous breasts covering up the steering wheel and housed in a dirty sweatshirt that says something about "EAT SHIT" on the front of it. Wanda sees where Jimmy's looking and smiles.

"You 'member these, Jimmy D.?" says Wanda.

"Sure do, sweet thing. Dreams about dem tatas all da time," Jimmy says with a husky laugh. He reaches in and gives them both a nice gentle squeeze.

"Where you been, Wanda, jail or some shit like dat?"

"Hell no, Jimmy D. I gots me a real job now. I works at da K-Mart hangin' shit back up after da peoples been throwin' shit on da floor they don't want. You be surprised how much shit peoples throw on da floors! It's a bitch, Jimmy D. I works hard for my money," Wanda fires back.

"So whatchu doin' here, Wanda? Off taday?"

"Yeah, Jimmy D. I came back to da JC Penney to get my baby Sharita one o' dem crawlin' Elmo mutherfuckas she been yellin' 'bout for da pass two weeks. And o' course dese motherfuckas ain't got one even when da man says he getting' a shit load of Elmos in this morning! I had me one yestaday, right here at da JC Penney and some trailer park cracker bitch ripped it right out my hands. And get dis shit, Jimmy D. Me and her goin' round and round – pretty even fight until I kick dis bitch right in her pussy and down she went like da great white whale hisself – you know – Mopy Assed Dick."

"Is dat how you loose more of your teefers?" asks Jimmy.

"No! Hell no! I lost a bunch o' teefers las' month when dis here big ass fight broke out at BINGO game at the V.A. hospital. Some clown think he a Marine or sompin' 'cuse me o' cheatin' and punch me inna mouth. Teefers be jumpin' all ova da floor. I got up though and threw dat skinny-ass Marine drunk right through da punch bowl and his big head smashed into da neon BINGO ball machine. Fucked them all up: da Marine, da punch bowl, and da big-ass neon BINGO ball machine. And dat neon shit fucked dat Marine up big time 'cause when he hit it, dat somebitch explodes wid all dem BINGO balls be shootin' out across da room like bullets. Da skinny ass Marine – he out cold, but me an' mose peoples in dere got whacked wid them damn BINGO balls. My titties and ass are still sore from dem BINGO balls be flyin' all over da place."

"You somepin else, Wanda," Jimmy laughs and lights up another Camel. "So did youse get da Elmo shit you wanted for Sharita?"

"No, Jimmy D., and dis here is da bitch of it all, cause jus' when I went to pick Elmo up off da floor – and I'm good at that from my K-Mart job – another sneaky bitch come in, snatch Elmo and run off before I could get to her! Sneaky bitch outran me and ran into da mall, pass da Santa and shit and out da door. Didn't even pay for da Elmo motherfucka! I runs hard too and coulda had her but I runs into some little elf what works wid Santa. Anyways, me an' dis little elf muthafucka go tumblin' down onna floor and knock over four or five reindeers and shit. Kids crying and screamin'. Santa yellin' shit at da elf. Peoples watchin' as I untangle this little elf fucka from my titties – had his little elf head all tangled up in my sweatshirt – even had one o' my bra straps cross his neck! Little elf fucka almos' pass out 'til I unhooks my bra strap – my titties damn nears hits da floor, and da little elf fucka comes to.

Now here somebody 'posed to be workin' wid Santa and kids, and shit and he gots one foul, nasty-ass mouth – callin' me 'dirty whore' and 'nasty bitch,' and shit like dat. Well, I took dat little elf boy by his scrawny head an' lifts that little motherfucka up and jammed his tiny ass on one o' dem reindeer still be standin' up. Little elf fucka be dazed and shit an' lookin' like he jus' won the Kentucky Derby an' waitin' for his picture be took by da newspaper or some shit. By da time I get back on my feets, da Elmo-stealin' bitch is gone! I gots a good look at her, dough, an' when I do see dat bitch again, she gonna get hers."

"Gees, Wanda," Jimmy D. says, "Sorry you din' get no Elmo shit for Sharita. Das a shame, man, a real shame. Say look, Wanda, can you takes Jimmy D. to St. Bignuts down on Pulaski Streets? Jimmy D. gots to get hisself some new pants and shit from da priess dere. My frien' Bee Bee, he da owner of da Cash and Carry joint. He say dis priess gives out free clothes an' shit to da poor peoples. You wanna go, Wanda? You can preten' you poorer 'an shit. Maybe da priess gives you some free shit too. You know where dat is, Wanda? – down in Polack town?"

"Sure, Jimmy. Hop on in an' give me a Camel," Wanda says.

"Shit, Wanda, you be nice an' Jimmy D. give youse more 'an dat!"

"Jimmy D., you always been a smooth talker. But where you goin' wid dat Santa shit on? You workin' somewhere? You workin' here at da mall?"

"Not yet, Wanda. But Jimmy D. workin' on it. *Jimmy D. Ain' be tellin' dis fat bitch about my 'heritance.* Got me a nice place to live in an' real close by," Jimmy says.

"You want me to go there first?" asks Wanda.

"No Wanda. Don't be goin' dere jus' yet. Maybes Girl Scouts or Jehovah Witness be comin' roun' ask for donations and shit"

They both laugh as the Lincoln slowly glides and parks in the last row under the trees.

"Why Jimmy D. you really is happy to see Wanda, ain't you!"

Houston, we have lift off!

It's early Saturday morning and Santa Don has his Santa suit and accessories and his first paid Santa gig. Don met earlier with all the other Santas (Santa Monica was late – probably got some of her chains tangled up), where Sal and Vic handed out the Santa gear and assignment sheets. Mr. Mimo-Momo, whatever, was not in sight. *He probably had to help Joey and Pauley park a few boats.* Everyone was jolly and excited to start playing Santa and be out of there in about ten minutes. Everyone but Santa Domingo, that is. Domingo is still pissed at the world and never said a word except and occasional "Gringo!"

So now the race was on and off to the parking lot this rag-tag group of Santas went. Off to their first assignments. Off to conquer the world of kids and Christmas. Off to spread cheer, happiness and "good will to all men" regardless of race, color, creed, number of limbs, number of chains, tattoos, prison terms, wives buried in the basement, you name it. *We're off to save the world from Scrooge and make a difference in lives of children! Oh yeah, and remember, Don, don't promise anything! Just say, "We'll see," and "I have to check the good list."*

Don's in the Volvo now. Santa gear is all safe in the back seat. He checks the assignment sheet just as the black-primered Chevy low-rider races by with a roar. Don sees Cheech and Chong in the front seat laughing and spies Santa Domingo in the back. "Mister Happy Claus" rolls down the window, gives Don the finger and yells out, "Gringo!" Don shakes his head and goes back to reading the assignment sheet. He sees he's to spend six hours at Fat Wang's Chinese Take-Out. "See Anita Wang, the owner." Don smiles at the name, "Anita Wang.*" I wonder what Mama Wang was thinking when she named her daughter "Anita Wang?"*

The assignment sheet indicates "No pictures will be taken by a hired photographer," but Don's sure some parents will have cell phones and want a picture of Fat Wang's. Don checks the address and didn't know this part of Chicago even existed as a commercial area. As far as he knew, this area is all warehouses and derelict old buildings up for sale. *Oh well. A gig is a gig and I still get sixty-five dollars an hour.* That brings a smile to his face. Don checks out the assignment sheet again and reads: "Just talk to the customers and be friendly with the kids and see if they want to sit on your lap and tell you what they want for Christmas – AND DON'T MAKE ANY PROMISES! And bring the suit back clean! – This means NO SHIT on the Santa suit or you won't get paid!"

Don plugs in the address to Fat Wang's Chinese Take-Out into his GPS and begins the drive. *Jesus,* he thinks. *It's too early to go there now. Maybe I'll stop off for some coffee. Do I dare go back to the Dunkin' Donuts? It's on my way. What the hell – Why not – Maybe they won't remember me.* Don turns on his Sirius satellite radio and selects the "Willie" channel for some good old country music. You couldn't ask for better. Willie himself is singing, "Blue Eyes Crying in the Rain."

It didn't seem long at all before Don's parking the Volvo at his favorite Dunkin' Donuts. The ride was great and so were the country-western tunes sung by the greats like: Loretta Lynn, Hank Williams, Johnny Cash, Conway Twitty, Jim Reeves, and on and on it went – Just perfect. *Love that Sirius radio!*

Don walks through the doors to Dunkin' Donuts and right off the bat he recognizes some of the customers who were there when he had his melt-down just yesterday. Ex-Detective Carlo DiSabatino is sitting with all his ex-cop friends again. Carlo is looking a little gray today and is sporting a new neck brace that looks a little too small and a whole lot painful. Carlo sees Don and instinctively reaches for his "piece" that he turned in years ago and again comes up with air. "Fucking retirement!" he mumbles. His buddies all recognize the lunatic from yesterday's scene and brace themselves for "Fort Apache, Part II." Not a word is spoken.

All eyes are on Don Kaminski, the walking time bomb. One re-tired cop, Sylvester Jardine, slips his right hand into his pants pocket and grabs hold of a two-shot Derringer with no safety. This old fool still carries around the "throw-down" piece he carried when he walked the beat as a patrolman downtown somewhere. Jardine figures if anything happens today, he's going to be ready for it. Ex-cop Sylvester Jardine squeezes the trigger ever so slightly.

The owner, Shuly Patel, comes out from the back with a fresh tray of Old Fashioned donuts and immediately recognizes Don. The donuts go on the shelf and Shuly is around the counter and in Don's face.

"We don't want any trouble from you today." He says.

"Believe me," Don says, "I am so sorry for …" Just then a shot rings out.

POW!

Immediately, everyone in the room looses his hearing. Seems ex-cop Sylvester Jardine squeezed a little too hard and fired the Derringer through his pants pocket and under the table. A quarter inch to the left and the head of Jardine's dick would be missing. Lucky for him this didn't happen and even luckier for Jardine, the piss, which is now flowing freely, helps to sooth the pain because his crotch is on fire! As luck would have it, when Jardine fired the Derringer, his crotch ignited in flames. Unlucky for DiSabatino, though, because the bullet bounced off the bottom of the table and landed in his right testicle (A quarter inch to the right and the head of DiSabatino's dick would be missing!).

Ears are ringing while ex-cops jump up knocking the table over. Hot coffee splashes onto everyone's lap. There's a whole bunch of hooting and hollering going on and grabbing for napkins.

"I'm shot!" DiSabatino screams. "The son of a bitch shot me in the balls!" and Carlo shrinks back down into his chair and slides off onto the floor with the donuts and the hot coffee. "He shot me in the balls!"

Don stands there in complete shock. Shuly looks at Don from head to toe and checks Don's hands but sees no gun. The ex-cops circle around DiSabatino trying to help. Shuly runs for the phone to dial 911. Jardine, temporarily hypnotized by the whole ordeal, finally throws the Derringer down onto the floor just like the old days when he could claim, "The perp drew a gun on me!" Except this time he's a bit late and everyone in the joint sees him do it and besides, his crotch is still on fire! Shuly sees the fire while he's on the phone and without hesitation grabs for a full pot of fresh, hot coffee and tosses the contents onto Jardine's crotch. It's a perfect shot and the fire goes out. And so does Jardine. Way beyond screaming for the life of his family jewels, which he hasn't used much these days anyway, Jardine grabs for his blistering crotch with both hands. To him it feels just like a hot plate of boiled spaghetti – *al dente*. Poor Sylvie's mouth is locked in a wide-open position with no sounds coming out at all. The boiling hot coffee saturated his boxer shorts and freely makes its way down into his shoes and socks. And now his feet feel like they are shoved into hot lava. Jardine stumbles back and slams into the back wall. He then slides down the wall in slow motion and passes out and is now lying next to DiSabatino who keeps screaming, "The bastard shot me in the balls!"

"Yeah," another ex-cop chimes in. "And poor Sylvie's dick is on fire!"

Don hears the sirens approaching and slumps to a chair. EMTs enter the shop like invading ants. Next come the real cops with real guns: Officers Patrick Malone and Sean O'Malley, with undoubtedly a couple more hidden "throw-downs."

All the cops, ex-cops, EMTs, and Shuly Patel exchange greetings and pat each other on the back like they just arrived for Thanksgiving dinner. They should – they know each other very well. One of the ex-cops explains the situation as if he were on the witness stand and they all look at one another and shake their heads in agreement that this is exactly what took place and they all had the same story for the witness stand.

Before long, two gurneys hastily go out the front door. Ex-Detective Carlo DiSabatino is lying on the first one, still in disbelief as he cries out yet again, "The son of a bitch shot me in the balls!" You can tell by his facial expressions that he is in excruciating pain. The second gurney carries ex-cop, Sylvester Jardine. Sylvie is lying in a fetal position with both hands cupping his privates. He still cannot make a sound and his mouth is now frozen open wide enough that you could probably fit a softball into it. Both of his eyes are rolled back into his head so far that you can only see the whites. As silent as poor Sylvie is, everyone there hears his bloody scream for some kind of help – except for Shuly Patel who is busy cleaning up the tables and chairs for the next customers. Shuly has done this countless times before and recognizes the value of keeping a neat place. He is oblivious to everyone and everything around him as he races for a mop as if on automatic pilot while muttering something no one hears but himself, "And now, because of this very rude customer, I am going to be late for my dental appointment with Dr. Saltzman!" He comes over to Don. All the ex-cops are looking his way with glares that warn Don, *Perhaps you should leave now, dickhead*!

"Excuse me, sir," Shuly says, "but I think you should leave now!" Shuly hands Don a bag. "Here are two complimentary Old Fashioned donuts. I'm sorry, but we are fresh out of coffee at the moment. Please leave now," Shuly says and gestures towards the door. Don doesn't say a word but simply turns and exits.

30

Somewhere in Chicago suburbia there's a children's Christmas party going on in full swing and the two children who live there (brother and sister), along with many neighborhood children and parents, are anxiously awaiting the arrival of Santa Claus. Dad checks his watch knowing that Santa's surprise visit should be any minute now. He warns the children to be on their best behavior because "You never know where Santa might turn up!"

The children all run to the window just as an old Harley pulls up and low and behold – Santa is the driver! Santa parks the HOG, which doesn't want to shut down and just sputters while Santa twists and turns levers and switches on the Harley.

BAM!!!!! With one giant HOG fart the Fat Boy shuts up. Santa heads up the walkway with a peculiar stride that indicates he might be in some kind of pain. The kids are all yelling and screaming. "Here he comes! Here comes Santa Claus! Here comes Santa Claus!" Mom races to the door just a few steps in front of the festive munchkins and opens it for Santa's big entrance. All the other parents in attendance have their cameras ready for Santa's grand entrance.

"Ho, Ho, Ho!" yells Santa in a different kind of voice other than what was expected. The children hush up a bit. *Maybe Santa is under the weather?*

"Ho, Ho, Ho!" is repeated in a muffled way and the children all get a better look at jolly old Saint Nick. Sure, it's Santa's red suit and hat. Yes, Santa said "Ho, Ho, Ho." – but something is definitely wrong here. As tiny eyes investigate the problem they notice that Santa has more than rosy red checks. Santa has many tiny silver chains running across his face, through his lips, in and out of his eyebrows, back into his ears, through his cheeks, and out his nose! Santa looks like a chromed Frankenstein!

"Waaaaaaaaaaaaaaaaah!" little Alice screams. She grabs brother Henry out of mom's grip and hand-in-hand they both race for the kitchen.

"Eeeeeeeeeeeeeeeeeeek!" little Kimberly yells in fright and hides behind the door wishing to become invisible. Other children have the same sentiment as they scream and run for cover in all directions.

"Holy shit!" little Chucky yells as he and buddy Patrick jump behind the couch wishing they had their Darth Vader deadly saber swords with them. All the parents stare in horror as Santa looks like something out of a Steven King movie.

"Jesus H. Christ!" Chucky's Dad blurts out. "What the hell is that?"

"Are you supposed to be Santa?" mom asks the chained creature.

"You betcha!" the chromed Santa replies with chains swinging and banging into each other. "You wanted a Santa this afternoon, right? Well, here I am. I'm Santa Anita," the Harley chick says as she tries to pull a wedgie out of her ass but it seems to be caught on something and makes her wiggle a little.

"Let's get the party started? What do you say?" says Anita – total silence.

Dad gently nudges Santa Anita back outside and onto the stoop careful not to get any chains hung up in the door. He steps out behind her and quickly closes the door for the safety of all those inside. Instantly the windows of the house are jammed with faces of all ages wanting to get a peek at the freak show Santa.

"Listen, Santa," Dad begins, not sure what to say but knowing damn-right well that, *Only one of us is going back into that house!*

"I think there must have been some kind of mistake here," dad says to Santa Anita. This is a CHILDREN'S Christmas party and I'm not sure...."

"Right, right, there's no mistake buddy, believe me. You're having a kid's party. You paid for a Santa. And I'm it – Merry Christmas!" Anita sings and smiles with a face that looks like a holiday party plate full of chromed spagetti.

"Tell you what, Santa," dad barters. "Why don't you just go the hell back to wherever you came from and let's just forget the whole thing shall we?" Dad peels out his wallet and hands Anita a twenty. "Just get the hell out of here before my neighbors start calling the cops – okay? What do you say?" He gestures Anita should head back towards the Harley.

"Suits me, mister," Santa Anita says. "Doesn't look like you people are having much fun here anyways, if you ask me. Screw you people!" She pockets the twenty, gives dad the finger with her oil-stained, white Santa gloves, and gingerly walks back to the Harley while trying again to pull out the snagged wedgie. *Something is definitely wrong here,* she thinks. *I'll bet I pulled another chain out and my fucking vagina is bleeding again! He we go off to the hospital with no fucking insurance and only a twenty! Jesus Christ!*

Dad turns, opens the door and walks back inside. *What do I tell the kids?*

"Santa had to go kids…"

31

Meanwhile, at the Church of the Always Open Door Daycare Center, a rather slender Santa is hunched over and is stealthily climbing over the peak of the school roof and softly creeps towards the gable overlooking the fenced-in playground. It is none other than Santa Lee who, although dressed like Santa Claus, has his face covered in a black hood with cutouts for his eyes and mouth – the kind that bank robbers and terrorists wear. Perhaps Santa Lee is a Ninja and related to Bruce Lee? Now there's a possibility.

The Church of the Always Open Door Daycare Center's Saturday daycare program has been a big success since they started it about three years ago and today there are about thirty-five children present at recess in the playground. The younger children are playing on the outdoor jungle gym and sliding boards, while the older children are racing back and forth in a game of kickball which has a tied score. One of the workers, Miss Mary, rings a bell for the children to listen up. She announces loud enough for all to hear, "Don't forget, boys and girls, we have a special visitor coming this afternoon, so if I were you I would be on my very best behavior." The kids all smile at Miss Mary, giggle and cheer, pretty certain that the surprise guest is going to be Santa Claus. This is no secret. They heard the teachers all talking about Santa's surprise visit this morning when they arrived at the daycare. The children all return to some heavy duty playing and everyone is as happy as can be, knowing that they will soon see the big guy himself and be able to personally tell him all their wishes and wants for Christmas. What a glorious day this is!

In a death-defying leap, Ninja Santa Lee jumps from the rooftop and lands in the middle of the kickball game right in front of Miss Mary. The stunned children all freeze in their tracks. Swings appear to have stopped mid flight and slides are halted half-way down the sliding board. The Ninja Santa yells out unfamiliar words and goes into an "advance and kill" Karate-type exercise complete with twirling Ninja sticks which came out of nowhere. Miss Mary faints without hesitation and collapses onto the turf which, lucky for her, consists of about four inches of chewed-up tires which soften her landing.

Ninja Santa Lee jumps over Miss Mary and while still swinging the Ninja sticks yells out, "Melly Klistmas!" and thirty-five kids
who just had the shit scared out of them scatter to the four points of the
Earth. Some make it through the gates to freedom while others vault
the short chain-linked fence and run for the hills and safety from an
obvious terrorist attack or invasion of the Santa from outer space.
Little Danny MacAdory vaults over the fence in one swift leap and
almost makes it but his coat gets caught and now he is unable to get
free and facing certain death from the Ninja Santa gone berserk.

A block away, a blue and white police car passes by and the officers
see children wildly running for cover and yelling things like, "Help us!
Santa's nuts!" and "Run for your lives! The Santa from Mars is after
us!" Five year old and tough guy, Eddie Minka, runs over to the blue
and white and yells to the officers, "There's a crazy Santa back there
in the playground and he made me poop my pants! Now Mom's going
to beat my ass when I get home!" And off he runs to collect his
beating right away and get it over with. *Better to face Mom than some
berserk Santa, that's for sure.*
    The police car makes an unexpected left turn on two tires, rac-
es up to the playground with lights flashing and sirens blaring and
comes to a screeching halt. Guns are drawn and two cops leap out of
the squad car and crouch down behind the open doors. They immediately see Miss Mary passed out on the ground and the back of a
skinny Santa who is still twirling sticks in the air. Officer Patrick
Malone thinks to himself, *What in the hell is going on here today?
First the shooting at the Dunkin' Donuts this morning and now this
fucked up Santa at the daycare center!*

"Put the sticks down and get on the ground!" orders Malone's partner,
Officer Sean O'Malley. The Ninja Santa stops and turns to face the
street and the police. Santa Lee is rather stunned that the children ran
off in the middle of his performance and now these two cops are going
to ruin the grand finale he has planned with the fireworks he has just
lit housed inside the Ninja sticks.
    "Put the sticks DOWN and get on the ground NOW!" repeats
Officer O'Malley. The Ninja Santa drops the sticks on the ground as
he is told. He begins to tear off the black hood when out of the blue a
foot comes flying up from behind and catches him deep in the crotch,

sending his testicles into his lower abdomen and down the Ninja Santa goes in so much Kung Fu pain that twenty Mr. Miyagis wouldn't be able to sooth the fire between his legs. Miss Mary stands there in triumph.

"Better call the meat wagon," one of the cops says.

Suddenly, the fireworks hidden in the two Ninja sticks goes off shooting numerous blue balls of fire which rocket across the playground in different directions with loud whistling noises. One blue ball knocks the hat off Malone and both officers hit the deck on instinct. O'Malley calls for backup. "Officer down! Officer down! Shots fired! ...Church of the Always Open Door Daycare Center!"

32

In another part of town, Santa Rick drives the VW Westphalia camper into an L-shaped stripmall parking lot in a grafitti-riddled section of Chicago. Although most of the shops are rented out to various businesses, the stripmall has seen better days, that's for sure, and business is really bad. Santa Rick is driving slowly for three reasons. One – he is looking for a photographer who is supposed to meet him here this afternoon. Two – the parking lot is in ruins and probably hasn't been patched or re-paved for the past twenty years. You could lose a front end or perhaps a small car like a Mini or a Smart Car in one of the potholes. Some say the slum lord who owns this place is some Russian religious nut who drives around in a fancy black car, kissing and blessing everybody. And three – Santa Rick just now notices that he is running out of gas as the VW camper sputters, jerks, lurches forward and finally quits with a bang.

The folks in this neighborhood know instinctively what to do when they hear a loud bang. The people in the parking lot dive for cover. Store owners go to the front door to lock out the looters. The patrons of the local watering hole, Wallowich's Frog Pond, empty out into the sunlight for a look-see. Most of the patrons are garbage men who frequent the Frog Pond every day for suds and lunch. The stripmall business association still complains about the stink from the garbage and the number of trucks parked right in the corner of the stripmall. And most of them are parked in the handicapped spots.

Habib Constantine, the owner of Bee Bee's Cash and Carry, is already standing by the doorway with his sawed-off 12-guage shotgun, awaiting the next attack. Standing sideways and trying to hide behind the door jamb (tough to do when you wear XXX clothes!), he surveys the parking lot and listens for sirens. Nothing. People are again walking in the lot and shaking their heads at each other as if to say, "false alarm." The garbage men return back into the darkness of the Frog Pond for more suds. Two winos go back to fighting over the few sips of Vampire wine left in a discarded bottle and are pushing and tugging at each other and groping for the bottle in the brown paper bag. Habib takes another look around to be perfectly sure and satisfied that all is well, returns to the counter to replace the shotgun under the cash register and grabs for more Reese's Peanut Butter Cups.

An oil-smoking, light-green, 1970's Plymouth station wagon pulls into the parking lot towing a long flatbed trailer which has a huge Santa seat bolted down on top of it. The chair has been hand-painted red, gold and green and whoever did the job did not use tape or even care, for that matter, where the paint landed – just slapped it on anywhere – and it looked it. The trailer has a faded-green skirting all around the base and looks as though it might have been a parade float many years ago.

Santa Rick watches as the driver parks the station wagon in the middle of the stripmall close to where the VW died. He has his choice of spots to park because the lot is darn near empty except for all the garbage trucks down by the taproom.

Out jumps a bald, wiry, old guy who needed a shave three days ago. He scratches the top of his head, his chin, and his ass as he looks around the lot. Next, the old coot proceeds to the rear of the trailer and lowers an attached set of steps. He opens up the tailgate to the Plymouth and begins to remove and set up several old Polaroid cameras. The cameras are mounted on a home-made stand which he places on the other end of the trailer, facing the Santa seat.

Santa Rick checks his assignment sheet and figures this has to be Sam Irving, the photographer. Rick slides off the driver's seat and onto the wheelchair which is attached to where the front passenger seat should be. He rolls back to the side door and with the controls mounted there, Rick presses several buttons and the side door automatically slides out of the way and the metal floor begins to fold outward. Rick easily rolls out onto the floor and with a push of a button he begins his short journey to the blacktop.

Sam Irving sees a Santa in a wheelchair rolling across the parking lot and doing a marvelous job avoiding the craters. Several people watch as the chair-bound Santa rolls to a stop next to the flatbed. Sam introduces himself and shakes hands with Santa Rick. He then reaches down under the side of the trailer and pulls out a sliding ramp. Between the two of them, Rick ends up on top of the flatbed and into the Santa seat – and there they wait, like two lepers whom no one is willing to approach. *Let them get their own water! What are a bald*

*skinny man and the Santa with no feet doing in THIS parking lot,
anyway? Are they crazy?*

Sam the photographer and Rick, the no-legged Santa, spend hours
exchanging life's interesting stories while waiting for all the local kids
to show up to meet and have their picture taken with Santa. Periodical-
ly they look around while chatting hoping to catch a glimpse of a
prospect – but nothing. One little tyke almost broke loose from mom
to check out the legless Santa on the trailer, but mom snatched him
just in time and tossed his tiny butt in the back seat of the car. No visit
with Santa here.

Hour after hour goes by and now there is nothing else to talk
about. They already agreed it was a darn good thing it wasn't as cold
out today as it could have been. More than once both Sam and Rick
checked their assignment sheets to make sure they are at the right
place, at the right time, and on the right date, and they are.

"My guess is, they didn't advertise it good enough," Sam says
in disgust.

"Sure looks it," Rick replies woefully and adds, "What do you
say we break down and skedaddle out of here?"

"That's a mighty fine idea, partner," Sam replies. "I'll see you
next time and maybe we will have better luck," Sam says and heads
for the cameras.

Before they begin to shut down for the day, about six inner-city
teens enter the parking lot on their bikes and spot the trailer.

"Hey look!" cries the leader. "Just like Lamar said. Look for
the trailer and check out the Santa with no feet!"

"No feet, hell you say! He ain't got no legs either!" from
another teen. They zero in on the safest route to make it to Santa
without losing a bicycle in the pot holes. They arrive safely, dismount
their bikes and look up at Santa Rick.

"Hey, Santa," one of them says. "Where are your feet? Did you
get hung up in a chimney or something?" The others laugh at the
thought of Santa tightly wedged in a smokestack somewhere.

"No boys, I didn't as a matter of fact. It happened during the
war," Santa Rick answers.

"Who's he calling 'boy?' comes from the back.

"Were you in World War II?" the leader asks.

"Yeah, did you kill any Russians?" another pipes in.

"No boys, I got wounded in Vietnam," answers the Santa with no legs.

"I am very lucky to be alive and happy to be here today just to visit with you boys, hear all about what you want for Christmas and take a picture which you can have for free. Come on up boys, but watch your step."

"There goes that 'boys' shit again," from the back.

"Free is cool," says the leader. They march up the steps and over to where Sam and the cameras are located.

"How did you end up staying alive, Santa?" another asks. "Were you captured by the Shaka Zulus, or something?" this from another kid. Santa Rick motions for the boys to come closer. "Actually, one of my buddies, Sgt. Jimmy Mays, made sure that none of us were captured that day and that we all made it home, God bless him. I'd sure like to find him one of these days."

Sam Irving sets the boys up for a picture with Santa Rick and it should have made the newspaper for the grand shot that it was. The boys all spend some time together talking with Santa Rick and telling him what they would like to see under the Christmas tree. Being older and more grown up than most school children, they didn't want to sit on Santa's lap and admitted they knew mom or grandmom was really Santa; but they were pleasant to talk to and very respectful of Santa once they accepted the 'boys' part wasn't meant as a racial slur.

Once the visit was over and the leader got the free picture, Sam began to pack away his cameras and equipment into the station wagon. The boys all pitched in and even held the wheelchair steady while Santa Rick shifted over to it. One young man got down and held onto the rear of the trailer to hold it steady as Rick wheeled over to go down the side ramp.

"Don't push down there!" Sam tried to warn the kids, but it was too late. The rusted tilt-trailer catch finally gave way and the entire flat bed tilted all the way down to the blacktop and away flew the legless Santa riding backwards in the wheelchair. Rick was simply caught off guard and didn't have much time to react. Instinctively, both arms flew out in an attempt to grab for the wheels, but they only went so far. As luck would have it, both sleeves of the Santa coat got caught onto the arms of the wheelchair. As hard as he tries, Rick cannot free his hands. The wheelchair flies backwards down the trailer ramp so fast that the ball on the Santa hat blows straight out in the wind, only in the wrong direction. "And away they all flew like the down of a thistle."

Down the trailer Santa Rick flies and onto the parking lot like a jet being launched from an aircraft carrier. Amazingly, he goes pretty far before running into trouble. The boys are all sure Santa Rick is a dead man flying backwards and all. The flying Santa eventually hits into one of the many potholes that almost swallows him up whole. Down goes the chair and out flies Rick. The boys and Sam the photographer run over as fast as they can. Sure enough, there is one dead, legless Santa lying in the parking lot.

They all surround Santa Rick and begin to turn him over on his back expecting to see a bloody mess. Miraculously, Santa Rick is not hurt much. In fact, he isn't even scratched from what they could tell. Just a tad dirty here and there, that's all. Sam turns the wheelchair right side up and rolls it back to where Santa Rick is.

"You're one lucky Santa," he says. "The wheelchair seems to be fine! Looks like all you did was scrape some white fur off the front of your jacket!"

"I'm fine, boys. I'm fine," Rick says as they help him up onto the wheelchair.

"Sorry, Santa," one of the boys says. "I sure am sorry."

"Hey, I'm fine. You were only trying to help. Don't worry about it."

They wheel Santa Rick back to the trailer and say their good-byes. The bikes are all mounted and the boys ride on out, eager to share their experience with the Santa with no feet.

Sam's all packed up and ready to roll.

"Need any help getting into the camper?" he asks Rick.

"No thanks, Sam. It's all automated and easy for me to use."

"Okay then. I'll be seeing you." Sam drives out of the lot careful to miss any more potholes.

Rick wheels on over to the van.

That's just great, he thinks.

I forgot – I'm out of gas! Now what?

Stay calm, Santa Rick. Help will come. And besides, you are really going to get mad when you see what's been spray painted all over the other side of your VW Westphalia!

The BINGO Party at the Ira Hayes Veteran's Administration Hospital is in full swing now. The place is packed to the gills with the locals, the "high rollers" of the local BINGO world, and the hospital veterans. Sue Kaminski is happy to see retired Gunny John L. Sargeant is behaving himself playing BINGO and sipping pure fruit punch – no chaser. It helps that he is flanked by the two biggest orderlies in the hospital who have explicit orders to "Watch Gunny Sargeant!" The punch bowl is secure and Sue sees no sign of the black lady with the big titties. All is well.

Santa Rajneesh has just unloaded a pound of quarters into the parking meter and is satisfied that his multi-colored Yugo is safe from harm. *Some of these days, Yugo will be classic hit with collectors and Rajneesh will be selling to rich American for maybe three millions of bucks or more!* Rajneesh is excited about being rich some day and begins the almost two-mile trek to the Sears Tower, and his first assignment as Santa (It's called the Willis Tower today because Sears moved out, but you ask any native of Chicago and they will all tell you it's the "Sears Tower"). He puts the Santa hat on his head and begins to jog, not wanting to be late for his first gig. He is stared at and laughed at by just about everyone who passes him this sunny, Saturday afternoon. More than one walker does a double-take at the unusual sight and turns back to take another look. It is not often you see a skinny dark-skinned man dressed in a full Santa suit jogging down the streets of Chicago.

Rajneesh continues jogging and picks up the pace. The Santa suit keeps him warm as he races along to his quest, and by the time he nears the tower, he is almost too hot to continue. He took the hat off long ago and without realizing it, lost it a half-mile back. The thick black belt is undone and hanging down the sides of his hips. The Santa jacket is unzipped and hangs on him like a wet blanket over a clothes line. Sweat rolls off his black curly hair and the fur around his collar is wet. He looks like a captured illegal alien without a green card.

   Shuly Patel, the owner of the Dunkin' Donuts, has just left the dentist's office and is now driving on S. Wacker Drive when he sees the Indian Santa. He blows the horn repeatedly and is waving his hand out the window and yelling something about praises to Vishnu, and very much excited over the rise of "his people."

   "Look at that! Look at that! – an Indian Santa Claus!" Shuly says with pride. "Some day, an Indian – perhaps that Indian Santa – will be President of this great country! Just you wait and see." Shuly tries not to smile so much because his jaw still hurts from the tooth extraction. He is a patient of Dr. Saltzman and so is just about every other Patel and Indian worker here in Chicago a patient of Dr.

Saltzman. The Myron Saltzman Dental Clinic has been around since the middle ages. Some say Dr. Saltzman made George Washington's false teeth, although no one has ever confirmed that to be true. One thing is for sure. Dr. Saltzman is cheap and fast. No appointment is necessary. Just come in off the streets and have a tooth pulled. Hell, it's even cheaper if you have more than one pulled!

Fact is, Dr. Saltzman has been dead for more than thirty-five years. The dentists who work at the clinic, and this has always been the practice, even when Dr. Saltzman was alive, are all new dental school graduates who have little to no experience. It has been suggested, and even investigated once or twice, that some of the dentists are still in dental school and perhaps a few working there have flunked out of dental school! And there are those who believe none of them went to dental school! Still – "Need a tooth pulled? Go to Dr. Saltzman," is always the answer – in and out – nothing to it. Good thing too, because Shuly got off to a late start today with the shooting this morning and all the paperwork the cops made him complete, not to mention the time spent on the phone with the insurance company, the Dunkin' Donuts people, and the Patel clan.

Shuly holds his jaw in pain from smiling too much and takes one last look at the Indian Santa. He later told the cops that perhaps he looked a little too long because that's when he slammed into the rear end of a black-primered Chevy low-rider.

Santa Rajneesh hears a horn blowing and waves out into the traffic not sure which car it came from. It wasn't long after that he hears the crash and Rajneesh sees the ass-end of a black-primered Chevy get pushed into the back seat. Both cars then veer out of control and the low-rider smashes into the front window of Pazzo's Cucina Italiano. Sirens are heard closing in from every street.

That will be costing somebody a whole bunches of American dollars, he thinks. Rajneesh watches and sees two more Indians come climbing out of a huge hole in the rear window of the Chevy. Dazed from the accident, they both stagger to the street and sit down at the curb. They are covered in blood and what looks like spaghetti. On second thought, that's not blood. It is Marinara sauce and the two men are not Indian, either. *They look more like Mexicans, perhaps?* Rajneesh wonders about this, but still proud of his new American know-how, street smarts, and quick ethnic identification.

Just then a third man rolls out of the rear window of the low-rider moaning and is cussing loudly in Spanish. He is wearing a Santa suit covered in sauce and meatballs. *He looks Mexican too,* Rajneesh thinks. "Holy Krishna," he says. Rajneesh recognizes Santa Domingo and yells over to him while waving his arms, excited to see a fellow Santa. "Hello Mexican Santa!" he yells. Domingo looks around and spots the red Santa suit on Rajneesh.

"Fuck you, Gringo!" Domingo yells back and gives Rajneesh the finger.

Gringo? Rajneesh thinks. *Rajneesh is an INDIAN! – not the Native American kind – the Seven-Eleven kind.*

Another man, and this one is also an Indian from India (*another* Seven-Elevin kind), gets out of the second car, an older faded-blue Mazda with very little left to the front end, and crashes down to the sidewalk in a heap. He is carrying a bag and Rajneesh watches as the Indian reaches into the bag, pulls out a donut and begins to eat it while sitting on the curb. A crowd of onlookers assembles as cop cars and fire trucks begin to pull up on the scene.

Rajneesh has seen enough and continues jogging. The Sears Tower is just up the block. Finally making it to the large enclosed glass entrance, Rajneesh leaps over to the main door ready to fulfill his Santa obligations. Too bad Sal or Vic gave him the wrong assignment sheet. This gig is for Monday not today. Rajneesh should have been sent to the inner-city YMCA, where a bunch of munchkins hyped up on Coke and chocolate-chip cookies are just about ready to tear up the joint over Santa's lateness.

Doug Stamboolian, USMC scout and sharpshooter, retired after 25 years service in Vietnam, Cambodia, North Korea, Turkey, Pakistan, a secret CIA training camp in Trenton, New Jersey, and God knows where else, is in charge of the weekend security team at the tower. Stamboolian, carrying his prized, well-oiled, super-charged and nickel-plated M-16 rifle with numerous notches in the stock, meets Rajneesh at the doorway and bars him from entering the building.

"Can I help you, sir?" he says politely but with authority.

"Yes, please be telling me where to be delivering cookies?" Rajneesh says.

"What cookies? What are you talking about?"

"This is Serious Towers, yes?"

"This is the WILLIS Tower, sir. What is your business here?" says Stamboolian.

"Where is Serious Towers?" Rajneesh is confused.

"You mean the SEARS Tower?"

"Yes! Serious Towers."

"This IS the Sears Tower."

"No, no, you just telling me this Willis Towers!" Rajneesh says in a confused state.

"Yes, this IS the Willis Tower now, but it used to be called the Sears Tower, before Sears moved out."

"Serious move out? Why Serious move out? I will be of the business of giving out cookies to all workers at Serious Towers!"

"Not today you won't because most of the offices are closed."

"Then please to telling me who has cookies?"

"What cookies?"

"The cookies I am to be giving to all peoples in the Serious Towers!" Rajneesh is starting to get a little hot under the collar.

"I told you, sir, most of the offices are closed. Today is Saturday, get it?"

"Get it? Why you talking to Rajneesh this way? I not foolish person from wetback country," Rajneesh says with indignation. "Today is Saturday, yes? This Serious Towers, yes? I am Santa Rajneesh, yes? So where are cookies?" Rajneesh dares to poke Stamboolian in the chest.

"Look, pal, I don't know anything about no goddamn cookies, and if I were you, I would keep my hands to myself and get the hell away from this door right now! Understand, Santa?"

"Does Rajneesh look the fools to you? Does Rajneesh look like terrorists with bombs in coat for Allah? Does Rajneesh ask for free ride for Skydick observations deck to be blowing up Serious Towers and be going home with one-hundred virgins? No! Santa Rajneesh here for cookies! – damn all to hell with you!" Santa Rajneesh throws up his hands in utter frustration and disgust.

Poor Rajneesh just finished his tirade when Stamboolian pushes the alarm button, drops to the floor and fires a round from his supercharged automatic rifle with numerous notches in the stock into each of Santa's kneecaps!

Swat teams members dressed all in black and armed with an assortment of weapons appear to drop out of nowhere. Weapons are drawn and all aimed at Santa Rajneesh who is rolling on the ground in shear agony.

"Ahhh!" he screams like a young girl on her first roller coaster ride alone. "Mr. Vic and Mr. Sal not to be liking so much blood on Santa suit! Ahhhhhhh!"

"Shut up, raghead." A fog of black darkness surrounds Santa Rajneesh as a black hood is roughly placed over his head. Next, both of his hands and feet are quickly cuffed with plastic wire straps. Just then the police and ambulance pull up with cops and EMTs running every which way.

"Wow, that was fast," thinks Stamboolian. *I think we set a record with this one!*

Meanwhile, across the street at Pazzo's Cucina Italiano, Shuly Patel is still sitting at the curb with his head tucked between his legs. He's already eaten four Old Fashioned donuts and is oblivious to the shots fired across the street and the ruckus that followed. With a tear in his eye, he continually shakes his head in disgust thinking about all the donuts he was going to make today. *"Now what will I give out to my customers?"* he thinks. *"They will probably stop coming and instead go to Khalid's Donut Emporium down the block where that rat-faced non-believer Amin will give them free pieces of stale baklava!*

35

Don Kaminski is finally composed enough to begin driving to Fat Wang's Chinese Take-Out. He made a pit stop for gas and a cup of coffee at a 7/11. *Ugh!* – Poured most of it out at a red light. Traffic is not all that bad but there are sirens all over the place this afternoon – police, fire trucks and ambulances going in every direction.

Are we being invaded? Don wonders.

The GPS tells Don to turn here and there and eventually Don's sees that he was right all along. Fat Wang's is located somewhere in the middle of a huge industrial area. Aside from a Hoover repair store, Womack's Steak Shop (closed by the looks of it), and the Mother Church of God in Jesus, Daycare, Rescue Mission and Sub Shop which sits in between a couple of seedy bars, there is nothing out here but fenced-in weeded lots, burnt-out factories, and old, worn-out buildings now converted into storage warehouses.

And now the GPS system shows the little car driving in a blank field of blue – no street line indicators at all on the monitor, let alone street names. Don has no clue where he is. He sees two older black men talking out front of the Mother Church of God in Jesus, Daycare, Rescue Mission and Sub Shop and he pulls over to ask directions. He lowers the driver's side window and asks, "Excuse me. Do either of you know Fat Wang's?"

"Fuck you honkey and your 'fat wang!'" One of them says. The other picks up a soda bottle filled with a yellow soda the color of which Don doesn't recognize, and heaves it at the car. He misses by a mile and by now Don is a moving target anyway.

None of the streets in this area are marked, so Don is driving around in a blind when, *Thank you Lord Jesus!* – There it is on the corner and with a number of cars parked out front and the field across the street is darn near full. *Business must be good!* Don is most grateful to see the red neon lights lit up in the window announcing, "Fat Wang's Chinese Take-Out." He parks the Volvo in the field and opens the trunk to get his Santa gear and into Fat Wang's he goes, after locking the car and checking it twice, as the Santa song says.

Don opens one of the double doors to walk in and is immediately hit with the most wonderful smells he has ever encountered.

His mouth is salivating as he enters the take-out. There are six people standing around and waiting for their food orders and all of them happen to be Chinese. *This must be a good Chinese Take-Out*, Don thinks, *but where are the drivers of the other cars? These six Chinese people didn't drive all those vehicles parked out front?* Don figures there has to be about thirty cars and trucks out there – and nice ones too! *None of this makes any sense*, he thinks.

The Chinese all turn in unison and look at Don. The quiet turns to laughter when one old lady says something in Chinese. Now it sounds like a Chinese hen house.

"Who you? Wha' you wan'? You no call for take-ou'? You no Chinese." – more laughter. Don looks to his side and then down a bit to see a little Chinese lady in a faded red satin dress complete with dirty apron drenched in soy sauce. She has dyed stringy jet-black hair all piled on the top of her head with at least four chop sticks and two pencils in it at different angles, holding all that hair in place. And now she begins poking Don in the chest with two more chop sticks which are greasing up Don's shirt.

"Who you? Wha' you wan'? You da powice? Powice already COME for donation. Wang give! Not now – Week ago – Wang give! Why you here? You wan' tase Genera' Tso's chicken?" fires the Chinese woman with her extra long painted finger nails and smoke-stained yellow teeth.

"Are you Anita Wang?" Don asks. "I am looking for Anita Wang," he says, getting a little annoyed that his shirt is now stained with soy sauce.

"I Wang. I Wang," says the dragon lady as she nods her head in affirmation. "Wha' you wan'? I pray parky tickies las' week!" Now she is starting to get a little too excited. "I pray powice donation and I pray parky tickies too! Why you here? Wha' you wan'?" Again, Anita Wang pokes Don in the chest with the greasy chop sticks.

"Hold on, Mrs. Wang," Don cautions as he backs away. "I am your Santa!"

"Centa? Wha' centa? Wha' you mean, centa? You here for trash? Trash come on Fliday – Fliday! – no today! Today no Fliday!"

"No Mrs. Wang, I am here to be Santa Claus. SANTA CLAUS – HO, HO, HO!" Don gestures holding on to his little round belly as he laughs.

"Santa Craws? Ah! Santa Craws!" Mrs. Wang gives Don a great big smile and nods her head as she now understands. "Today Santa Craws day? You Santa Craws? Ah! Today Santa Craws Day! You Santa Craws! Wang forget today Santa Craws day!" She continues to smile and rapidly fires off something in Chinese to the others. Don hears the words "Santa Craws" in the middle of it.

"Ah-so!" the take-out customers say in recognition. "Santa Craws! Santa Craws!" They all bow in unison. Don returns the bow.

"How come no send Chinese Santa Craws like las' time?" Mrs. Wang asks.

"I really don't know," says Don, "but that's a good idea. I have the Santa suit right here, look." Don unzips the bag and shows her the red suit inside. "Do you want me to go?"

"No, No," says Anita Wang. "You stay. You stay. Put crows on; be Santa Craws for customers. Here – Here!" She points to kitchen housed behind a greasy pink bed-sheet curtain, splattered with soy sauce, where Don can change. Don smiles and slips behind the bed sheet careful not to get any more soy sauce on his shirt. The kitchen is hot, steamy and manned by three men yelling at each other in Chinese and running back and forth with boxed eggs, fresh long noodles, bags of fortune cookies, duck sauce, take-out cartons and such, while cooking in large woks and boxing up take-out orders at the same time. *Talk about multi-tasking!* In walks Anita who screams something to them in Chinese about "Santa Craws."

"Ah-so!" They all smile and bow to Don. "Santa Craws! Santa Craws!" Again, Don returns the bow. Anita points to a tiny door Don figures is the wash room and he opens it. The dragon lady barkes at the smiling cooks and off they go back to work like a Chinese fire drill.

Whoa! This washroom isn't big enough to get into, let alone try to change in. Don looks back and Madam Wang is gone. He can hear her out front with the customers jabbering away in Chinese and every other word seems to be "Santa Craws," followed by laughter from the customers and, "Ah-so! Santa Craws! Santa Craws!"

Don sees another door off to the left and opens it. It is a cool, well-lit hallway that travels the length of the building and then angles downstairs without any steps. *What the hell,* he considers. *Might as well go down here and find a place to change.* The hallway leads to a large metal door. *Sure hope this isn't a meat locker! Watch me get locked in here and never be found until after Easter! Happy Passover!*

I can see the headlines now, "Missing Santa Claus Found Frozen in Chinese Freezer!" No Christmas this year, kids!

Don is surprised how easily the large metal door opens and instantly feels the heat and cigarette smoke rush out into the cool hallway. His eyes begin to tear. *Christ, that burns! Maybe Jackie's in here!* He steps into a dimly-lit, humongous room and hears voices – lots of voices, and different languages as well: English, the inner-city type, Spanish, perhaps Russian, and definitely Chinese voices. Don has walked clean into a Chinese gambling den, and these boys are some serious gamblers. And are they noisy! That door Don came through must be heavily insulated because he never heard a peep on the other side. This mob is boisterously cheering on each card dealt and every pair of dice thrown. He recognizes Black Jack and poker tables – two tables are Texas Hold'em. Next, Don sees two tables playing "Sic Bo" (the sign says). He watches a minute and figures this Chinese dice game is played with six dice in a cage that can be flipped over on its axis for each new roll. It looks as though you can bet any combination of dice: highs, lows, pairs, three of a kind, etc. Each of these tables has about four to six players sitting around it excitedly throwing casino chips, dollar bills (very few "ones", however) onto the marked playing table designating their wagers. One gambler, outfitted in a turban and looking like he's part of the Taliban, tries to through down his gold watch as a bet and is waved off with a grunt from the dealer.

Ah-so! Don puts two and two together. *Here are all the car owners!* Two more tables are playing Chinese poker, "Pai Gow," where you have to make two hands out of the five cards you get – a high hand and a low hand. *Interesting little game and only twenty-five dollars a hand. I could go broke playing that game in about three minutes!*

With all of the cheering and yelling going on, absolutely no one is interested in Don or why he is here. He could strip naked in this cellar, walk up to one of the craps tables, buy some chips, and begin playing without anyone noticing. *At least probably not until I lost all my money. Then they would throw my bare ass out into the street!*

Don spots the men's room off to one side and enters to change into the Santa suit. *Smart move, Don. Plenty of room here and not much smoke.* Don takes his time, notices the four open toilet stalls which are immaculately clean. He opens up his Santa bag and begins the transformation into Santa. He checks to see he has all the accessories with him: jacket, pants, hat, boot tops, black shoes, belt, white gloves and even some of Sue's bright red lipstick to put a little color in his cheeks, lips and tip of his nose. *I wonder if I am going to be Santa down here for the gamblers or upstairs for the take-out crowd? No doubt the dragon lady will direct me.*

Don is just about ready now and surveys himself in the mirror. *Man-oh-man, do I look like "Santa Craws," or what?* Don practices his "Ho, Ho, Ho, Melly Klistmas!" a few times when all of a sudden there is a loud crash at the door and in runs a tall, skinny Chinese guy followed by three other Chinese men all racing for one particular toilet stall. Don turns, frozen in terror, as the first man climbs up on top of the toilet, and while standing on top of the toilet tank, cranks open a small widow looking out to an alleyway, and crawls out the window. One man after the other hoists himself up and is out the window in record time, and racing away down the alley. Don can't believe what he just saw. *These guys had to have been Chinese acrobats or gymnasts from the Olympics!* He looks up at the tiny window knowing that if he had to do that, his ass would be stuck in the window!

The door crashes in again, and in rush four Chicago policemen with guns drawn.

"Up against the wall, Santa, and assume the position!" one officer shouts.

Don spots Officers Patrick Malone and Sean O'Malley from this morning's shootout and the Dunkin' Donuts.

Holy Christ, I'm going to jail now! Maybe they won't recognize me in the Santa getup.

"Look, Sean. Another Santa gone ape-shit." Malone says.

"Say, weren't you at the shootout this morning at the Dunkin' Donuts?" O'Malley questions Don.

"Yes, Officer, I was there, quietly enjoying my coffee and an Old Fashioned donut, and seated by myself. I had, and still have, nothing to do with that shooting!" Don is beginning to sweat a little.

"All the same, you're coming with us, Santa. Turn around."

"Look Officer, I was not gambling. I am here to be Santa Claus upstairs. I was only changing, honest!" Don pleads.

"Yeah, right. Who ever heard of a Santa Claus at a Chinese take-out?" The cops laugh at that one.

"Now, turn around, Santa. You're going for a little ride with the rest of the elves here."

Don does what he is told, is cuffed and led out the building along with about thirty others, including Anita Wang. All are briskly escorted to awaiting police vans.

"You people should all know better!" Don says in frustration to the other men and women captured in the raid.

"Don't you know that it is illegal to gamble in Chicago?"

"Fuck you, Santa!" one says.

"Hey, you! Don' go tell Santa Craws 'fluck you!' You no get no plesents!" Anita Wang yells out and pokes mid-air with a set of chop sticks to make the point.

"Hey, Santa," from another of the incarcerated. "I want the key to these cuffs for a Christmas present, but I want it now. Christmas is too far off to wait!" They all laugh at Don as the vans pull away.

"Fluck you, you big plick!" Anita Wang yells out.

36

Jimmy D. Mays is sitting comfortably in Wanda's old Lincoln, enjoying the good weather and other things when Wanda's head pops up from his lap. "Come on, Jimmy D." she says. "I ain't gots all day. I has to get Sharita to the Christmas party they's havin' at the Black Elk's Club. Maybe I can get her one of those red disappearin' Elmo suckers if I'm lucky?

"Don't stop now, Wanda. Jimmy D. almos' ready."

Wanda gets back down to business and it isn't long before Jimmy starts singing.

"Here come Sanda Claus. Here come Sanda Claus. Right on Wanda's car seat."

Wanda jumps back up and starts yelling at Jimmy while reaching for the Windex and paper towels she keeps in the back seat of the Lincoln.

"Jimmy D., you nasty-ass bastard. You be cleanin' up all this nasty shit before I drives you anywhere! You hear me?"

"Calms down, Wanda. Look. Is already clean up and we ready to roll," says Jimmy.

A blue and white Cushman scooter with Chicago Police written on it with blue and white lights flashing pulls up to Wanda's Lincoln like a major drug bust is in progress.

"Hey, Wanda," says Jimmy. "Youse din' do sompin crazy in da mall like steal any fuzzy toys or shit for Sharita did youse?"

"Fuck you, Jimmy D.!" Wanda fires back. "Maybe I did cop a couple a batteries for the smoke alarms, but ain't nobody seen what I did."

"Well, somepin wrong somewheres 'cause da cops is here wid da lights flashin' all over your Lincoln."

"Step out of the car with your hands up!" Jimmy and Wanda hear from a bullhorn. Startled, both do as they are told. Standing by the doors of the Lincoln they are ordered to put their hands on the roof of the car by Officer Sammy Gomez, who just graduated from the police academy this month.

The lone officer spots the Santa suit and immediately calls for backup and a quick ID on the license plate. Gomez then proceeds to Jimmy D. and Wanda and cuffs them just like he did a hundred times in practice; only this time it's for real and it feels good. Gomez almost laughs out loud at cuffing the skinny, black Santa and the big-breasted lady but he quickly maintains his posture as an officer of the law and does a neat job of it.

Officer Gomez should be riding in a squad car with a veteran officer for training today, but all that got changed in a hurry since the shooting at the Dunkin' Donuts this morning and a raft of shit coming down the pike involving the arrest and hospitalization of a shit-load of demented Santas of all shapes and sizes; and so Gomez got shifted to light duty in the mall parking lot riding around in a rinky-dink scooter and bored out of his mind. And now this – another Santa incident.

Something must be up, he thinks. *What the world is going on with all these fucked-up Santas? Did they all escape from some lunatic asylum and rob a costume shop? Has the Salvation Army put something in the Kool-Aid before sending these wacked-out Santas on the road with their buckets and bells? Is there a terrorist organization tied in with the Santa business? There has to be something to make all these Santas go nuts!*

"Were either of you at a Dunkin' Donuts this morning?" Gomez asks.

"No, Jimmy D. wasn't at no damn Dunkin' Donuss!" says Jimmy. "I be workin' pan-handlin' for rent money an' beside, Jimmy D. ain' got no time be sittin' 'round drinkin' coffee an' dunkin' donuss. Jimmy D. didn' dunk shit!"

"Me neither," says Wanda. "I don't even like no damn donuts! I do like them bear claw things but I got to watch my figure," Wanda says while showing off her big ass and titties jammed into a triple-x sweat pants and top. "What's this all about, Officer?"

"Is this your car, ma'am?" the Officer Gomez asks.

"No, Officer," Wanda says. "This here my boyfrien's car. My car's in the shop."

"May I see your driver's license and do you have the registration for the car?" asks Officer Gomez.

"Officer, I lost my driver's license about two year ago and I been waitin' to get a new one in the mail any day now," says Wanda.

"Wanda, bitch. Youse dummer an shit!" Jimmy adds softly.

"Well, ma'am, according to the information I have on this clipboard, this car has been identified in connection with several liquor store hold-ups, drug transportation, and fake Gucci handbag distribution among other things." Wanda spots her handbag on the front seat of the Lincoln, praying that she might have switched bags last night or this morning. "Damn," she says quietly as she spots the fake Gucci. *Don' be makin' no difference anyways,* she thinks. *Wait until he opens up the trunk and fines all kind a shit in there. Wanda in deep shit now!*

"I'm afraid we are going to have to impound the car and bring you two in for questioning," Gomez says.

"Holds on! Holds on! You ain' been saying shit about no Sanda Claus! Why you got Jimmy D. in han'cuffs? Jimmy D. ain' done shit!"

"Watch your mouth, Santa," Gomez warns Jimmy. "I'm holding you as an accessory to the crimes mentioned."

"Assessory? Assessory! Jimmy D. ain' no assessory! Can't youse see Jimmy D. a black Sanda? An' da firs' black Sanda in da Chicago vicinity! And dat's da truth, so helps me to Jesus H. Chrise!" Jimmy tries to raise his right hand up to swear the oath but the handcuffs do not allow this to happen, and so Jimmy turns sideways so Officer Gomez can see his right hand is straight up and pointing to the sky in swearing that this is the truth. "Jimmy D. didn' commits no crimes, Officer. Jimmy D. didn' do shit!"

"Both of you remain quiet while my backup gets here and we will sort this all out. In the meantime I'm going to read you your rights." Officer Sammy Gomez feels he has complete control of the situation and reaches for the plastic card with the Miranda rights on it that he left in his locker back at the station. As he rapidly searches all of his uniform pockets, Gomez realizes that the Miranda card is nowhere to be found and he visualizes it lying on the bottom of his locker. Now he's a bit nervous knowing that he has to recite the Miranda rights from memory.

"You have the right to remain silent," he begins. So far so good.

"Wanda, don' be sayin' shit," says Jimmy.

"Anything you do…I mean do and say – No, just SAY. Anything you SAY can be used against you in court…in a court of law."

"Wanda, don' be doin' or sayin'' shit, I'm tellin' youse! An' if we ends up in da court, Wanda, you be tellin' da judge da honess truff." *Ain' dis some shit! Now Jimmy D. missin' his meetin' wif da priess an' ain' gonna get hisself some new pants an' shit for da holidays.* Jimmy sure wishes he could light up a Camel right now. "Wanda, you sure youse didn' steal no shit for Sharita?"

"Honest, Jimmy, honest," she says and then turns to the officer. "Now you listen to me, young man, we ain' done nuttin' about breakin' no laws. We just be here in the parking lot talkin' 'bout old times, that's all," Wanda pipes up.

Officer Sammy Gomez doesn't even hear Wanda because his mind is racing back and forth for the next Miranda right and draws a blank. Gomez nervously looks around for his police backup, a squad car, another Cushman scooter, a rookie cop like himself, or better yet, an off-duty cop walking through the parking lot, anything looking official-like. No such luck.

"Look you two, I'm not going to tell you again to remain silent and just be patient." Gomez is flustered now and it shows. "We will get this all sorted out when my backup gets here so how about we all just shut the fuck up for the time being and wait real friendly like, okay?"

Jimmy D. and Wanda freeze and stare at Officer Gomez knowing damn right well that "shut the fuck up" is not one of the Miranda rights.

"Wanda," Jimmy whispers. Don' move or dis motha-fucka will shoot us, hear?"

Wanda, too afraid to open her mouth, nods her head up and down.

"You have other rights too," Gomez adds. "I just can't remember them all right now. Do either of you know the Miranda rights?

"I heard them once when I used to work tricks, Officer, but I that was a long time ago," says Wanda. "They might have changed a lot since then."

Yeah, right, Wanda, you fat fuck. Jimmy D. hears youse been doin' tricks jus' last week! Mirana rights ain't changed none since las' week, bitch! Hell, ol' man Mirana ain' even shaved yet since you done your las' trick! Jimmy thinks to himself. "Listen Officer, Jimmy D. an' Wanda here jus' catchin' up on old times. Das all."

"Looks to me like you're losing your pants, Santa. Are you sure that's all you two were up to?" Gomez looks to Wanda for any tell-tale signs that he is right.

"Look, Officer," Wanda tries to turn on the charm. "We just real happy to see each other again, that's all."

"Shut up, Wanda. Tell da man youse got yourself a real job down at the K-mart."

"Maybe we was foolin' around a bit Officer..." she leans over to read the name plate on his shirt, "...Gomez. Me and Jimmy D. go back a long ways, and we really happy to see each other, honest."

"Yeah, Officer Gomez, Jimmy D. an' Wanda go way back. Way back. Shit, Jimmy D. know Wanda when she only weighs a hunert and sixty-five pound! Looks at her now, Officer Gomez. Shit, she gotta be over three hunert pounds by now!" Jimmy smiles and gives Wanda the "once over" *Shit, dat ass o' hers gotta be a hunert and sixty-five pounds all be isself!*

"Fuck you, Jimmy D.!" Wanda fires back with a vengeance. "I on Weight Watchin' an' right now I stuck in one o' them plateaus they's always talkin' 'bout."

"How you bein' on Weight Watchin', Wanda? You goes there? Where ats?"

"No! I don't '*goes there.*' I be doin' Weight Watchin' on the computer at home! – you dumb shit!"

"Oh yeah, Wanda? Wassa e-mail for da Weight Watchin' shit?"

"WWW.KISS-MY-MUTHA-FUCKIN'-ASS.COM! – Jimmy D.!"

"Whoa, whoa, whoa! Calm down both of you! Just calm the FUCK down and nobody gets hurt! Understand!"

Absolute silence and NO movement from anyone!

"Do you have any objections if I open up the trunk of the car?" Gomez asks.

"No, Officer. You go right ahead," Wanda says as nice as can be. "I ain't been in that trunk for four or five years now. I never use that trunk. I don't even know why they have 'em. Seems like such a waste of space if you ask me."

"Thas right, Officer." Jimmy sees a chance to make things right again. "Wanda ain' never use her trunk since Sharita come home from da hossital an' she had a lot of shit wid her. Ain't dat right, Wanda?"

"That's exactly right, Jimmy D. We lives near the hospital and so Sharita only rode in the trunk for about six blocks," Wanda fondly remembers. "And that was a long time ago, Officer Gomez. She cough for a few days, Officer, but she fine now, honest."

"Thas right, Officer. Shit, Sharita ain' cough for about two year now! An' she about forty-six now, ain' she, Wanda?"

"Shut the fuck up! Sharita ain't no damn forty-six, you dumb-ass black Santa Claus, wino-mutha-fucka!"

"What did I just finish saying to you two Niggahs?" from Officer Gomez who now begins swinging his nightstick in the air and over his head like a veteran Ninja preparing for action.

Jimmy D. and Wanda are both ducking their heads repeatedly, just missing being hit by the flying baton.

"Get in the back of the Lincoln and shut the fuck up – both of you!"

Gomez opens the two rear doors one at a time and helps Jimmy D. and Wanda into the backseat of the Lincoln.

"I at least got you for prostitution and maybe more." he says. "We'll just have to wait here for my backup to arrive. In the meantime – just be still and SHUT THE FUCK UP!" Gomez slams the car door.

"I'm scared, Jimmy D. What we gonna do?" cries Wanda.

"We's gonna shut da fuck up!" Jimmy answers.

37

Patriarch Zoltan Shimko is now donning his Santa suit with real white fox trim on jacket and hat. Two orthodox altar boys dressed in white robes are attending to "his excellency" as one brushes down the Santa jacket to be sure no loose hair might by lying about – and please don't even insult the Patriarch by suggesting he might have a bit of dandruff on his collar! Not the way this man meticulously grooms himself with the best of everything. Even his after shave, "Holier Than Thou," is exclusively made for him by Christian Dior and flown in from Paris way before he runs out.

The second altar boy is busy quietly chanting, "Here comes Santa Claus. Here comes Santa Claus," while circling the Patriarch and anointing him with holiday incense that smells like holly berry and old money.

The Santa suit, by the way, was custom made especially for him by Sax 5th. Avenue in New York City where he worked as Santa back in 1995. He didn't last the season at Sax due to numerous questions about missing Gucci handbags from the same floor the Santa set was on, only to be replaced with fake ones. All this came about when Gina Mangarecabassa, Shimko's ex-elf who looks more like one of Hugh Heffner's top-shelf bunnies rather than Santa's little helper (There are those employees at Sax who questioned how exactly Gina "helped" Santa?), ratted out the Patriarch as the culprit who had been switching the handbags over the past two weeks. Seems Zoltan was a little tardy in giving Gina her cut of the take and so she turned him in to the store detective. Sure enough, about twenty-five to thirty bags had been switched, but the quality was so good that it was very difficult to tell the difference. However, there are always some tell-tale clues when the product in question is a fake. It appears that the South Koreans who manufacture the fake Gucci bags, as compared to the Chinese who make the real Gucci bags, spelled "Gucci" with only one "c." Too bad – they were so close! Zoltan still made a killing because they never did catch on to the fake Gucci wallets, clutch bags, umbrellas, gloves and headscarves which, by the way, were spelled correctly, (Gina didn't know about these).

Sax was embarrassed, to say the least, and never reported the switch to the police – too much bad press – too far into the holidays – and besides, how many fake "Guci's" and "Gucci's" were already sold by Sax? No, the Patriarch walked away clean and in so doing took the custom-made Santa suit with him including a pair of really nice hand-tooled Mexican leather Santa boots with ermine tops. He left New York in the dust along with Gina, whom he forgave after they made a new deal, and rebuilt his empire in Chicago (after all, that's where the "real" Playboy Bunnies are!) – saving orthodox souls and selling fake Gucci handbags and whatever else he could get his holy hands on.

This morning the Patriarch was headed over to the Black Elk's Pride of Chicago Hall in some seedy part of the south-side for a grand breakfast with Santa for all the poor inner-city kids who knew this was their only shot at getting something good for Christmas. Most of them walked over to the hall or car-pooled together with a mom or a granny they found who wasn't on crack or out on the streets this early, hooking. Needless to say, the place was packed and Santa had better show up soon and give up the loot or some serious shit was going to happen.

Inner Pride Guard, Eustice Pinson, approaches the Grand Exalted Pride Ruler, Leroy Maxwell, with a worried look on his face.

"Boss," he says (and Leroy really is his boss down at the "Six Brothers, Three Sisters and a Truck – Moving and Hauling Service," where Leroy is one of the Maxwell brothers and Eustice married one of his sisters, Clarice – the ugly one).

"Boss, we got troubles!" says Eustice with a look on his face that shows he's damn-well worried. "These kids done ate up all the breakfast! All the eggs and hot cakes are gone! They inhaled all the Jimmy Dean sausages in the first ten minutes, and some of them were still frozen! They devoured all the toast and drank up every bit of juice in the house, and they're looking around and yelling for more! And what's worse, Santa ain't even here yet and I don't think we bought enough presents for all these little bastards! What in hell are we going to do?" While Pinson is talking, he takes out a clean, white hanky and begins to wipe off the highly polished, gold regalia and jeweled emblems that Maxwell is proudly wearing around his neck showing that he *is* the "Grand Poobah." Next, Pinson begins to shine his own, much smaller, silver regalia around his neck proving that he is the Inner Pride Guard.

Both Pinson and Maxwell turn and watch as the kids begin pounding on the tabletops and tossing paper plates like Frisbees across the hall and chanting, "Bring on Santa! Bring on Santa! Bring his fat ass here!"

"I knew we shouldn't have hired that priest again this year," Maxwell says shaking his head.

"Ah, NO, Boss, NO! Please don't tell me you hired that white-Russian, thieving priest again this year?" says Pinson. "Don't you remember the riot we had last year not to mention the expense we had in cleaning up the hall and the new paint job! And what about the rape charge the Washington sisters threatened us with? We had to pay them off! Remember that? And you hired this clown again! What in the hell were you thinking?"

"Don't talk to me in that tone of voice, Pinson," Maxwell warns. "I am *still* the Grand Exalted Pride Ruler and I'm wearing my jewels to prove it!" he quips while fingering his jewels. And you, on the other hand, are still just the Inner Pride Guard. Let's not forget that, Pinson. My jewels are bigger than yours!"

"I'm sorry, Boss, I really am." Pinson turns back to view the unruly crowd then quickly ducks as a paper plate full of syrup-laden, half-eaten Jimmy Dean sausages flies past his head and lands on the Grand Exalted Pride Ruler's suit, shirt, tie and highly-polished regalia (the "Grand Poobah," as he is known around the club, always did dress in the best of clothes and today was no exception).

Pinson is horrified that the Grand Poobah now had little bits of sausage bouncing off his suit and warm syrup oozing down the front of him and dripping off his Black Pride jewels. He takes the hanky and begins to try to clean the up mess. Maxwell stares at Pinson with disgust that first of all this happened to ruin his clothes and jewels, and secondly that Pinson didn't take the "hit" for the Grand Poobah and block the flying syrup missile as he should have out of respect for Maxwell's highly polished regalia!

Just then Pinson gets an un-planned bath when several full cups of cheap grape juice come flying at him from different directions and hit him in the back of the neck and on the right side of his head. His open-collared, hand-made Panama shirt allows the purple shower to quickly run down his body on the inside of his clothes. His boxer shorts soak up a lot of the liquid but there is still enough to escape down to his socks and shoes. The kids roar at this and soon food, juice, pancakes and little Jimmy Deans are flying in all directions. Pinson immediately freezes and knows he does not feel comfortable at all – now that his socks were soggy. "Little bastards!" Pinson growls and turns.

BANG! The hall doors burst open and in bounds an almost seven-foot tall, dazzling and sparkling Santa Claus in the best Santa outfit ever seen on the face of this Earth! The Patriarch-Santa begins yelling **"Ho, Ho, Ho"** in that deep, commanding voice of his and all the little "bastards" begin to cheer and yell, "It's him! He's real! He's here! It's really Santa!"

Little Ollie Muse puts down the plate of half-eaten pancakes he loaded up with syrup to hurl at the two adults with the "fagot chains" around their necks. Tears begin to well up in his eyes as he looks reverently at the Patriarch and declares, "And Santa's white just like my Me-Maw says he is…white!"

The Patriarch-Santa flies around all the tables like magic, bellowing "Ho, Ho, Ho" and "Merry Christmas to all the good boys and girls!" followed by the two altar boys brushing down and incensing the entire crowd of ruffians.

"Hey man, quit brushing me with that shit!" yells Willie Jefferson to one of the altar boys. "And what's with all the damn smoke! You trying to kill the niggahs like they did the Jews?" Jefferson begins to cough, gag and spits on the floor.

Outside, the Patriarch's shiny black Russian-made car is gently lowered down onto cinder blocks as the notorious "no-face gang" rolls four almost-new tires, complete with custom, chromed rims, around the block to a waiting truck and sets a record in under two minutes. One hooded thief whispers to another, "Hey, man. Does your tire smell like holly berry?"

"Man, shut the fuck up and throw the damn tire in the truck, moron!" came the reply.

38

Officers Patrick Malone and Sean O'Malley help unload and escort the thirty or so hand-cuffed criminals from the paddy wagons to the underground booking desk at the local precinct. The Duty Sargeant in charge of the precinct, Sgt. Alphonso Pasquale LaManna, was alerted before they got there so there is plenty of help on hand to make sure things go smoothly in booking those arrested in the raid at Fat Wangs. LaManna looks over the mob of pissed-off gamblers and Chinese and just shakes his head. "It's going to be a long day, and it's far from over," he ponders.

"Hey, Sarge," shouts Malone. "Here's another fucked-up Santa for you!"

Malone looks up from his desk and spots Don Kaminski cuffed to Anita Wang.

"And what do we have here? Another Santa Claus to add to the collection and Madame Chiang Kai-shek!" The cops all laugh at this one as they continue to herd the mob into the booking area.

"Hey, Malone!" shouts LaManna. "Un-cuff Santa and throw him in with the other Santas. Lock up all the Chinks together, and put the rest of the losers in the big cell. We'll get to them one-at-a time. And for Christ's sake, Malone, take the damn chopsticks out of Madame Chiang's hair!"

"Yes, sir!" Malone answers as he grabs for the chopsticks sticking out of Anita Wang's dyed black crow's nest.

"No touch!" Anita Wang yells. "No touch Wang! No touch Wang!" She begins swinging her arms about to fight off Malone.

"Yeah, Malone," a fellow officer shouts, "Don't touch your wang, buddy!" – more laughter.

"You no get plesent from Santa Craws!" yells Anita Wang. "Santa Craws bling you more shit again dis year!" – even more laughter.

Malone and O'Malley help the other officers separate the crowd into identifiable ethnic groups and begin to lock them up. Malone then grabs Don Kaminski by the arm and says, "Come with me, Santa. I want to take you to the North Pole." More laughter from the officers.

O'Malley unlocks a cell door with a key that must weigh half a pound and both officers shove Don into what looks like the North Pole segment from the Disney ride, "It's a Small World!" The tiny cell is loaded with a wild assortment of Santas of all colors, shapes and sizes, and all dressed in red suits and looking like they'd been in a Civil War battle!

If these guys start singing "It's a small world after all," I'm going to start banging on the bars with my tin cup, Don says to himself.

"Greetings, fellow Santas," Don says in jest as he waves to his fallen comrades.

39

"Hey, Malone, O'Malley! Get your asses back here" barks Sgt. LaManna down the hallway. After a few minutes both come strolling into the squad room and hang up the keys to the cells.

"Do either of you know where the Black Elks Club is on the bad side of town?" LaManna asks.

"Which 'bad side' are you talking about, Sarge?" pipes O'Malley.

"Very funny, O'Malley. Remind me to have you clean up the drunk tank when you get back!"

"I know where it is, Sarge," answers Malone. "Didn't we go there last year to break up a riot at a kids' Christmas party?"

"Right you are, Malone. And guess why you're going back there right now?" quips LaManna.

"Don't tell me?"

"Yep. Better take a few of the boys here, lots of cuffs and several vans. Besides another riot breaking out when Santa shows up with twenty presents for about a hundred kids – Santa goes ballistic when he finds out his "sleigh" is missing four chromed, hi-tech tires and he proceeds to join in the riot and whips up on two black Elks, the custodian, three kitchen workers, and those two fat Washington sisters who claimed they got raped at the party last year. And something else I didn't get about some jewels that got man-handled and broken, and a stuffed elk's head that got torn off the wall and thrown out a window into the street. Find out what the hell is going on over there!"

"Don't worry, Sarge. We'll have it all under control," says Malone as he motions to the others and heads out the door to the back parking lot.

"Better hurry boys. The fire department and paramedics are already on their way. And be sure to isolate the Washington sisters first!" fires LaManna.

The same group of officers that made the raid on Fat Wangs grab for more handcuffs, race out the back door into the awaiting police vans, and take off with sirens blaring to save whatever black Elks were still standing. As they exit, Sergeant LaManna sees two rookie cops hustling in some drunk they probably picked up at the accident they were assigned to check out hours ago. There were no more squad cars left at the time LaManna assigned the rookies and so the Sergeant threw the rookies the keys to an old Pontiac they impounded years ago from an out-of-work drug pusher and occasionally use the car for undercover work. The damn thing never ran right and smoked up the streets as it darn near reached forty miles per hour.

"And where in the hell have you two been?" barks LaManna as he swivels his chair from the desk behind the booking counter to get a better look and sees the two rookies escorting another hand-cuffed Santa – Santa Domingo.

"Well I'll be damned!" LaManna almost grins at the novelty of it all. "Another Santa in cuffs! Only this one is covered in marinara sauce, is it? Smells pretty good too. Don't say one word boys. I don't even want to know." LaManna turns to the side and says to another booking officer, "Hal, would you kindly take Mr. Kringle here down to our Santa lounge?"

"Sure thing, Sarge," Hal replies.

The rookies hand over Santa Domingo and both begin speaking one right after the other in rapid fire.

"First of all Sergeant, that there Pontiac don't go but thirty miles an hour. It took us half the day to get there and back!"

"That's for sure Sergeant. And this Santa here was in the accident we investigated down at Pazzo's Cucina Italiano." LaManna folds his arms on his chest and listens to the two rookies unfold the new Santa mystery.

"That's right, Sergeant. He's not hurt much at all. Just a few scrapes and bumps – that's all," says rookie one.

"Santa didn't cause the accident from what we can tell Sergeant, but he doesn't speak English too good and we can't understand what he's saying," pipes in rookie two.

"That's right, Sergeant. We had to cuff him 'cause he was beating the hell out of this Indian fellow," from rookie one again.

"Indian? Indian!" bellows LaManna. "Now we got Indians running around town with all the screwed-up Santas! Is that it? What's next? Cowboys and Easter bunnies hopping all over the fucking place?"

"No, Sergeant, No. He's not a Native American Indian. He's the Seven-Eleven kind," says rookie two. "And we didn't see any Easter bunnies, did we?" Rookie two looks over at rookie one.

"Yes and no," from rookie one. "Yes, he's the kind from India. You know, Sergeant – India, the country? – and no, we didn't see any Easter bunnies – at least I didn't," rookie one tries to clarify the matter.

"I know where India is, son. I'm not that stupid!" LaManna blasts.

"Yes, sir, Sergeant. But anyway, this here Indian, the Seven-Eleven kind mind you, not the Native American kind, well he's the one who caused the accident," from rookie one.

"So where the hell is this Indian, the Seven-Eleven kind, who caused the accident?" LaManna looks around the room for another "perp." "What did you two do, take him to the movies?" LaManna shouts letting the rookies know he is beginning to get really pissed-off.

"No sir, Sergeant! We had to take him to the hospital. I mean that's where we took him – to the hospital and he's still there," number two admits.

"That's right, Sergeant. We had to take him to the hospital," number one confirms. "He got banged up pretty good."

"From the accident?" LaManna asks.

"No, Sergeant. Not from the accident; from when Santa here who don't speak English so good went ape shit and started to pound the hell out of the Seven-Eleven Indian for causing the accident," says one again.

"That's exactly right, Sergeant. I think Santa here was going to a gig somewhere and now he can't make it because he's covered in marinara sauce and meatballs," from rookie two.

"Not if he beat the crap out of the Seven-Eleven Indian, he isn't," LaManna answers.

"Listen, Sergeant, this here Indian fellow we're talking about is a pretty nice guy," from rookie one.

"That's right, Sergeant. He's a darn nice fellow if you ask me. You know he kept offering us some Old Fashioned donuts he had in a bag all the time they were stitching him up in the E.R." says rookie two.

"That's exactly right. A couple of those Old Fashioned donuts had blood on them, but the ones that didn't were really good," rookie one admits.

"Exactly, exactly. You could tell they were freshly made this morning and not the frozen kind," rookie two again.

"Right, right," says rookie one. "He even offered an Old Fashioned donut to the Santa who don't speak English so good while he was kicking the shit out of him. Now that's what I call being pretty nice, wouldn't you say, Sergeant? Come to think of it, where did those Old Fashioned donuts go we didn't eat yet? They were pretty good."

"Beats the hell out of me," rookie two answers while scratching the top of his head. "Did we leave them at the hospital?"

Rookie one shakes his head in disgust, "Yeah, maybe we did – damn!"

"Okay, okay," LaManna surrenders. "How about the two of you super crime solvers put your heads together and complete an easy-to-read report that makes some sense out of all this bullshit so that I don't get my ass fired by the commissioner!" *This ought to be good!* thinks LaManna. *I'll probably be on a forced retirement next week and these two idiots will be in charge! Wonder how much I can get a month?*

40

Here it comes, Sue. Don't look now, but your worst nightmare is about to take place – again!

CRASH! The punch bowl just hit the deck and there's no apparent reason for it. *Did it slip? Was it pushed? There's no one standing by the table? How in the hell did it happen?* Sue can't figure it out, but something is definitely wrong here and she's going to get to the bottom of it before anything else happens.

All heads turn to see what was wrong. The BINGO caller, eighty-seven year old Raymond Schwartz, complete with VFW cap, an official Naval Shore Patrol night stick tucked in his belt, and an Oscar Mayer weenie whistle tied around his neck in case of an emergency, stops in the middle of a number. Ray Schwartz has called out BINGO numbers at the Ira Hayes Veteran's Administration Hospital since he was discharged in 1947 and he knows when there's a problem, that's for sure. So far all is quiet as Ray instinctively reaches for the night stick and the weenie whistle, and then...

"**G** what? **G** WHAT?" comes thundering from the middle of the room. "What's the number for Christ's sake?" yells Charlie Rupnicki who figures he just won a thousand dollars. He jumps up out of his chair blocking Gunny Sergeant's view.

"Hey, man. Sit your ass back in the chair!" Gunny yells wishing he had a drink of anything but this fruit shit.

Charlie turns and gives Gunny a sour look.

"Go to hell, you rummy, you!"

That was it. No decent lifer U.S. Marine, John Wayne watching, "Sands of Iwo Jima" lovin', veteran of this wonderful United ball-busting States of America is gonna sit here and take any crap from a liberal, card-carrying, pinko, friend of Jane Fonda, commie puke who probably burned his damn draft card during Vietnam while Gunny was knee-deep in Gooks!

"Semper Fi!" Gunny belts out and springs over two rows of BINGO players like Errol Flynn did in "Robin Hood," and had poor Charlie Rupnicki by the throat. Tables and chairs flipped over, BINGO cards and chips flying everywhere, and old farts bolting down aisles between tables leaving their walkers behind as the two went at it. Seems old Charlie here has a quick temper as well and half a brown belt to boot! He would have gotten his brown belt in Karate if his old lady, Bernice, had only stuck around to help him practice more instead of running off with the bagger from the ACME. Bernice, it seems, was tired of getting hit and kicked by *accident* – at least that's what Charlie told her and the judge.

Don't count Gunny out yet. His style maybe crude, but Gunny's a street fighter having grown up in the Irish neighborhood of South Philadelphia. Danny O'Brian, Sr., long-time owner of O'Brian's Pub on Shunk Street, backed him up for fight lessons back then and Gunny ended up a "Golden Gloves" contender. Not to mention Gunny's experiences in hand-to-hand combat during the Tet Offensive back in 'Nam. And besides, no one is faster at kicking you in the balls than Gunny. And after receiving at least three well-delivered karate chops to the head and torso by Ninja Charlie, Gunny faked to the left, intentionally dropped down to the floor on his back and landed his right foot with a powerful blow right into Charlie's nuts! And Charlie goes down for the count while holding his aching balls.

Too bad that wasn't the end of it all, because several other professional BINGO players, who also thought they too had won with this last ball, got into it and all hell broke loose again as just about every able-bodied gambler, and some not so able-bodied, got into the ruckus for old time's sake. And what about the new BINGO ball machine you ask? The glass top was completely shattered with BINGO balls shooting out in every direction at about a mach-1 velocity, hitting unsuspecting BINGO players in the head, face, chest, back, you name it; and them flying BINGO balls stung pretty damn good.

Sue reaches for her cell phone and dials 911 and asks for the police.

"Sergeant LaManna speaking…"

Santa Bruce has just left the Tres Bon Fashion Boutique where all the "old money broads" go for the latest in designer clothes and classic originals hand-crafted by Monsieur Roland LaPuff, whose real name is Reginald Watson. Seems Watson designed a Santa suit for Bruce like no other. First of all, it isn't red. It's a flaming, glittery reddish-purple all trimmed in bright pink fur. You could see it for miles. The exaggeratedly long Santa hat had a huge gold ball on the end that was spring-wired to remain up in the air and bounce up and down as Santa moved forward. There are oodles of long, gold and green-sprayed ostrich feathers flaked in silver which are mounted on a harness on Santa Bruce's back. He looks like the NBC peacock on acid. The boots (the only things that are red, candy-apple at that) are also trimmed in pink fur and have six inch high heels. The entire outfit is adorned with a gold, lame cape and a matching custom-made shoulder bag which contains expensive multi-colored and liquor-flavored candy canes, candy-flavored lip glosses shaped like little penises, and designer condoms.

Santa Bruce looks more like a Vegas showgirl than he does Santa. His makeup is just right – especially the purple and pink glittery eye shadow, perfectly applied by Watson. And to top it off, Bruce has his nails done in "Hot Pink" and has a pair of satin gloves tucked away smartly in his purple sash. What a sight!

Creating quite a scene on the sidewalk, Santa Bruce races down the street to hail a cab. Once inside he orders the driver, Amjad – that's what it says on the visor – to dash away as quickly as possible to his first gig downtown at the Pipefitters, Local 812, for a Christmas bash that will go down in the history books as one of the most memorable the pipefitters ever had.

"Off you go Ramjet. I'm late as it is."

Back in the "Santa tank," Santa Domingo is tossed in with the rest of the brotherhood and immediately recognizes Don Kaminski. Jimmy D. thinks he knows this demented looking Santa from somewhere but can't recall where or when. Jimmy still has enough street smarts to know to stay away and nudges himself through the crowd to the back of the cell.

"Jimmy D. ain' gonna get fucked up by dis wacked-out Sanda. Dat's for damn sure!" he says quietly to himself and lights up another Camel.

From another cell Anita Wang is rapidly mouthing off in Chinese and every other word seems to be "Santa Craws!"

"For Christ's sake – shut the fuck up, chink bitch!" Wanda yells from the back of the cell.

"Hey, fluck you!" yells Anita. "You no get no plesents flum Santa Craws either!"

Sergeant Alphonso LaManna returns from the restroom just in time to see the parade of officers returning from the riot at the Black Elks Club. And what does he see? – another Santa – and a great big one at that. The tightly cuffed, Patriarch-Santa, Zoltan Shimko, is stumbling – unsure of where he is. He is dressed as Santa but has a huge elk's head stuffed on his head, which is turned to the side and missing one antler. The Patriarch is sneezing and coughing away inside the furry helmet as the one antler, pointing up and towards the front, charges this way and that – almost goring officers O'Malley and Malone who are trying to hold him steady and guide him into the squad room.

"We had to mace this one, Sarge," O'Malley says as he struggles with Malone in steering Zoltan to the center of the room so that the one antler left on the elk's head doesn't injure anyone or knock into any of the rather large hanging globe ceiling lights.

"Yeh, Sarge," O'Malley adds. "He's the one we had to mace after he went crazy and cleared out the Black Elks Club of all the inner-city kids and any black Elks who happened to be standing around."

"Right," Malone continues. "The place is a complete mess. Chairs and tables tipped over, trash all over, windows smashed..."

"And food and juice tossed all over the joint," O'Malley jumps back in. "Looked like those tiny sausages we always get down there for the free Police Appreciation Day breakfast they have each year."

"Sure did, Sarge," Malone again. "Them damn things always give me heartburn," he says quietly to LaManna. "Anyways, we got the "skinny" from two Black Elk leaders who, by the way, are covered in pancake syrup. They will be down here later to press charges as soon as they clean up a bit. And, get this, we got the Washington sisters on the way to the hospital for some rape tests – just like last year."

"Wait a minute! Wait one fucking minute! The Washington sisters, from last year, got raped again?" LaManna asks.

"Actually, Sarge, if you recall, they weren't really raped last year. The whole thing was an act and the judge threw it out of court for lack of evidence," Malone answers.

"Seems to me they won't have any evidence this year either," O'Malley says while shaking his head in wonderment. "Both them Washington girls is covered in heavy maple syrup as well! And as big as they both are, it would take an army to hold them down to do anything sexual! And besides, Sarge, how are they going to do a rape test when everything, and I mean every *thing*, is full of maple syrup! You know what I mean, Sarge?" O'Malley raises his eyebrows and tilts his head. "You might find one of them little Jimmy Dean sausages stuffed in there, but that's about it!"

"One! You could probably fit a case of them sausages in either one of the Washington sisters," Malone pipes in. Several officers start to chuckle but LaManna looks around the room with that, *Do you see me laughing?* look on his face and all becomes deadly silent.

Malone looks down at his note pad. "So far Sarge, we got Moosehead Santa here who keeps yelling about the wheels stolen off his car – some big, black foreign job I've never seen before. It's missing all its wheels for sure, Sarge, and right now the black beast is up on milk crates. It won't be long before it's picked clean, that's for sure. Looks to me like another hit from the "no-face gang.""

"Better send a flat-bed over and get that damn thing the hell out of there, or whatever's left of it and haul it to our secure lot," LaManna fires over his shoulder to rookies one and two. "And make sure Moosehead Santa here gets the bill for all this!"

"We'll get right on it, Sergeant, sir," one of the rookies responds.

While all this is going on, more officers come into the squad room escorting the two altar boys. They are handcuffed to each other and are carrying an assortment of brushes, lint rollers, car polish, and a smoking censer which is furiously spewing sweet, holy fumes and smoke throughout the squad room.

LaManna stops in his tracks with his mouth open and nothing coming out. His eyes begin to tear as he watches the farce unfold in front of him when his voice finally breaks through.

"Put that shit out right now!" he yells while pointing to the censer and literally jumping up and down. "And get that damn moose head off of Santa!"

"That's not a moose head, sir," rookie one calls out from a desk in the back of the squad room. "That there is definitely an elk,

Sergeant. I got chased by a moose once in Alaska and that there ain't no moose head."

"Well I don't give a rat's ass what that thing is! Get it the hell off his head and get rid of that smoke bomb and I mean now!" La-Manna bellows. Losing his voice, he begins to cough and finishes, "What the hell is wrong with you people? And why are these boys handcuffed? Were they saying high mass in the street tonight?"

Rookies and old-timers alike recognize that Sarge is hot and at least six officers tackle the Patriarch-Santa and struggle to free him from the elk's head.

CLANG – BANG – CRASH! – as one huge light globe shatters mid air sending shards of glass showering the entire squad room like rice at a big Polack wedding in the 1950's.

The rain of glass settles as O'Malley tosses the elk's head to the floor when the other antler snaps off. Everyone is brushing glass bits off their uniforms except the Patriarch who is still cuffed and dazed. Rookie one quickly picks up the broken antler and waves it in triumph for all to see while pretending to get the bigger half of the Thanksgiving turkey wishbone, and says, "Look boys, I get my wish!" Sergeant LaManna gives rookie one such a look that he immediately puts his arm down and quickly tosses the antler to the floor as if he'd never touched it or even seen the damned thing. Rookie one then disappears back to his paperwork in the back of the squad room with rookie two.

While all this takes place, Officer Malone grabs the burning censer from one of the altar boys, runs into the men's room and tosses the incense into one of the toilets. It sizzles and fizzles and finally goes out. "There, that did the trick," he laughs as he flushes the toilet and adds, "Now that's some holy shit!"

Sergeant LaManna gives the Patriarch-Santa the once over as Zoltan slowly comes out of a funk from the macing with tears still streaming down his face wondering what in the world has happened.

"*Moi ZIL! Moi ZIL!* Dose *schwarzes* stole *mein* wheels! *Moi ZIL! Bozhe Moi!*" the Patriarch cries out loud in a prayer to God himself.

"What the hell is he saying?" says rookie number two.

"I think he's praying for a new set of Schwartz tires? I never heard of that brand?" from rookie one.

"Yeah, Sergeant, don't interrupt him or he might put a mojo on your ass and you might be excommunicated or become impotent or something," from rookie two again.

LaManna looks over in the corner and barks, "If I hear another peep out of you two, you both will be on the graveyard shift down at the missions! Is that clear enough?" LaManna pats Zoltan on the back and says, "I know, Santa. Some bad boys stole your tires and now they won't get any presents for Christmas. Don't worry now. We'll find what's left of your fancy car and box it up for you with a big red bow."

Sarge looks at the two altar boys and yells, "O'Malley! Unlock these two boys here, get them a Hershey bar for Christ's sake; and get in touch with their parents, NOW!"

"Right on it, Sarge," O'Malley gently guides the boys over to the break room complete with the assortment of brushes, lint rollers, and car polish.

"Malone, please show Mr. Moose where our 'Santa lounge' is located," LaManna points down the hallway to the cells.

"Sure thing, Sarge." Malone guides the Patriarch down the beaten path to the Santa cell.

"Let's see now," LaManna looks over at Hal behind the booking desk while reaching for the in-take blotter. "We got the Russian Black Elk Santa, alias "Moosehead," the little, black, blow-job Santa with the 300lb. Mrs. Claus, the Fat Wang Santa and all those gambling chinks, and the lunatic Puerto Rican Santa who doesn't speak English so good and only grunts. Is that it?" He looks around for confirmation.

"It's still early yet, Sargeant," from the rookie corner.

LaManna throws the clipboard down on the desk, cocks his leg and lets out a mighty fart.

"Fuck Christmas!"

44

"All available staff to emergency, STAT," comes booming over the sound system throughout St. Joseph's Hospital. And once again, "All available staff to emergency, STAT."

Please God, tell me what's going on with all these emergencies? Nurse Practitioner Roman Sigurdson asks himself as he responds to the call and races down the hallway. *Wonder if it's another wounded Santa or ex-cop with a groin injury? Something is definitely up tonight and I hope it ends soon! I can't take much more of this. It's starting to feel like 'Nam, man!* He turns the corner near one of the ORs and sees the flashing lights of the ambulance at the end of the corridor. The E.R. has been jammed up all evening with emergency medical staff, cops, ex-cops, ethnic Santas, a Dunkin' Donuts owner complete with free samples, and two very overweight, black girls covered in maple syrup. What a night!

The ambulance crew wheels in a gurney with a male patient moaning in agony. Sigurdson can't believe his eyes. It appears this poor soul has been tarred and feathered!

"It's really not as bad as it looks," pipes one of the crew. "He doesn't appear to have any internal injuries and that's not really tar – it's melted chocolate. The feathers are part of his fancy Santa outfit."

Feathers on a Santa suit?

"The other colored bits you see all over him are multi-colored jimmies like you put on ice cream," the EMT continues.

Sigurdson bends over to get a whiff of the chocolate and spots the red high-heeled Santa boots trimmed in pink. Then he begins to see the hint of glitter peeking out from all the chocolate and jimmies. He looks up questioning his find.

"Look Doc, all we know is the union hall hired this flamer here to be Santa for the kids' party and the pipefitters weren't exactly thrilled with his costume, table dance, or choice of party favors," says the ambulance attendant while holding up a chocolate pop in the shape of a penis. "I'm sure all the drinking that went on at the party tonight didn't help much either. My brother-in-law Horace is a member of the union and he was there drinking at the bar. He told me that shortly after Santa Bruce here entered the union hall with strip music blaring from his boom box, he immediately jumps up onto the ice cream fixins table and begins a strip tease while handing out these cocksucker lollipops to all the kids who are frozen in total silence." That's when all the pipefitters at the bar took Santa, punched him in his nuts, dipped him into the three-tiered melted chocolate display, covered his ass in jimmies, and threw him out into the parking lot!"

Sigurdson just shakes his head and wheels the gurney into the E.R. where he hands him off to the E.R. team wondering what in God's name this was?

"Here you go folks – one chocolate-covered Santa complete with jimmies and NO nuts!" He does an about face and leaves. *Figures,* he thinks. *Another Santa to add to the collection! Let's see,* he wonders, *what's the Santa tally now? We have: one chocolate covered Santa with no nuts, one Ninja Santa with his balls shoved up his ass, one questionable, female Santa with her vagina chained to her biker's wallet and other body parts, and one very tall and skinny, Indian Santa (the Seven-Eleven kind), with a bullet in each kneecap. There now – that about does it for the Santas.* Sigurdson now finds himself chuckling and breaks out singing, "Here comes Santa Claus. Here comes Santa Claus. Right down Santa Claus Lane." Several nurses in the hallway break out in smiles and laughter.

Roman, old buddy, he says to himself. *You never saw anything like this in 'Nam now did you?* "Nope, sure haven't," he says out loud while entering into the "Cop Ward", as he calls it anyway. *And what do we have here in ex-cops and cop-wannabe section? Ah, yes: one ex-cop shot in the nuts, one ex-cop with the scalded dick, and one rent-a-cop with serious head injuries! Sorry boys – can't do anything for you today – it's quitting time!*

Nurse Practitioner Roman Sigurdson does a smart about face and marches out of the room and into the hallway headed for the male staff changing room. While marching through the hallway he begins to hum the theme song from *Bridge on the River Qui* and marches the way the British do with arms swinging high in the air. He spots and picks up a Dunkin' Donuts bag on his way while never missing a beat. He opens it up while he continues his march and spots a half dozen or so plain-looking donuts with, what looks like blood on them. In the trash bin they go as he smartly makes a left flank maneuver into the changing room and comes to a stiff British halt in front of his locker.

"Fuck Christmas!" he announces to his face on his locker door mirror. "What I need is a stiff drink and a good piece of ass!"

"Amen, brother!" comes from an orderly trying to sleep in the corner of the room.

Laughter...

45

Junior and Annie find their way into the precinct hall and with worried faces approach the booking desk and guess who? – Sgt. Alfonso LaManna. Who else!

"We're looking for our dad," Annie belts out barely holding back the tears.

"How long has he been missing, Miss?" questions LaManna in a voice that conveys a most sincere and caring manner while at the same time giving them both the once over for weapons like brass knuckles, axes, and the like.

"Oh, he's not missing, sir. He's in here!" adds Junior.

"Here!" LaManna responds sounding more like the real Sgt. LaManna.

"You mean like here in jail? Locked up! – as in HERE!"

"That's what he told me when he called me from his cell phone about half an hour ago," says Junior.

"Cell phone? Cell phone!" LaManna's face begins to redden again as he turns to the officers in the room. "You mean them Santas back there have cell phones? No one here bothered to search them?" he roars to the stillness of the room. Everyone is in a freeze-frame status.

"What the hell else they got back there, boys? Uzis? Alcohol? A popcorn machine?" LaManna points down the hall and the entire roomful of officers goes running back to the cells. He turns to Junior and Annie and tries to regain his composure.

"Your father wouldn't by any chance be dressed up like Santa, would he?"

"Why yes he would," Junior said. "He was on his way to his first Santa gig at some Chinese place and ended up here. I don't know the complete story. He couldn't talk long. Said something about some crazy guy in the cell with him and to get down here *pronto* with his checkbook for bail."

"Is he in any trouble?" Annie asks shaking with worry. "What's this all about? We didn't say a word to Mom about any of this believe me. She's still very upset over the fight at the BINGO game today – with all the damage and all her balls missing. This would put her over the edge for sure!"

"Wait a minute. Wait a minute. Was this Santa, your father I mean, at a BINGO game today down at the V.A. hospital?"

"No, no, no! He wasn't at a BINGO game. I told you, he was sent to some Chinese place to play Santa and got locked up," Junior said.

"Mom was the one at the BINGO game!" Annie jumps in. "I told you that! She lost her balls there! And why is Daddy locked up? What did he do? Why is he here?" Annie and Junior are as confused as LaManna is.

LaManna nods his head pretending to understand but in reality he's not listening to Annie's ranting at all. He's still stuck on the statement and trying to picture how "Mom lost her balls at the BINGO game." He pauses a moment and thinks perhaps he didn't hear that one right and decides to let it go.

"Your Dad is Don Kaminski, right?" LaManna asks. "The white Santa who looks like he's normal, right?"

"Yes, sir," Junior says.

"Actually, we don't have anything concrete to hold him on. I honestly think he was at the wrong place at the wrong time, as they say; so there's no need for bail." Sergeant LaManna pats Annie lightly on the arm. "Don't worry Miss, we'll have your Dad released in about five minutes and you can take him right home. In fact, PLEASE take him right home." LaManna turns away to give the order to release Don but turns quickly back to Annie and Junior. "He will probably have to pay to get his car released and for the towing, however. He can do that right here before he leaves. And if I were you I'd get him to change his clothes before he sees your mother – or sneak him in through the back door or something." He turns away but quickly turns back again. "You don't have any guns in the house do you?"

"Harbor master," Mimo Gigante, Jr. answers the phone. He is seated behind his gigantic wooden desk once owned by Lucky Luciano. He cradles the phone with his left shoulder and listens a bit while still cleaning and oiling up his antique American Flyer locomotive. He stops mid-wipe and jumps out of the chair still holding the engine and cleaning rag.

"You gotta be shittin' me, right?" Mimo drops the rag and grabs the phone with his left hand and throws the train engine across the room with his right. It hits the door with a loud **BANG** and a classic American Flyer Atlantic Coastline steam locomotive with oiled parts goes flying all over the room.

"What the hell do you mean we didn't make a dime today because 'Our Santas got locked up or are in the hospital?'" Mimo starts screaming into the phone, "What the fuck are you talking about?" He listens to more bad news.

"Let me tell you something…" He's more than flustered now and starts to stutter.

"Say what?...Say that again!...How many fucking Santa suits are ruined?" Mimo can't believe what he's hearing.

"You get the boys in here right now and you'd better have some good, goddamn reasons for why all this shit is coming down the pike now or I'm going to have your balls on a silver platter! Do you hear me, motherfucker?"

"Poor Wanda," Jimmy D. Mays thinks as he strolls out of the jail with no fines, no bail, no fees at all, and free as a bird. He strolls down Main Street smoking a cigarette, blowing out tons of thick gray smoke, and talking to himself. It's a mild Saturday evening for November and most of Chicago is outside enjoying the unusually warm weather. Passers-by snicker, joke and poke one another pointing to the little black Santa but Jimmy D. is in a world of his own. One passer-by, strolling arm-in-arm with her husband, leans closer and whispers, "I think I had that Golden Book when I was a child?"

"What book was that?"

"Little Black Santa."

Both are hysterical as they turn around to take another look.

"With all that smoke," says hubby, "he looks like 'The Little Engine That Could.'"

Jimmy D. keeps on walking and blowing smoke all over the sidewalk.

"If it wasn't for bad lucks, Wanda have shit for luck anyhow. Dumb bitch! Boyfrien' car my ass! An' a trunk full-a knockoff Gucci shit. Dumb-ass bitch!" Jimmy stops at the corner and bends over to light up another cigarette from the one he's holding while trying to shield them both against the wind, which has picked up considerably the past five minutes.

"Look Emma!" Miss Martha says while strolling arm in arm with Miss Martha. "It's that wonderful, black Santa we met at the mall. He must still be out collecting for all the poor little pickaninnies." Miss Martha claps hers hands in excitement.

"You're right Martha," Miss Emma says while trying to focus her eyes a little better to see what Jimmy D. is up to. "Why bless his soul. It is him – our black Santa. What a kind old negro he is for sure." They stop right in front of Jimmy and almost knock him backwards into the Salvation Army donation tri-pod with the pot missing (the real Santa must be on a pee break).

"Oh Santa…Hello Santa Claus," Miss Emma sings as they plow into Jimmy D.

"Remember us?" Miss Martha says as they both grab for Jimmy D.'s hands before he falls over. In the process, both cigarettes go flying out in different directions.

"Jesus H. Chrise, bitch! What da fuck you doin' knockin' Jimmy D. shit all ova?"

"What did he say, Martha?" Miss Emma says with a puzzled look on her face.

"Something about 'praise Jesus' or other."

"Oh, isn't he just precious! It's us, Santa – Miss Martha and Miss Emma from the shopping center. Remember?"

Jimmy takes a better look at the two old gals and a smile brightens up his face.

"Ladies. Ladies! So nice to see youse bof," Jimmy D. smiles showing off all those white teeth of his. That's one thing about Jimmy D. – he always takes good care of his teeth. Brushes them at least three times each and every day (when he is sober enough to do so that is). And today his smile just sparkles and lights up the street.

"Oh, our lovely black Santa," Miss Martha sings out. "Miss Emma and I talk about you all the time and the wonderful things you do for all the poor little pickaninnies."

"Lil' what? What youse say? Picka what?" Jimmy D. asks.

"That's right, Santa," Miss Martha says opening her purse latching onto a twenty.

"Wait Martha," Miss Emma says, doing the same. "I have one too!"

"Where is your pot?" says Miss Martha waving the twenty and eyeing the Salvation Army tri-pod missing the red donation pot.

"My what?"

"Your pot? Your pot?" Miss Martha repeats.

"My pot?" *Shit, Jimmy D. ain' smoke no pot since last' week! Doan go tellin' me dese little ol' white ladies lookin' to buy POT!*

"Your pot! Your Salvation Army pot!" Miss Emma says while jingling the empty chain. "Where's your pot?"

"Oh, my Salivatin' Army pot!" Jimmy spots the white tri-pod with missing pot. "You had Jimmy D. all confuse, tha's for sure," says Jimmy. "Well, ladies, I gave dat pot o' monies to some ol' man had four chil'ren to feed cause they was tire of the food down at da mission. So nows he gonna have Kentuckies Fry Chicken. All them chil'ren gonna eats chicken tonight from da Colonel."

"Isn't that just a lovely story? We just think you're grand, Santa," says Miss Martha.

"Well here you go, Santa," says Miss Emma, "and may God bless you for all your wonderful deeds." She hands Jimmy the two bills, which he gladly takes.

"You be sure and buy something nice to give to the precious little darkies who need a little something on Christmas," says Miss Emma.

"We just love what you do for the black folks in our town," Miss Martha adds.

"Doan you worries none, ladies. Jimmy D. makin' damn sure all da niggahs gets a present for da holidays!" He smiles, winks, and bows to them both as they sally down the block arm in arm again.

Jimmy D. smiles so big now it almost hurts his face. He's looking at the two twenties and wondering where the nearest liquor store might be. Jimmy begins to sing and stroll down the block looking in the store windows for telltale cans and bottles.

"Here come Sanda Claus. Here come Sanda Claus. Right to da liquor store. Gonna buy some hooch an' bran new smokes an' maybe a little more. Ha Ha Ha!"

48

Later that Saturday evening, a tired and down-trodden Donald Kaminski, still in his not-so-fresh Santa suit, sneaks into the house behind Junior and Annie hoping to avoid Susan and the interrogation about what went wrong – *simple – everything!*

"The coast is clear, Pop," says Junior. "I don't see Mom anywhere so you'd better hop on upstairs and take off the Santa garb before she sees you and starts asking too many questions."

"I'm sorry it didn't work out for you, Daddy," Annie adds. "Maybe you'll have better luck next time around."

"Not with the mob Santa group I won't," Don says. "I'm going to quit tomorrow first thing and try to hook up with a professional Santa organization like the one who hired the Santa down at the mall."

"He's cool, Pop," Junior says. "He really does look like Santa. And that elf of his, Buddy the Elf. He really knows his business and he's good with the kids."

"You're right about that, Junior," says Don. "You know Buddy the Elf?"

"Sure, Pop. Everyone knows Buddy the Elf. He's more popular than Santa, I think."

"You're right, Junior. He's something else. I saw him in action a while back. They are both a class act. I might just head on over to the mall tomorrow and see if I can get any information on whether or not they need any more Santas."

"Good for you, Pop. Don't let the small stuff get you down." Junior pats Don on the back. "After all, you're a Kaminski and grandpa says, 'We Kaminskis come from good stock – after all, we made it through Hitler!'"

"He's right about that, Junior. We made it through Hitler. I just hope I can make it past the mob!"

"How much longer do you have to do this, Daddy? Didn't they say you would get your old job back?" Susan asks.

"That's what they're telling me, Annie. Just as soon as they pass the referendum scheduled this January. All I have to do is make it past Christmas and New Years," says Don.

"If this Santa group is really tied into the mob, how are you going to just quit?" asks Junior.

"You'll see, son," Don says. "I'll just make them an offer they can't refuse."

A little later, over a glass of wine or two, Sue pours her heart out to Don and tells him about the BINGO riot, the cops, the flying BINGO balls, the mess, the wounded, the sirens, and the busted BINGO ball machine. Don listens and decides not to say a word about his day. Instead, he hugs Sue and tells her: he understands, she did the right thing, no one was really hurt all that badly, the mess can be cleaned up, and she can always buy another BINGO ball machine.

"I'll even make the first donation," he says reaching for his wallet.

"No dear, no," Sue says. "I think perhaps my BINGO days are numbered."

"Yes they are," says Don. "B-6!"

Sue and Don break out in laughter. Don pours some more wine.

"Don, how did your day go with the Santa gig? Wasn't it today?"

"You're right, Sue. It was today and I really don't want to talk about it now. Let's just say it was a Chinese fire drill and leave it at that."

They clink glasses in a toast.

"You'll always be my Santa." Sue kisses Don on the cheek and downs the wine.

49

Finally, it's Sunday – a day of rest and prayer, family and togetherness; time for solitude, planning, and just reading a good book. In Jimmy D's case – two empty bottles of Fat Bastard and a little purple snow.

Rest easy, Jimmy. Nice to see you've come up a shelf or two.

Part 2

IT CONTINUES

Santa Claus is generally depicted as a plump, jolly, white-bearded man wearing a red coat with white collar and cuffs, white-cuffed red trousers, and black leather belt and boots (images of him rarely have a beard with no mustache). This image became popular in the United States and Canada in the 19th century due to the significant influence of caricaturist and political cartoonist Thomas Nast. This image has been maintained and reinforced through song, radio, television, children's books and films. The North American depiction of Santa Claus in the 19th and 20th century in turn influenced the modern perceptions of Father Christmas, Sinterklaas and Saint Nicholas in European culture.

From Wikipedia, the free encyclopedia

"You can't make chicken salad out of chicken shit!"

Frank McDermott

50

Monday morning is a bright and sunny day; another unseasonably warm day for November. Don decides it might be better if he travels a little farther to the new Dunkin' Donuts just opened up down the highway a bit. *Better not stir up the Patels and the retired cops any more than you already have,* he thinks. *Why half of them are in jail or in the hospital, anyway!*

Let's see – first I have to return the Santa suit to the mob: no soy sauce stains, no bullet holes, and no blood – that's good. Next I'll drop by the mall and see if I can milk Santa for some info. Maybe I should talk to Buddy the Elf rather than interrupt the big guy. Yeah, that ought to work. Buddy looks like a cool little dude. Maybe I'll bring him a small soda and half a sandwich. They can't eat much, can they?

There are no problems at the new Dunkin' Donuts as Don quickly goes through the drive-thru and gets his coffee the way he likes it and a couple of Old Fashioned donuts. Don had such a good time thinking about his first Santa experience and laughing to himself that he hadn't realized he was already at the Belmont Yacht Club. He pulls into the parking lot and drives around to the rear.

Thank God, Don thinks. *No goofy-assed cars. Guess all the other Santa fuck-ups got another assignment.*

Carrying the box of Santa suit and accessories, Don treks through the lot and onto the portico of the "White House." The restaurant and lounge appear to be doing a booming business as Don manages to elbow the door open and enters the Harbor Master's Suite and is immediately hit with a dense cloud of cigarette smoke.

"Jackie, you in here?"

"Walk this way, Mr. Kaminski. I saw you on the monitor."

VVVVVVVERRRRRROOOOOOOOOOOOOOOM!

The two Pratt and Whitney smoke-eaters suck up the smoke in seconds.

Miss Jackie is reaching for her feather pen as it floats back down to her desk.

"Good morning, Mr. Kaminski. I understand you ran into a bit of trouble yesterday?"

"Hi Jackie." Don checks to see if his Cubs ball cap is still on top of his head. "I guess you could say there was a wee bit of excitement."

"Well, just as long as you weren't hurt or shot or anything, and the Santa suit is okay." Miss Jackie bolts out of the chair and grabs for the box almost breaking an orange-colored fingernail. "You didn't fuck up the Santa suit. Did you?" She grabs the box and begins to inspect the contents.

"No, no, Jackie. See for yourself. The Santa suit is just fine and it's all there, believe me."

"Well, it had better be, Mr. Kaminski. Mr. Mimo Gigante, Jr. – you know, Momo, Jr. He gets really pissed and crazy when the Santa suits are fucked up!"

Don checks the room from corner to corner looking for Sal and Vic – *or was it Joey and Paulie? No, Sal and Vic. Joey and Pauley are too busy parking the boats.*

"Good thing for you, Mr. Kaminski. This one looks just fine. I'll get your next assignment." Miss Jackie starts to turn when Don says:

"Hold on, Miss Jackie. Hold on a minute. I don't think that's going to be necessary. You see I don't think I'm cut out for the Santa business and so I think I should just quit while I'm ahead and the Santa suit is still in good shape."

"Gee, Mr. Kaminski, I'm real sorry to hear that. I mean you are one of our better Santas. It would be a real shame to lose you." Jackie is now clicking her orange fingernails on the desk top.

"Do you need more money, free bus tokens, a complimentary lunch or something?" Jackie lights up another Marlboro and inhales the smoke clear to her toes.

"No, thank you, Miss Jackie. None of that is necessary. I just think it would be best if I looked for another job." Don smiles at Jackie trying not to breathe too deeply.

"Well, okay Mr. Kaminski. If that's what you want. We will sure miss you." Jackie reaches into her desk and pulls out a wad of papers. "We'll just need you to fill out these forms before you go: another disclaimer, a receipt for the Santa suit, and a promise not to sue or compete with Gigante and Associates, LLC.

"Does this mean I can't work as a Santa for someone else?" Don asks.

"Well, I'm not really sure about that, Mr. Kaminski. I do know that you won't be able to open your own Santa business and go back to any site we service and play Santa, but I think it's okay for you to work for someone else." Jackie exhales.

"You don't have to worry none about that, Miss Jackie. I'll leave the business end of it to you." Don signs all the papers and is beginning to lose sight of Miss Jackie in the Marlboro haze.

VVVVVVERRRRRROOOOOOOOOOOOOOOM!

The two Pratt and Whitney smoke-eaters suck up the smoke again as Don shakes Miss Jackie's hand and watches as the feather pen floats back down onto Miss Jackie's highly polished desk.

"Best of luck, Mr. Kaminski. Nice working with you." – exhales.

"Bye, Miss Jackie." Don exits the office and heads to the car while searching for Sal, Vic, Joey, Paulie, any sort of weird car, or any fucked-up looking Santa. The coast is clear and Don is already thinking about Buddy the Elf down at the mall.

51

Jimmy D. Mays hears the bell tingle at Bee Bee's Cash and Carry as he enters. Habib Constantine, the owner, is standing behind the cash register checking to see who just entered the store.

"Jimmy D., Jimmy D.!" sings Habib. "Where you been, Jimmy D?"

"Hey, Bee Bee," Jimmy says. "How youse been?"

"Fine, Jimmy. Have a nice Easter?"

Yeah, Bee Bee – real nice – real nice."

"Just got in a fresh shipment of Fat Bastard, Jimmy – the red, not the white. How many bottles you want today? Six? Eight?"

"Ha, Ha, Ha, Bee Bee. Das very funny seein' as how Jimmy D. wearin' his Santa shit an' come in here wif more 'heritage money to spen'. No Fat Bastid for me, Bee Bee. Today Jimmy D. jumpin' up a shelf or two. Gimme a fifth o' Early Times. Tha's whiskey, Bee Bee, case you ain't sold some recen'ly." Jimmy laughs at his own joke.

"You got the money, right, Jimmy D.?"

"I gots it. I gots it." Jimmy reaches into his Santa pants pocket and pulls out the two twenties. "I gots more 'an enough, Bee Bee." Jimmy starts marching up the aisle waving the twenties around like an American flag in a Fourth of July parade. "Tol' youse I got more 'heritage money, Bee Bee. An' give Jimmy D. THREE pack o' Camels an' some free matches!"

"Jimmy D. Jimmy D. You pumped up pretty good, Jimmy D. Your ship come in, huh, Jimmy D.?"

"Yeah, Bee Bee, my ship done come in and dump plenty o' good shit at Jimmy D. house. My 'heritage be layin' all over da groun'. So much 'heritage, Jimmy D. had to buy a shovel to shovel all dat 'heritage shit into da house."

"Say, Jimmy. You got any extra inheritance? Remember, I got three kids going to St. Ignatz the Martyr Orthodox Catholic School and the tuition I pay there is expensive as hell. In fact, I could send each one to Michigan State with a private room for all the money it costs me to send them to St. Ignatz! That tight-ass priest there, Father Zoltan, he must be making a ton of dough, all them kids going to St. Ignatz. I wonder what he does with all that money? He sure don't put it into the church or the school, that's for sure. Last Sunday at mass, they had a THIRD collection 'cause the school roof is caving in! And the history books end with President Eisenhower and talk about the possibility of space flight! Ain't that some shit? Oh yeah, and I still need to save up to get my wife, Fatima, over here from the old country. The kids miss her." Habib looks down in disgust and mutters, "I don't miss her all that much but the kids do. They keep yelling about 'When's Mommy coming? When's Mommy coming?' I'm glad they're over at St. Ignatz all day. They drive me fucking crazy with all the yelling about seeing their Mama, and they do it in both English and Arabic – the little fuckers! So if you have any extra inheritance, maybe you could help out old Bee Bee some?"

"Ah, Bee Bee. You bein' a good frien' to Jimmy D. for a long time now, but to be ahness' Jimmy D. jus' been braggin' 'bout my 'heritance. Jus' two little ol' ladies give Jimmy D. some monies once in awhile, das all." Jimmy walks over to the shelf where Habib is selecting a fifth of Early Times.

"Sure you don't want a quart, Jimmy. It ain't that much more. Just a couple of bucks."

"Yeah, sure, Bee Bee. Gimme da quart. Jimmy D. almost a top-shelf guy. Marks my words, Bee Bee. One day soon, Jimmy D. gonna come in heres and buy a bottle o' Crown Royal. Ain' dat sompin'? Jimmy D. an' some Crown Royal. Jimmy D. be a top-shelf muthafucka for sure! Ain' dat right Bee Bee?"

Just then the bells tingle as two local children come in and start yelling at each other in Arabic about the candy they want to buy with arms swinging in every direction.

"Hold it! Hold it!" Habib yells in their dialect. "What the hell is going on? Did you come here to buy something?" he asks.

"Yes, Mr. Habibee. We came to buy candy," the littlest one pipes up.

"Where's your money?" asks Habib.

"That's the problem," the elder brother says. "This dumb shit lost our money on the way to your store!"

"Then get the fuck out of here, the both of you!" Habib yells and points to the door. "Go down to the Dunkin' Donuts store and try that bullshit story on the Patels. Maybe they'll give you some stale Old Fashioned donuts! Out!" Habib ushers the two dark-haired boys out the door, then turns around to Jimmy D. "Those two are mine – the little bastards!"

Jimmy D. shakes his head in confusion. "Hey, Bee Bee. Dat priess-fella over St. Bignuts…"

"You mean Father Zoltan over at St. Ignatz the Martyr?"

"Yeh, Bee Bee, Father Suntan over St. Bignuts. Youse think he still be given out free clothes and unnerwears an' shit to da homeless peoples?

"Jimmy D., you homeless? I thought you had a place to stay somewhere."

"Well, yeah, Bee Bee. I gots a small place das warm an' cozy-like and make Jimmy D. feel all at home, except when it snows, but I still needs me some new unnerwears an' shit, see?"

"That tight-ass priest's so tight, Jimmy. I don't think he givin' out nothing free anymore, but you could go check. I hear he's charging a dollar for the free razors he gets from the Polack war vets! But, you could always go down and try, Right, Jimmy D.? You know where the church is, right? Down behind the Polack war vets."

'I knows, Bee Bee. I knows." Jimmy collects his change and a plain brown bag of goodies including the free matches and heads on out the store.

"See ya, Bee Bee. Be cool."

"Okay, Jimmy D. You the man!"

"No, Bee Bee. YOU da man. I da Santa! Ho, Ho, Ho!"

The bells tingle as Jimmy exits.

Don pulls into the mall parking lot and has to drive around a bit to find a parking place. He attempts to pull into an end slot when an old lady in a big silver car cuts him off and gives Don the finger. Don shakes his head in disbelief. "Screw you lady!" he yells inside the car. *Ain't that a bitch? – Old lady in a Buick! I'll be damned! You got to have eyes in the back of your head to drive around in here today. People are crazy!* Don's way back behind the mall when he spots a place to park over near the dumpsters. *Figures,* he thinks. *Every nut in the world has come here today for the Christmas sales.*

He carefully parks his Volvo, and reaches for the key in the ignition. Out of the corner of his eye, he swears he sees what looks like a little black Santa, smoking a cigarette, complete with Santa suit and carrying a plain brown paper bag, crawl over the top of the last dumpster, and then reach out and pull the lid of the dumpster closed. Don sits there frozen in thought and mesmerized buy what he thinks he just saw.

"What the hell was that? Great! Now I'm seeing things!" Don says out loud. "Just great. Real great. Just what the hell I need. Seeing little black Santas jumping into dumpsters. And why not? After all, it's Christmas and Santa can do whatever the hell he wants...even little black ones!"

Don shuts off the Volvo and locks it up tight. *After all,* he thinks, *I got a date with an elf; and not just any elf – Santa's number one elf – Buddy!*

Back at the police precinct, Sgt. Alphonso LaManna sits quietly at his desk and takes a sip of his fresh hot Dunkin' Donuts coffee and bites into a warm Old Fashioned donut just delivered by some Indian fellow (the Seven-Eleven kind, not the Native American kind) and reads an attached thank you note about how great Chicago's police are in fighting hate crimes and keeping young hoodlums off the streets.

"How right you are, Hapu. And we can kick the shit out of any trouble-making Santa Claus within a hundred miles of Lake Michigan. Bet your ass!"

"What's that, Sergeant?" from a rookie in the back of the room.

"Nothing. Nothing. Just talking to myself. Get back to work!"

"Yes, sir!" from the rookie in the back.

LaManna takes another bite and washes it down with the coffee. *All is well,* he thinks. *It's nice and quiet here. Nothing going on. The boys are out hiding somewhere. All the Santas have been cleared out: released to the local bondsmen, or simply released to go the fuck home, the mental hospital, Sri Lanka, or wherever the fuck! That one crazy-fucking Santa should have been locked up in a padded cell! I'll bet we see that asshole back here before long.*

What luck for Don. Santa is gone on a lunch break and Don sees Buddy the Elf closing up the set and is just about to leave.

"Hey, Buddy!" Don yells as he picks up the pace and reaches the set. "Done for the day already?" he says knowing full well that Santa had better get his chubby ass back on time because the line is getting longer and no one's leaving.

Buddy turns quickly from the closed Santa gate, "Are you kidding me!" Buddy looks around to spot the wise guy. "Oh, hi there – no, we're just closing down for a lunch break. The kids are still in line, see them?" Buddy waves to all the children and pissed-off parents who are lined up and darn near circle the entire Santa set – kids crying, moms and dads yelling at the kids to behave themselves, moms and dads yelling at each other for the hell of it, or just not talking at all – and all with such unhappy faces.

They look like a bunch of Jews ready to board the train cars to Auschwitz! Don looks back at Buddy. The kids see Buddy and are happy again. They scream and wave back to the smiling little elf.

"We'll be right back! Don't go anywhere!" yells Buddy.

"Fuck you!" comes from somewhere way back at the end of the line followed by a nicotine coughing fit.

Buddy pretends he didn't hear it. "Santa here, is a real *prima-dona*. He worked out a deal to get a free lunch every day down at the Burger and Brew if he waves to all the patrons in the restaurant. Buddy starts to walk away then hesitates, "Say mister, didn't I see you here once before? I'm good at remembering faces. Are you looking for a job or something? You've got a great beard and I can spot a good Santa from a mile away."

"You have a good memory, Buddy. I was here a while back and watched you work for a minute or two. You are really great with the kids."

"Oh, you have to be in this business. It's fast and furious. Seems the photo outfit wants to sell a record number of pictures and lots of picture frames this season. Listen, I don't have long so I'm headed over to Orange Julius to get a cold drink," *and to take another long look at the new girl – Patsy with the big tits.* "Want to come along?"

"Sure, Buddy. If you don't mind."

"No, heck no." Buddy turns and makes a beeline down the mall concourse.

For a little shit, this is one fast elf, Don thinks as he quickens the pace to come up along side Buddy. *He might wobble side to side like a Weeble but he's making damn good time!*

"You're right, Buddy, but I need a real Santa job. I've been working for an organization that's kind of odd and sends its people to all the wrong places. Not necessarily wrong places but they send the wrong Santa. For example, they sent me to a Chinese Take-Out and they actually have a Chinese Santa they sent to an almost all-white daycare! Get it? It just doesn't make any sense. And the guys running the show were very questionable, if you know what I mean." Don is still quick-stepping along side Buddy who is waving to all the kids while he wobbles down the mall and still listens to Don. "By the way, Buddy, I'm Don Kaminski."

"Good to see you, Don. As you know, I'm Buddy the Elf," Buddy says with a sideways glance as they approach the Orange Julius. Buddy's the next in line but he doesn't see Patsy.

Then, all of a sudden, Patsy races in from the back room and up to the counter, "Sorry I'm late," she says to the fat lady behind the register – probably the boss.

"See that it doesn't happen again," comes from the boss.

Patsy looks over the counter and then down. "Oh, Hi Buddy. Your usual – a large 3-Berry Blast?"

"You got it, babe. How've you been, Patsy? You're looking awful good today!"

"Fine, Buddy. How's the Santa business?" Patsy looks over at Don. "Are you two together?"

Don takes one look at Patsy with her long, curly, jet-black hair, velvety skin, and red lipstick – a knockout for sure! And all dressed up for work in a clean starched white shirt with way too many top buttons unbuttoned and colorful Orange Julius vest pointing severely almost due North and has trouble remembering where he is and what the question was. All Don can think about is his old man's 1955 Cadillac Eldorado with the big chrome tits.

"Ah...yes...and I'm paying," pipes Don. "Give me the same," as he throws a ten on the counter hoping Patsy doesn't see him looking at her gigantic chest, the tops of which offer more than a hint of two glorious golden orbs hidden down under.

Buddy the Elf chuckles as he takes his large drink from Patsy. Good thing there's a lid on it or Don would have spilled his drink on his shoes. *Those can't be real!* Don thinks.

"Sir, here's your change...Sir?...Here's your change...Sir?"

"Oh...yes...yes...my change. Thank you." Don takes his change from Patsy and gives her great big adoring smile thinking again about the old man's Cadillac.

Patsy looks back at Don, admires his good looks for being an older man, returns the smile, winks at Don and whispers, "And yes, they *are* real." Patsy blows Don a kiss and turns to greet the next customer – another wide-eyed, all-American male who isn't looking at the Orange Julius menu posted on the wall.

Don turns beet red, does a quick about-face and heads to the table where Buddy the Elf has already sucked down half of his 3-Berry Blast and is feeling the rush of a frozen-brain ache.

"Man, that's good," Buddy says looking up to the heavens cross-eyed.

Jimmy D. Mays has already smoked a half pack of Camels along with numerous big gulps of Early Times wiskey, and Jimmy D. is in a heavy-duty yuletide buzz. In fact he's "half shot in the ass," as the saying goes.

"Here's to you, Moms! I misses you da mos' an' das for sure." He takes another swig and lights up another Camel. Jimmy D. feels a bit light headed and is careful to put the whiskey bottle flat down on the floor, away from him as far as he can reach, just in case he passes out again – which he does. The cigarette falls from his lips onto the floor and lucky for Jimmy, the Camel lands in some strange liquid on the dumpster floor and fizzles out.

"So what's up, Don? What do you want from me?" says Buddy the Elf as his eyeballs begin to focus on reality after the brain freeze. "I can tell already by what you said that you've been working for the mob Santa group across town," Buddy chuckles. "They care more for the damn Santa suits than they do the Santas!"

"You hit the nail on the head, Buddy. Can you help me in any way make some connections with businesses that might need a good Santa? I mean do you work for the mall or the photographer? What can you tell me to steer me in the right direction? I'm one of those striking schoolteachers you've been reading about in the newspapers and I really need the help. Christmas is here already and I'm flat out broke!" Don shakes his head and looks Buddy straight in the eyes to prove his point.

"Listen Don, let me ask you a couple of questions first. Do you belong to any unions or professional Santa groups?"

"No, nothing to do with Santa. I do belong to the National Education Association, but that's got nothing to do with the Santa business. In fact, other than take my money once a month, I don't think they do much at all. Tell you the truth."

"Okay, that's great. Let me ask if you've signed any contracts or agreements with anyone for 'exclusivity in representation' or any thing like that?"

"No. No one. I did sign a contract with Gigante and Associates not to compete at the same locations…"

"That's a bullshit contract, Don. It won't hold up in any court. And besides, you don't want to go to any of the places they send you anyway." Buddy leans over the table closer to Don and whispers, "You look like a decent guy, Don. Maybe I can help." Buddy looks Don in the eyes like a stockbroker who has the million-dollar insider tip of the century, and Don gets ready for it.

"I appreciate anything you can do for me, Buddy."

"First of all, I don't work for the mall, the photographer, or the Santa, for that matter. I work for the Amalgamated Society of Santas. And that's all I'm going to say right now, 'cause I got to get back to the set."

"Well how do I get in touch with these people?"

"That's just it, Don – you don't. They get in touch with you. You see, you have to be invited. This is a very close-knit group. Look Don, I really have to go now. Listen, do you know where Pippin's Tavern is on North Rush St.?"

"Sure, I know that place."

"Well, right next door to Pippin's is a little place called The Mini Bar. Suppose you meet me there about ten o'clock this evening. Can you do that? I'll fill you in on all the details when we can talk in private. How's that sound?" Buddy spreads his arms open, palms up as if to say, *What the hell else do you want from me, pal?*

"Yes, sure, Buddy. I can do that; about ten o'clock. I'll be there at The Mini Bar next to Pippin's on Rush St."

Both Don and Buddy are out of their seats and shaking hands. Don being careful not to hurt the midget's hand (or is he a dwarf?). Buddy the Elf cocks his head and gives Don his elfish grin, winks and off he goes – wobbling down the concourse at record speed and waving to all the kids.

"See you around ten, Don," echoes down the mall.

"Sure thing, Buddy," Don yells back as he turns to take one more look at Patsy with the big tits, when the biggest brain freeze Don's ever experienced hits him between the eyes – Don flops back down in the chair and grabs for his head.

57

Dinnertime at the Kaminskis and all are gathered around the table this evening for some of Mom's chicken and rice skillet with cream of mushroom soup on the top and a side of asparagus. Annie made a quick salad – dry because everyone likes a different dressing, and Junior has poured each one a glass of diet iced tea. Tonight's dinner is a quick one but all agree it's a favorite, especially when Annie whips up her special Hollandaise sauce for the asparagus.

The Kaminskis make it a habit to at least eat dinner together and catch up on all the news on "What happened today," and "Who's doing what tomorrow?" It didn't used to be this way with everyone going off in different directions. They hardly saw each other. And they all ate poorly as a result – usually fast-food, and most of it eaten in the car. They usually only saw one another in the mornings and briefly at that: on the fly to start the dryer for some forgotten item that was still wet, running down the stairs to throw a bagel in the toaster, popping their heads in each others room to ask a question that couldn't be understood because of teeth brushing, hopping up and down while trying to put on a sock, dental flossing, and Junior once tried to ask Mom a question while gargling with Listerine. Don put an end to all that at a pow-wow he called for several months ago where he laid down the law, "I don't care where we are all headed but let's at least plan to have dinner together as a family, if at all possible." They all agreed that this sounded like a good idea and besides they all were beginning to feel like a fraternity member rather than a family. So they tried it out and they loved it – dinner became *the* major family event of the day and they were usually all there. If they weren't – someone had better have been notified – and those were the rules.

"Where were you this morning, Don? You got up awful early." Sue asks as she finishes making his plate and hands it to him at the table.

"Ah," he says, "That's a secret." Don grins as if he's onto something really good.

"You know I'm sworn to the sacred oath of secrecy when it comes to the Santa business, but I will say this..." He looks around the entire table at everyone's faces with a big grin on his.

"I have made contact with a very, and I say VERY top-secret Santa group AND I have a clandestine meeting to go to tonight at ten o'clock!"

"We know all about it, Pop," says Junior. "Buddy the Elf called to remind you to meet him at The Mini Bar at ten sharp."

"Buddy the Elf!" Sue spits out with a chuckle.

"The Mini Bar!" Annie follows with a mouth full of rice.

Hysterics all around the table. Even Don is laughing.

"Alright, alright," Don holds his hands up surrendering to the ridicule. "Let's come to order here."

"What's going on, Don?" Sue says as she sits at the table. "And who's Buddy the Elf?"

"Oh Mom," Junior shakes his head in disbelief. "I can't believe you don't know Buddy the Elf. "Why he's Santa's number one elf!"

"Yeah, and he likes to hang out at the *Mini* Bar with all the other elves!" Annie adds. Junior and Annie crack up over that one.

"Well, it just so happens that I've made a connection to an 'invitation only,' exclusive Santa Claus club called The Amalgamated Society of Santas."

"The Amalgamated Society of Santas?" in three-part harmony.

Junior thinks for a second or two, "Say, Pop, you do realize that the acronym for the Amalgamated Society of Santas is *ASS*, don't you? Do you really want to be one of the *ASS* Santas?"

"Ass Santa?" Don says out loud.

"Ah ha!" says Susan. "Are you sure you know what you're getting into?"

Total silence – then complete hysterics drowning out poor Don as he barely whispers, "I don't think they call it that?"

After a quick shower and change, Don getting ready for his big meeting at The Mini Bar. He peeks into the den where the family is entrenched watching "Dancing With the Stars."

"Can you believe that grossly overweight guy, and who is he anyway? I can't believe he is still in this competition," Sue says.

"That's Steve Woz...something-or-other. He helped invent Apple Computers, Mom," answers Junior.

"Well, he's too fat to be out there with all those good dancers. Why do they keep voting him back in?"

"It's like anything else, Mon," adds Annie. "It's a popularity contest that has very little to do with dancing."

"I don't know about that," Sue fires back. "The rest of these people dance pretty darn good if you ask me!"

"Especially Cheryl Burke!" Junior says hardly able to keep his tongue in his mouth.

"What's she wearing tonight?" Don joins in from the doorway.

"Hardly anything, Pop!"

"That's my girl. Say, listen up gang. I'm off to my meeting. I won't be late. See you later." Don gives Sue a quick peck on the cheek.

"Cheryl's up next, Pop," from Junior.

Don spots Cheryl's next-to-nothing outfit as they go to commercial. "Sorry gang. Got to go. See you later." He heads towards the front door. *Damn, I have to miss Cheryl Burke!*

"So long, Don. And be careful."

"Bye, Daddy."

"See ya, Pop. Watch out for any loose reindeer, and if you do have a beer, have a *short* one!

"Maybe the drinks there are *half-off?*"

Mass hysterics as Don grabs his car keys off the counter and an almost naked Cheryl Burke grabs her partner to begin the tango.

Don pulls into a parking garage around the corner from Rush St. The drive into town is a pleasant one. The weather is back to being seasonably cold again. *Thank God the wind has died down!* That's always a relief in Chicago. With the economy being questionable again this season, the downtown businesses pulled out all the stops on Christmas displays and colored lights, especially outside. The whole town seems to sparkle with holiday warmth and joy. Carols could be heard on the streets as retailers welcomed shoppers to come in, and buy, buy, buy. Hopefully this would be a good season after all.

As Don is about to pull into a nice corner spot in the parking garage, he hears the loud blare of car horn as a large silver Buick darts into his space.

"What the shit! Screw you lady!" he yells from inside the car.

An older woman with short blonde hair and stylishly dressed gets out of the Buick with her leather business bag and gives Don the dirtiest look ever.

Well I'll be damned! It's the same old lady in a Buick who cut me off this afternoon. Kiss my ass!

Don settles down and finds another spot. He carefully looks around for any more Buicks and parks the Volvo. He's a little early but that's better than showing up late. Don locks the car, strolls out to the street and crosses at the corner. He spots The Mini Bar and gives it the once over.

Now I see why they call it the Mini Bar. Looks like the front of the building is no longer than twenty feet wide – big enough for a door and a very small glass block window with a neon Budweiser logo shining through from the inside. And, to top it off, it's only one story tall and sandwiched in between much larger buildings making it appear even smaller than it is. Just perfect for Santa's elves! Don laughs out loud as he enters the bar.

Yepper, typical, small-time Chicago watering hole: small, dark, noisy, and smoky...smoky? Hell, you can't even smoke in a public park any more. Why the hell is it smoky in here?

Don looks around but doesn't spot Buddy the Elf. He heads towards the bar when someone taps him on the right butt cheek. He turns around and looks down at Buddy. "Hey, Buddy. How's it going?" Buddy has a huge glass of beer that Don figures is a full liter. He's holding on to it with both pudgy hands, so Don pats him on the shoulder as a greeting. Then Don wonders how Buddy tapped him on the ass to get his attention when his little chubby fingers barely manage to hold onto the liter of beer? He reaches back and feels a wet spot on his ass from the beer glass. *Oh well, now I get it.*

"Good to see you, Don. I'm glad you came. Follow me." Buddy swings to his left and begins weaving in and out through the crowded bar, spilling beer all over people's feet but careful enough not to get stepped on.

"Hey, watch it, buddy!" they yell at Don not seeing Buddy the Elf at all. Don scrambles to keep up with the little guy, losing him once or twice in the process. Buddy ends up in the back corner of the bar and is frantically waving to Don to catch up.

"Down here, Don." Buddy leads the way to a full bar in the basement complete with live rock band and flashing disco lights. That's when it hits him.

"Well I'll be damned!" Don says unbelieving as to what he is seeing. Buddy turns to Don, takes a big gulp of beer and cracks a broad grin. The entire room, even the band, is made up of little people! Midgets and dwarfs alike – all of them! – drinking, dancing, laughing, and partying big time. The band members are rocking out with instruments that look far too big for them. Even the drummer has specially adapted pedal blocks for the bass drum and crash cymbals. On stage one little lady is dressed to kill, complete with long blonde wig, and is belting out the latest Lady Gaga hit and the crowd is loving it.

Several little people stare at Don and wonder, *What's this freak doing here?* A couple of tiny bar girls comment on how big Don is and begin to giggle. Don just smiles and takes it all in.

"Over here, Don. Yo, Don – over here!" He spots Buddy in the corner motioning to an empty chair at a large table full of Buddy's partying friends.

Don walks over to the table, looks around and gives everyone a big smile and says, "Hello." They all smile back as Buddy begins the introductions pointing at each from left to right.

"Guys, this is Don Kaminski."

"Hi, Don," they all say almost in unison in their higher pitched voices.

"Don, these are my roommates, Marty and Billy." They wave to Don. "This is Sally and her fiancé, Danny." Both smile and nod. "Next we have Ginny and her companion, Betty." They both wave and smile at Don. "And finally, we have Mary and next to her, her boy-friend, Miroslav."

Miroslav?

"Miroslav is from Bulgaria and doesn't speak English very well, but he's a hell of a polka dancer."

Miroslav shakes his head in agreement as he gulps down his beer, burps out loud like a Mississippi truck driver, and says through his newly acquired beer foam mustache, "*Zdravy*, Meester Don." The mini-pack laughs at this. Miroslav is always worth a few laughs.

Don grabs the empty chair next to Buddy and sits down. That's when he notices that the chair legs, and the table legs for that matter, are all shorter than normal. The result is that the back of his chair ends about four inches up from the crack of his ass, and his knees hit the front edge of the table and won't fit under it; forcing him to be about two feet farther from the table than everyone else. Don definitely looks like a circus freak among all the little people who all notice the predicament and grin.

Without thinking, Don surveys his situation and says, "This reminds me of going to the Open House when my children were in kindergarten." He looks up at the others, "Oops! Sorry, gang. Hope I didn't say anything to offend anyone."

"Don't worry about it, Don," Buddy says. "You're the outcast here!" All have a good laugh at that one along with Don.

"What do you do for a living, Don?" asks Marty.

Don chuckles, "Well right now, Marty, I'm a school teacher out on strike and hoping to make it past Christmas."

"This is a tough time to be out of work," says Billy.

"Say Don, you've got a great-looking beard. Why don't you get a Santa job?" from Betty.

She's probably the male role player of the two little lesbian midgets, or are they dwarfs?

"Don't worry. Don't worry," Buddy chimes in. "I'm going to hook Don up with the right people. He was working for the mob Santa group. You know the one I mean?"

"Oh, that bunch of spaghetti-eating losers!" from Danny. "I worked for those *goombahs* for two days and quit. They cared more about the friggin' elf costume than they did about me!" Danny looks around the table as all the mini guests shake their heads in agreement looking like, "Bobble heads gone wild."

"I almost got my ass kicked at a Chinese Take-Out if it hadn't been for my escape though the men's room widow!" Danny continues. Don laughs along with the others and orders a Bud Lite from the mini bar girl who gives Don the eye.

"Been there. Done that. Got the T-shirt!" Don says.

"Don't worry one bit, Don," Buddy responds. "I've got connections."

"Yep," says Billy. "If Buddy says it's happening – it's HAPPENING!" More laughter as they all clink glasses in a toast.

"Here's to Buddy," Ginny says.

Don listens as the minicrew spends the next couple of minutes telling stories about working on the Santa set.

60

Don orders another Bud Lite from the mini bar girl who teases him, "Sure you can handle a Lite, big guy?" This brings on another round of laughter from the munchkins.

Don just takes it in stride and laughs along with the mini crowd. Some of the little partiers get up to dance and others are locked in conversations about this and that, when Buddy seizes the opportunity to talk to Don personally.

"Again, Don, I'm really glad you made it here tonight." Buddy leans over into Don's face. "This shows me you are an upright person and I'm going to help get you into the real Santa business." Buddy looks him in the eye and gets ready to divulge top-secret information.

"Thanks, Buddy. I really do appreciate all you can do in helping me make the connections I need. Believe me when I tell you – I'm flat broke!"

"I know, Don. I know. Been there myself once or twice." Buddy leans over even closer. Don also tries to lean over as close to the table as he can but his knees are in the way. Buddy the Elf looks from side to side to see who's watching – No one is. Good. He takes out a small scrap of paper from inside his mini jacket pocket, lays it on the table, still covering the paper with his pudgy hand, and slides it over to Don. He looks around again. Still no witnesses.

"Take this phone number. Don't look at it now and don't lose it. Just put it in your pocket and don't forget it's there. Hear me?"

Don shakes his head afraid to say a word.

"Remember I told you I belong to the Amalgamated Society of Santas?"

Don shakes his head again.

"Well I want you to call this number tomorrow morning sometime between the hours of ten and eleven o'clock. It's important that you call during that time frame, Don. Don't forget!"

"I won't. I promise," Don says as he takes the paper and carefully places it in his jacket pocket, patting it on the outside for safe keeping. "Between ten and eleven – got it."

"You'll be speaking to the Grand Exalted Santa, himself!" Buddy raises a finger to the heavens as a warning to Don. He continues, "You are to mention my name, Buddy Holly..."

Buddy Holly? What was your Mama thinking?

"... and tell the Grand Exalted Santa that I *myself* gave you this number and instructed you to call him. Introduce yourself, Don, and tell the Grand Ex., that's what we call him, but not to his face, that you have a real Santa beard and would like to interview to become a member of the association. Got that?"

"Sure, I got it."

"Don't say another word and do everything the Grand Ex. tells you to do, and be sure to follow his directions, okay? This man is very important and has a very busy schedule to keep."

"I will. I will."

"If he wants to meet you, he'll set up the meeting and put it on his calendar. But don't worry, Don. I know once the Grand Ex. talks with you a bit, he will see all the good qualities you have and what a great addition you will make the society." Buddy reaches over to shake Don's hand and Don takes this as a sign that the meeting is over and he needs to leave so the little people can party on.

Don rises up out of the uncomfortable tiny wooden chair and reaches down to shake Buddy's hand which, by the way, feels a lot like about a half-pound of cold hamburger ready to throw on the grill.

"Thanks a million, Buddy." Don gulps down the rest of his beer and reaches for his wallet.

"Beer's on me," says Buddy the Elf.

"Thanks again, Buddy." Don says goodbye to all the little people and turns to head on out.

"Bye!" comes from the entire room as the misfit heads on up the stairs.

"I'll bet he's hung like a racehorse," the mini bar girl says to another.

"Nah," the other responds. "Probably more like a pony."

More mini laughter.

It's early Tuesday morning and it looks like another unusually mild day today for the good people of Chicago. Jimmy D. wouldn't know that because his "early time," like his empty bottle of "Early Times," is spent! Jimmy's sound asleep in his Santa house and snoring like a well-oiled Craftsman weed whacker. He's lucky if he sees any daylight at all after drinking up a whole quart of almost top-shelf whiskey. Sweet dreams, Jimmy.

Don's at the kitchen counter pouring two large glasses of orange juice. He's got the coffee going and two bowls of healthy all-natural, multi-grain cereal poured out for him and Sue. He checked earlier to be sure they had low-fat milk in the fridge. Annie had already left for her methods of teaching class at the college.

"Big test today," she yelled going out the door. She and Don often discussed different methods of teaching along with how and when to use them. Don informed her that a good teacher had to be like the old house-visiting doctor was years ago with his large black bag.

"What do you mean by that, Daddy?" she asked.

Don explained that in the old days, the doctor had to carry around all that he needed in order to make house visits. Once the doctor made the diagnosis, he (and it usually was a *he*), would reach inside the bag and pull out some pills, an ointment or salve, or maybe some Castor Oil.

"That crap," Don explained, "was like drinking a mixture of fish oil and motor oil! But somehow, with the grace of God, you got it down and before long you got better. The point is, if one remedy didn't work, he always had something else in that old black bag of his that would do the trick. As a teacher, not only do you have to choose the right method, (and remember what works for Dick might not work for Jane), but you also have to keep it interesting as well, *and*, especially remember this one, if you can't prove to the students that they really need to learn this concept and here's why – you've lost them. You have to answer for them every time, 'What's in this for me?' and 'Why do I need to learn this?'"

"I get it," Sue said. "If one teaching method doesn't seem to be working, then try another until you see that the kids understand what it is you are trying to teach."

"Smart girl – but just wait until you run out of methods!"

"Then what do you do?"

"Listen, sweetie – every good teacher knows how to tap dance."

"Tap dance!"

"That's right – tap dance. Remember I said you had to keep it interesting. Well, if the message doesn't get across, at least make the show entertaining. Do SOMETHING – tap dance, tell a joke, stand on your head – but don't lose the audience!"Annie got a big kick out of that one.

Sue is headed down the stairs, ready for undoubtedly another interesting day at the Ira Hayes Veteran's Administration Hospital. She looks great with her new shorter hairstyle, all fluffed up on one side. Half way down the stairs she is passed by Junior who is running late for school.

"Look out Mom – I don't want to miss the bus! Bye! Love you!"

Sue gives the "moving freight train" plenty of room as he bounds out the front door and sprints down to the corner. Other neighborhood doors are slamming at the same time and a mass of "America's future" run to the bus stop. They all make it in time just as the school bus pulls up; and one might suppose America will make it as well.

"You look charming today," Don says as he hands Sue a fresh hot cup of coffee with a little milk – just the way she likes it.

"Why thank you, dearest." Sue takes a welcomed sip. "And what's in store for you this fine day?"

"Well, funny you should ask, but I have right here in my pocket…" Don pats his right pants pocket. "…a very highly-classified, top secret phone number, hermetically sealed in a plastic envelope, and known *only* by only the President, the CIA, and me!"

"And whose phone number, pray tell, might that be?"

"Honestly, Hon, if I told you I would have to shoot you! It's that confidential. But, I will tell you this. It has a lot to do with the Santa business." Don winks at Sue and pats his pocket again.

"Good luck, Don," Sue says. "And please don't end up in jail again!"

"How did you know that I ended up …"

"Don't ask! Don't tell! Just be careful, okay?"

"Yes, Dear, I will." Don slinks back to the counter for the two cereal bowls like a hen-pecked husband, which he isn't. It's just for another laugh, and it works. Sue chuckles as he hands her a bowl.

"Actually, I do have the phone number for the agent who places the mall Santas."

"That's great, Don. Are you calling him today?" Sue eats a little cereal.

"Sure am – just as soon as ten o'clock rolls around."

"That's great, Don. Keep me posted, will you?" Another bite of cereal and a quick gulp of coffee and Sue's putting on her hat and coat. "Have a great day, Hon, and good luck again."

"Sue, you've hardly eaten anything!"

"Got to go, Don. Father Zoltan over at St. Ignatz got me a great deal on a new BINGO ball machine. See you later…Oh Don, you don't know any one who needs a liver transplant, do you?"

"A what? A LIVER transplant! No – why do you ask?"

"Oh nothing important. Just something Father Zoltan was asking me about. Bye. Love you." Sue's out the door and Don is still standing there with a confused look on his face.

Liver transplant?

63

Sam Robinson is just finishing up his ritual mid-morning tea. He dabs his lips with a warmed lilac-scented linen napkin made from Egyptian cotton. His tea, a custom blend of Earl Grey and Moroccan mint specially prepared for him by Harrods of London and shipped overnight should he ever run out. The tea is served in a fine, hand-painted, gold-banded, china cup, circa 1890's, made by Royal Doulton, and is accompanied by an antique, highly-polished silver spoon. The ornate French-provincial phone on his Louis IVX desk pleasantly rings – not like the Radio Shack phone on your desk blaring away and interrupting everything to alert you that you have a call from a bank wanting "not to sell you anything," but to make you aware of a special program so you can earn points to cash in at Disney World, (perhaps a free refill of the soda of your choice – now *that's* worth listening to!). No, No, not that ring, but a pleasant tinkling as a subtle reminder that a desperate soul out there values your leadership and needs your expertise on an important subject.

"Sam Robinson here. To whom am I speaking?"

"Good morning, Mr. Robinson. My name is Don Kaminski. I was given your number by Buddy Holly, the elf at the mall. He said I should give you a call about the Santa organization you supervise and how I might be able to work as a Santa."

"Good morning, Mr. Kaminski. Buddy the Elf is one of our finest Santa's helpers and a stellar member here at the Amalgamated Society of Santas. If Buddy recommends you, that means you have a great-looking Santa beard and well, we'll just have to do all we can to set up an interview."

"Gee, that's great, Mr. Robinson. I really appreciate this."

"Please, call me Sam."

"Okay, Sam, and please call me Don."

"Great, Don. Listen, I just happen to have some free time later today, say about four o'clock. Could you make it then?"

"Sure can. Where are you located?"

"Do you know where St. Ignatz the Martyr Orthodox Church is located down on Pulaski Street?...just down the street from the Polish-American Veterans.

"Yes, I do."

"We are to the right of St. Ignatz in the large green granite, federal-style building behind the tall wrought iron fence."

"Everyone knows where that is. I often wondered what that building was all about. It looks so majestic."

"It truly is an old, beautiful and historic building. It's named the John Brown Building because it used to be the headquarters for the John Brown Society for Unfit Mothers, but after they folded due to some unfortunate law suits, Johnson and Johnson took over the building and used it to store talcum powder during World War II. Some even believe the Johnson brothers developed and manufactured a secret talcum powder that would incapacitate a human, especially a soldier, for at least fifteen hours. Believe me, this is all documented in the Library of Congress and in the personal library of the Johnson family. Seems they sent a boxcar full of the special talc to Hitler just before D-Day. Who knows? Maybe that's why we eventually took the beach. Anyway, after Johnson and Johnson moved out, we picked up the place for a song and a dance. It took us quite some time to renovate the old gal – especially the interior, with all the built-in baby changing stations and about four tons of talcum powder spilled all over the place. Actually, you can still smell the slightest hint of talcum powder down in the cellar by the south wall; something to do with a minor explosion there towards the end of the war.

Well, that's about all I know about this place, Don. Sorry to bore you with all the details, but you'll see for yourself this truly is a beautifully restored federal-style building. We have our lodge meetings here for the Amalgamated Society of Santas. Hopefully you'll get to see the interior of our grand lodge hall."

"Sure thing, Sam. That's really interesting info about the building and its history. Can't wait to see you later at four. Don't worry. I'll be on time."

"Great, Don. Just come up to the entrance gate and ring the buzzer for entry. Looking forward to meeting you. See you at four."

"Four it is. So long, Sam."

CLICK

Don spends some time paying whatever bills he can pay and calling up companies to explain why he can't pay the others. This strike is becoming quite expensive and Don's beginning to think the teacher's union and the school system are in cahoots and have the strike time frame all figured out. *You do this and we'll do that. You say this and we'll say that. No matter how this works out, the teachers will get screwed in the end, just like the last strike five years ago when we had to give up some benefits and extra pay for extra responsibilities.*

The phone rings.

"Hello."

"Hi Don. It's Sam Robinson again. Sorry to bother you but I had some cancellations this afternoon and so if by chance you could make it, we could meet earlier this afternoon if you like?"

"I'll be right down, Sam. I can be there in about half an hour if that's okay with you?"

"That works out fine, Don. No hurry. See you when you get here."

CLICK

Don drives by St. Ignatz the Martyr on Pulaski St. and thinks he sees the Tsar of Russia himself in the back driveway to the rectory frantically waving his arms in directing the deliverymen who are emptying a large cargo van. The attached lift begins to lower onto the driveway what looks like two large BINGO ball machines. There are already three or four theatre-sized popcorn machines on the driveway along with a photo booth and three child-size mannequins dressed in summer shorts and matching tops.

This guy's into everything! Don thinks. *I'll bet one of those is Susan's.*

From down the street a heavy steel door comes crashing open and someone is pushed out onto the parking lot of the Polish-American Veterans Hall. Polka music blares out onto the street as someone yells, "And stay the fuck out of here you Slovak piece of shit!"

"Fuck you, you dumb Polack bastard!" comes the reply from the parking lot. "I've been thrown outta better places than this!" The door slams shut and Don sees the reveler swaying to his car while fumbling for his keys. Even though he's a block away, Don swears he can smell beer!

Kind of early to party, isn't it? And on a Tuesday? Must be some sort of retirement party or celebration of some sort. Maybe some poor Polish martyr like St. Ignatz made it to sainthood! Actually, I think St. Ignatz was Russian, Don ponders.

Oh well, maybe someone's getting married this weekend and they're starting early. Hell, he might be the lucky groom!

Don parks the Volvo, careful not to scuff up the tires and locks the doors. Up close, the green granite of the ASS Mansion is quite stately.

Oh, that's right – They don't call it that!

He approaches the tall wrought-iron gate and notices the security buzzer along with camera.

Probably being watched by a bunch of deranged elves!

BUZZ...CLICK.

"Come on in, Don. The gate will close itself," Don hears over a speaker hidden somewhere.

CLICK

As he walks up to the entrance, Don notices a set of large ornately hammered-silver doors that have to be over ten feet high. Don studies the intricate artwork and is amazed by the dazzling beauty of all the different designs of sparkling snowflakes on both doors. This brings a wide grin to his face on seeing such a vast display of Christmas fantasy that he misses the buzz to enter.

BUZZ...CLICK

"Nice doors, aren't they, Don? I love them too," says the voice. "Just push open the right door, Don, and come on in. My office is just inside to the right."

BUZZ...CLICK

66

For such a cold afternoon, with overcast skies, Patriarch Zoltan Shimko has worked up a sweat in directing the unloading of the cargo van. The back yard of the rectory looked like a Sears "scratch and dent" store with the wild assortment of fryers, cookers, candy and soda dispensers, and machines of all types including three of the latest electronic slot machines hidden under a tarp, not to mention the five large cases of fake Gucci handbags with only one "c".

"Don't let BINGO machines fall off lift! Careful! *Boshe moi! Oui*, vatch out! Be careful! Be careful!" The Patriarch is frantic now that his profit margin may be reduced by a careless accident.

The two BINGO ball machines juke left and then right as the truck lift jerks downward with squeaks and squeals that indicate a good squirt of WD40 or a nice glob of white lithium grease is in order.

"*Oui, Boshe moi! Boshe moi!* Vatch out vat you're doink!"

One of the altar boys runs over with an ornate silver tray carrying a tall crystal glass of something that looks like water but in fact is vodka, the imported and very expensive kind, "Jewel of Russia Classic Vodka," at $44.99 a liter. Bee Bee's Cash and Carry doesn't carry this brand of vodka and you won't find it anywhere near the Fat Bastard shelf, so don't even look.

"Your Excellency," the altar boy empties the last of the vodka into a chilled glass and serves up the cool drink to the Patriarch. He gulps it down in a flash and returns the empty glass.

The second altar boy is rapidly going up and down each row of "wery waluable merchandise," as Zoltan calls it, with the incense burner and is incensing and chanting a blessing for all the "wery waluable merchandise." The two men on the truck stop to watch the holy rite and are taken aback by the ritual.

"Vat! Vat are you vating for, the second coming? Go boys, go!" the Patriarch calls out. "Get last of *boychick* dummies off truck! That heathen Bee Bee needs these dummies to show off his new line of slightly-used clothes I sold to him last time." The Patriarch sneezes several times as a waft of incense curls just under his nose. He turns toward the altar boy with the incense.

"Enough, Dimitri! Enough, *dupah!* Save some for the high holidays!" *Dumb peasant!* "Both of you," the Patriarch points over to the black limo, "vashing the car now, please." And off they go, back into the vestry to return the incense burner and the silver tray, while carefully taking turns tilting the glass back to eek out any remaining drops of vodka.

"Don't worry, Kolya. There's a whole bottle opened under the sink!" They both laugh and rush off in a cloud of incense.

"Okay, boys. Dat's it. Off you go for another load," Zoltan orders. "Here is monies for gas and lunch. Eat someting. You need energy to do God's vork." The Patriarch peels off several twenties from a fat wad and hands them to one of the workers.

"Thanks, Faddah," says Stanley Piesecki, "We'll get right on it. Don't youse worry none," he says as he heads back to the truck. His partner, Willard Meekins and he bought this used Chevy step van about four years ago and have been doing a tremendous business hauling freight, mostly thanks to the Patriarch and all the BINGO ball machines he's been selling.

"Good boys. Good boys. See you ven you get back." Zoltan heads into the vestry when immediately there's a loud scuffle inside with the Patriarch yelling at the altar boys in Russian with every other word sounding like a cuss word and most assuredly the word "vodka."

"What's all this shit about "doing God's work?" Meekins asks Piesecki.

"You got me there, Willard," says Stanley. "Say, do you think we can get lunch and enough gas to get this job done with a twenty?"

"Is that all that cheap bastard gave you is a twenty?"

"That's it pal. We gotta make do somehow." Piesecki secretly pockets the extra twenties.

"Well, how 'bouts we go over to Wallowich's Frog Pond and grab a couple o' beers and a hot sausage sandwich. Don't cost much to eat there. What do ya say?" says Meekins. "And besides I pulled a fast one on Father Zorro, here. I got a case of nice handbags hidden in the truck. Must be about twenty of 'em in the box. We can probably unload these at Fat Wangs for maybe five bucks apiece. That ought to pay for a whole bunch of lunches and gas."

"Willard, you always was the smart one. Let's go."

The vestry door swings open with a crash and the two altar boys appear to be thrown out onto the lawn, complete with white vestments, buckets and sponges. Inside – more cussing in Russian and definitely the word "vodka."

67

Don Kaminski steps into the lavish foyer of the "ASS Palace." *Oh right! I forgot. We don't call it that!* He is struck by the beauty and grandeur of the décor. The eye-pleasing color scheme of the tall mint green walls with white and gold trim along with the highly polished dark oak floors enhances the beautiful Hapsburg furnishings, floral paintings, and Italian marble statues carefully placed throughout the hall.

I wish Susan and the gang could see this. It's just breath taking.

He half expects the Empress, Maria Theresa herself, to come waltzing around the marble pillars at any moment. Don feels the plush Armenian carpet below his feet and checks out the ceiling and sees a huge crystal chandelier that must weigh about three hundred pounds. *This has to be a Tiffany. It sparkles too much not to be.*

"Right this way, Mr. Kaminski," from a valet complete with white beard, white serving jacket and white gloves. "I'll take your coat for you, sir."

Don slips off his coat and scarf and hands them to Jeeves, or whatever his name is, with a "Thank you."

"Right this way, sir." Jeeves leads the way to the beautiful carved oak door on the right.

"Mr. Robinson is waiting for you inside, sir." Jeeves knocks twice then opens the door all the way and announces, "Mr. Kaminski to see you, sir."

"Fine. Fine. Show him in Clement," from Robinson. Don takes a step inside the room and immediately notices it is more ornate and beautiful than the grand hall. He can't help but look all around and inspect the majesty of it all.

"That will be all, Clement," says Robinson…"Oh, Clement, would you please bring us some tea?" He turns to Don. "You do drink tea, Don, you not?"

"Why yes, I do. Thank you very much. That would be grand." Don offers his hand to Robinson as Jeeves exits for the tea and hopefully a tasty little snack to go with it.

"I'm so happy to finally meet you, Mr. Robinson…"

"Please. Please. Remember? 'Sam' and 'Don'"

"Right you are, Sam." They shake hands cordially.

"Please have a seat, Don." Robinson gestures to the French-Provincial style coffee table in front of his desk with four Queen Anne styled chairs. "Come join me and we will chat a while."

Don and Sam make themselves comfortable which isn't hard to do in this surrounding. Another gorgeous room decked out in a peach and tan color scheme with red and green trim that blend well together. Don notices the oil paintings of at least eight or ten different Santas hung throughout the room in ornate gold and silver frames. *This must be 'ASS Headquarters,'* he thinks. *A guy probably could get a lot of 'ASS' in here. This Robinson dude looks like he lives the life of Hugh Heffner.* Don does another quick once-around. *This place is probably NICER than the Playboy mansion.*

Sam Robinson is dressed in a burgundy suede smoking jacket on top of a satiny Armani cotton shirt open at the collar (People who know Robinson often hear him say buys a lot of his clothing from some orthodox priest, of all people, from down the block at St. Ignatz the Martyr). Robinson is about the same age as Don, has dark brown hair (all of it is his with a very professional, and no doubt very costly, dye job), nice skin, manicured nails, lean – no fat on him at all, blue eyes and clean shaven – no Santa beard. He's a little on the short side but overall he's quite handsome and has an award-winning smile – just like Hugh Heffner.

"Don," Sam begins. "Buddy was right in sending you to me. You have a great Santa beard and a wonderful smile. Don't worry that your eyes are brown and not blue. The kids will still think that you are Santa."

"Why, thank you, Sam. That's kind of you to say," Don replies. "I believe I mentioned to you over the phone that I got hooked up with the wrong Santa outfit…"

"That's history, Don," Robinson cuts him off with a wave of the hand. "We're going to change all that this evening and you're going to become an active member of the Amalgamated Society of Santas. By the way, Don, I don't need to explain to you why we do NOT use the acronym, do I?"

"No, Sam. No. I get it." *We don't call it that!*

"Right. Right. We probably should have thought about that years ago when we first began the organization but after all these years, it seems a bit late now to change our name. Don't you agree?"

"Probably so, Sam. Probably so. *Although I would!*

Jeeves knocks twice and enters then room with a sterling silver tea set complete with an assortment of imported Italian cookies and sets it down gingerly on the coffee table. "Will that be all, sir?"

Yes, Clement. Thank you."

"Your very welcome, sir." Jeeves exits, stage left.

"Help yourself, Don."

There's a fire in the fireplace; just enough to keep the room comfortable, not the kind that drives you into the next room or down the cellar just to cool off. Sam pours tea for both and offers Don: lemon, cream, sugar, cookies, "Or perhaps you'd like something stronger?"

"Oh no, Sam," Don says. "I hardly ever drink."

"Good answer, Don. This is a test. If you're going to be one of our Santas, you have to watch your drinking; and certainly NO DRINKING AT ALL on the days you wear 'the suit'!"

"The suit?"

"The Santa suit, Don. The Santa suit!"

"Oh, yes – of course, the SANTA suit. No drinking in the Santa suit – of course. Well you won't have to worry about that, Sam. Not one bit."

"Good. Good, Don. Our Santas take an oath that they will not drink the day they are performing. One young Santa thought he could get away with breaking his oath to the association and he got a big surprise waiting for him when he returned to the lodge hall."

"What was that, Sam?"

"First he was formally accused of drinking in front of his lodge brothers and he did not deny the accusation. Next, in front of everyone, he was stripped of his Santa suit and all the trimmings: belt, hat, gloves, boots, were all taken away from him. He stood there in just his red Santa underwear, in front of everyone in the grand lodge hall. It was such a disgrace!"

Sounds like the old black and white TV show with Chuck Connors, "Branded." I wonder if they broke his sword as well?

Sam leans over closer to Don with a puzzled look on his face.

"Did I tell you we use real fur-lined Santa boots made in Texas and not those fake boot tops you see all the other Santas wear?"

"I noticed that at the mall the other day. You guys are a class act, that's for sure."

"More than a 'class act,' Don; much more than a 'class act.' We are a brotherhood – a brotherhood of Santas, and we take an oath to uphold the truths we so genuinely believe in."

Yeah, like "truth, justice, and the American way," Don thinks.

"What are you thinking, Don?"

"I was just thinking how *super* your group really is – and every *man* in it."

"That's right, Don. We really are SUPER MEN. But not just when we wear the 'suit' – all the time! Remember, we take an oath."

"I got it – an oath!"..."Say, Sam. I know this might seem kind of crazy and all, but, ah, do you have to pay anything to join the society? I mean, is there an initiation fee or any annual dues or such to plan for? I was just curious since you are such an elite group."

"Good heavens NO Don. The answer is NO! – no dues, no fees, EVER. As I said, we are a brotherhood of Santas. We take an oath to do the right thing and to watch out for one another. We are all believers here, Don. It's vitally important that you understand this from the very beginning. Got it?"

"Sure. Sure. You take an oath. You are a brotherhood of Santas, and you are all believers. Nothing hard to understand about that...except, what is it exactly that you believe in?" Don asks.

"I just told you, Don. We believe in doing the right thing and we support one another. That's it! That's all! There is no mystery here. We are not a political-action group. We do not concern ourselves with *anything* outside of the Santa business. We are a brotherhood of Santas doing what we do best – making children happy."

"I get it," Don says. *Truth, justice, and the American Santa way!*

"Great, Don – I want YOU to be part of our brotherhood if you would like that."

"Sure I would, Sam. Sounds like a great organization to belong to. Sure – count me in. What do I have to do?"

"Simple, Don." Robinson reaches over and pulls a pink file folder from the top of his desk and opens it.

Pink must be for the new guys – the neophytes, Don thinks. *I'll bet there are red files for the fully-initiated Santas.*

Robinson hands Kaminski a one-sided form.

"Don, we need to do a simple background check and so we need some basic information. Therefore, you need to complete this form today before you leave." He hands Don the form. "Don't worry, Don. Our people can do a full check in a matter of hours and if you are approved, you can be initiated this evening in our grand lodge hall. If you think what you've seen so far is impressive, wait until you see the grand lodge hall – it's simply majestic!"

Don takes the form and reaches in his front shirt pocket for a pen. "I'll fill this in right now if that's okay, Sam?"

"Absolutely." Sam reaches towards the desk again and grabs an ornate granite clipboard and hands it to Don. "Here, use this. It will make life easier." He smiles and hands Don the clipboard.

"While you're doing that I'd like to ask you a few questions if you don't mind."

"Go ahead," says Don as he begins the form. *Not much to answer here. Just some very basic information: name, address, phone number, etc.*

"Let's see now…Kaminski – that has to be Polish, right?"

"Right you are, Sam. My father emigrated from Poland and met my mother in the United States – Hoboken, New Jersey as a matter of fact. They were both in line to buy sweets at Carlo's Bakery on Washington Street when my mother bent over to look in the display case and knocked the *cannolis* right out of my father's hand. That was the beginning of a life-long love affair and to this day they still go to Carlo's to buy *cannolis*."

Sam laughs as he envisions the story in his mind. "That's funny, Don. That's a great story." He pauses just enough to change his expression back to serious. "So your parents raised you to be a good Catholic boy, right?"

"Catholic! Oh no, Sam. We're not Catholic." Don laughs at the idea of his parents, especially his father with his *yarmulke* sitting cock-eyed on his head, raising him Catholic. "We're not Catholic, Sam, we're Jewish."

CRASH!

The Queen Anne cup, or Louis IVX mug, or whatever the hell it is comes crashing down on the French-Provincial coffee table, breaks into smithereens and hot tea splatters all over the table, Don's pants, the "ASS" form, and the Armenian carpet.

Sam Robinson stands up so quickly that Don sits dazed and motionless to trying to understand the situation.

Oh, oh – anti-Semite!

"**Jewish!** Oh No, Don, No, No, No! There is no such thing as a Jewish Santa! It's totally against what we believe in. You can not join our brotherhood if you are Jewish! It simply is not allowed! It is written in our by-laws and in our oath. We do not allow Jews to become part of our association! We take an oath and we take it very seriously."

Donald Kaminski, backed by all his Jewish heritage chock-filled with a history of enslavement, mistreatment, and suffering; in honor of Hiram and Saul Kaminski, Camp Slivovitz in Lithuania, Simon Wiesenthal, Moshe Dayan, and even the Little Sisters of the Poor, stands up and towers over this maggot of a man, Sam Robinson, and begins to unleash a little bit of kosher "brotherhood."

"Why you little hypocrite! 'Do the right thing!' 'Brotherhood of Santas!' 'Making children happy!' Which children? – the ARIAN children? Is that part of the oath, Herr Robinson? – making the ARIAN children happy? Is *fuck the Jews* part of the oath, Herr Robinson? – or is it *death to the Jews*? Is that it, you little unworthy, prejudice, hypocrite bastard!"

Don turns to exit the room as he rips the "ASS" information sheet off of the granite clipboard and tears it up flinging the pieces across the floor; and with one mighty arm-fling the clipboard goes flying across the room towards Robinson's anti-Semitic head. Sam ducks the clipboard as it narrowly misses his right ear and crashes to the rear of the room as Robinson bends down and frantically begins pushing a buzzer hidden below the coffee table.

"Mr. Kaminski, I am truly sorry if I have offended you in any way, but I am going to have to ask you to leave this room and building immediately, sir." Robinson quickly moves back behind his desk and away from Don.

"If you do not leave right now I will be forced to call the authorities! Please, Mr. Kaminski, leave now!" Robinson points to the door but ready to duck should another Jewish missile come his way.

"The authorities? And who might *they* be, Herr Robinson? – the Gestapo? the S.S.? the camp commandant?"

Robinson is frantic now hoping that the silent alarm went off to alert Clement. Sam turns abruptly and heads for the door and turns back for a parting shot but he's so damn pissed-off he can hardly think of anything to say. But when he does, he lets Robinson have it.

"Listen, you little wimp! You haven't heard the last of this, my Nazi friend. You'll soon be hearing from my attorneys, Abramowitz, Abramowitz and Laganelli!" Don remembered this group from Mimo, Jr. "And one more thing, Herr Robinson, I've got the Little Sisters of the Poor on my side, you asshole!"

Little Sisters of the Poor?

Don exits the "Arians only" room and bumps into Clement who has his scarf and coat. He swiftly grabs for the items and tears them away from the valet.

"Give me those, Jeeves, Himmler, Gehrig or whatever the fuck your Nazi-assed name is!" Clement lets loose of the garments and quickly heads for the front doors to open them before Don tears them off the hinges.

"Thank you, you Nazi Santa mother-fucker," Don says to Clement as he heads down the front walk.

BUZZ…CLICK

The front gate swings open.

Don unlocks the Volvo and guns it down the street.

The drunk down the block is still fumbling for his keys and yelling at the Polish Am-vets building, "Dumb stupid Polacks!"

"Christ! I need a drink!" Don says out loud.

Sam Robinson sits down at his desk, shaken a bit, and reaches for a black colored file folder.

Don's driving God knows where when he hears, "Call from…Max Kaminski," over his car radio speakers. He pushes a button on his built-in Sirius radio he had specially installed last year, the one with the G.P.S. and phone package, and he speaks towards the built-in speaker.

"Hello, Pop."

"Is this my favorite son?"

"You got that right. Even though you know damn right well I'm your *only* son. What gives? Everything okay?"

"Everything is fine – fine. Can't I call you up to say 'Hello' and 'How the hell are you?' without something being wrong?"

"Sure, Pop. Sure. I'm sorry, I really am, but right now I'm madder than a wet hen! – those Nazi bastards!"

"Nazi bastards? Son, that was years ago!"

"No, Pop. Listen. Are you wearing your *yarmulke* by any chance?"

"Sure, I'm sitting *shiva*, but what's that got to do with anything?"

"Sitting *Shiva?* Who died?" Don pulls over to the side of the road in a panic.

"Moses died."

"Moses? Moses who?"

"Moses – Moses! – your Aunt Sadie's cat on your mother's side. Moses. You remember Moses? You used to play with him all the time when you were a kid."

"Pop, Aunt Sadie's had about fifteen different cats by now, all named Moses! I really don't think *this* Moses is the one I played with as a kid."

"Okay, son. You're probably right. I get things all mixed up as it is. Anyway, Moses, whatever number he was, died this morning. She called about three o'clock to tell us. Woke me and your mother up to tell us the dumb cat died! She was crying her eyes out which really upset your mother, I'll tell you."

"So how's Mom now?"

"Well, she got up and got dressed right after the phone call and as we speak she's over at Sadie's house in Brooklyn."

"Brooklyn?"

"Brooklyn! She took a cab."

"A cab? – all the way to Brooklyn!"

"A cab! You know how your mother gets. There's no talking to her once she gets something in that head of hers."

"Is Mom okay? Have you heard from her?"

"She's fine. They're both fine. She called about ten minutes ago. She and Sadie are going to Myer's Puss and Boots store to buy a new Moses, if they have one in black. Moses has to be black you know – maybe with white feet, but mostly black. She said not to worry, she'll call later, and Sadie asked me to sit *shiva*, since they wouldn't have time because they had other chores to do before they get back to the city. You know: shop, lunch, visit with relatives to tell them about poor Moses, shop, dinner, *et cetera*." Max pauses to think a bit. "You know for a dead cat, I think you only have to sit *shiva* for two days and not a whole week like for humans; but I'm not so sure about that. Maybe I'll call the Rabbi up on that one." Max pauses again and then says excitedly, "Say, did you know Rabbi Peckerman got off on the Gucci handbag thing and the hot liver transplants? He got off clean as a whistle. He had a good lawyer – that's why. A good lawyer does the trick every time! Remember that, son. Always have a good lawyer in your back pocket."

"I'll remember that, Pop. Say, I'm glad you brought that up. Who is Rabbi Peckerman's attorney? Do you know?"

"Of course I know! Everybody knows – Abramowitz, Abramowitz and Laganelli, who else! They have offices all over the United States: New York, San Francisco, Washington, DC, Marcus Hook, Pennsylvania – you name the place – they're there!"

"Right. I should have known – Abramowitz, Abramowitz and Laganelli. 'Who else' for sure. Why am I not surprised?" *Marcus Hook, Pennsylvania? Where the hell is that?*

"So how come you're sitting *shiva*?" Don asks.

"Why not? I already had my *yarmulke* on from breakfast. I ate a soft-boiled egg, one kipper, a piece of rye bread with grape jelly and black coffee – one cup because of my stomach…"

"It's Tuesday, Pop. I know what you eat for breakfast on Tuesdays – and every other day of the week for that matter."

"Right, son. You know I have been following the same diet for over forty-five years now – you know, cereal every other day. I really like that Kashi. Your mother, on the other hand – I mean there's no rhyme or reason as to how she eats and that's why she always has stomach troubles and needs to see Dr. Finklestein every other week. We spend a small fortune because she doesn't know how to eat right! Not like me, anyways. And then, every other day, I eat my soft-boiled egg and one kipper for breakfast and look at me – a picture of health, right? Dr. Finklestein says I'm fit as a fiddle and he ought to know. He's been our doctor since we were married in Hoboken and he was trained in the old country – not like these Indian doctors you see today running all over the place. You can't understand half of them!"

"Right. God bless you, Pop."

"And really I had nothing else to do. I already read the newspaper from front to back. Lies and bullshit – all of it – and so I'm sitting *shiva* for the dumb cat, Moses. My good friend, something Patel. What the hell is his first name? Vishtu or Vixen or Nixon – no, not Nixon, but something like that. He owns the Dunkin' Donuts near me…"

"Pop, the Patels own practically every Dunkin' Donuts and every Seven-Eleven store in the United States."

"Maybe so, but he made a special trip to come by the house and dropped off some Old Fashioned donuts. I have no idea what-so-ever how he found out Moses the cat died! It's a real mystery, believe me when I tell you that. He said he would come back later to sit *shiva* with me and he isn't even a Jew! Now go figure! Now that's something, isn't it?"

"Sure is, Pop"…*Old Fashioned donuts? Why does that sound familiar?*

"Say, listen, Pop, I might need some legal help. Do you personally recommend the Rabbi's lawyers?"

"Without question, son. They are the best! And you want Abramowitz, the second one – Junior – the son. He's the best! The old man isn't bad mind you, after all he's the one who trained Junior, but Abramowitz, Junior is the one you want. He's the chosen one! Never lost a case yet and he's had some doozies: Detroit vs. General Motors, Dombrowski vs. Weight Watchers, Shimko vs. Gucci, Ben vs. Jerry, and so on and so forth. Won every one of them, he did – perfect record! Stay away from Laganelli, though. He's only there to keep an eye on Abramowitz and Abramowitz. That's the word on the street. Story is the mob put Laganelli there to make sure things were on the 'up and up' and went the way the mob wanted. I'm not even sure he has a law degree! He's got a lot of friends in high places, if you know what I mean. A.A.&L. do all the mob work in court and that's why the mob always comes out on top. But listen, son, you aren't in any trouble with the Nazis are you? You mentioned the Nazis."

"No, Pop. Nothing like that. I do think I have a good case against a card-carrying ant-Semitic group of Santa Clauses though."

"Santa Clauses? – anti-Semite Santa Clauses? Sure, the Nazis were anti-Semites. You know all about that. I taught you well enough about them, but I had no idea that there was a group of anti-Semite Santa Clauses! *Meshugana!*"

"Listen, Pop – I'll call you later and explain the whole thing when I have more time. Right now I have to go"

"You're absolutely sure you're not in any trouble? Want me to make a couple of calls? Maybe you should talk to Laganelli? No – on second thought stick with Abramowitz, Junior. You do that and you're in good hands – just like Allstate."

"Thanks for the advice, Pop. You go ahead and sit *shiva* and eat Old Fashioned donuts and I'll give Abramowitz, Junior a call. I'll give you a call later – I promise."

"Okay, son. If you're sure."

"I'm sure, Pop. Say hello to Mom and Aunt Sadie for me."

"Will do, son. My best to all of you. So long. I love you."

"So long, Pop. I love you too."

CLICK

Late Tuesday evening the Chicago's winter temperature had plummeted to where it should be this time of year, and maybe even a little farther down the thermometer. Jimmy D. Mays wakes up with more aches and pains than any man has a right to.

"Chrise, it's col' in here! An' feels like some som-bitch done fucked wid all Jimmy D. bones, das for sure." He rubs his arthritic shoulders and the back of his sore head as he tries to rise up from his cardboard bed but flops back down with a groan.

"Oh Lawd. Please helps Jimmy D. gets up. Please Lawd – if you gots any feelin's for the peoples who need yo' help – please help Jimmy D. up off dis floor widout breakin' my ass or somepin' – Please!"

Jimmy tries real slow this time to roll over in the proper position to get up off the floor. Next he puts his arms out to brace himself and scoots up a knee. He's on both knees now and struggles to plant a foot firmly on the floor. He reaches for the Santa chair and is pulling himself up while at the same time he brings his right leg up and pushes as hard as he can to lift his little, black Santa frame to a full upright position.

"Made it, Lawd – made it! Thanks be to Chrise an' Holy Jesus." Miraculously, as if the Lord above personally heard Jimmy's plea for help, his aches and pains appear to instantly vanish and it feels pretty darn good. He stands erect and is perfectly still knowing that at any second now all his pain will return with a vengeance and cripple him down to the floor. He waits and braces himself for the hit. Nothing! Jimmy D. is shocked and is genuinely most thankful. He looks down on the floor and sees there's a tiny bit of Early Times left in the bottle; so he reaches for it and brings it to his lips.

"Here's to ya, Jesus, and many mores." And down the last drops go. Down – down – down – making Jimmy, "even mo' better, but it still col'er 'an shit in here!"

"Don, what's wrong?" Sue says. "Something's up. What is it? You've done nothing but mope around the house since I got home. You've hardly said one word to me or the children. What's wrong, Don?" Sue faces Don squarely and puts her hand softly on his shoulder.

"Ah, Susan," (he hardly ever calls her 'Susan'). "Tell you what," he smiles and grabs hold of her shoulders. "You and the kids go ahead and eat. There's something I have to do and I have to do it now." Don turns to grab his coat and scarf from the rack in the pantry and turns back to face Sue.

He looks normal, she thinks. "Are you in any trouble?"

"Don't worry, Susan. I'm not in any trouble," he chuckles. "I'm not going out to do something stupid like rob a bank or something." *Maybe a Dunkin' Donuts or a Seven-Eleven on the way home, but nothing STUPID like a bank!* "I just need to get out for an hour or so to sort some things out in my mind. I'll be back soon. Keep my supper warm and tell the kids I'm fine."

"Don, are you sure?" Sue looks into his eyes for any hint as to what gives.

"I'm fine, Sue. Believe me, I'm fine." He gives her a peck on the cheek and heads out the back door.

Jimmy D. Mays is in good spirits and feeling mighty fine as he heads through the mall parking lot to the highway. His 'good luck' Santa suit looks better than ever on him as he wonders where he should go looking for some easy pickings and a hot dinner. He begins to sing:

"Here come Sanda Claus. Here come Sanda Claus. Right down Sanda Claus Lane. He gonna bring youse lots 'o presents iffin youse do da same. Ho, Ho, Hoes to all you peoples who gots da moneys to buy. Gives Jimmy a ten and he'll be yo' frien'. And tha's no big-ass lie." Jimmy stops to light up a Camel.

After circling the neighborhood several times – just driving – somewhere – anywhere – and faster now to try and outrun the hurt – and feeling like the Lone Ranger with a pounding headache, Don now knows exactly where he's headed.

"Ha, ha, ha," *NO!* – "Ho, Ho, Ho!" he laughs like a deranged Santa and checks his playful demented look in the rearview mirror. "To the ASS Lodge! That's where! Now dash away, dash away, dash away all!"

Don makes a hard right to correct his new target course. He swears he can hear sleigh bells.

"I'm going to the ASS Lodge and I'm going to surprise all the ASS-HOLES! That's what!"

He slows down a bit when he realizes he's a bit over the speed limit. No one is going to spoil his fun now. He's on a mission. "No coffee! No Dunkin' Donuts! And no free, complementary Old Fashioned donuts!" He turns left at the corner to take a short cut that saves him all of two minutes.

"On Comet, on Cupid, on Donder…" *And yes, kids, it is Donder in the original version – not Donner. Guess old Gene Autry didn't know that one!*

"I'm going to crash that secret Santa society tonight and blow the lid on all those white bearded anti-Semites – especially their leader, Herr Robinson, the head Nazi!" Don looks at himself in the rearview mirror again and sees "Dr. Dementia!" The tires squeal in a hard right turn on Pulaski Street. He's almost there and it's dark out. "Perfect!"

After a couple of hours of bumming rides, smokes, and panhandling, and not a whole lot to show for it, Jimmy D. Mays hits pay dirt. On the suggestion of the driver of the Hanson Brothers trash truck, good old Jerome something or other, his last ride, Jimmy D. ends up at Wallowich's Frog Pond, a sleazy bar in the same neglected stripmall where Bee Bee's Cash and Carry is located. The parking lot is full of Hanson Brothers trash trucks (Thank God it isn't summer!) At least a dozen drivers and helpers are inside because they "need to unwind" on their way home after a "hard day's work," as they put it. Some of them are unwound half way to oblivion already and probably won't make it back to the parking lot, let alone home.

Anyway, they are all enamored with Jimmy D. all dressed up in his Santa suit and they have him elevated up on a bar stool, thanks to two telephone books, and are feeding him cold beer, spicy shrimp, plenty of whiskey. Not Crown Royal, mind you, but, *If Seagram's Seven ain't good enough for the little nigger Santa, he can get the fuck out!* – plenty of mozzarella sticks and French fries follow – a wino's smorgasbord, for sure! Oh, yes, and, when the nostalgia hits the Hanson trash men, a fiver comes floating down the bar in between toasts, "To our own little trash man Santa!"

"Here's to the little black Santa!"

"Here's looking at you, nigger!"

"HEY! Watch your mouth!"

Jimmy D. is eating it up: the toasts, the chow, and the fivers. He hasn't counted yet, but he figures he's up to about forty dollars, and that ain't hay! And he's washing it down with plenty of cold beer and Seagram's.

The Volvo eases over to the curb on a quiet side street. The engine is already off and the door is shut without a sound. *Only two blocks from the ASS Lodge.* It's dark out. The streets are quiet, and Don can't help but notice there are a number of parked cars on all the streets nearest "Nazi Santa Central." He spots decals repeated on many of the cars that read, "Have You Got Toys?" and "NP".

So, Herr Robinson; you weren't kidding when you said I could be initiated this evening, were you? Don's not sure, but he thinks the two men about a block ahead of him have natural Santa beards. He can't tell for sure because the wind has picked up this evening and anyone out tonight is bundled up from head to toe – except Don, that is. He didn't dress as warmly as he should have and right now is freezing his ass off. He doesn't feel it though; he's so damn pissed off and besides, he's on a mission.

Let's just see what the bearded Nazis are up to, shall we? Don quickens his pace and catches up to the Santas headed for the ASS Lodge. He steps up along side them and keeps pace. "Hi, fellas. This sure is exciting isn't it?"

Quick side glances and Don's white beard put the Santas at ease as they continue to the wrought iron gate.

"You must be a neophyte. Are you ready to be initiated?" asks one of the Santas.

"Why sure I am. I'm as ready as I'll ever be!" Don says excitedly. "This is going to be one of the best days of my life!"

"That's the attitude, young man. You'll do fine in our brotherhood as long as you think like that."

"Exactly!" says the other Santa. "We need more men like you to round out the association and counter act some of the older, less jolly Santas who just hang around and complain about kids and all the medications they're on."

"And you're right about that, Santa Christopher. I really don't know why they don't take advantage of our retirement package? We all have it as a benefit. I mean right now instead of putting up with all this foul weather, they could be rocking comfortable on that large porch at the Home for Retired Santas in Bangor, Maine. Right, Santa Christopher?"

"Exactly!" from Santa Christopher. "Have you seen the pictures of the retirement home that were posted on the bulletin board recently? This place is beautiful! Private rooms with bath for over a hundred and fifty Santas; gourmet dinners, lovely dining facilities, Santa library, free hot chocolate and two nearby golf courses – for free! What else could you ask for, Santa James?"

"Well, Santa Christopher, there are no women allowed in the facility at all. Perhaps a few broads once in a while might not be such a bad idea."

"Now, now, Santa James. Remember, we took an oath!" They both laugh as the gate swings open and all three walk up to the main doors where Jeeves is waiting for them.

"Evening, gentlemen. Good evening to you all."

"Evening, Clement," one of them says.

Jeeves opens up the large door to the right and gestures for the Santas to enter not noticing Don who has the same coat and scarf he had on earlier today.

Great! So far – so good. The two "made" Santas lead Don through the entry hall where he spots other Santas joyfully conversing to one another as they make their way over to a huge holiday display that wasn't there earlier today. It is simply breathtaking! Featuring a full-sized, stuffed Rudolph complete with lighted red nose and an antique red sleigh from the 1800's beautifully trimmed in green and red holly with silver-glittered bells and a gigantic red bag overflowing with wrapped packages, the display is backed by six white-flocked Blue Spruce pine trees which have to be over eight feet tall. Breathtaking! And "Here Comes Santa Claus" softly playing over the sound system. Don felt like a tourist in New York City for the first time; keeping his eyes straight ahead but wanting desperately to look high above to the tops of the skyscrapers.

Without hesitation the Santa parade wound around the last Blue Spruce and into a rather tiny, dimly-lit hallway which Don didn't even know existed. He went along with the flow and realized that it got quiet all of a sudden. The Santas knew the way all right. The silence seemed to be more out of reverence than anything else. They are all just about single file in the tiny hallway, and facing forward, moving quite slowly and not a sound is heard. Don was beginning to feel a little claustrophobic when the line begins to move a little quicker. Don passes through another door and now finds himself in a rather large locker room complete with benches and showers. The Santas all begin to chatter again and get loud with excitement as they each find and open their own full-sized locker and begin to shed their outer coats, gloves, winter boots, etc. Don checks out the brass nameplates on the locker doors: Matthew Christianson, Daniel Baker, Luke Miller, Christopher Goodman, Matthew Mitchell, Mark Krystopolski...*Krystopolski?*

Don looks around puzzled *And where the hell are we, anyway? Are we going to play volleyball? Take a swim lesson? Are we at the YMCA? YMCA?* He immediately thinks of the Village People, the gay, all-male recording group. *Oh, no!* Don thinks. *Don't tell me all these fuckers are gay! If these faggot Santas take their clothes off for the BIG initiation – I'm outta here!* He begins to sing in his head, *Don we now our GAY apparel. Fa la la, la la la, la la la...*That's when Don turns and casually checks to find the nearest exit.

He begins to weave through the Santa's towards the tiny hallway to exit the room. This isn't easy since most of the Santas don't require padding in their Santa suits. That's when he spots the multitude of robes hanging on heavy cast-iron hooks hung high along the far wall. *Christ! There must be a hundred of them!*

These were not ordinary robes for sure. They were not bathrobes or lounging robes. They were not robes for boxers or even the nice complimentary robes you got at one of the high-end casinos in Las Vegas or Tahoe. These were Santa robes. And they were not your run-of-the-mill Santa robes either. These robes were majestic! The first thing Don notices about the robes is that they are not red. They are a dark burgundy color, hinting on violet; and they are trimmed in metallic silver. He reaches out to touch one. They are made of a thick plush material that is gentle to the touch. They are full length, down-to-the-floor robes and are very full in width. The sleeves are huge and bellow down past were the hands would be. *Just like monk robes,* Don thinks. That's when he checks and sure enough there's a full sized hood which, by the size of it, must hang low over one's head to the point of completely shading the face. All of the robes are hung neatly on wooden pegs just below more nameplates above them indicating the Santa they belong to and they are lined up in alphabetical order.

One by one the Santas make their way over to the robes and begin to get dressed for the grand initiation. That's when things get quiet again.

"All novices to be initiated this evening will find their white robes at the end of the robbing area. Please select an empty un-named locker to store your coats in," comes bellowing over the sound system. Don spots half a dozen Santas heading over to the white robes a little nervous about the initiation.

I'd be damn nervous if I were in their shoes, or should I say robes.

"Initiates will line up at the end of the procession, please," another announcement.

Don hangs back behind a row of lockers and observes the quiet Santas lining up in their robes. He's right. Their hands are locked together in front of them inside the long flowing sleeves and their heads are bowed in silence and reverence. The new guys follow suit in their white and green trimmed robes. Everyone is perfectly still and faces the same direction.

"Lead off Brother Daniel. It is the hour," someone says.

A door opens and the entire assembly paces off down another long narrow and dark hallway. As the last "made" Santa enters the hallway, the "wannabes" follow in a single line. Don grabs one of the left-over robes and quickly follows at a safe distance. He's donning his "gay apparel" as he rushes down the hallway.

I guess Krystopolski couldn't make it. Probably found out HE's a Jew!

Don catches up to the end of the Santa parade and sees flickering lights up ahead. To a man, or actually, to a Santa, each participant in the parade of Santas is carrying a battery-powered candle in front of them, just visible, and sticking up from the folds of the robe helping to light the way to the ASS ritual.

Hmmmmmm. Must be high mass.

Next the Santas begin to chant as they process in a slow step into the abyss. Don listens to the almost silent chant.

"Ho, Ho, Hooooo," step, "Ho, Ho, Hooooo," step, "Ho, Ho, Hooooo," step...

What the fuck?

"Stop." They all stop and no more chanting – Dead silence.

BOOM! BOOM! BOOM! Three loud bangs on the outer door to the grand lodge hall and the door cracks open a bit so that the Inner Santa Guard can challenge the interference.

"Who dares knock on the chamber door?" from inside the grand lodge hall.

"Brothers of the Amalgamated Society of Santas with six neophyte Santas wish to enter," the first Santa in line bellows out.

"What is the password?" comes the challenge from inside.

"Balls on the tree!"

"Be still and meditate," comes the reply as the door closes.

After several minutes which seem like hours, the door opens again – all the way this time, and the Inner Santa Guard announces, "Enter brothers, and prepare for the initiation."

The line quickly moves forward into the light and the door is closed shut.

75

Lord, oh Lord, there goes Jimmy D. Mays trying to light up a Camel and walk a straight line through the stripmall parking lot over to Bee Bee's Cash and Carry. It ain't working, Jimmy. Your Camel isn't lit but you sure are!

"Here come Sanda Claus. Here come da Sanda. Righ' down Bee Bee's Lane." He staggers trying to pull his new silver Zippo lighter with "Hanson Brothers" etched on it and a color image of a trash truck. He can't seem to find the damn thing and begins to check his other Santa pockets. Meanwhile he's laughing at the situation and the Camel in his mouth is beginning to get soggy from all the saliva.

"Aha! Here you is!" He fishes out the lighter from his back pocket careful not to drop any of his new-found loot. Jimmy successfully opens the lighter but try as he may, he can't get the damn thing to work. "Come on, bitch! Shit!" It won't light. The cigarette completely falls apart in his mouth and drops down to the cement in a wet lump. "Tha's alright. Is alright. No big shit." He slowly puts the lighter away knowing full well he's a bit incapacitated and doesn't want to lose the lighter on the day he got it. His new friend Jerome gave it to him.

As cold as it is, Jimmy D. spots Bee Bee standing in the open doorway of the Cash and Carry, and laughing his ass off as he watches Jimmy try to walk a straight line.

"Hey, Jimmy D.! You need some help, buddy? You need a seeing-eye dog?" Bee Bee slaps his side and bends over laughing at that one.

"Fuck you, Bee Bees," Jimmy waves him off and begins to laugh at himself. "Jimmy D. been worse 'an this, tha's for sure." He staggers a little more closer to the store. "Jus' gives me a little more time an' Jimmy D. be there! You hears me, you dumb…whatever the fuck you is!"

After five minutes or so, Jimmy D. makes it to where Bee Bee stands and barrels into the store.

"Whoeeeee, Jimmy D. You smells like a spilt beer in a garbage can ain't been emptied in three months!" Bee Bee says as he lets the door close. "How long you been over the Frog Pond, Jimmy?"

Jimmy pulls out another big wad of cash and shows Bee Bee. "Long enoughs!"

He heads on down the liquor isle and doesn't bend over either for the bottom shelf. He spots what he's looking for. "Say, Bee Bee; how much is dis?" He holds up a fifth of Wild Turkey Kentucky bourbon – eighty proof.

"For you Jimmy, twenty bucks."

"I'll takes it and gimme four packs o' Camels, Bee Bee."

"You need matches, Jimmy?"

"Not no more, Bee Bee. I gots dis new fancy-ass lighter…" he stops to think about the wet Camel. "Hold on, Bee Bee. Hold on," he thinks a bit. "Yeah, Bee Bee – better gives Jimmy D. some matches." He marches off to the counter and throws down two twenties.

"More inheritance, Jimmy?"

"Nah, Bee Bee. Jus' some dirty monies from da trash guys over at da Frog Pond." He laughs thinking that's funny, *dirty money from the trash guys.*

76

Don finds his way in the dimly lit hallway to the large door leading to the grand lodge hall. He places his ear up to the crack of the door hoping to hear anything at all. He can't. The door is solid oak and fits snugly into the framing.

I can't just knock like I'm the local census taker or door-to-door salesman! 'AVON calling!' 'Fuller Brush man!' The door is probably locked anyway. And who knows how many Santa goons are just on the other side?

Don checks the door knowing full well it is locked. The handle turns freely and Don turns it ever so slowly all the way to the left. He gives it a little nudge and realizes he can enter the room any time he feels like it.

Now what? Do I actually open this door and just walk in like I was invited? Why not? 'Hi guys, Santa Joe sent me.' 'Balls on the tree' and all that! Ready or not, here I come! Here goes nothing.

Slowly now, Don eases the door open just inches. He puts one eye to the crack to survey the premises. He's in luck. The grand lodge hall is much larger than he had imagined. The inner area is surrounded by huge Italian marble columns that ring the center floor.

This looks like the insides of the Capitol Building in Washington!

Don opens the door even wider and looks at the backs of the robed Santas who are standing quite some distance from him. He hears more chanting but can't quite understand what is being said. Don covers his head with the large attached hood and enters the grand hall. Slowly and quietly he closes the door behind him. He spots a bin to the right of him containing all the discarded battery-powered candles. Carefully, Don turns and steps behind one of the columns.

The grand lodge hall is just that – grand! The walls and many columns in the hall, tower clear up to the second story where there's an evening winter sky painted on the entire ceiling complete with stars that electrically twinkle on and off. The effect is spellbinding. Don spends five minutes enjoying the ceiling and finds himself smiling like a kid at Disney World for the first time. The outer four walls are painted a pristine white with all sorts of holiday designs on them. Don sees gigantic crossed red and white candy canes that must be about six feet in length every ten feet or so. All around the room, about three feet above the candy canes, he sees a large garland of fresh green holly with strikingly bright red holly berries on the walls. Every so often there's a huge red satin bow tied to the holly with bellowing streamers that almost reach the floor. The chanting stops and Don's attention is drawn to the center of the room which he is having trouble seeing due to the multitude of Santas. The base of the Corinthian column Don is hiding behind sits high up on a marble base about two feet from the floor and so he easily steps up to view the proceedings.

The center of the grand hall is magnificent. Everyone is standing except for the Grand Exalted Santa, Sam Robinson himself, dressed in an elaborate crimson robe outlined in white ermine fur. Robinson is seated on an elevated gold throne located at the north end of the hall.

I'll bet the Pope doesn't know his chair is missing!

Behind Robinson is a larger-than-life, beautifully painted statue of St. Christopher up high on a pedestal for all to view as their patron saint. To Robinson's left is a gigantic, grossly over-sized, white marble open-hearth fireplace that must measure six feet high by ten feet wide. Three immense logs, almost too heavy for one man to move, are blazing in the fireplace. The entire hall is toasty and smells like bayberry. Both sides of the fireplace are outlined in more snow-flocked Christmas trees of gargantuan heights, but tastefully done and professionally decorated. Overall – magical! Everyone becomes quiet and they all focus on the Grand Exalted Santa. Robinson stands up, holds up both white-gloved hands for absolute silence, and as a sign of supremacy, and begins.

"Brothers of the Amalgamated Society of Santas." Robinson uses his Toastmaster's voice which commands attention. "We are gathered here in the grand lodge hall to initiate six new Santas into our brotherhood." He pauses to allow the severity of the rite to strike home. "Brother Initiator will now bring forth the initiates for the final test." Don sees the six new guys being led up to the center of the main floor by Brother Initiator to face the Grand Exalted Santa.

Okay fellows, time to witness the ASS ritual! Don thinks as he holds on tightly to the column and up on his tippy-toes to get the best view of the secret initiation about to unfold.

Brother Initiator stops and the conga line of Santa wannabes follows suit. They all turn and face Robinson. The Santa initiates are lined up to his right, eyes raised to the "Grand" himself still standing next to the gold throne.

"Brothers – Give the sign!" barks Robinson.

In unison, except for the new guys, all the brothers raise both hands and plant the bottoms of them on their foreheads. Their fingers are spread out like reindeer antlers and they buck their heads up and down three times while shuffling their feet and making a snorting sound like reindeer in heat. The grand lodge hall sounds like the Black Forest during rutting season.

Robinson answers the mating call with a loud whining sound as he makes the antler sign with his fingers and turns his head to exhibit the sign to the entire room from left to right.

SLAP! All hands go down in unison.

Then, out of nowhere, the Grand Exalted Santa raises a large six-foot candy cane over the heads of the flock for quiet and continues the ritual.

"Brothers – Recite the creed!"

They repeat back, again in unison:

"I am Santa."

"Santa is always jolly."

"Santa always smiles."

"Santa never says bad words on the set."

"Santa never touches the children or their parents in secret places."

Robinson lowers the giant candy cane and all are silent again.

"Brother Initiator, are the initiates ready for the final test?" Robinson asks.

"Yes, Grand Exalted Santa. All six initiates have been tested. They know the names of the reindeer. They can sing "Jingle Bells" on key. And the can recite "The Night Before Christmas" without the aid of references. All this I certify before you and my brothers."

Satisfied with the response, Robinson steps down from the throne and taps each initiate on the head three times with the huge candy cane. Then he announces, "Pay close attention, brother initiates. The final test is not as easy as it appears." Robinson turns to face the huge fireplace with blazing fire. Four exaggeratedly large Christmas stockings with glittered names on them are now being hung by the fireplace with care. They read: "Billy," "Bobby," "Mary," and "Sue."

"Brother Daniel will now exhibit the correct procedure for the final test." The entire room observes Brother Daniel who walks to the side of the room, picks up a rather large wrapped package, complete with tag and bow. He checks the name on the tag and walks over to the fireplace, and while holding the top of the stocking open with one hand, Brother Daniel drops the present into it. The stocking holds with the weight of the present as it swings a bit from side to side. A log in the fireplace spits and pops with a loud **CRACK.** Brother Daniel steps back from the fireplace and the intense heat.

Piece of cake! Don thinks. *What kind of test is that? I've done that myself many a time on Christmas Eve and usually half-loaded!*

"Brother Initiates," Robinson continues. "You will each be given a turn at completing this task. Place one present, WITH CARE, in the correct stocking hung by the fireplace. Do this so that the package is secure and that the stocking doesn't come loose and fall into the fireplace and burn up!" he pauses for effect. "There is one difference, however." They all look back and forth between Robinson and the roaring fireplace. "Once you read the name tag on the present, you will be blindfolded and have to walk carefully to the fireplace and place the package in the correct stocking."

Dead silence in the room.

"Brother Initiates… please take the time now to memorize the order of the stockings, for in a few minutes you will be lead out of the grand lodge hall until your time comes for the final test." All the novices begin to memorize the order of the stockings and get an idea as to their spacing.

"Brother Initiator…Please escort the initiates to the anteroom at this time." Brother Initiator steps forward and quietly informs the new guys to follow him in single file. They exit the room through a different set of doors behind the columns to the right.

Well now, thinks Don, *this should be interesting! Wonder if there's a fire truck and an ambulance or two waiting out back?*

Jimmy D. Mays makes his way back to the dumpster thanks to Jerome the trash man. On his way out of Bee Bee's Cash and Carry with his stash of Wild Turkey and smokes, Jimmy D. spots Jerome climbing into his trash truck parked out front of Wallowich's Frog Pond.

"Hey, Jeromes!" he yells out. "Yo, Jeromes! Youse leavin'? Can youse give Jimmy D. a ride to da mall?"

"The mall's closed, Jimmy! It's almost eleven!" Jerome yells back trying to squeeze behind the steering wheel. Seems good old Jerome's been snacking and beering it up way too much lately at the Frog Pond since his old lady through him out and his body is suffering for it.

"Jimmy D. knows dat, Jeromes. Jus' gets me to da mall, okay?"

"Sure, Jimmy. Hop on in."

Jimmy trots on over to the truck and gets inside for another free ride.

"Thanks, Jeromes. Youse alright, man!"

"Yeh, tell that to that old bag I live with!"

"Brother Initiator," Robinson orders in a commanding voice. "Bring out the first initiate for the final test." Brother Initiator advances to the anteroom door and returns with the first novice to attempt the final challenge. Side by side, they face the Grand Exalted Santa.

"Is the initiate ready?"

"The initiate IS ready, Grand Exalted Santa," responds Brother Initiator.

"The initiate will now silently read the name on the wrapped package." Brother Initiator hands the present to the novice Santa. He quickly reads the name on the label, "Mary" and then quickly eyeballs Mary's stocking on the fireplace from where he is standing.

"The initiate will now be blindfolded." From behind another Santa slips a black hood securely over the novice Santa's head.

"The initiate will begin the trial," orders Robinson. The novice steps off quickly at first heading slightly to the right about seven full paces.

Holy Christ! Don thinks. *This dumb fuck is headed right smack into the middle of the fireplace!*

The novice stops abruptly and turns forty-five degrees to the left and slowly, ever so slowly he moves forward about three half-steps, then stops.

I think he's right on. From where he stands, Don can't see the names on the stockings clear enough, but he believes the stocking the novice is blindly reaching for is in fact "Mary's."

Slowly now, the novice reaches and feels for the top of the stocking. As luck would have it, he finds it with no problems and while juggling the package, he manages to open up the top of the stocking and slip in the present. The wrapped present drops to the bottom of the exaggeratedly oversized stocking and it holds! Good thing too because the novice is just about to scream in pain from the hotfoot he's getting for being too near the fireplace. It appears his right foot is embedded in some cinders that are still aglow. Feeling he's succeeded in the final test, the novice quickly backs out of the fireplace and stomps his right foot several times hoping his shoe isn't on fire.

"Brother Initiator will now inspect the stocking," from Robinson.

Brother Initiator does just that and upon seeing that the name on the stocking matches the name on the package announces, "CORRECT!"

The grand hall erupts into cheers and wild hand clapping as the hood is removed from the *new* Santa's head. He checks his shoes first for any flames or fire damage and then grins from ear to ear at his success. The newly "made" Santa is now escorted over to the Grand Exalted Santa by Brother Initiator and Robinson shakes his hand and congratulates him for a job well done. Next, Robinson directs the new Santa to stand by him and watch the proceedings as another novice is brought out for the final test. This one looks a little shaky and unsure of himself. Even Brother Initiator whispers to the Santa wannabe, "You'll do fine," as he pats him on the back. They both face the Grand Exalted Santa and the process begins anew.

The novice Santa reads the present label, "Billy." He quickly looks up to spot where the stocking is, and before he can zero in on the correct one, the black hood is placed over his head.

First one! It's the first stocking to the left! He thinks.

"The initiate will begin the trial," again, from Robinson.

The novice Santa hesitates, second-guessing himself, and then takes four giant steps forward as if he magically sees through the hood and knows exactly where to go. He stops abruptly, unsure now of where to proceed. He then takes two steps to the left – hesitates, then three tiny steps to the right.

This guy's WAY off! Don continues to watch while holding his breath. The novice holds up the present with both hands trying to feel for the stocking, the mantle, anything but the roaring fire!

POP! – another sound from the fireplace and the novice is beginning to shake a little. Several startled Santas cry out loud in alarm.

"SILENCE!" barks Robinson.

The novice takes two more short steps slowly towards the fire, still feeling for some resistance – NONE – two more tiny steps and success. He feels a stocking! *This has to be it.* Now he's fumbling with the present while trying to open the top of the stocking. He almost drops the present into the fireplace. The front of his body is beginning to warm up quite a bit and he begins to sweat. He's still fumbling with the present while trying desperately to open the top of the stocking. He fumbles again and loses the package!

"UGH!" The gaggle of Santas cry out, but in a fraction of a second he catches the package before it lands in the roaring fire and burns up! He quickly tosses the wrapped package into the stocking and it *too* holds the present! The Santas are all smiling and talking to one another about the miracle they just witnessed. The hood is removed and the initiate returns to the starting point smiling and nodding to the other Santas.

"SILENCE!" from Robinson.

"Brother Initiator will now inspect the stocking." Once more, Brother Initiator steps forward and checks the name of the stocking against the name on the label. He shakes his head and checks it again to be sure he hasn't made a mistake.

"INCORRECT!"

"UGH!" from the multitude as the ex-novice is lead out of the grand hall with his eyes to the floor.

Wonder what happens to the losers? Don ponders. *Maybe they make him walk the gauntlet and beat him with belts of jingle bells...OUCH!*

Low and behold, a third Santa wannabe is escorted to the starting point, smiling to beat the band and awful cock-sure of himself.

Somehow a magical feeling – an aura of some sort – perhaps a message from St. Nicholas himself envelopes the entire grand lodge hall and everyone there, Don included, gets the same message: *This guy's a loser!*

The same process unfolds and the novice Santa reads the label, "Sam.*"* The hood goes on, the novice begins, and right now you're saying to yourself, *Wait a minute? There is NO 'SAM'!* And right you are! There IS NO 'SAM'! Go figure? No one in the hall knows that this dunce read the name wrong. So where is he going to put the present? There is no stocking with the name 'SAM'! Beats me! Read on.

In less than ten seconds, the hooded novice walks right up to where the fireplace is located. He reaches out with one hand and immediately touches one of the stockings. Somehow he manages to open it with just one hand and with the other hand holding the present, he quickly dumps the present for a score and for going down in the record books as the quickest stocking-stuffer Santa in the history of ASS! Oh, but don't cheer yet. You see, he was a little too sure of himself as the present tips off the rim of the stocking and lands directly into the fire!

SNAP! CRACKLE! PUFFFT! Bye-bye present, and bye-bye Santa. He's quickly escorted out of the hall, still hooded mind you, and tossed into the anteroom. Everyone is shocked and there is dead silence in the grand lodge hall.

"HEY – YOU!" A startled Don Kaminski turns his head to see who's yelling at him.

"HEY! Who the hell are YOU!" The Inner Santa Guard has just returned to his post near the door. He should have been there the entire time but his quick dinner at the nearby Mexican restaurant, *Los Indios Ilegales,* where he wolfed down two hot pork burritos mixed with spicy cheese smothered in hot sauce made it necessary for him to run like hell to the men's room shortly after the parade of Santas entered the grand lodge hall. As it is, he's wearing no underwear and his ass is still stinging!

"We have an intruder!" he yells out in alarm. **"WE HAVE AN INTRUDER!"** The Inner Santa Guard races towards Don with arms open to apprehend the spy. Don fakes to the right then runs left bypassing the charging Santa. The Inner Santa Guard just misses latching onto Don's robe with a passing hand. Don races for the exit. The entire room turns wondering what has so abruptly interrupted the sacred ritual.

"We have an intruder! Stop him! STOP HIM!" Robinson yells and Santas begin running every which way.

Great God Almighty! Don't let that door be locked! Don prays. It isn't! Don just about knocks over Jeeves who stands completely stunned in the foyer. The hall door crashes open as the multitude of Santas race out. Too late! Don is already out the front door and leaping down to the gate, robe flying in all directions. What luck! The gate opens quicker than at Belmont! Don races around the block to where the Volvo is parked. The street is now covered with hooded Santas, hooting and yelling, and all headed in his direction. He fumbles for his keys through the folds of the robe and finally gets them out of his pants pocket. The Santa mob rounds the corner and spot Don as he enters the car.

BAM! The car door slams shut leaving about three feet of the robe hanging outside the Volvo. Quicker than Dale Earnhardt, Don starts the car and races right into the center of the Santa mass. They all dive for cover as Don passes them roaring down the street. He swears he heard some cuss words from behind. Don's pushing sixty-five miles per hour in a residential area. He even passes a pizza delivery car! Don finally comes to his senses and slows down desperately trying to get his heart rate back to normal. Somehow he makes it home alive, but he is all shook up from the chase and nearly being caught. He parks the Volvo out back and quickly rushes for the kitchen door. Sue and the kids are seated at the table playing gin, drinking hot tea, and making plans for the holidays – you know: dinner menu, who to invite this year, Christmas presents, buy plenty of Mogen David – room temperature of course, and the like, when Don comes crashing in with this weird expression on his face looking like he just saw the fourth horse of the Apocalypse in the back yard! Junior and Annie are dumb struck to say the least and can't get a word out.

"Nice robe, honey – GIN!" says Sue.

Early Wednesday morning ushers in one beautiful winter day for the good people of Chicago. The sun is shining brightly, the temperature is just right, and there is very little wind in the "Windy City" – very unusual!

Don is up and out early and can't decide what he wants to do on two fronts: first of all – where to get coffee? He's still a little gun shy about going to ANY Dunkin' Donuts. *The Patels probably put up a Wanted Poster with a black and white photo of me taken from the store surveillance camera and the notice, 'SHOOT ON SIGHT.'* Next, and more importantly, what to do about the covey of anti-Semitic Santas he's discovered in his own back yard. *Maybe I should just forget it and go on my merry way?* he thinks. But that thought doesn't fit right this morning. *Something is wrong here, and my finances are still a mess over this damn strike. Hell no. Hell no! I'm just as good a Santa as any of those guys and I deserve a chance to work in a good location and earn an income as Santa Claus even if I am a Jew!* Poor Don, he's pissed off again.

Don spots a diner up ahead and realizes it's Guilday's where Annie works.

By golly, I think she got called in today to cover for some wai-tress who went to visit her family in Rhode Island. That's great! Breakfast with Annie serving her Pop and I don't have to do the dishes, he chuckles.

Don carefully parks the Volvo and is headed into the restaurant when he spots a big black limo with lots of chrome pulling in that looks awful familiar.

Well if it isn't the Patriarch Santa! Probably has a gig here.

He waits by the door while Zoltan parks the "black beauty" and hurries up to the door.

"Hallo to you, Meester Donald. And how are you this blessed morning?"

"Just fine, Zoltan is it?"

"That's exactly right, exactly right – ZolTAN," the Patriarch repeats accenting the second syllable.

"Sorry, ZolTAN. I'll try to remember that. ZolTAN," Don practices the correct pronunciation.

"Eeez okay, Meester Donald. Everybody say 'Zoltan' instead of 'ZolTAN.' Eeez wery much okay. Good seeing you, Meester Donald, sir. You come for breakfast? You join Zoltan and be my guest. Food is wery good here. Just like Mama make! You know?...like Mama make in old country." The Patriarch gives out with a hearty laugh.

"You're right, Zoltan, just like Mama makes." Don holds the door open as the Patriarch enters first. They walk inside a bit and who do they see sitting at the counter but the skinny black Santa they met the other day in jail. They both recognize Jimmy D. Mays because he's still wearing his good luck Santa suit.

"Hello, Meester Jimmy Dees! Hallo, hallo," Zoltan pats Jimmy on the back as Jimmy looks up and grins at his jailhouse friends.

"Hey, Jimmy," Don adds.

"Hey, Zagnuts and say..." Jimmy looks over at Don. Wha's your name, man? Jimmy D. forgots, sorry."

"Donald, Jimmy. How are you doing?"

"Oh yeah, Donals. Thas right, Donals....Hey, fellas – Jimmy D. fine as wine and a shelf or two higher up. Ha ha ha." Jimmy finds that funny. "Say, man, sits here wif Jimmy D. and get some breakfass, okay?" Both Don and Zoltan flank Jimmy at the counter and Annie appears out of nowhere with placemats and silverware.

"Hi, Pop!" Annie beams with joy seeing her Dad in much better shape this morning. "What are you up to today? I see you are in good company with Jimmy D. and the Patriarch here. Coffee for all?"

"Yes, Meese," Zoltan says. "Coffee for all, please." Zoltan turns to Don and says, "She is your daughter, yes?" Annie gives them all a great big smile.

"She is my daughter, YES," answers Don.

"She is wery beautiful...wery beautiful!" Annie begins to blush.

"Yeah, Dons, Jimmy D. never in his whole lifes seen a girls as beautiful as dat. Tha's for sure!" Jimmy smiles flashing his set of perfect white teeth.

"Thanks, fellows," Don says. "I agree! She IS beautiful!" Annie blushes and smiles as if to say, *Aw, shucks!*

"I'll bet you guys say that to all the waitresses," Annie says.

"I do not like de fat one, I'm thinking," fires Zoltan.

"She's the new girl and she happens to be very nice," from Annie.

"Maybe she nice to *you* – yesterday she no nice to *me*," Zoltan fires back. "She no fill my coffee cup maybe one, two times most. And all my eggs get broken up like getting hit with *Katusha roketa,* and even toast coming late to counter!"

"Sorry for that, Patriarch," Annie gives him another smile. "I can't answer for the coffee and toast, but the eggs were probably broken by the cook, Mr. Mike."

"Yeah, Zagnut, Mikes can't cooks no eggs without bustin' 'em all up, bro. Ha ha ha."

"Ez no wery funny when eggs broke!"

"Well, relax, Patriarch," Annie says. "Mr. Mike's not here. Today's his day off. What are you having?" All three order breakfast for a small army and the Patriarch spouts, "Pleeze, Misses Annie. You give to me bill when ready. Zoltan buying my wery good friends breakfast today. Be sure you giving me bill, okay?"

"Okay, Patriarch. Breakfast is on you today. I've got it," says Annie.

"Thanks, Zoltan. That's nice of you," from Don.

"Yeah, Zagnuts. Jimmy D. be thankin' youse for the res' o' his lifes, man."

"Mein pleasures. Mein pleasures," the Patriarch pipes back.

"Say, Zoltan," from Don. "Where are your altar boys this morning? I usually see you with two boys all dressed up and fussing over you. I don't see them this morning?"

"Ach, dose boys – dose boys. Vat they doink to Zoltan is shame – shame, shame, shame!...dose boychicks." The Patriarch makes the orthodox sign of the cross three times. "You vant know vat dose boys doing yesterdays to Zoltan? Shame on dose boys. We spending nice day vashing up car and odder tings, and later in day I finding them behind church in small graveyard for peoples wid moneys for church. And guess vat? They drunk! They both drunk! They steal wine from sacristy and wodka from mein house, and go hide in graveyards in front mine good friend mausoleum – Masha Sokolova – from old country. Dose boys sit down in front of poor Masha – dead now for fourteen years – and drinking themselves silly wid holy wine from church and wery expensive wodka from old country. Both passing out on dead Masha's front steps."

"Das a shame, Zagnuts. Say, youse giving out any unnerwears over St. Bignuts? Jimmy D. could sure use some clean unnerwears, man."

"Vat you talking, unnervears? *Vas ist* 'unnervears?' Ah, *katori* 'unnervears?' *Yah ne znayu! Boshe moi!*"

"Unnerwears, man. Unnerwears! You know, unnerwears?" Jimmy pulls his Santa pants out a bit and tries to point inside. "Unnerwears! Drawers, man!" *Dumb-ass Polack!*

"Unnervears?" Zoltan is utterly confused now.

"Zoltan. Zoltan!" Don's trying to get the Patriarch's attention. "Under *wear*," he pulls at the top of his exposed T-shirt. "*Underwear.* What you have on UNDER your shirt and pants, okay?

"*Tak!* Undervear! Undervear! *Ya znayu! Ya znayu!* Undervear! I very sorry, Jimmy Dees, but-a ve no got-ed no more undervear for to give out. Maybe one, maybe two pair wery large lady undervear, but no fit Jimmy Dees. No fit. Is too beeeg for Jimmy Dees. Sorry. Sorry."

"Yeah, Zagnuts. Looks like Jimmy D. da sorry one. No clean unnerwears again. Somethin' better happen soon or Jimmy D. be outta socks next!"

"Socks! Jimmy Dees, you need socks? Zoltan have plenty socks and Gucci handbags. You need BINGO ball machine?"

"No, Zagnuts. Jimmy D. doan needs no BINGO shit, but I will take some socks. Are they free for the homeless?"

"I didn't know you were homeless, Jimmy. I thought you had a place to stay?" Don says with concern for the little black Santa.

"Is like this here, Dons. Jimmy D. has dis little place behind the mall an' all, but it ain' much and it always be snowin' and shit, so yeah, Jimmy D. be pretty much homeless."

"I likes you, Jimmy Dees," Zoltan adds. "You homeless no more." You come living with Zoltan. I have apartment just right for you over garages next to cemetery. You live there for free if you help Zoltan keep church ground nice and keep boys out of cemetery and no drinking on poor dead Masha's front steps."

"Thas sound pretty good, Zagnuts. Jimmy D. thinks about it. One thing…Jimmy D. ain' bein' NO Jew an' ain' be doin' no Jew shit in da cemetery! But Jimmy D. takes dem socks if they are free!"

"No vorry. No vorry, Jimmy Dees. We work it all out later. First we eat." Annie shows up with hot food for all and refills of steaming hot coffee. They all eat like it's their last meal.

"Just like-a Mama make and NO busted-up eggs!"

Laughter.

80

The Kaminski house appears to be calm this morning. Annie is at work and Don's off somewhere. Just Junior and Sue in the kitchen wondering if they should have a full breakfast or just a quick bowl of cereal.

"Don't go to any trouble, Mom. I'll just have some Cheerios," Junior says. I have to get to school early today. Another girl thinks I asked her to the prom."

"Oh, Junior. Not again! How do you get yourself in these jams?"

"I don't know, Mom. Maybe I take after Pop!"

"That you do, my boy – that you do." Sue reaches under the kitchen counter for the Cheerios box. "I think I'll have some Cheerios too. I need to get off to an early start. Did your father mention where he was going this morning?"

"Not sure, Mom. He seemed to be upset and kept mumbling something about 'Abramowitz and Abramowitz.' Who are they? You know, Mom?"

"God only knows with your father dear. They might be the new Rabbis in town or a new discount house just opened up." Sue is pouring out the Cheerios.

"Looks like another nice day out, Mom." Junior is looking out the kitchen window and admiring the refreshing early-morning sunshine. "We sure are lucky to have such nice weather this morning."

"We sure are, Junior. Here's your bowl of Cheerios." She hands him the bowl. "Need anything else?"

"No thanks, Mom. Say is there anything wrong with the house phone?" Junior looks at his Mom with a funny look on his face.

"What do you mean? I haven't picked up the phone yet and neither have you? So what are you talking about?" Sue stops pouring the milk as Junior picks up the wall-mounted phone and checks for a dial tone.

"That's funny? Everything is fine here," he says.

"Junior, what's wrong with you?" Sue grabs the phone from his hand and hears the dial tone as well. "Why are you asking about the phones all of a sudden?"

"Come over here, Mom, and see for yourself."

Sue moves over to the window and looks out into the driveway.

"What? I don't see anything? Are you cracking up on me, Junior? I can just about handle your father!"

"Over there," Junior points. "Look up the telephone pole across the street. Look, you can see him from here."

Sue looks again but strains to look down the drive.

"See who? I don't see anyone."

"Look up the telephone pole, Mom – across the street in front of the Jamison house. There's a guy up on the telephone pole." She looks one more time.

"Oh, yeah – I see him now. There's a worker up there probably fixing something – so what?" Sue looks at Junior as though he's lost his mind.

"The power is on so it can't be that," Junior questions.

"Maybe it's the cable company? Maybe he just fixed whatever the problem was. I don't know. What's gotten into you, Junior? Eat your Cheerios – will you!" Sue gives Junior a slight swat behind his head – more of a love tap than anything.

"Where's his truck, I wonder?" Junior stretches his neck as far as he can to look up and down the block.

Sue looks at Junior in wonderment.

"Junior, you're freaking me out! How the heck should I know where his truck is?" Sue comes back to the window to look again. *Yeah, where is his truck?*

Now they both are looking out the window to see if they spot a ConEd truck, cable truck or any other city utility or work truck – NOTHING – no trucks at all! They both look up at the worker high up on the pole. He's wearing a hard hat and a fully loaded utility belt.

"Eat your Cheerios, Junior. Maybe his partner went for coffee or some parts or something."

"Look, Mom. He's talking on a phone to someone."

Sue strains to look up as high as she can.

That's when they both notice that the utility worker has a full-blown Santa beard! They both bust out laughing at seeing Santa Claus up high on a telephone pole.

"He must be talking to the elves, Junior. Wait until I tell your father this one," Sue chuckles.

"Hey, Mom. I wonder if Dad pissed off the new Santa group he was going to join and now they're disconnecting our phone lines! Ha, ha, ha!"

"That's a good one, Junior. You know how your father can get when he gets angry." Sue takes another look. "Sure is a nice looking Santa beard, I'll say."

They both go back to the table and eat Cheerios in silence with smiles on their faces.

I wonder if Don did do something to piss them off?

81

RING...RING...RING

"Hello?...Hello!...Who is it?"

"Hi, Pop. How are you?"

"Hello, Donald. I'm fine, thank you for asking. How are things with the Nazi Santas going? You're not in any trouble, are you?"

"No, Pop, no. I'm not in any trouble, but do you remember me asking about lawyers the other day?"

"Sure, son, sure – Abramowitz, Abramowitz and Laganelli – only you want the second Abramowitz – Junior. He's the best. Remember I told you? Junior Abramowitz is the chosen one. He always wins...in court or out."

"I remember, Pop. Well I think I need him. I checked on the internet and they have an office in the downtown Chicago area in the old Sears Tower."

"Of course they do! They're everywhere! These Jews don't mess around, son. You call them and they come running. Especially if they smell money, and with these boys, there's ALWAYS money in it. Did you know that pure-blooded Jews can smell money? You didn't know that did you?" Max blows his nose.

"No, Pop. I never heard that one."

Well, it's true. Real, pure-blooded Jews can smell money – and that's a fact. I never could smell it myself and neither could your mother, but that because I think we've got some mixed blood way back in our ancestry – probably some Gypsy or Mongol or something. Who knows? But, that doesn't change the fact that real Jews can smell money! I've seen it with my own eyes, I tell you." Max pauses to fix his *yarmulke*.

"So listen, Son, you got a good case against these Nazis right? You'd better look into this real hard before you see Abramowitz, Jr. Don't fuck with these Jews, Donald. I'm warning you! These Jews really are the 'Chosen Ones,' and not only can they smell money – but they can smell it a mile away! Believe me they can, so don't fuck with these people, Donald. Make damn sure you have a good case!"

"Yeah, Pop. I think I have a real good case. Do you think I can use Rabbi Peckermen as a reference?"

"Sure, son, use Rabbi Peckerman, me, *and* Aunt Sadie as references. He knows all of us personally.

"How's that, Pop – from the congregation?"

"That and the fact that we all hired him in the past."

"I didn't know that, Pop. How did that happen?"

"Well," the old man coughs up some phlegm. "Excuse me, son." More silence. "You obviously know about the case against Rabbi Peckermen.

"Sure, Pop, but what about you and Aunt Sadie?"

"Here's the story – many years ago, when I was a young man, your mother and I had just gotten married, and I rented out a flat on the East side of town from the Fusco brothers. They were connected. You know what I mean – *connected?*"

"Sure, Pop, I know what you mean."

"Well, they had this junk yard in Jersey with all this rusted junk in it that just sat around for years and years and never moved an inch – and yet everyday questionable people, mostly Italians I might add, went to the junk yard office and got paid for the junk they supposedly dropped off – get it?"

"Pop – What the hell are you talking about?"

"The junk yard, dummy! The junk yard was a front for laundering money!"

"What's that got to do with you and Aunt Sadie?"

"Nothing! I'm just telling you – that's all. They didn't think anyone knew about this, but the truth was, we ALL knew about it!"

"So what about you and Aunt Sadie? You guys didn't go into the junk business, did you?"

"Donald – shut up and listen once, will you? I'll explain."

"Go ahead, Pop."

"So anyway, the Fusco brothers were in tight with the 'boys' and your mother and I were struggling to make a living. Hell, we were struggling to survive!" Max holds the phone away from his face as he sneezes.

"God bless you, Pop."

"Thank you, Donald. Wait – I dropped my *yarmulke*." More silence as Max fumbles with the phone.

"Okay – you with me so far?"

"I think so, Pop."

"Okay, where was I? Oh yeah, your mother and I didn't have two pennies to rub together and we were both working! Things were just so damn expensive then. It seems as fast as we earned our money, it all went away. Don't ask me where it went? It just went. That's the way it was for all of us immigrants. We worked and we paid. Your mother worked at the Ranger Joe Cereal factory on the waterfront. She spent all day making cereal boxes. Her job was to operate this big press with cutters that would cut the cardboard into the shape they needed to make the box – get it?"

"Sure, Pop. I got it."

"So anyways, this big machine was all foot powered and so she had to push down hard on the foot pedal to punch out a new box for Ranger Joe. And believe me, son, this was hard work – especially for your mother. You see, she had to cut six or ten boxes at a time! I forget the amount." Max doesn't talk as he cuts a long fart. It's silent – but deadly.

"Pop, you there?"

"Yes, Donald – I'm here. Phew! – that stinks! Anyways, she worked long and hard every day of the work week using her foot and punching out boxes for Ranger Joe. You should have seen the muscles in her right leg! If she kicked you – she could stop an elephant!"

Another sneeze – more silence.

"Pop, you okay?"

"Sure, Donald – quit interrupting." Max takes a sip of cold coffee. "And, me? I was working for the Long Island Railroad loading ice and toilet paper into the bar cars. You know, the train cars where you could get a drink and a salami sandwich? That was a hard, sweaty job, Donald – lifting huge blocks of ice – and we're not talking cubes here. I'm talking about fifty-pound blocks of ice that had to be loaded one at a time onto a cart which you then wheeled from the ice house to the bar cars and then unload them, one at a time, on your shoulder, and carried them *into* the bar cars and dump them into the ice chest. Believe me this was hard work – all day long. The toilet paper was easier because it didn't weigh anything, but that ice was a killer! You have no idea how much ice and toilet paper the passengers went through in a day. They must have done a lot of drinking and a lot of shitting!

"That's nice, Pop."

"Nice? You think so? No, son, it was *not* nice, believe me. Do you know that in the old days the toilets on the trains emptied right onto tracks? I'll bet you didn't know that, did you?"

"No, Pop, I didn't know that."

"Well, it did – right on the tracks. You could look down the toilet and see the railroad tracks. Well, you couldn't see the tracks per se but you could see the stone and the wood cross ties." Max takes another sip of cold coffee. "Damn, wish I had another Old Fashioned donut."

"And...?"

"And? I'll tell you AND! The entire rail line from Grand Central Station to Long Island was full of shit! All of it! Shit and toilet paper along the whole route! People who lived along the rail lines from here to Long Island complained all the time about the smell. In the summer time, it was overwhelming! You could hardly breathe from all the stink!"

"Pop, what does all this have to do with Abramowitz, Abramowitz and Laganelli?"

"Nothing! I'm just telling you so you have the background, that's all. Now stop interrupting, Donald! You're making me nuts already! Let me finish – will you?"

"Okay, Pop – go ahead."

"So anyway, with the tracks full of shit from here to Long Island, and all the people who lived along the tracks complaining all the time...I mean, wouldn't you? Well, that's when they started to design rail cars with toilets that held all the shit and toilet paper until it could be unloaded." Max tries to muffle the phone but Don hears him yell, "I'm talking to Donald...What?...He's fine...What?...I will...What?...What the hell do I care she lost the damn cat again?...What?...He doesn't give a shit either!...What?...I will! – Now let me finish with Donald, for Christ's sake!...Okay, okay, I won't forget...What?...He's fine I said – Really!...He's fine, I tell you!...Okay, I will, already!...Hello, Donald?"

"I'm here, Pop."

"So they tried to stick me with that job once too, you know – empty the shit from the cars. 'Hell NO' I said and so I stayed on with the ice and toilet paper. Anyway, son, to make a long story short, your mother comes home one day, tired as hell and with about four inches of Ranger Joe cereal all stuck to her shoes making her look a lot taller than she really is, and she tells me she's pregnant. She's pregnant with YOU of all people. Now what do we do? We're just making it as it is! She can't afford to take off from work. In those days there was no such thing as 'maternity leave,' and we didn't have any insurance as is was." Don hears his mother talking in the background...

"What is it now?" Max says. "Not now, later!...Yes, I said LATER we would go for some ice cream...Yes – at the new place – not Mayers...Can I PLEASE finish my story here?...What?...Donald, you know, your son, Donald?...What?...Of course I'm still on the phone with Donald!...He's fine!...I told you already!" Max ends up in a coughing spell.

"You okay, Pop?"

"I'm fine, Donald. Your mother makes me nuts sometimes, that's all. So anyway, where was I? Oh, yeah – your mother and I, we were very excited about having a baby and all but we weren't so sure how all this was going to work out. Somehow word got back to the Fusco brothers that your mother was pregnant. It probably happened because your mother got as big as a house and was still working making cereal boxes for Ranger Joe. Somehow she kept her foot up on the pedal and kept on punching out boxes day after day, but eventually she got so damn big with *you* she couldn't get her foot up that high to work the peddle and so she got fired and came home. It wasn't long after that, the Fusco brothers started a bunch of shit. You see, the problem was the Fusco brothers considered our flat to be one of their better ones and they didn't want children in there to tear up the place, and that's when they tried to throw us out!" Max clears his throat and finishes the cold coffee.

"Listen, Pop – I got to pee and I'm sitting in my car outside the restaurant where Annie works."

"Hold on, son. I'm getting to the end of the story. So, your mother and I contacted Abramowitz, Jr. who in turn informed Laganelli. Laganelli wasn't a partner then. He just worked there doing odd jobs I suppose. So, Laganelli somehow made things nice with the Fusco brothers and nothing was ever said again – no court, no nothing! Somehow we got through it. You were born and your mother went back to work for Ranger Joe and we stayed in that crummy flat for another two years."

"And Aunt Sadie?"

"Aunt Sadie? Oh, *Sadie*. Your Aunt Sadie didn't sue anyone. I made a mistake on that one, Donald. Sadie was sweet on Abramowitz, Jr. ever since she met him at Uptown Brother's Dance Hall, but his family stopped the courting when they found out we didn't have any money, and so, Sadie had to settle for Uncle Hershel who was worse off than we were. You probably don't remember Uncle Hershel. He died a long time ago in the explosion at the munitions dump down on the wharf. Did you ever hear about that one?"

"Listen, Pop. I got to go bad! I love you."

BUZZ

Don pockets the phone and races back inside Guilday's Family Restaurant.

"Love you too, son. Good luck!" Max puts the phone down and hears his wife, Marsha, calling again from the kitchen.

"What?...What?...Another what? Another cat?...When? Absolutely not!...No, I am NOT going into the city to look for the cat!...YOU go!...What?...Then you and Sadie go get ice cream!...I don't give a shit!...Because I have to watch 'The Price Is Right' with Drew Carey, that's why...What?...Drew Carey!...No, not Jim Carey!...Drew Carey!...DREW CAREY! – the funny Jew on TV!...He is too!"

Sue's on her way out the door and off to work in her old Pontiac. *Sure hope the men are well behaved today.* She backs out the driveway and looks up at the worker still perched high up on the telephone pole and still talking on the phone. The worker spots Sue and turns his head as if to hide his face from her. *That's odd,* she thinks. *Donald, what kind of a mess have you gotten us into now?*

RING...RING...RING

Don checks his cell phone while trying to pee at the same time. He sees it's Susan on the other end.

"Hello, Sue? Can you give me a minute here?...Oh, shit!"

"Don, are you okay?...Don?"

"I'm fine. I'm fine. I'm just trying to pee, that's all. And now I just peed on my pant leg and shoes. Shit!"

"Donald, did you poop your pants too?"

"What? No, Sue, I just said the word 'shit' because I peed down my pant leg!"

"What's going on?"

"I told you, Sue. I just peed down my pant leg!"

"Where are you?"

"Well I'm not in the middle of Daley Center, Sue. I'm trying to pee! I'm in the men's room at Guilday's; third urinal from the left! The one with the soggy floor!"

"Gee wiz, Don. You don't have to get so upset with me. I thought something was wrong."

"Susan, I'm sorry; honest I am," Don says trying to calm down. "I just got off the phone with Pop..."

"Is everything okay? Is someone ill?"

"No, Hon – everyone is fine. Let's just say the conversation went a little longer than my bladder could wait, that's all. What's up?"

"Tell me the truth, Donald. Did you do anything to upset the Santa group the other night?"

"Well, I did crash their secret meeting and interrupted the initiation."

"Oh, Donald..."

"Why do you ask?"

"Well, I think they tapped our phones."

"What the hell are you talking about?...tapped our phones. How do you know that?"

"This morning Junior and I saw a repair man up the telephone pole across the street and he was talking to someone..."

"Susan, you're not making any sense."

"Listen, Don. When I pulled out of the driveway five minutes ago he hid his face from me. I'm sure of it."

"Susan, your getting paranoid. Hid his face from you? Maybe he was trying to block out the wind? How do you know he wasn't up there checking on a phone line or fixing something? – Come on, Susan. This doesn't make any sense!"

"Don, there was NO truck."

"NO truck? That doesn't mean anything…"

"Don, he had a white beard!"

Don thinks a second about that one. "So he had a white beard. So what? That doesn't mean anything either."

"Listen to me, Don. He had a full Santa beard and he's up our telephone pole! Now what's going on?"

"It's probably nothing, Sue. I'll be home in about ten minutes or so and I'll see if he's still there."

"I know I'm right about this, Don. I think they tapped our phone!"

"I'll be right home."

"Well, I'm on my way to work, Don."

"So what is it you want me to do, Susan?"

"I don't know, dear. I'm just telling you that's all. Don't kill the messenger, okay?"

"Tell you what, Susan darling. Suppose I go home and see if Santa is up OUR pole instead of the NORTH Pole, okay? And if I do see his fat ass up there talking on the phone or checking some list twice, I'm going to grab my chain saw and topple his chocolate chip cookie-filled ass onto the street! How's that sound?"

"Fine, Don. And the kids can go down and bail you out of jail again…Bye…Love you…Don't do any thing stupid, Donald!"

BUZZ

Now how do you suppose she knew about the kids bailing me out of jail? Don ponders.

Try that one on for size, Don. Didn't think I knew that one did you? Susan smiles.

84

Don's racing home to catch a glimpse of Santa up the pole when he realizes he's being tailed by an unmarked police cruiser. *Great! Just what I need a speeding ticket.* He slows down to well below the speed limit and the cop car does the same and continues to follow him through traffic. Don's straining to check out the light green, stealth cruiser. *Looks like one of those Dodge Chargers all the cops are getting with the souped-up engine. He's probably waiting for me to make one little mistake like running a red light or not fully stopping at a stop sign. I got your number, buddy.* Don drives the rest of the way like he's re-taking his driver's test. *He's still there and there are two of them in the car.* Don starts making random turns through the rural streets. *They're a few cars back, but they're still following me. Maybe it's some sort of training for a rookie cop? Yeah, that's it. The experienced cop is driving and showing the 'new guy' how to tail somebody. I'll show them.* Don pulls over to the side. The tail is only two cars behind him and as it passes Don clearly sees that both the driver and the passenger have long white beards. They know they've been spotted but they look straight ahead anyway as if Don didn't exist and continue to drive down the street and out of sight. *I'm being followed by Santas from ASS!*

Don pulls back into traffic and heads for home. He keeps a sharp eye out for the green Santa cruiser and sees no sign of it. He relaxes a bit and laughs at himself for being so paranoid. *And I was accusing Susan for being the paranoid one. I guess the laugh's on me.* He turns down his street and just as he expected, there are *no* Santas up any telephone poles that he can spot. *Oh well, guess Santa had another house call; or would that be pole call?* Don's almost home and starts singing along now with the radio; Sonny and Cher's "I Got You, Babe." He makes the turn onto his street, glances in the rear-view mirror, and spots a Mr. Softee truck make the same turn. *What the hell is a Mister Softee truck doing cruising the neighborhood in December?* Don's not far from his house but he pulls over to the curb instead and waits to see what Mister Softee does. The Mister Softee truck does the very same thing about a half a block back. The truck's front window is big enough that Don can clearly see ANOTHER bearded Santa behind the wheel. Pissed, Don rapidly zips the Volvo out into the street and up the block to his home. He all but bounces the Volvo into his driveway and throws it in park. He quickly gets out of the car and runs back into the street. His car door is open and the motor's still running. Don looks directly at the Mr. Softee truck and sees the ASS Santa glaring back. *That's it!* Don's madder than hell and starts taking giant steps towards the Mr. Softee truck. That's when the music starts playing from the truck loudspeaker to alert the kids that Mr. Softee is here – "da da, da da da, da dat da da – da dat da da, da daaa da." *Nobody buys Mr. Softee in December!*

As Don nears the Mr. Softee truck, the ASS Santa disappears from behind the driver's seat. Peripherally, Don sees several children race out of doorways and headed for the truck waving dollar bills. The Mr. Softee music is still blaring and the truck generator kicks into overdrive. Several more front doors open showing more kids with confused looks on their faces which quickly turn to joy as they turn and race for their parents leaving the doors wide open. *It's December, kids! No one eats a Mr. Softee in December! And close the damn door – the heat's on! Where were you raised? – In a barn!* By now there's a line of kids at the truck and the ASS Santa starts handing out popsicles and soft-serve cones – chocolate, vanilla, half and half. It's a regular ice cream party. *You'd think it was ninety degrees out here!*

Don stops just in front of the truck and whips out his cell phone like Clint Eastwood draws his 44 Magnum in "Dirty Harry." He dials a number from the piece of paper he has in his other hand.

"Hello, is this the law firm Abramowitz, Abramowitz and Laganelli?...Is Abramowitz, Junior there?"

85

"Good afternoon – Abramowitz, Abramowitz and Laganelli – Rosalie speaking – How may I help you?"

"Hello, is this the law firm Abramowitz, Abramowitz and Laganelli?"

"Yes, sir, it is. How may I assist you?"

"Is Abramowitz, Junior there?"

"As a matter of fact he is. Is he expecting your call, sir?"

"No, not really. I never met the guy, but Pop says he's the best. Pop says Abramowitz, Senior is good, but Junior...Junior is 'The Chosen One,' that's what Pop says...ah, listen, this isn't coming out right. Let me start over."

"Go ahead, sir, and take your time. I'm here to help you."

"Thanks, Rosalie. My name is Donald Kaminski and ah...I'm not sure how to put this without you thinking I'm out of my mind."

"Just take your time, Mr. Kaminski. Explain your problem as best you can and I'll direct you to one of our attorneys."

"Oh no! – I don't want just *anyone* to handle my case. I want Abramowitz, Jr. That's it. It's JUNIOR or no one!"

"I understand, Mr. Kaminski. I take it you would like a consultation with Jacob Abramowitz, Jr. Is that correct, sir?"

"Yes, yes – that's it – Jacob Abramowitz, JUNIOR! It has to be Junior."

"I understand, Mr. Kaminski. Now, can you briefly tell me what this concerns? Again, take your time."

"Well, Rosalie...you see I am a school teacher on strike and I look like Santa, and the strike will be over soon, but I need money for Christmas and for Susan's ring because she made the seven-ten split, and so I hooked up with a mob Santa group and they sent me to a Chinese Take-Out for my first gig. It was on the bad side of town and the place really wasn't a Chinese Take-Out – well, it was but it really wasn't, know what I mean? – because downstairs was this gambling den complete with *Pai Gow* poker, and wouldn't you know it, while I was changing into my Santa gear, three Chinese guys ran into the men's room and climbed up onto the toilet, shimmied out the window and went running down the alley – that's when the cops got there.

They arrested me along with all the other gamblers, only I wasn't gambling mind you, and we were all tossed in a paddy wagon along with Anita Wang, the owner of the Chinese Take-Out, and for that matter, the gambling den. The cell I was in was full of Santas, see? – Wall to wall Santas. They all got locked up just like I did because they joined up with the same mob Santa group. Anyway, Junior and Annie had to come down to the police station to bail me out so Susan wouldn't find out, but there was no bail because they released me and there were no charges either. Somehow, Susan found out about it anyway. Don't ask me how she did, but she did. That's when I went to the mall to see Buddy the Elf and later I met him and all his little friends at the Mini Bar on Rush Street. All of them are midgets or dwarfs, I can't tell the difference, can you? Anyway, I just had to get the lowdown on how I could get to be a real Santa at one of the local malls, so they put me in touch with the Amalgamated Society of Santas – ASS – only they don't call it that. I guess you can see why. So, I met with the Grand Exalted Santa who in fact is a Jew-hating Nazi son of a bitch, and because I'm Jewish, he refused to let me join! Later that night I crashed the ASS party and secretly observed the initiation of the new Santas. Most of them passed the final test except one who dropped the present into the fireplace and it went up in smoke – **PUFFFT!** Just like that – burned to a crisp! That's when the Inner Santa Guard spotted me from behind and gave the alarm to all the other Santas at the initiation. They chased me out of the ASS lodge but I outran them and got home to safety. I thought it was all over until Susan – you remember Susan don't you? My wife? The one who made the seven-ten split? Well, she saw a Santa up the telephone pole across the street who was probably in the process of tapping our phones and wouldn't show his face to her as she pulled out the driveway to hide his Santa beard. Then, on my way home to catch the Santa up the pole, I was tailed by two more real-bearded Santas in an unmarked police cruiser. Actually it wasn't a police cruiser but it looked like one. You know, one of those Dodge Chargers all the cops like? Well I pulled over to the side of the road and they passed me by like I wasn't even there, so I thought it was all a mistake and Susan and I were just getting paranoid about the whole Santa thing and I was singing along with the radio – I remember the song: "I Got You Babe," by Sonny and Cher. I'm on my street, see, and there was no Santa up the telephone pole like Susan said there was, and I'm ready to pull into my driveway when I spot another Santa following me in a Mr. Softee truck. That's when I got out of the car and started to approach the ASS Santa in the Mr. Softee truck. And guess what the ASS Santa did? He turned on the Mr. Softee music! You know: 'da da, da da da, da dat da da – da dat da da, da daaa da.' And when he did that all the children came running out of the houses to buy ice cream! I'm watching it right now! The ASS Santa is selling ice cream to all the neighborhood kids! And so, here I am in the middle of the street talking to you. Got it?"

"Can you be here in half an hour, Mr. Kaminski? We're in the old Sears Tower, on the thirty-fourth floor."

"I'll be right there!"

86

It didn't take Don very long to go downtown, park, and walk over to the Sears Tower. And no wonder! Don's not really sure how he got there at all! He certainly doesn't remember driving! Don's mind is spinning thinking so many crazy thoughts about Santas, elves, midgets (or are they dwarfs?), cops, Chinese, gamblers, Jews, lawyers, jewelry salesmen, Rabbi Peckerman, the Little Sisters of the Poor, St. Ignatz the Martyr, and in-laws, not to mention the Hatfields, the McCoys, and little black Santas! Well, his head is just about ready to explode right there in the car when he thinks of one word that saves him – REVENGE!

Don reaches the main entry and asks the guard at the desk if in fact the law office for Abramowitz, Abramowitz and Laganelli is located on the thirty-fourth floor. The spit and polish guard on duty is none other than Doug Stamboolian, USMC scout and sharpshooter, retired. Stamboolian can spot a wacko a mile away, but he's not quite sure about Don Kaminski, and so, to be on the safe side, he has one finger on the alarm button under his desk while his other hand inches towards his super-charged automatic rifle with two new notches on it for poor Santa Rajneesh's kneecaps!

"Yes, sir," Stamboolian says with a big grin on his face. *Go ahead – make my day!* "Abramowitz, Abramowitz and Laganelli are located on the thirty-fourth floor. The elevators are behind me and to the left."

"Thank you, officer." Don walks smartly over to the elevators while Stamboolian follows his every move ready for more action and a few more notches.

Don's on his way up to see Abramowitz, Junior and realizes he's humming "Here Comes Santa Claus" on the elevator. Two very shapely young secretaries bust out laughing and smile at Don.

"I hope you two are on the good list?" he says.

"We do too, Santa!" one of them says, "But I think she's on the naughty one!"

"Remember, Santa's watching," Don says as he exits the elevator.

Don finds the office quickly and enters. He marches right up to the woman at the reception desk.

"Hello, my name is..."

"Donald Kaminski," she says with a smile. "Hello, Mr. Kaminski. I'm Rosalie." She holds out her hand and Don shakes it. "We talked earlier on the phone."

"Sure, Rosalie; Good to meet you in person."

"The same here, Mr. Kaminski. Please have a seat. Mr. Abramowitz, *Junior* will be with you shortly." Don grabs a seat and glances around the waiting area. *Nice, but not extravagant like I thought.* He reaches for a magazine and starts to thumb through the latest issue of the duPont Registry showing the latest exotic cars, homes and boats. He sighs a little when he sees a red, 1989 Ferrari 328 GTS for only $79,900. *Only $79,900! Hell, I'll just write a check! NOT!*

RING...RING

Rosalie picks up the phone and before she can say a word...

"Hi, Rosalie, it's Doug Stamboolian. Did a Mr. Kaminski just show up at your office?"

"Yes, that's right. Is there a problem?"

"That's why I'm calling you, Rosalie. Is everything okay? Is he acting normal-like?"

"Everything is fine here, Doug."

"Well call me if he gets a little crazy, will you?"

"Will do. Goodbye Doug, and thank you for calling."

"You got it, babe. We still on for Friday night?"

"Roger that."

BUZZ

87

The inner-office door opens and out steps Jacob Abramowitz, Junior. A rather short, but handsome man, about fortyish, very trim with Roman features, olive skin, full head of dark brown hair with just a hint of being recently planted in neat little rows. He is dressed in a shark-skin colored suit with a designer name only Donald Trump and King Faisal would recognize. His hand-crafted silk shirt is a beautiful light pink with matching pink and black silk tie – Windsor knot, of course, complete with a specially designed Rolex watch.

I probably couldn't afford the highly polished, platformed shoes he's wearing, Don thinks. In fact, these shoes were specially made for him in Morocco. The wooden carved model of his feet for making his hand-crafted shoes, complete with his full name engraved on top, sit on a shelf in the back of the store in Casablanca next to those marked "Bill Gates" and a dusty "Frank Sinatra."

Abramowitz walks right up to Don and offers his hand.

"Good Afternoon, Mr. Kaminski. My name is Jacob Abramowitz, Junior. I understand you have a bit of a problem."

Don stands and returns the handshake.

"Yes, sir, I surely do." They both smile a one another and Don immediately has the feeling that everything is going to be okay.

"Please come this way, Mr. Kaminski and let's talk about this problem, shall we?" Abramowitz ushers Don into an inner hallway where there are a number of office doors and a whole lot of traffic with lawyers, clients, and secretaries coming and going.

Busy place! Don thinks.

"In here, please, Mr. Kaminski." Abramowitz opens the door to a very plush and cozy office where they sit at the coffee table in big leather chairs.

"Please, call me Don."

"Great, Don. Please call me Jake."

Coffee is served by an assistant while Don takes his time and explains to Jake Abramowitz his never-ending story, how he is trying so hard to make it through Christmas, and how he feels his basic rights as an

American have been violated. After several hours of talking back and forth with questions and answers being posed from both sides, Abramowitz stands up, indicating Don should do the same, shakes Don's hand and says, "Don, I've got everything I need. I'm glad you're here with me today. Please don't worry about a thing. I've got it all under control, Don. You will be hearing from me, personally, very soon."

Don stands, shakes Abramowitz, Junior's hand and feels like the weight of the world has been lifted from his shoulders. They walk out to the reception area where Abramowitz, Junior pats Don on his shoulder and says,

"Good to meet you, Don. Call you soon!"

"Thanks, Jake. I really am happy I came here today."

"Rosalie," Abramowitz says, "please take good care of Mr. Kaminski." He turns and exits back into the inner-sanctum. Don reaches for his wallet.

88

As luck would have it, Don spots another ASS Santa tailing him on a Honda Goldwing as he drives home. *Keep it up you ASS-holes! I'll see you ALL in court!* He speeds up a bit and loses the tail. *Does it make a difference? They know where I live!* Don makes it home in record time. As he pulls into the driveway he sees yet another real-bearded Santa across the street with clipboard and dressed in work clothes acting like he's some kind of meter reader. Don's now out of the Volvo. The motor is running as he races across the front lawn.

"Hey, asshole!" The ASS Santa stops dead in his tracks and faces Don from across the street while attempting to hide his beard with the clipboard.

"That's right – YOU!" Don's getting red in the face and points his finger at the ASS Santa.

"You come any closer and I'll shave your fucking beard off! You hear me?" The ASS Santa drops the clipboard and hightails it up the street and out of sight as Don yells after him.

"And go tell the head Nazi-Santa son-of-a-bitch that I'll see him in court!" Sue comes out the back door and is trying to smile at Don but it isn't working.

"Everything okay, dear?" She looks at her husband for any signs of normalcy. Don's face is fire engine red and his hands are shaking.

"Who are you yelling at, Dear?"

"It's okay, Susan. I'm fine. I'm fine! I really am, honest." He raises his arms, palms out as if to show he isn't carrying any weapons.

"Really, Don? I wouldn't have guessed that you're fine by the tone of your voice just now."

"… just some asshole up the block, that's all. I'm okay, honest."

"Don, your language lately has really become atrocious and I've been meaning to talk to you about it."

"I'm sorry, Sue. I really am and I'll try to keep a check on things and choose my words more carefully in the future. I promise." Just then an old Ford passes by rapidly. It's the ASS Santa, and he gives Don the finger.

"Fuck you too, Santa!" Don yells at the car. Sue walks back into the house.

RING…RING…RING

"Hello…" Sue answers…Yes he is – just a second." Sue goes to the kitchen door and sees a disgruntled Don moping around in the yard. "Don, it's for you, dear."

"Who is it?" he barks back.

"A Mr. Abraham or something, I believe he said." Don races across the yard and grabs the phone from Sue.

"Hello, Jake? Is that you?"

"Sure is, Don. Got good news for you, buddy."

"Yes…?"

"There's going to be an arbitration hearing before Judge Daniel Herbert, this coming Monday at ten o'clock in courtroom six, down at the Richard J. Daley Center. Judge Herbert is a just about to retire from the bench and wants to go out in style. He figures if he can end the Santa wars and get to the bottom of all this, and if all parties involved can reach an agreement where we all win, well…that's what he's after – a win–win situation. He wants to be remembered as the judge who saved Christmas and the Chicago Santas. That's the way he wants to go out – saving Chicago's Santas and keeping as many of them as he can out of jail and out of the hospital. Is this agreeable to you, Don?"

"Why sure, sure! I'd like nothing better than to end this thing, Jake. How in the hell did you get this done so fast!" *'Good'?…This guy is unbelievable!'* Don thinks a bit, "Ah…Jake, hold on a minute. You said something about other Santas? Are there other Santas involved in this? I thought this case was about me personally being excluded from working at the local malls because I'm Jewish? Isn't this our case? Why are there other Santas involved? I don't get it?"

"You're right, Don. This is our case, but you're just the tip of the iceberg, buddy, believe me. This Santa problem has gotten out of hand. Important people, and I mean at the top, are talking about doing away with Santas and Christmas this year unless this mess is straightened out right now! That's why Judge Herbert is involved. This bench hearing is going to involve *you* along with ALL the Santas, and little elves – dwarfs – midgets – whatever the hell they are, I'm not really sure! Anyway, all the Santas and elves who work in the Chicago area will be subpoenaed to appear before the judge whether they belong to the Amalgamated Society of Santas or not; even the misfits who work for Gigante and Associates, LLC, along with Mimo Gigante, Sr., some Rabbi from New York City – go figure that one out – a local group Puerto Ricans who call themselves the 'Puerto Rican Civil Rights Battalion and Low-Rider Association,' the 'Black Elks Pride of Chicago,' the Greek Orthodox Church – don't even ask me about that connection – about half the local police department, some little black Santa who's supposedly hustling a bunch of old ladies out of their Social Security checks, and one Indian fellow – not an Native American kind, the Seven-Eleven kind – who owns a Dunkin' Donuts and claims he has evidence about some missing Old Fashioned donuts and wants to be involved, and, last but not least, the star of the show, the Exalted Santa himself, Sam Robinson.

"Yeah?" Don is shocked. *I think I know that Indian fellow – the Seven-Eleven one.*

"Well, they're all going to be there. Judge Herbert legally invited them all to participate at the hearing. I suppose with all the notoriety this will get from the press conference being held tomorrow afternoon by Judge Herbert down on Daley Plaza, there should be enough press there to cover the event and plaster it all over the news for the next two weeks. It's going to be a real circus, Don, but at least we will get to the bottom of this once and for all."

"So, listen, Jake…will I be able to work as a Santa at the mall?"

"Don't know, Don. I didn't plan for all of this, Judge Herbert did, and to tell you the truth, if this doesn't go quite the way he's planning, saving Christmas and Santas and all…Chicago might end up having to cancel Christmas this year!"

"Cancel Christmas!"

"Look, Don, if things get nasty in the courtroom, this could all end up in litigation and tie up the court system for the next year or so. This is big, buddy! There's even talk about money laundering, selling fake Gucci handbags, and even black market sales of living body organs to the medical profession! This is way bigger than Don Kaminski needing a part-time Santa job to hold him over for the holidays. There could be indictments if Judge Herbert can't keep this under wraps and end up with a peaceful solution. He says he can, but I have my doubts. Anyway, I'm your attorney and I'll make darn sure you come out of this unscathed."

"ME?"

"Yes, YOU, Don. Weren't you locked up the other day? – or did I just imagine that part of our discussion?"

"Yes, but I didn't do anything wrong! What do they want ME for?"

"Look, Don, you and I know you are just an innocent bystander, but the court system doesn't know that! Judge Herbert doesn't know that! This is why you have me as your lawyer. I promise you, you will be okay when this is all over. Trust me!"

"Okay, Jake. I trust you. You're my man and I'm glad you are representing me."

"Good, Don. Relax. I've got our part of this under control. See you down at the courthouse on Friday, okay?"

"Sure thing, Jake, and thank you."

"You're welcome, Don. You'll be hearing from Rosalie this week."

That's a given!

Part 3

IT ENDS

According to a tradition which can be traced to the 1820s, Santa Claus lives at the North Pole, with a large number of magical elves, and nine (originally eight) flying reindeer. Since the 20th century, in an idea popularized by the 1934 song "Santa Claus Is Coming to Town,' Santa Claus has been believed to make a list of children throughout the world, categorizing them according top their behavior ("naughty" or "nice") and to deliver presents, including toys, and candy to all of the good boys and girls in the world, and sometimes coal to the naughty children, on the single night of Christmas Eve. He accomplishes this feat with the aid of the elves who make the toys in the workshop and the reindeer who pull the sleigh.

From Wikipedia, the free encyclopedia

"Sometimes the bumper sticker is right:
SHIT HAPPENS!"

Dan Slipetsky

89

High noon on Daley Plaza and Judge Daniel Albright Herbert steps to the special lectern set up for his proclamation to the world – if not the world, at least all of Chicago.

This is big! He can see the press now, "JUDGE HERBERT SAVES CHRISTMAS!" *Ah, yes – this is BIG alright and I'm just the man to do it!*

The press is here, the politicians are here, the bankers and insurance bigwigs are here, the police and firefighters are here, and the Patels are all here, except for the ones who have to stay back to watch the tills at all the Dunkin' Donuts throughout Chicago. And *everyone* is excited to see how Judge Herbert is going to pull this one off. Not too long ago, some un-named trial judge who wanted to make a name for himself, tried the same approach about accepting gay marriages was met with a barrage of eggs and fruit. This created so much bad press, he moved to Rehoboth, Delaware to get lost.

The sun is out and it's a glorious day. Still many of the onlookers were wearing raincoats just in case the judge says something stupid and it starts raining fruit and eggs again. The U.S. and Illinois flags proudly wave on each side of the lectern almost daring any lowlife to toss an egg or rotten orange is this direction. *Go ahead! Who dares throw anything at these grand old flags and soil the sacred ground of Daley Plaza!*

"Good afternoon. My name is Daniel Herbert and I am a superior court judge for Cook County."

Everyone on the plaza knows that. In fact, just about everyone in Chicago knows, has read about, and can recognize Judge Herbert from the positive press he's received over these many years from the high-profile cases he's presided over. Daniel Herbert, for as short as he is, about five feet-two, is one *very big man* in Chicago politics and carries a lot of weight at the State House as well. He's a senior citizen for sure, but has never let his age slow him down. Well built and exercising daily, some say Daniel Herbert looks like a middle-aged Tom Cruise, the actor. He's smooth alright. Socializes with all the "Who's Who," and goes to all the gala parties with his attractive wife,

Jean. He's been invited to the White House several times for his opinions on matters important to the president and for sure, he has the ear of the governor and both senators when he needs it.

"First of all, I wish to thank all of the men and women of the press for being here this gorgeous afternoon. I promise I won't keep you very long. First, I am going to make a brief statement and then will take questions." Judge Herbert pauses to gather his thoughts. *This is my shining moment in the sun!*

"You, members of the press, have been reporting, and all of you have been reading in the news lately, about the rash of incidents around our fair city involving, what appears to be, a gaggle of lunatic Santas."

The audience can't help but laugh a little here. Some of the more recent headlines include: "Ninja Santa Attacks Children," "Santa Arrested in Gambling Den," "Al-Qaeda Trained Santa Unleashed in Chicago," "Orthodox Santa Crowned with Antlers," and who can forget, "Cell Full O' Santas!" just to mention a few.

"Some of you have even reported, unsubstantiated, I might add, that these incidents and their perpetrators are part of a larger conspiracy to keep Christ out of Christmas." This comment brings on even more laughter. Judge Herbert smiles and holds up his hands for silence as he continues. "I can assure all of you that this is not the case. There is no conspiracy of any sort as I see things, but there are many misunderstandings, injustices, and perhaps even criminal acts against the citizens of this great city that have, unfortunately, taken place within the past week or so."

Judge Herbert again pauses for effect. "This kind of behavior will not be tolerated and IS going to stop right now, I assure you!" Eyebrows raise. Several rain-coated spectators crouch down in a huddle to avoid any flying missiles.

"This Friday, at ten a.m. sharp, I will be holding an open hearing where all the parties involved will have their say. I promise you the court system will get to the bottom of this and try to make some sense of it all. Damages will be paid for and time may be served by Santas, elves or anyone else who decides to break the law in the City of Chicago. Are there any questions?"

The reporters surge forward towards the platform, raising their hands and trying to get in the first question.

"Judge Herbert! Judge Herbert!" they all shout.

"Yes." The judge points to a woman in the front row.

"Is it true that you are only doing this because you intend to run for governor in the next election?" This question is from Madeline Wilson from the Chicago Tribune.

"Madeline, you and I have known each other for many years now, and you have always been fair in reporting about me – and I greatly appreciate that." She shakes her head in agreement but still remains silent waiting for an answer. "It's true that I will be retiring from the bench, and very soon. This should be no secret to anyone. I announced this fact at least four months ago and you people printed it." Judge Herbert pauses again. "It is true, the notion of running for political office *has* crossed my mind several times over the years, but I can honestly say to you today, that I have NO designs on running for *anything*, once I retire. I may perhaps teach a few courses here and there" The judge looks directly at Madeline Wilson. "You know what I'm going to do when I retire, Madeline?" She smiles. "I'm going to travel throughout this great land of ours with my lovely wife, Jean. That's what I'm going to do when I retire. Does that answer your question?"

"Judge Herbert! Judge Herbert!"

"You, sir – go ahead." He points to a young man with long stringy, unkept hair on the far right of the group dressed in what looks like a Daniel Boone buckskin outfit with matching buckskin boots.

"What about the rumor that you were recently turned down for starting an off-shore hedge fund using money obtained from city pension funds?" This question comes from a new guy to the press corps representing some off-the-wall monthly paper professing the end of capitalism called, "Students for Industrial Workers of the World."

"Son, I have no idea what you are talking about? I have a simple IRA for my retirement. I have a checking account with about a thousand dollars in it. My savings account amounts to roughly eight thousand dollars. I own one car – an American one at that – an older Cadillac with about a hundred and fifty-five thousand miles on it and it's still a beauty – just waxed it myself a month ago. Original paint job – can you imagine that? And it still looks like new!" More laughter from the crowd. "I own a relatively expensive apartment here in the city. I admit that. And believe me, young man, when I tell you this. I *earned* it – through a lot of hard work…I have a small vacation bungalow where I go fishing somewhere in Michigan, and I won't tell you where it is so that it can remain a private spot – and besides, the fishing's great! It has an outside well for water and an outhouse with two holes in the seat." Judge Herbert wishes he could say but doesn't, *In the cool summer evenings, my wife Jean and I like to go out there, leave the doors open, take a shit together, and watch the ducks land!* The total value of this property, including rustic cabin, is about fifteen to twenty thousand, at most." More chuckles from the reporters. "Believe me, son, I personally have no extra money to sink into a hedge fund. I have *not* made any loans from city pension funds. And I have *not* absconded with anyone else's money! Furthermore, young man, I don't even *know* what a hedge fund does! As it is, I have a hard enough time just trying to balance my checkbook!" Several reporters begin to clap at this comment as others laugh out loud again. *Now go the fuck home, get out of that Buffalo Bob outfit and wash that greasy-assed hair of yours and get a haircut, you commie fuck!*

"Judge Herbert! Judge Herbert!"

"Okay." Herbert points to a rather tall man in the center of the group.

"What about the ties to al-Qaeda in the recent shooting at the tower." This question is from Wayne Richardson of the Chicago Sun-Times – a "gun slinger" itching to put Judge Herbert on the spot.

"Any time the word 'al-Qaeda' comes into play, the Department of Homeland Security becomes involved. This incident, along with the suspicion that this may be the case, was already reported and investigated by Homeland Security. The facts are, based on the rapid and yet thorough investigation performed, that there are NO, I'll repeat that, NO connections to al-Qaeda with the shooting incident that took place this past Saturday at the Willis Tower."

"Judge Herbert! Judge Herbert!"

"Yes, madam." Herbert singles out a woman towards the left.

"Judge Herbert, the Daily Herald would like to know how and why you made the decision you did against the Carlucci Small Arms Manufacturers last month, which in essence, put them out of business?" The crowd of reporters all turned to get a look at the dumb broad who had the nerve to open up this juicy can of worms. It was none other than Suzanne King, the shapely, blonde reporter from the Herald who broke darn near every news-worthy story since she was hired out of Washington, DC.

"Good afternoon, Suzanne. Something told me you would be here today. Good to see you."

"Good to see you too, Judge Herbert – got an answer?"

"Yes, Suzanne, as a matter of fact, I do." The judge pauses, smiles, and stares directly at Ms. King. "This news briefing is not about that. This news…"

"Still, Judge Herbert, I'm darn sure the good people of Chicago, as you put it, would more than love to hear your explanation for your surprising actions in this case…Judge?"

"Again, Suzanne, if you will kindly allow me to finish. This news briefing is about the Santa crises. As to the latter, I would be more than willing to meet with you on a one-to-one basis to explain why I did what I did. Fair enough? Just call and set up the appointment at your convenience. Thank you, Suzanne."…*you fucking cunt!*

"Judge Herbert! Judge Herbert!"

"Yes, sir…you in the back there…yes, you."

"Dale Leslie from the Chicago Free Press – Judge Herbert, what can you tell us about the unfortunate gay Santa who was tarred and feathered down at the pipefitter's union hall recently?" The crowd tries real hard not to laugh at this one, but you could still hear a few sniggers here and there.

"All I know right now is that the young man in question is improving nicely under hospital supervision and expects to recover soon with a hundred percent mobility. I might add, however, that he wasn't really tarred and feathered…he was covered in dark chocolate and jimmies, I believe that's what you call them." No stifling the laughter now. The entire audience, including reporters, is in an uproar with poor Leslie looking all around and not understanding at all such insensitivity. *Oh, the inhumanity of it all!*

"Judge Herbert! Judge Herbert!"

"Okay, last question." He points to a chubby old guy in the second row.

"Judge Hairbert…I vas vanting to know eef true dat orthodox Santas are treated different from udder Santas in de jails, wid dat moose atlers on head? How you see dat, your honor, sir?"

"Yes, I believe I got that and understand the drift of your question, but first of all, allow me to ask who you are, sir, and what paper do you represent."

"Yes, your honor, sir...I am Stash Brodzinski from da Polish Daily News. Da Polish peoples in Chicago wery upset dat a real priest who work like Santa, being treated like low-life, even if he is orthodox and not real Catholic like regular Polish peoples."

"Well, Mr. Brodzinski..."

"Please, your honor, sir, calling me Stash."

"Okay, Stash. I'm not sure how to answer that one. I wasn't there to witness the incident...but I will say this. My dealings with the Chicago Police department over the years have demonstrated to me that these men and women are nothing but professional and that their treatment of the public has been, for the most part, fair, equal, and very professional. I would like to think that all the citizens of Chicago get fair and equal treatment by the police, fire, and all other departments of city government and services. I hope that answers your question, Stash."

"No, sir, but thanks to you all da same, your honor, sir." Judge Herbert looks around puzzled and decides to move on and close the briefing.

"Again, ladies and gentlemen of the press, thank you very much for being here and covering this important news briefing. You are all invited to the open hearing, right here, this coming Monday morning at ten o'clock, in courtroom six. Thank you." And with that success, Judge Daniel Albright Herbert steps away from the lectern and proceeds down off the riser and into the arms of his lovely wife, Jean. He receives a hug and a kiss from Jean as she whispers, "Good Job, Herbie. I hope for your sake Christmas isn't cancelled."

"Thanks, Jeannie, I'm hungry. Let's go to lunch."

"You buying?"

"Sure thing, babe. Just got another check from that off-shore deal I was telling you about."

90

The big day finally arrives – Monday – another bright and sunny day with very little wind for the "Windy City" – and Daley Plaza is packed with people rushing inside, passing through security, and trying to get a good seat for the hearing of the century. What a great day to make all kinds of decisions that will impact a great many people in this fine City of Chicago. There's a crowd of people mingling outside on Daley Plaza. The place is buzzing with excitement. Several protestors have signs which read, "Judge Herbert on Naughty List!" "Don't Cancel Christmas," "Free Santa Now," "Santa Answers to a Higher Authority," and "Puerto Ricans for Equality."

Courtroom six, the largest one in the building, is opened early and it's already darn-near filled to capacity; even the newly renovated balcony, which completely surrounds the courtroom, is filling up quickly. Extra court ushers and bailiffs have been assigned to make sure all remain civil. Police patrols have been beefed up inside the building and outside on Daley Plaza. Security is the optimum word. Folding chairs have been gathered from the four corners of the Earth and set up in expectation of a record crowd. No doubt about it, everyone in Chicago is tuning in to the Santa debacle.

Don Kaminski is here with his entire family: Susan, Annie and Junior. His parents, Marsha and Max, have come along for support, and besides Max wouldn't miss this for anything. This is much better than "The Price Is Right." As soon as they enter the building and finally make their way through a rather thorough security check, they nudge through the crowd and enter courtroom six. Don sees the press corps and court reporters all gathered in the back of the courtroom, no doubt discussing the hearing and coming up with more catchy headlines like "Nix on Saint Nick," "No Presents This Year Kids, Santa's In the Slammer!" and "Kringle In a Pickle!"

"Are you sure you got Abramowitz, JUNIOR, Donald?" Max asks while adjusting his *yarmulke.*

"Yes, Pop – for the tenth time, I hired Jacob Abramowitz, JUNIOR to be my attorney."

"Jacob? How about that? I didn't even know he had a first name. All I ever heard was Abramowitz, Junior."

Don just shakes his head and smiles at his father. He sees his long-time buddy from school, Chick Falzone, the phys. ed. teacher, up in the balcony section with old Millie Cramer, the librarian. Don waves to them and smiles. You just can't see Millie Cramer without thinking of the "Dick Hurts" incident.

"Look, Donald," Max says in surprise and points ahead to the large oak tables for the prosecution and defense. "They're all here – Abramowitz, Abramowitz AND Laganelli. This is a big thing, I'm telling you! Laganelli never shows himself in public. Just look at how he keeps looking at Abramowitz and Abramowitz? Told you he's just here to keep an eye on things for the mob, didn't I?"

Max invited Rabbi Peckerman to attend the formalities all the way from New York City and darn if he didn't show up complete with a large fedora hat which they allowed him to wear inside but only until Judge Herbert enters the courtroom. Then he has to take it off. Judge Herbert has the last "say" in this room – not God.

Max looks at the Rabbi and asks, "Rabbi, do you like Drew Carey?"

"Who?"

"Drew Carey...Drew Carey! – the big TV star from 'The Price Is Right' – Drew Carey."

"Of course I do!" the Rabbi smiles. "He's the funniest Jew on TV today!"

"You're right! You're right about that, Rabbi! I keep telling everybody that, but they don't listen!"

"Look guys," Don addresses family and the Rabbi, "Find a place to sit and get comfortable. I think this might take some time. I have to sit at the table with my attorneys."

"Good luck, Donald."

"Give 'em hell, son!"

"Good luck, Daddy."

"Try not to get angry and say something stupid, Don."

"Don't say anything bad about ASS, Pop!" The Rabbi stares at Junior with a frown on his face, then back to Don, Senior.

"*Mozel tov*, Mr. Kaminski."

Don makes his way to center stage and sees all the Santas he attended class with at Gigante and Sons. *Look, there's Mimo, Sr. having a heated discussion with Mimo, Jr. Guess Sal and Vic had to stay back home parking the boats...or was that Joey and Paulie? I can't remember. I get them all mixed up anyway. Good thing Jackie's not here or the place would be covered in smoke!*

"Hola, gringo!" comes from the side somewhere and Don spots the crazy, Puerto Rican, Santa Domingo, wheeling in the Santa in the wheelchair with no legs, Santa Rick. *Good Lord, he's actually smiling and waving at me.* Santa Rick also gives Don a big smile, nods and gives the peace sign. Don waves back while at the same time wondering if Santa Domingo did something to the Volvo in the parking lot. Behind them stroll the two Puerto Ricans who smashed up the Chevy low-rider, Tito and Carlos, waving some kind of banner about Puerto Rican pride. A security guard, squeezed into a uniform about two sizes too small, rushes up to them and convinces them that they should surrender the banner, which they do without any grief. It's none other than ex-mall Security Chief, Paul Simpkins. And who's that behind him to make sure all is complied with? – His new boss, ex-mall cop, Billy Watkins. My, my – how things can change.

Anita Wang, the owner of Fat Wang's Chinese Take-Out, is present in a new vibrant red, satin dress complete with about six chopsticks planted in her black dyed, crows-nest hairdo. *Wonder how she got all those chopsticks past security?* Santa Rajneesh is here as well and hobbles in on two crutches. He's still experiencing a lot of pain in his knees but he's smiling anyway and nodding to everyone in the courtroom whether he knows them or not. The motorcycle chic, Santa Anita, swaggers in dressed all in black leather and it looks as though some of her chains have been removed. *She probably had a tough time with security,* Don thinks. *She IS walking a lot better, I'll say that for her.*

Ninja Santa Lee is over there with them and doesn't look too happy considering he might end up doing a little time when this is all over. Shuly Patel, the owner of the Dunkin' Donuts, is present and carrying a large bag of Old Fashioned donuts. *He probably had to bribe the guards to get those in here.* And sure enough, Don sees Shuly handing out donuts and flyers to anyone who will have one. The Patriarch, Zoltan Shimko glides in next and looks around as if waiting for an usher to escort him to the best seat in the house. The two altar boys follow him and Don notices they aren't carrying a thing – no brushes, no incense burners, nothing. Don guesses security wouldn't allow brushes and incense in the courtroom.

Sue's parents, Eunice and Bobby Lee, called early last evening to wish Don the best of luck. Bobby repeated the offer he made last week to be present with Doke Candy, who according to Bobby, "Done some fancy lawyerin' for hisself when the cock fights got raided last year," and they "busted up his still real good." Don thanked him anyway and said that wouldn't be necessary.

"I'm-a tellin' you, Don, this here boy is about the smartest Chambers we got down on the mountain. He can really help!"

"No, thanks, Pop. No doubt he is one of the smartest of the Chambers clan, but I think we got things pretty much under control here. Thanks anyway."

"Well, Don, if you need anything, I mean especially if you have to spend some time in jail, be sure to give us a call, that's if you can. All us Chambers boys know what it's like to be in jail, you know."

"Will do, Pop. And thanks again."

"Oh, and by the way. Tell SuzyAnn that cousin Tammy got knocked-up for sure this time at the last revival meetin' an' she blowed up bigger 'an a refrigerator already! She ain't tellin' who the father is. Tell you the truth, I don't think she knows. Some folks around here are sayin' it was one of the snake handlers or that young preacher fella who just about milked this town out of every dime we had. It's a real mystery, for sure."

"Okay, Pop. I'll be sure to tell her. Got to go, Pop. See you, and thanks for calling."

Along the right wall, Don spots some of Chicago's finest, deep in discussion. Led by Sgt. Alphonso LaManna, Officers Patrick Malone and Sean O'Malley lead fellow officers in discussing the recent rash of Santa capers and the possible outcome of the hearing. Malone brings up the crowning of the Russian Santa with the Moose antlers.

"No, Malone. Those were Elk antlers."

"Whatever!"

The police men and women present are all smiling and laughing at story after story but Sgt. Alphonso LaManna doesn't look very happy. *He's probably wondering if the Washington sisters will sue the police department again.* Not far from them stands ex-cop, Sylvester Jardine, who is out free on bail pending the investigation, and ex-Detective Carlo DiSabatino, who looks as though he's wearing a huge medical wrap over his crotch. *Sure hope Sylvester left his throw-down weapon at home!* Don thinks. In walk the Inner Pride Guard, Eustice Pinson along with the Grand Exalted Pride Ruler, Leroy Maxwell, from the Black Elk's Pride of Chicago. *Probably here to make sure they can collect for the damages done at the lodge hall when they had the Moose Crowning Ceremony.*

A parade of midgets (or are they dwarfs?), led by Buddy Holly the Elf, and fresh from the Mini Bar down on Rush Street, by the smell of it, are making their way to some front-row seats in the balcony: Marty and Billy, Sally and Danny, Ginny and Betty, and finally Mary and Miroslav the Bulgarian who doesn't speak English very well. They are busy talking and laughing, and waving to the crowd who become a little excited to see all the elves appear in courtroom six.

Paul Waxman and Wayne Jarusinski from the mall are here seated next to Mitsy Guilday. *Waxman and Jarusinski are hoping they still have a mall Santa when this is over. Mike Guilday probably had to stay back at the restaurant to break more eggs for the customers?* Not far from where they are sits the nurse-practitioner from the hospital, Roman Sigurdson. *Hope he brought some medical supplies with him. We might need them!*

There's a slight disturbance at the entrance to courtroom six. Several security officers appear to be shoving someone around and all hear, "Youse don' needs to be friskin' Jimmy D. for no kinda shit! Jimmy D. asked to be here and now Jimmy D. here! What youse gonna do, send my ass back to da dumpster?" The next thing you know, Jimmy D. comes plowing through the officers and the crowd at the door and heads straight into the center of the room all decked out in his newly-cleaned Santa suit.

"Look, Miss Martha! There's our little black Santa!" says Miss Emma. Jimmy is followed by his good friends Wanda, and Habib Constantine, owner of Bee Bee's Cash and Carry.

So you see, they're ALL here – well almost all. Things quiet down a bit and most people take to their seats, when in walks the ASS Santas with the Grand Exalted Santa leading the pack, Sam Robinson.

"I think I know this man," says Rabbi Peckerman.

"What did you say, Rabbi?" from Max.

"Nothing, Max – I was just thinking out loud. That man who just walked in with the bearded Santas – He looks familiar. He looks like someone I know from a long time ago, but it can't be."

Behind Robinson, all the good Christian, Nazi Santas march to their seats: Matthew, Daniel, Luke, Christopher, Mark and the rest. Even Clement, the butler is here, complete with white gloves.

Shuly Patel is passing by Max, the Rabbi, and the Kaminskis offering each of them a free Old Fashioned donut. In fact, just about everyone in the courtroom is eating one by now. For sure, the cops all have one. Sue declines but both Annie and Junior help themselves and Shuly hands them a half-page flyer with coupons for a new holiday coffee he wants to try out this season.

"No, thank you," the Rabbi declines the offer.

"Are they kosher?" asks Max.

"You didn't ask me that last night when you came into my store, Mr. Max!"

Marsha reaches over and smacks Max's hand as he reaches for the bag of donuts. Max stops and abruptly waves off Shuly like he never met the man before in his life.

"He's got me confused with someone else," he says to the Rabbi.

"No doubt about it, Max."

91

"All rise!" says the bailiff and everyone is quickly up out of their seats.

BUZZ! Goes the court alarm announcing the entry of Judge Herbert. The door behind the judge's bench opens and out comes the judge in his freshly pressed black robe. He doesn't have that professional stern look on his face that he usually has that warns all those present, especially the attorneys, "Don't hand me any of your bullshit today, boys and girls, because it's not going to work!" Instead, he has a mellow look about him. There's almost a smile on his face. *This is my crowning glory*, he thinks.

The bailiff announces in a stately voice, "The special hearing in the Superior Court of Cook County is now in session – the Honorable Judge Daniel Albright Herbert presiding. May God preserve and protect the City of Chicago and the State of Illinois."

"Please be seated," the judge announces as he takes his seat in the large, black leather chair behind the bench. "Ladies and gentlemen, before we begin I would like to make a few comments on these proceedings. This is a special bench hearing, and one that I personally called for. It is not a jury trial. In fact, it is not a trial at all. Yes, there are people seated in the jury box, but that's because they got here early and so they got the best seats in the house."

Nice to see the judge hasn't lost his sense of humor, Don thinks.

"I called for this special hearing because of a complaint lodged by a Mr. Donald Kaminski who claims he was turned down from being a mall Santa simply because he is Jewish. Upon investigation of the claim, Pandora's Box has been opened, you might say. There appears to be much, much more to all of this than you can imagine and there appears to be some connection between the recent rash of negative incidents involving Santas all over our city and the complaint made by Mr. Kaminski. It seems you can't pick up a newspaper without reading something naughty about some poor unfortunate Santa." This brings on a few chuckles.

"Many of them ended up in jail or in the hospital. This, to me, doesn't make any sense at all! What's happening here? Is there something in the water? Is there something behind all of this, or are these truly isolated incidents? Well, I aim to find out." Judge Herbert pauses to pour a cup of water and wet his whistle.

"My goal today is to try to sort this all out in order to find out if there *is* a connection to all these negative incidents and to see if the law has been broken, and if so, by whom; and if not, come to some sort of agreeable compromise so that we all can leave here today, hopefully, in a win-win situation." More water for the judge. "My mind is open. I will hear everyone's testimony. And I have no intent to cancel Christmas for Chicago!"

Applause and cheering abound in the courtroom as Judge Herbert gavels loudly for order several times. The balcony is buzzing with excitement.

"Many individuals have been invited here today to give testimony. Many have brought with them legal counsel – and rightly so; and I might add, many of them have white beards." Now there is laughter in the courtroom.

BANG!...BANG!...BANG!

Judge Herbert bangs the gavel and calls for order. "Sorry, folks; couldn't help myself. Please forgive me."

"We will begin this special hearing by calling Mr. Donald Kaminski to the stand. Mr. Kaminski, if you will, sir, please come forward." The courtroom comes even more alive as Don stands, has a few words with Abramowitz, Junior, and steps forward to the witness box.

"Just tell it like it is, Don," says the high-priced attorney.

"Don't worry, I intend to." Don reaches the witness stand and turns to face the Bailiff.

"Please raise your right hand, sir," from the Bailiff. He does.

"Do you swear to tell the truth, the whole truth, and nothing but the truth, so help you God?"

"I do."

"Please be seated."

"Please state your name for the record," says Judge Herbert.

"Donald Kaminski."

"Do you have a middle name, Mr. Kaminski?"

"No, your honor, I do not."

"What do you do for a living, sir?"

"I am a public school English teacher who is currently on strike."

"Hopefully that will end soon and all our teachers and children can get back to school soon."

"I sure hope so, your honor – I'm broke!" The packed courtroom laughs out loud on that one.

"Order please," cautions Judge Herbert. "Well, Mr. Kaminski, would you please explain to the court, in as few words as possible, just what is it that took place which made you feel that your rights have been violated."

"Certainly, your honor…recently, I contacted Mr. Sam Robinson, the Grand Exalted Santa of the Amalgamated Society of Santas, *Good thing I didn't say 'ASS'*, about the prospect of joining the association and getting a Santa job at one of the malls they represent. He invited me to meet with him at their grand lodge and interview for membership into the group. We did meet not long ago and everything went well, or so I thought, when he asked me about my last name – Kaminski. He wanted to know if I was Catholic. I said no, I am Jewish. Well your honor, that's when things changed in a hurry. Robinson turned into something other than inviting. He told me that there is no such thing as a Jewish Santa and I fully got the hint that I was not welcome there any longer. It became clear to me that I was never going to be admitted into the association and would never be employed as a mall Santa through this organization, anyway – not as long as I was Jewish. In fact, I was told point black to leave the building immediately or the police would be called. This is what I did, your honor. As you can imagine there's a lot more to this story, such as my family being followed by a number of Santas from the group and the suspicion that they even tapped our phones in order to monitor our conversations. Who knows what else this group did to me and my family or tried to do?"

"Mr. Kaminski," Judge Herbert begins, "do you have proof of any of these allegations? I mean this could end up being a "he said – she said" situation. Are their any eye witnesses?"

"Yes, your honor. Both my son, Junior, and my wife, Susan saw the repairman up the telephone pole with a white beard."

"And that proves 'what,' Mr. Kaminski?"

"It proves they are watching me and tapped into my phone lines!"

"Couldn't it just be a coincidence that a repair man had a white beard, Mr. Kaminski? Did you alert the phone company over your suspicions? Did anyone come to your house, say, to check to see if in fact the phones had been tapped?"

"No, your honor, I guess not."

"You guess not or you know not, Mr. Kaminski – which is it?"

"I did not notify the phone company, your honor, and I did not have the phones checked out, but the guy with the Santa beard was still up that pole! We saw him! And several Santas followed me throughout the day. One of them even sold ice cream on our street as a diversion!" Courtroom six is again overcome with laughter.

BANG!...BANG!...BANG!

Judge Herbert bangs the gavel a little harder this time.

"Order in the court, ladies and gentlemen, please!"

"Mr. Kaminski, are you telling me that a man in a white beard followed you to your street and began selling ice cream in December?"

"That's exactly what I'm telling you, judge. He did it in a Mr. Softee Truck." A large number of loud coughs and other noises made their way into the courtroom as those listening tried to stifle their laughs which came out as coughs, gags, and sneezes as well. Judge Herbert looked around the room for quiet, and he got it.

"Let me get this straight, Mr. Kaminski. You were followed by a Mr. Softee truck driven by a man with a Santa beard who then began to sell ice cream on your street in December. Is that it?"

"I object, your honor," from Abramowitz, Jr. "With all due respect, your honor, it appears you are leading my client into statements which, in turn, make my client appear to be quite deranged."

"It's all right here, Mr. Abramowitz." Judge Herbert is waving several sheets of paper for Abramowitz to see. "I got this information from a statement your client wrote and signed. I, sir, am doing the best I can to air this information for my benefit and the benefit of the court in order to better understand specifically what took place. I didn't make this up and I am not leading your client into making a false statement. As a matter of fact, Mr. Abramowitz, your signature is at the bottom of this statement as well! Did you happen to forget what exactly took place and what your client has written? I can give you a copy of this if in fact you need it. Furthermore, since I am shedding light on the truth, as you two see it, that is, why is it that you make the objection to begin with? Can you explain yourself, Mr. Abramowitz?" All eyes in the courtroom focus on Abramowitz, Jr. and he looks like the kid who just got caught stealing money out of Mom's purse – guilty as hell!

"No, your honor, I can't, and I respectfully withdraw my objection at this time and would ask the court to forgive my zealousness when it comes to protecting my client, your honor."

"So noted, Mr. Abramowitz and, I might add, the court *very much* appreciates your duty to your client." Judge Herbert reaches for the water pitcher again in hopes that the dust has settled once more and he can get back to hearing from Don Kaminski.

"Mr. Kaminski, would you like me to repeat my question to you, sir?"

"No, your honor, that won't be necessary. Everything you just said is the truth. Santa was selling ice cream on my street in December and that's why I feel he was using that as an excuse to follow me home and spy on me and my family."

"I see, Mr. Kaminski. Did anyone else witness the Santa selling ice cream?"

"Of course! All the kids on the block! And I would guess all the parents and grandparents who had to shell out the money to buy the ice cream!" More stifled laughter erupts into coughs, gags and even a couple of farts.

"Thank you, Mr. Kaminski. You may step down now." Don leaves the witness chair and heads back to Abramowitz. Both of them feel as though things didn't necessarily go their way and that they both ended up looking like a couple of nuts. Courtroom six is convinced of it as well!

92

"Would Mr. Sam Robinson please take the stand," Judge Herbert announces as he reaches for more water wishing it were something a little bit stronger. Robinson leans over to a man who looks a lot like Joseph Goebbles, the Nazi Reich Minister of Propaganda, and listens while "Goebbles" whispers something to him. Robinson shakes his head in agreement, stands and almost marches to the podium.

Go ahead, you Nazi bastard, you – give Judge Herbert here the good old Nazi salute, why don't you! Don is pissed. *I see you got yourself a good Nazi lawyer!*

"Please raise your right hand, sir," from the Bailiff. Robinson does.

"Do you swear to tell the truth, the whole truth, and nothing but the truth, so help you God?"

"I do."

"Please be seated."

"Thank you for being here today," Judge Herbert begins. "Would you mind stating your full name for the record?"

"Certainly, my name is Sam Robinson."

"Is that your legal name – not Samuel, by chance?"

"No, Sam Robinson is it."

"Mr. Robinson, did you in fact meet with Mr. Kaminski as he says?"

"Yes I did meet with Mr. Kaminski."

"Can you tell us what took place at this meeting?"

Rabbi Peckerman leans way over in his seat to try to get a better view of Sam Robinson, the ASS leader, and is shaking his head in disbelief.

"What's wrong, Rabbi?" Marsha asks in concern. Max looks to the Rabbi for some explanation of his strange behavior. "Are you ill, Rabbi?"

"I swear, I know this man but I can't figure out how? Still, there's something about his name that sounds familiar…Sam Robinson…Sam Robinson?"

"Rabbi," Max says, "You meet a lot of people every day. This guy might look like someone you met, perhaps years ago. Probably someone you helped or sold something to, you know what I mean?

Maybe you rented him one of your apartments over by the synagogue, or some such." *Maybe this poor schmuck bought one of your discounted hearts or livers along with a Gucci handbag for the old lady?* Max thinks.

"You're right, Max. He probably reminds me of someone I know from the past. Happens all the time, doesn't it? You get people all mixed up over the years...you're right, Max, you are right." The Rabbi ends the conversation and still he can't get over the notion that he really does know this man, and personally...but how?

"Mr. Robinson, would you please begin by telling the court about the organization you lead, the Amalgamated Society of Santas." With a proud look on his face, Robinson talks about ASS, only he doesn't call it that.

"I started the Amalgamated Society of Santas back in 1978 in the cellar of my home with just four local Santas and about a hundred bucks. Three of the founding Santas have since passed on, God rest their souls. The other has long since retired and is living in our Santa Retirement Village located in Bangor, Maine where he is very active organizing trips to the Indian casinos – not the Seven-Eleven kind, the Native American kind." Judge Herbert raises his eyes in disbelief.

"Since its inception," Robinson continues, "I have worked tirelessly to recruit the best-looking Santas to join the organization and live up to our very high standards. At the present time, I am proud to say, we have over three hundred natural-bearded Santas who are active members and reside all over the United States, not just here in Chicago, although I will mention that we have over sixty who live in Illinois and many in the Chicago area. Several years ago we made a bid and purchased the old federal-style building on Pulaski St. named after John Brown. It took us years to renovate the building to where it is today – a shining example of good deeds and hard work."

"That's quite some operation you must have there, Mr. Robinson, but let me ask you this: Is it the purpose of your organization to simply place Santas at the mall or is there more to it?"

"There's much more to our society. We are a fraternal organization and we have rules to live by. We try our hardest to set examples for others to follow through our beliefs and how we conduct ourselves in our daily lives."

"That's commendable, Mr. Robinson, providing these rules you mention do not violate the law or the constitutional rights of others. Can you at this time give us some examples of the rules you live by, Mr. Robinson?"

"Our rules for daily living are quite simple. We believe in keeping to ourselves and not getting involved in other people's business. We are not a political action group but we are conservative in our views and in our voting. We believe in living a simple life. We believe in working hard and in paying our bills and taxes. We like to keep things organized at home and recognize the importance of family values and support. Each member in our fraternity looks out for his brother and their families. We are a tight knit group and we are proud of our organization, its principles and its practices."

"Very good, Mr. Robinson, very good ideals I must say, but do you allow anyone to become a member of your fraternity?"

"No, we do not. Our standards are quite high, you see. Since this is a fraternity, we do not allow women to join. The wives of our Santas, I might add, are very supportive of our organization as we focus on old-time family values. Our Santas do not abuse alcohol or their families. The only drugs they take are the prescription kind and most all of us are veterans of our armed forces."

Robinson is on a roll now and has a lot more to say about ASS but he's getting a little parched and looks at Judge Herbert and quacks, "Say, do you think I could get some water around here?" Clement, Robinson's personal man-servant, looks around for a cup, a container, a jug, anything he can put water into to serve the boss but he is pinned down in the middle of the crowd so even if he had water for Robinson, he wouldn't be able to get within fifty feet of him to serve it.

Judge Herbert's raises his eyebrows a bit at the brisk way the water request was made and he smiles back at Sam Robinson. "That's no problem at all, Mr. Robinson." He turns to the Bailiff. "Scotty, would you mind pouring a cup of water for Mr. Robinson." Scotty the Bailiff reaches for a paper cup and begins to fill it with water. He hands the cup to Robinson. Now it's Judge Herbert's turn to serve up something to Mr. Robinson.

"There you are, Mr. Robinson. I hope it is cool enough for you. Oh, and by the way, Mr. Robinson, you WILL from now on acknowledge my presence here and address me as 'Your Honor.' You see, I too have rules which we live by here in MY courtroom. Is that understood, Mr. Robinson?"

"Yes, your honor." Robinson, along with the rest of courtroom six, sits up straighter and the smug look he wore all morning vanishes from his face. Now he looks like a scared little boy.

Stuff that in your pipe, you Nazi bastard, Don says to himself.

"By the way, Mr. Robinson, you mentioned 'veterans.' Are you a veteran, Mr. Robinson?"

"No, your honor, I have flat feet." Courtroom six laughs a little at this one.

"I see," Judge Herbert is still smiling as he directs Robinson, "You may continue with your dissertation."

"Yes, sir, your honor," Robinson downs the entire cup of water.

"The first requirement to belong to the Amalgamated Society of Santas is that you maintain a natural beard and that it be registered with the National Beard Registry."

"Excuse me please, Mr. Robinson, but I see you are clean shaven. Now I *am* a bit confused about your first requirement."

Robinson slightly flustered, "Well, you see, your honor, I…I can't grow a beard…never have been able to."

"So have you ever played Santa Claus with a fake beard, Mr. Robinson?"

"Well…no, your honor, I never have."

"I see…are you married, Mr. Robinson?" asks the judge. "Do you have a wife, children?"

"No, your honor, I never married."

"What about children, Mr. Robinson? You didn't answer that part of the question." The courtroom chortles over that one.

"No, your honor, I don't have any children."

"Again, I am confused, Mr. Robinson. I hear about all these old-time family values and yet you, Mr. Robinson, seem to have no family at all? Is this the case?"

"Yes, your honor, I live by myself…but I do have a man servant, Clement, who lives in the house with me."

"Is Clement paid for his services?" More laughter erupts from the crowd.

"Of course he is, your honor. Clement is paid quite well for his services."

"So then, the rules set up for the association, the fraternity as you call it, these rules, the rules YOU no doubt personally penned, are meant for everyone in the fraternity except you? Is that it, Mr. Robinson?"

"No, judge, no! – absolutely not! Other than being a Santa and being married, I follow ALL the rules just like all the other members." Robinson reaches for the empty water cup and Judge Herbert nods to Scotty to refill the cup.

"Let's get right to the point, shall we, Mr. Robinson? Did you in fact not allow Donald Kaminski to join your Santa group, the Amalgamated Society of Santas, because he is Jewish?"

"Yes, your honor, yes – I admit that. That is the truth. Who ever heard of a Jewish Santa? There is NO SUCH THING! Everyone knows that!"

As you can imagine, the entire courtroom is buzzing with all kinds of comments. The ASS Santas are all in agreement with Robinson as they nod their heads as they openly voice their comments to one another about keeping their society "pure." The misfit Santas are all confused and are asking one another, "Did you get that? How come no Jews?" Even the midgets (or are they dwarfs?) are all abuzz about the revelation.

"Didn't you once tell me you are Jewish?" Little Sally asks Buddy the Elf.

"Hell no!" he responds. "My mother might have been Jewish, once removed, but my father was adopted by Slovak Gypsies and forced into the circus business."

Buddy didn't realize how loud he was when he made that remark, but the entire upper gallery heard it and begins to laugh as they point to Buddy. The little people are all laughing as well. Judge Herbert has had enough of this and reaches for the gavel prepared to empty the entire courtroom if he needs to when all of a sudden Rabbi Peckerman jumps up out of his seat, points to Robinson and yells loud enough for everyone to hear.

"I remember you now! And you are a FRAUD!" Courtroom six is startled by the Rabbi and some begin to panic anticipating the Rabbi exposing some sort of automatic weapon and begin firing into the crowd. Security, from all over the room, begin to zero in on where the Rabbi is standing. They are talking into shoulder microphones, barking orders, and moving in for a quick takedown while never taking their eyes off the rabid Rabbi. Rabbi Peckerman continues to wave his finger at Robinson and it's all coming back to him now. He truly does know this so-called "Sam Robinson." Poor Robinson is white with fear. You can see the blood drain from his face as he looks at his accuser from across the courtroom. The Kaminskis seated next to the Rabbi look up at him in utter surprise. *The Rabbi has totally flipped out!* Judge Herbert is, for the moment, frozen in shock as he watches the Rabbi and waits to see what's next. His gavel is frozen mid air.

"I know YOU and I know WHO you are!" bellows Rabbi Peckerman. **"Your name is NOT Sam Robinson! Your name is SHMUEL ROBINOWITZ and YOU are a JEW!"**

Noise and pandemonium fill the courtroom. The ASS Santas are horrified at the revelation. They look at one another in pain not understanding any of this at all.

"He lied to us?" They can't believe the deceit!

"We remained pure and true to the cause and he was a phony all along!"

"The Grand Exalted Santa is a JEW!"

"What's next? The Easter Bunny is an Arab terrorist?"

BANG!...BANG!...BANG!...BANG!

Judge Herbert pounds the bench with his gavel so hard he could have driven an eight penny nail clean through the top. One more **BANG**, and the head of the gavel breaks off and flies into the crowd in a wicked curve.

"Ouch, goddamn that hurt!" Marco Foniolli yells out from his seat while rubbing the side of his head. "Hey, Abramowitz, I think I got one for you." Abramowitz, Jr. quickly acknowledges the call to arms with a quick nod of the head as he jots down the time on his legal pad. Scotty comes to Judge Herbert's aid with a new gavel he keeps on hand for just such an occasion.

"ORDER IN THE COURT! ORDER IN THE COURT!" Judge Herbert yells at the top of his lungs. The judge grabs the gavel from Scotty.

BANG!...BANG!...BANG! The new gavel rings out better than the old one did.

At least three security guards reach the Rabbi at the same time and grab for his shoulders and arms holding him secure while squeezing Kaminskis out all over the place. Junior is knocked clean off the bench and ends up on the floor dazed while some big fat oaf in a security uniform way too small for him is standing on Marsha's foot and grinding it into the floor while he struggles with the Rabbi. The cheeks of his big fat ass are pounding into Marsha's face from both sides as he tries to control the enraged Rabbi wrestling to get free of the guards who are all over him. Marsha is in a lot of pain and is struggling to scream and breathe at the same time but can't because of where her nose is stuck – right smack in the crack of ex-mall Security Chief, Paul Simpkins' big fat, smelly ass! Realizing that she's in trouble, can't speak, and about to pass out from the smell and lack of oxygen, Marsha is backhanding her left fist squarely into Max's chest with blows that Mohammed Ali would be proud of. Max begins to cough, spit, and double over in pain unsure of what the hell is happening. He tries desperately to gulp down some air as Marsha continues to knock the wind out of him. Finally, in shear panic, he begins to punch the fat security guard in the ass as hard as he can while being ever so careful not to deck Marsha. "Get your fat ass out of my wife's face!" he screams. "She can't breathe, you fat shit you!" Eventually he manages a right hook into the security guard's balls. That did it.

Annie is also screaming, "Watch it, fatso!" in trying to protect her mother from the onslaught. Sue has been forced out of her seat and is now straddling the arm of the bench in front or her. As uncomfortable as it is, there is a certain amount of sexual excitement as she is rocked back and forth by the movement of the struggle around her. She stops yelling for a minute and is beginning to enjoy the ride.

Don is watching the circus unfold before his eyes while hoping the family is okay. He stretches to see that everyone in the family is okay, but he can't tell from his position. He sees everyone but Junior, who remains on the floor underneath the Rabbi and what appears to be a heard of elephants jostling each other for position. Junior's okay, for the most part, and is concentrating on covering his head and his balls as the mob tangos above him trying to control Rabbi Peckerman.

"ORDER IN THE COURT! ORDER IN THE COURT!"
BANG!...BANG!...BANG!...BANG!

Judge Herbert about snaps his vocal chords as he hammers away with the gavel. Eventually things begin to settle down. The tango is over and Junior stands up. Don is relieved to see him. Ex-mall Security Chief, Paul Simpkins, happy that he wore his cup today because this isn't the first time he's been punched in the balls, removes his steel-toed boot from Marsha's foot and turns to the side allowing her to get a breath of fresh air that doesn't smell like shit. She immediately grabs for her foot. Max, however, is still pounding the hell out of the Simpkins' fat ass when the guard looks down at him and punches Max squarely on the top of his head.

BAM! Max almost goes blind with the pain. The golden griffin atop the blue stone of the security guard's high school class ring (class of '63), dents the top of Max's head and a bolt of searing white hot pain goes clean through his body to the tip of his toes. Max farts out loud and believes he might have soiled his pants. He gasps for air and grabs for Marsha.

"Max, are you okay?" she screams.

"What?…Well, I think so…you?"

"What's that smell?"

"I think I shit my pants, Marsha. We have to go home." Three rows of onlookers all glare at Max while trying to not breathe.

"Hey, buddy," from the side. "What the fuck did you eat?"

93

BANG!...BANG!...BANG!

"Order in the court, ladies and gentlemen, PLEASE, for the last time!" Judge Herbert looks over towards the surrounded Rabbi and sees that he has calmed down and appears to pose no threat to the proceedings.

"May I ask who you are, and why you are interrupting my hearing?" Judge Herbert asks the Rabbi.

"My name is Rabbi Joseph Peckerman of the Shalom Synagogue located in the Lower East Side of New York City, your honor."

"And you know this man?" Judge Herbert asks while pointing to Robinson.

"I've known him and his entire family since they escaped from Lithuania after World War II, your honor. I helped them get established with work and a place to stay."

"Did they escape from the Nazi's, Rabbi Peckerman?"

"No, your honor, they escaped from the Russians. They ARE the Nazis! – or at least the father was." The courtroom is abuzz once more.

"Are you telling me that Sam Robinson, here, is himself a JEW and that his father is a NAZI? I don't get that at all, Rabbi. Can you explain yourself to the court?"

"Certainly, your honor – Robinson's father changed his Jewish identity and his religion to avoid persecution. He joined the Nazi party in Lithuania to show his support for the new order and worked his way through the party ranks. He did such a good job of it that they made him head of a secret factory in Lithuania – Camp Slivovitz!"

"What did they manufacture at this secret factory? Do you know?"

"No, your honor, I do not, but it must have been something the Allies wanted like uranium-enriched water for nuclear testing – 'heavy water,' they called it. Had to be something special because the little town of Slivovitz was never bombed during the war. Actually, there was one small explosion at the lederhosen factory on the outskirts of town but many think this was due to a gas leak, your honor."

"I see, Rabbi. Please continue."

A light bulb goes on in Max's sore head as he listens to all of this. He stands up and yells out to the judge.

"I know what they made there, Judge Herbert! I KNOW WHAT THEY MADE THERE AT THAT SECRET FACTORY IN CAMP SLIVOVITZ!"

People in courtroom six are wondering if they should hit the floor in preparation for another attack from some other lunatic security has allowed to invade the courtroom this morning. Judge Herbert decides to take a chance and see what else he can find out and points over towards Max.

"Will you please identify yourself for the court?" Judge Herbert asks.

"Yes, I will your honor." Max stands up a little straighter now that he realizes he didn't shit his pants and the smell is gone. He reaches to adjust his *yarmulke* which isn't on top of his head where it should be. He pats around on his nearly bald pate, which is still sore as hell, and realizes it's in his pocket. He grins at the judge and announces,

"My name is Max Kaminski. I'm Donald's father."

"How do you know about the secret factory in Lithuania, Mr. Kaminski?"

"I know about it because my father almost got sent there and my Uncle Saul was held prisoner there for many years. Why he even helped run the factory, your honor."

"Well, Mr. Kaminski, do you know what they made there at this factory, secret bombs for the war perhaps?"

"No, sir, not secret bombs – they made hubcaps for the Mercedes people, your honor." Courtroom six, expecting to hear some deep secret revelation, cracks up with that one and Judge Herbert is sorry he went with his gut feeling instead of realizing that the court was full of crazies this morning.

"Please, Judge Herbert, you've got to believe me. This IS the big secret and has been for a long time, but the Mercedes people are so powerful that they arranged for Camp Slivovitz to be left alone during the war. The plant is still there today, and Uncle Saul, as old as he is now, is STILL in charge of production. They make hubcaps, I'm telling you; no tanks, no cannons, no guns and NO heavy water – HUBCAPS!" More laughter erupts from the audience. Max just waves the room off with both hands in disgust and sits down. Marsha pats him gently on the back.

"*Feh! Kish mir en tooches!*" Max says aloud from his seat.

"Max, don't get yourself all worked up – you'll get heartburn!" Marsha scolds him with a frown. "Take some Rolaids!"

"You did what you could, Max. Forget about it," says the Rabbi. Max fishes for the Rolaids and scans the crowd. "What a bunch of morons," he says while shaking his head.

"He's right, your honor," Robinson says barely audible.

"Say that again, Mr. Robinson," orders Judge Herbert.

"I said, *he's right*," Robinson is a little louder now and ready to come clean. "The Slivovitz plant did make hubcaps for Mercedes Benz and my father was in charge of the entire operation for the Nazis and like Mr. Kaminski said, his Uncle Saul was in charge of production."

"Are you now telling the court that YOU are a Jew, Mr. Robinson, or is it Robinowitz?" asks Judge Herbert.

"It is Robinson, judge. It was legally changed years ago. We did manage to escape from the Soviets just as the war was ending. In all the confusion, we made it to New York with the help of the secret Nazi underground Hitler had set up. My father thought it might be more to our advantage if we continued to lie about our heritage and we kept the last name. As I said, we did legally change it later on. We weren't practicing Jews anyway. It was just my father and me who were able to escape. Many ex-Nazi higher ups made it to Argentina but my father thought we would have an easier time getting lost in New York City, and besides he wanted to see the Statue of Liberty. My mother and sister, Michelle, never made it. They were detained at Bremerhaven and not permitted on the boat because their pictures weren't pasted on the fake passports correctly and you could still see the original pictures underneath theirs. We couldn't acknowledge that they were with us because all hell broke loose and they were hauled off by the secret police for interrogation. That was the last time I saw my mother and sister." Robinson wipes a tear from his eye. "Eventually, we made it safely on board the Dutch ship, "*Witte Olifant*," where we remained hidden the entire passage in the hold of the ship, like rats. We never did hear from my mother and sister again but we did find out through sources that they survived being incarcerated for one year in a East German prison and were released. I have tried repeatedly but could find out nothing more about them. One source reported, but could not verify, that they hooked up with a band of roving Gypsies and took off for parts unknown." Robinson hangs his head down in memory of the family he once had.

"Please continue, Mr. Robinson, and tell us how this all unfolds to the present day," asks Judge Herbert.

"Life with my father was very difficult, to say the least. We had to be careful not to expose ourselves for who we are. We were always looking over our shoulders for someone who might recognize us from the hubcap plant. One man did, a while back, and we moved to another location before anything happened." Robinson drinks the little bit of water he has left and continues. "We had nothing – no family, no home to speak of, and no love, your honor. As a result, my father became a very bitter man. We didn't go to church. We didn't go to synagogue. We didn't go anywhere. He went to work as a butcher and made sausage all day for Oscar Meyer and came home. I went to school and came home and we would eat a dinner in silence – usually sausage. I would do my homework and go to bed. The next day it was the same thing all over again; over and over and over – day after day, month after month, year after year. The weekends were worse. We just stayed in the house and did nothing. We couldn't even look out the window because he kept the shades down. He wouldn't even buy us a radio." Sam Robinson is beginning to shake a little as more tears roll down his cheek. Courtroom six felt the emotions of a scared little boy.

"It was a miserable existence."

"Can you continue, Mr. Robinson, or do we need to take a recess?" asks the judge. Scotty hands him another cup of water which he immediately gulps down.

"No, your honor, I'll continue." Robinson takes a huge breath of air and looks over the courtroom with sad eyes.

"Most of the children I went to school with were Christians and so when Christmas came around, well, that was a time for celebration. After all, Santa Claus was coming to town and bringing presents to ALL the good boys and girls. In school we would make and hang up decorations all over the classroom. We even had a real live tree in our room and it sure looked swell when we put all the hand-made ornaments that we made on it. There was this store-bought lighted star on the top. I can still see that star today sparkling way up on top of the tree."

Courtroom six is perfectly still. Some spectators reach for handkerchiefs and tissues. Max Kaminski blows his nose and Don recognizes where the semi, tractor-trailer sounds came from over the holidays.

"The teacher even let us pop popcorn and string it all over the tree. All the hoopla and excitement reached its peak just before we left for Christmas break. All the kids did was talk about food, Santa, and presents. And when we did return from the holidays, everyone would ask, 'What did you get?' and the toy lists went on and on. They all talked about the neat presents they played with and the wonderful parties and home-cooked dinners they had. I used to drool just listening to all the good food that was eaten." Robinson stops for a second. You could see he saw the whole thing in his head – just like he's describing it. Smiling some, he begins again.

"I had to lie and make up presents that I never got. It wasn't hard to do. I did a lot of pretending when I was a kid. I think that's how I managed to survive it all – I did a lot of pretending. I had to! We didn't have fancy food – just Oscar Meyer sausages. We didn't have a tree at Christmas. We didn't have decorations and we certainly didn't have presents. We didn't acknowledge Christmas, Hanukah or any other holiday, for that matter. My father was a 'dead man walking' and I guess, to some extent, I was dead too. But somehow I survived it all. Even after my father passed away, I survived. I swore to myself that some day I was going to have Christmas! Some day I was going to have presents! I was going to have the biggest Christmas tree and the best decorations anyone had ever seen! I was going to have it ALL and I was going to control it so that it could NEVER EVER be taken away from me – NEVER!" Robinson looks down at the floor and shakes his head in remorse.

"I was so afraid that someone would catch on…that someone would find out about my past and who I really am…and ruin it all by taking it all away from me…Santa, Christmas, presents, decorations, holiday foods, and decorated trees. It was too much for me to think about and the more I did, the more obsessed I became, and the more I worked to control it all! And now this! – The end! – My end. I have nothing – I am nothing."

"That's not true!" Max yells to Robinson while standing up. **"You're alive! You're breathing!** You just made a mistake, that's all! We all make mistakes, ask the Rabbi here. Even HE makes mistakes." Max looks at the Rabbi for some acknowledgment. Rabbi Peckerman keeps looking straight ahead as if his name wasn't the one mentioned by Max.

"Live your life, already! Ask for some forgiveness. Jews celebrate Christmas as well as Gentiles. Don't believe me? Just go to Disney World after the holidays and see all the Jews celebrating their asses off and spending your money! There's your proof. So why can't a Jew work as a Santa?" Max looks around the courtroom for an answer and just about everyone nods their heads in agreement. "And why can't a Jew run a Santa business or fraternity, or whatever the hell you want to call it? Truth is, I'll bet if you checked to see the large mall Santa outfits, and pictures with the Easter Bunny groups are mostly run by Jews! Why not? Jesus was a Jew, wasn't he? And it was his birthday that started the whole thing to begin with, wasn't it?" Max Kaminski has the entire courtroom listening and he's about the only one who's made any sense the entire morning.

"Listen, folks, for God's sake listen!" Max continues to address the court better than any experienced lawyer could...better than Abramowitz, Junior could...better than Clarence Darrow could...better than Ol' Abe Lincoln could!...well, maybe not better than Abe.

"We have to learn to share and to get along for our *own* sake...for our *children's* sake, and for the *world's* sake...and for true 'Peace on Earth' or we will end up destroying ourselves and everyone else on this planet and here in Chicago. Forget the mistakes already and live! LIVE! Live each and every day as if it were your last! Life is a gift – a gift from God! And many of us throw it away in anger and hurt. Life was meant to be lived and enjoyed! – so go enjoy yourself!" Max looks over at Judge Herbert and says, "I rest my case, your honor." Max sits down wishing he had a tall glass of Mogen David – room temperature.

"Marsha, you got any aspirin?" Max whispers.

Sam Robinson stands up from the witness chair and faces the entire room. "I am truly sorry for all that I have done, especially to you, Mr. Kaminski." He looks at Don for forgiveness. "I hope you can forgive me. We would love to have you represent us as a Santa in one of our local malls. Please come see me." Now he looks to Max. "And you,

Mr. Kaminski, are a very smart man. Thank you, sir, for your insight and for helping to pave the way towards love and peace." Max waves him off and reaches for more Rolaids.

"It was nothing," says Max. "Don't mention it. Now can we start all over and have a nice holiday? What do you say, Judge Herbert?" Max asks.

"I think that's a wonderful idea, Max. Let's forget about all the negativity, go forth and live our lives the best that we can as brothers and sisters should. Let Christmas be restored to the great city of Chicago. Merry Christmas and happy holidays to everyone! And God bless us one and all!"

BANG!...BANG!...BANG!

"This special hearing is now closed. Several of you may still be hearing from the court, but as far as I am concerned, these proceedings are over and we are adjourned." Everyone begins cheering. Judge Herbert rises with a big grin on his face. Flashbulbs are going off repeatedly and reporters are scrambling out of courtroom six to report their stories about the *two* men who saved Christmas for Chicago – Judge Daniel Albright Herbert and Max Kaminski.

Judge Herbert waves to his wife, Jean, and turns to exit into his private chambers for a victory Scotch.

"All rise," from Scotty the Bailiff. "This special hearing in the Superior Court of Cook County is now over. May God preserve and protect the City of Chicago and the State of Illinois and Merry Christmas Chicago!" Judge Herbert glances over his shoulder and winks at Scotty as he approaches his wife just below the bench.

The Kaminskis are stunned and look at Max in awe. Don's never been so proud of his father. He is lost in his amazement of his father's foresight and heart-felt comments when he realizes that all of courtroom six is on their feet and applauding Max Kaminski. Don stands and raises his hands to applaud his father along with everyone else. Max seems oblivious to it all. He's more concerned about beating the traffic home to catch Drew Carey on "The Price Is Right."

"Come on Marsha," Max says. He finds his *yarmulke* folded up in his pocket and he places it atop his head, dried snot and all. "Hurry up, Marsha or we will miss Drew Carey!"

"I'm going as fast as I can! No one's moving! They're all clapping for you Max! Don't you hear that?" The noises of hand clapping,

joyous laughter, cheers, words of agreement and praise to Max Kaminski all blend together and for some reason, in a small part of Don's
brain not caught up in all of this yet, he can hear Gene Autry singing,
"Here comes Santa Claus. Here comes Santa Claus – Right down
Santa Claus Lane." just as plain as day. Don is smiling. *Merry Christmas Chicago!*

"Corporal Mays? Corporal Mays! Is that really you, Jimmy?" Santa
Rick yells from his wheel chair at the black Santa in the red suit.
Jimmy D. Mays stops mid-sentence in commenting to Habib Constantine on how great it is to be an American today when he hears his
military title and he looks around to see who's calling him "Corporal
Mays." Instantly he recognizes Private Richard Dempsey, one of the
wounded men he saved in 'Nam many years ago."

"Hey, Rick!" Jimmy is grinning from ear to ear as he rushes
over to Rick and Santa Domingo. Jimmy bends over the wheelchair
and both men embrace while talking at the same time.

"I can't believe it's really you, Jimmy! It's been so long." Santa Rick is chocked up with emotion now and can't talk.

"I knew youse was gonna make it, man. I jus' knew it!" Jimmy
hugs Rick for dear life. Both men are quiet but many words of gratitude are spoken and shared in their hearts as they embrace like the
long lost brothers they are. They're laughing and crying and making
no sense at all – just enjoying the jubilation of seeing one another
knowing how close to death's door they once were and how grateful to
God almighty that they are alive and enjoying life today.

"Jimmy Mays! Jimmy Mays! Say, Jimmy, did you ever come
across 'skimo'? You know, Jay what's-his-name?...the Eskimo...or
Sgt. Sargeant by any chance?"

"Nah, Rick. I ain't seen 'em since 'Nam, man. I'll bet Jays
went back to 'Laska somewheres and Sarge, well, he jus' fell off da
planet, I guess. I miss 'em, though. I really do."

"God blessed us, Jimmy."

"Yeah, man...God really did."

94

Courtroom six is buzzing with good will and excitement as people begin to file out onto Daley Plaza. What a glorious day for Chicago, for Christmas has been saved! Marshall Fields does a record breaking-day in holiday shopping and extra workers are called in to help handle the traffic.

Susan and the rest of the Kaminskis are making their way over to Don, in the center of the courtroom. She passes by Rabbi Pecker-man who is in deep conversation with Patriarch Shimko and she thinks she hears something about Armani suits and cadaver parts. She passes them by looking straight forward and pretends she didn't hear a word. Don is all smiles as Sue rushes up to him and he hugs her like he just got out of prison. He feels like a new man. They kiss as Max, Marsha and the kids catch up to them and all begin to speak at once.

"I love you, Don."

"I love you too, Susan."

"Your Mom and I are proud of you, Son."

"I'm so happy for you, Dad."

"Good thing you didn't say ASS, Pop."

"Did we miss Drew Carey? What time is it?"

They all weave their way through the crowd as they make their way outside. It's not even noon yet, but with the overcast skies it appears to be much later in the evening. The holiday lights that decorate the plaza and all of downtown Chicago are all on. The trees are all aglow with twinkling lights. It looks like a scene from a Disney movie when like magic, it begins to snow. There is no wind at all and people are enjoying the crisp chill in the air and the fine snow that is falling. Like being anointed from heaven, every man, woman and child is smiling as they walk along, arm in arm. Then, as if on cue, the sound system kicks in and guess who's singing? Why, Gene Autry, that's who:

"Here comes Santa Claus. Here comes Santa Claus. Right down Santa Claus Lane..."

"It's here! It's here!" proclaims Buddy the Elf to all his little friends.

"What's here?" laughs Mary.

"The Christmas spirit, that's what! The holiday spirit with all its magic has just descended upon the entire city of Chicago. The people can feel it. I can feel it. Can you feel it?"

Buddy begins to skip across the plaza as all his little friends laugh and skip after him.

"Come on," says Buddy. "Let's go to the Mini Bar – I'm buying!"

Epilogue

It wasn't long after the hearing that Don got a call from Sam Robinson asking if he might be interested in being Santa at the mall for a whole bunch of days – and for a good price too. Don accepts happily at the thought of finally getting to the big time, and what's even better? He gets to work with Buddy the Elf.

The whole family is there one Tuesday evening before Christmas to watch Don's performance. He's doing just great and having a ball. The kids love him. The parents love him and so do Waxman and Jarusinski who are smiling at all the moms buying the silver picture frames.

Annie and Junior wave as they laugh at Don doing his Santa impersonation. Max stares with half a smile wondering what Rabbi Peckerman would say if he saw this.

"Fuck Rabbi Peckerman," Max says to himself.

"What did you say, Max?" Marsha asks.

"Nothing, dear – nothing at all," Max answers as he smiles at Don, shrugs his shoulders and adjusts the *yarmulke* atop his head.

Sue observes Don in all his glory and gives him a loving smile. She waves and flashes him the seven-ten split, diamond ring. He sees the ring and nods lovingly to her.

"Be darn careful you don't shoot your eye out," he yells after the little guy skipping down to his parents.

Jimmy D. Mays is a happy man these days. He has a full-time job – at least for now. He has a nice warm place to stay thanks to Anita Wang. It's a small studio apartment on top of Fat Wang's Chinese Take-Out. It isn't much but the food is great and his place always smells good. Jimmy gets free eats because at night he sweeps the floor and takes out the trash. He's been cutting back on his drinking somewhat and he attends counseling weekly for his addictions and post-stress syndrome. He and Santa Rick have dinner together at least once a week. Usually Rick stops over to Jimmy's place and they eat at Fat Wang's.

And where is Jimmy D. right now, you ask? Take a look. He's dressed up in a brand new Santa suit and sitting in the middle of the stripmall in a gold colored Santa chair on top of a trailer. Neighbor-hood kids are lined up and anxious to see the little black Santa. All the trash men are waving to him from the doorway to Wallowich's Frog Pond.

"I told you Santa was black?" Little Sharita tells her Mom.

"I hope so for your sake, Sharita honey," says Wanda. "Why don't you ask him for that Elmo doll you wants?"

"Nah, that's not what I want, mommy. I want Baby Alive!"

"You're lucky you alive, Sharita!"

Jimmy is busy explaining to one young man how important it is to go to school, listen to your teacher, and to treat others the way you want to be treated.

"Oh, yeah – an' stay off drugs an' don't drink too much booze!"

"I won't, Santa. I promise."

"Good boy! – Now go on home an' cleans up your room before I gets there." Like a flash, the boy is off the trailer and racing through the lot on his way home. Habib Constantine is watching Jimmy from the door of Bee Bee's Cash and Carry and laughing his behind off wondering what Jimmy told that kid to make him race on out of the lot so fast.

Jimmy laughs too as he motions for the next child to come sit on his lap. It's Sharita's turn and she leaves Mom's side, runs over to Jimmy D. and gives him a great big bear hug.

"Hi, Santa Claus! I love you, Santa Claus!" Sharita gives Jim-my a big smile as he lifts her onto his lap.

"Hello, Sharita – Sanda loves you too, baby – Ho Ho Ho!"

"I seen you before, Santa Claus."

"Wheres 'at, Sharita, honey?"

"I seen you last week at the mall. I seen you getting in the am-bulance downtown, and I seen you get locked up on Friday! And you's was white then!"

"Well, dis here da real Sanda and I's black!" Jimmy D. shows off his pearly whites and minty breath to Sharita.

"Then you must be the real Santa!" Sharita hugs Jimmy D. again and kisses him on the cheek.

They both smile as photographer Sam Irving takes the shot with his Polaroid.

"Look this way," Sam the photographer says. "Great!" Sam is snapping away and giving free pictures to all the kids and parents who are delighted to have a Santa this year that looks the part and knows what the kids need to hear – simply put, "Do the right thing, listen to your elders, and stay in school!" This is part of Judge Herbert's penance handed down to the Gigantes, Mimo, Sr. and Mimo, Jr. for their part in the recent Santa invasion in filling up the hospital and the police lock-up. They are paying Jimmy D. time and a half for all his hard work with the inner-city youth. Something that Jimmy D. hopes to be able to do in the future – like next week when Christmas is over and the red suit won't do him much good.

Sharita hops down off of Jimmy's lap after she tells him what she wants this year and that she is going to leave him just some home-made cookies because the milk is sour. Being the big girl that she is, for a second grader (damn near a hundred and eighty pounds – takes after her Mama); Sharita almost topples both her and Jimmy D. out of the Santa Chair as she scoots off his lap. Lucky for Jimmy he braces himself before he keels over onto the flatbed trailer and at the same time reaches under the Santa chair to hold onto his new bottle of Crown Royal in the purple bag.

Good job, Jimmy D. – all is saved...you, Sharita, and the Crown Royal. Now this is what you call a "happy ending."

Sharita goes off skipping towards her Mama while singing, "Here comes Santa Claus. Here comes Santa Claus. Here comes Santa Claus...AGAIN!"

ACKNOWLEDGEMENTS

Writing this book has been a wonderful experience for me at this stage of my life. Maybe it is not as funny as I think it is, but it made me laugh anyway. And a few times it brought tears to my eyes. Sure, I know it may never go anywhere and probably few people will read it – I honestly do not care. I had a ball creating it! My family and friends are probably tired of my ramblings on about writing a book and the characters I've created, especially my lovely wife Shirley, who, on many occasions, had to stop whatever she was doing only to listen to a reading of my latest creation. She seemed to like it when I read to her, or maybe she just wanted to get back to whatever she was doing when I interrupted her. I'm not sure – but she listened all the same and I love her for it.

Additionally I wish to thank my father-in-law, Shirley Lockhart who passed away last year. And yes, his name was Shirley, just like my wife's name. Pop taught me all I know about the Hatfields and the McCoys, living on a mountain in West Virginia, the snake handlers, and running moon shine. Thanks, Pop. You are definitely one of the most interesting men I have ever known and one hell of a storyteller. We all miss you very much.

I spent many hours at Guilday's Restaurant (I know, I kept that name), and at the Oh La La Café (please don't tell Regina from Guilday's) in thinking, creating, and typing out with my two sore fingers many chapters and edits to my creation on a laptop. I'm about coffeed out! Thank you all so much, and a special thanks to you Mark for always busting my eggs and trying to hide them on the bottom of the pile. Why don't you take a lesson from Kelly? Seriously, your food is great and your friendship even greater. And a special thank you to all the guys and gals I sit with at the counter for listening to all my stories and ramblings. I can only imagine what you say about me behind my back, "That son-of-a-bitch is crazy!" Maybe so, but I never pretended to be anything else!

Thank you to my friend Pete Freyburger for all his suggestions, useful tips, and countless hours in helping to edit my manuscript and in trying to make me a better writer. A special thanks goes to Robert Rodebaugh, Russell Steedley, and Frank Rivera, who, many years ago, listened to all my crazy ideas about writing a book about a guy trying to get into the Santa business and inspired me to write this story.

And now for all you Santas and clowns I'm friends with on Facebook. I want you all to go out there and buy my book. It's cheap! It's funny! And you can upload it to your e-reader, if this works out the way I want it to.

A special thank you to my granddaughter, Hope – just for being you!

Love and gratitude to all,

Santa Dan

About the Author

Dan Slipetsky is a retired teacher having taught a variety of disciplines for over 30 years: from business and marketing to English and math courses in public high schools and local colleges, to adult basic education and GED classes at night school and in prison facilities. Additionally, he has taught for Junior Achievement, the Department of Elections and the Department of Labor. He received a Doctorate in Educational Leadership from the University of Delaware in 1999.

Born in Delaware County, Pennsylvania in 1945, Dan spent most of his adult years in the State of Delaware, "The State That Started a Nation," where he now resides with his wife, Shirley Lockhart. He served in the United States Air Force during Vietnam and the Cold War Era as a Russian Voice Intercept Processing Specialist.

Since 1999, Dan Slipetsky has marketed himself as a professional Santa Claus and has acquired many experiences and wonderful stories working in different venues: from mall work to daycare centers, business parties and promotions to nursing facilities and home visits. He also participates in reenacting the court scene from, "Miracle on 34th. Street," in courthouses throughout the state.

Dan belongs to numerous Santa organizations such as: The Fraternal Order of Real Bearded Santas, The Royal Order of Santa Claus, Santas Across the Globe, The Alumni of Real Bearded Santas, NorthEast Santas, Real Santas, The Kringle Group, ClausNet, and Santas on Facebook. His beard is registered with the National Beard Registry.

This is his first attempt at writing a novel.

Made in the USA
Charleston, SC
27 March 2012